Garfield ®

BY JIM DAVIS

VOLUME 2

Garfield

ROSS RICHIE Chief Executive Officer • MATT GAGNON Editor-in-Chief • FILIP SABLIK VP-Publishing & Marketing • LANCE KREITER VP-Licensing & Merchandising
PHIL BARBARO Director of Finance BRYCE CARLSON Managing Editor • DAFNA PLEBAN Editor • SHANNON WATTERS Editor • ERIC HARBURN Editor • CHRIS ROSA Assistant Editor
STEPHANIE GONZAGA Graphic Designer • JASMINE AMIRI Operations Coordinator • DEVIN FUNCHES E-Commerce & Inventory Coordinator • BRIANNA HART Executive Assistant

kaboom!

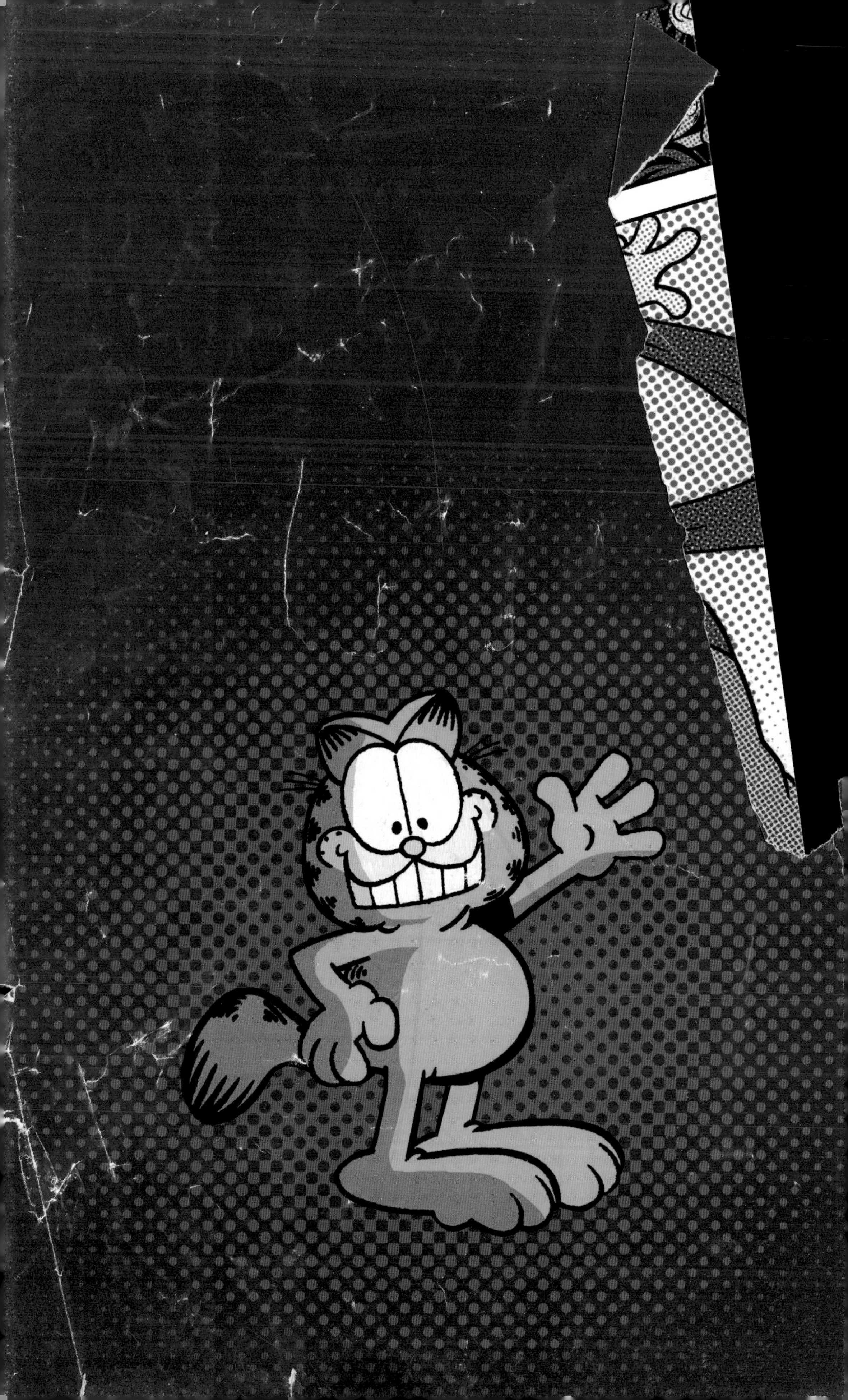

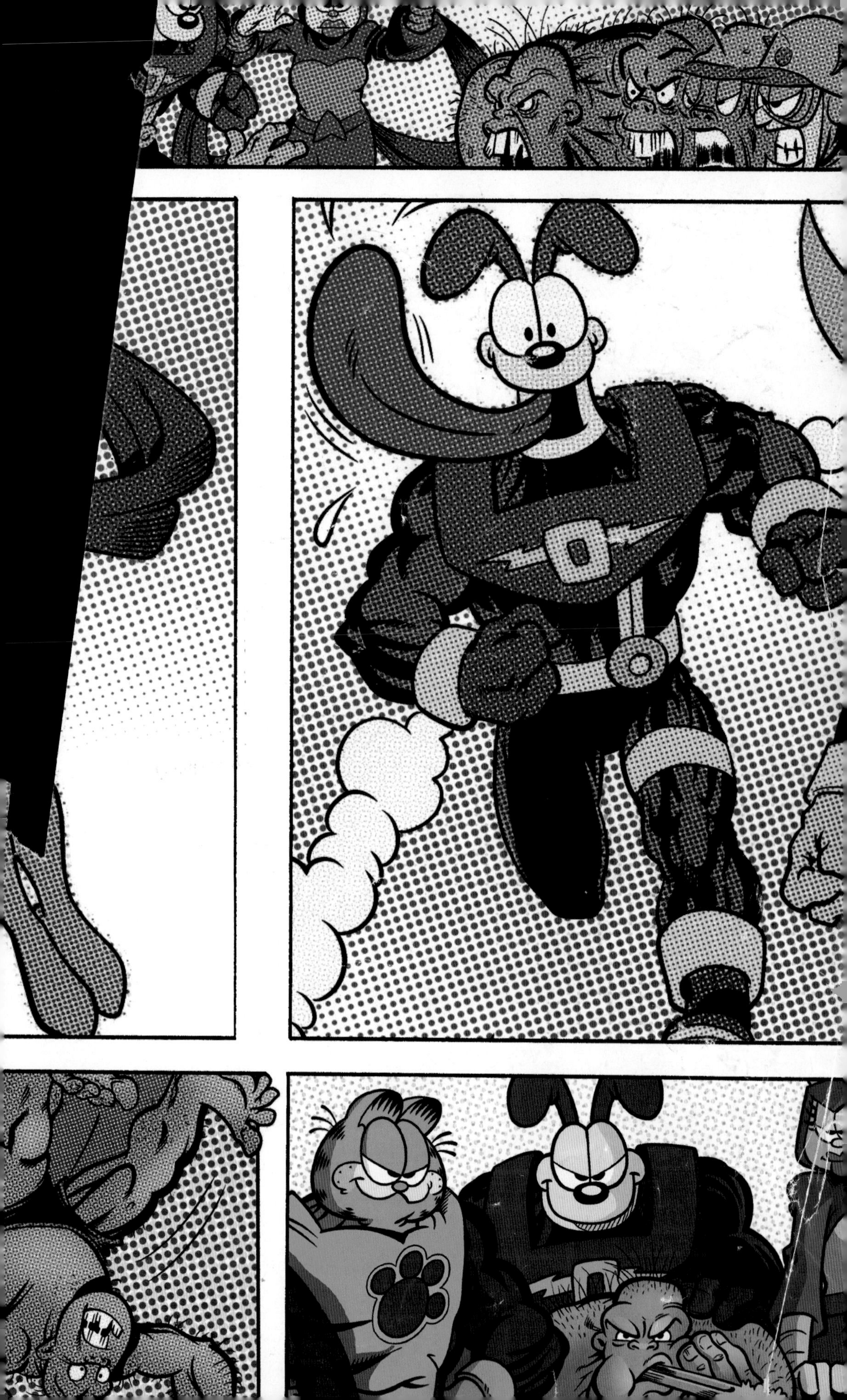

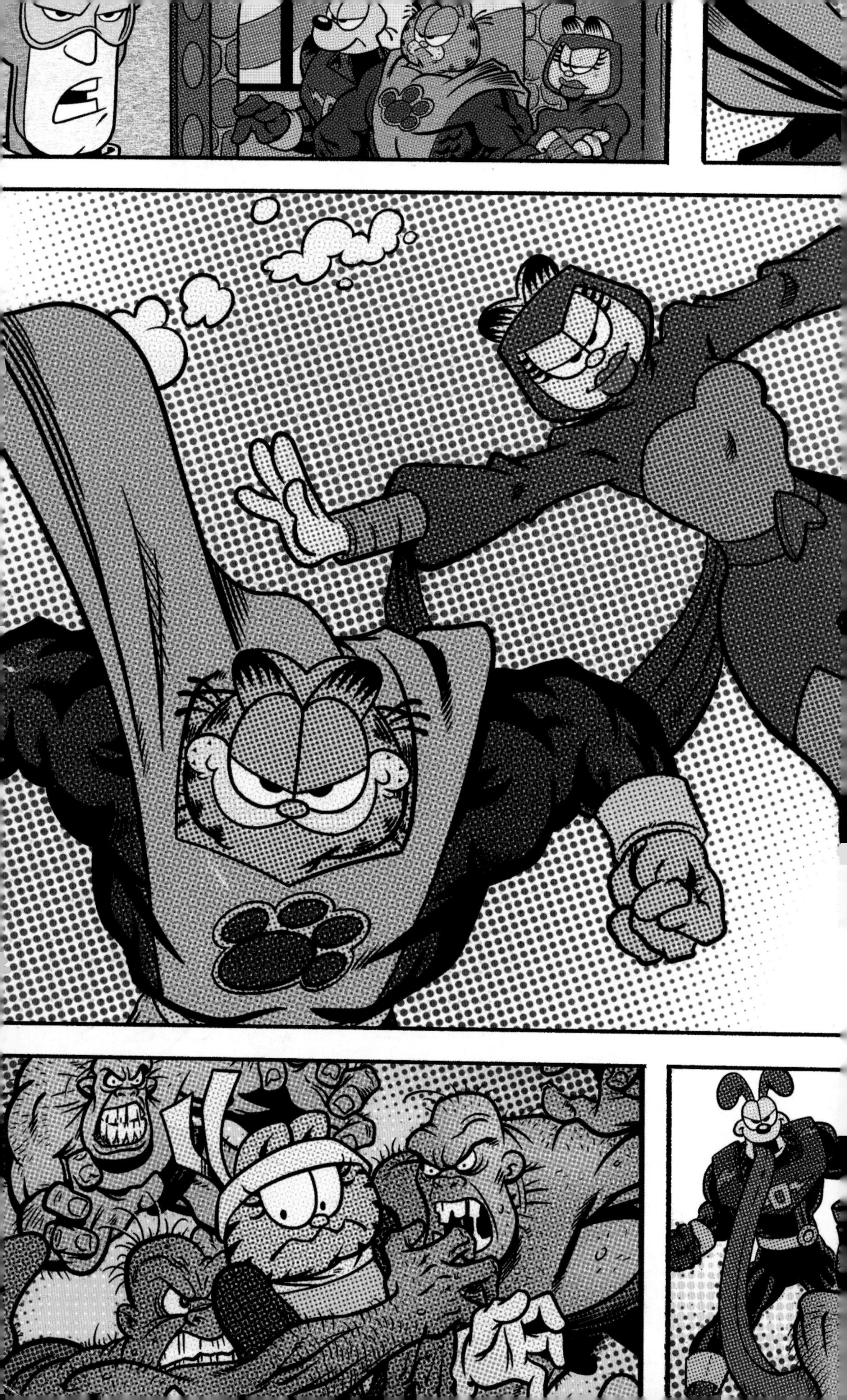

ISSUE 8B COVER BY
GARY BARKER & DAN DAVIS
COLORS BY **LISA MOORE**

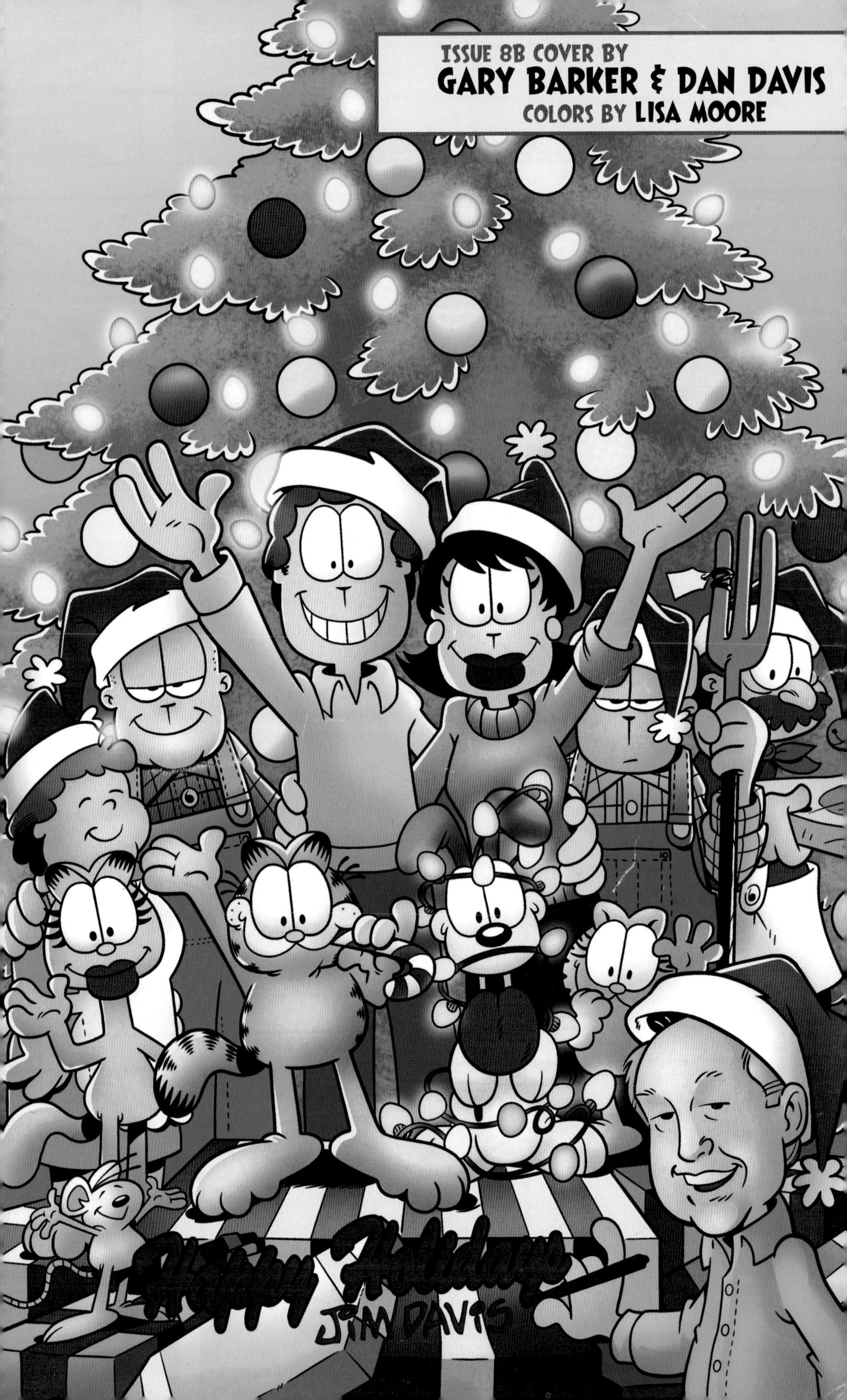
Happy Holidays
JIM DAVIS

ISSUE 8A COVER BY
GARY BARKER & DAN DAVIS
COLORS BY **LISA MOORE**

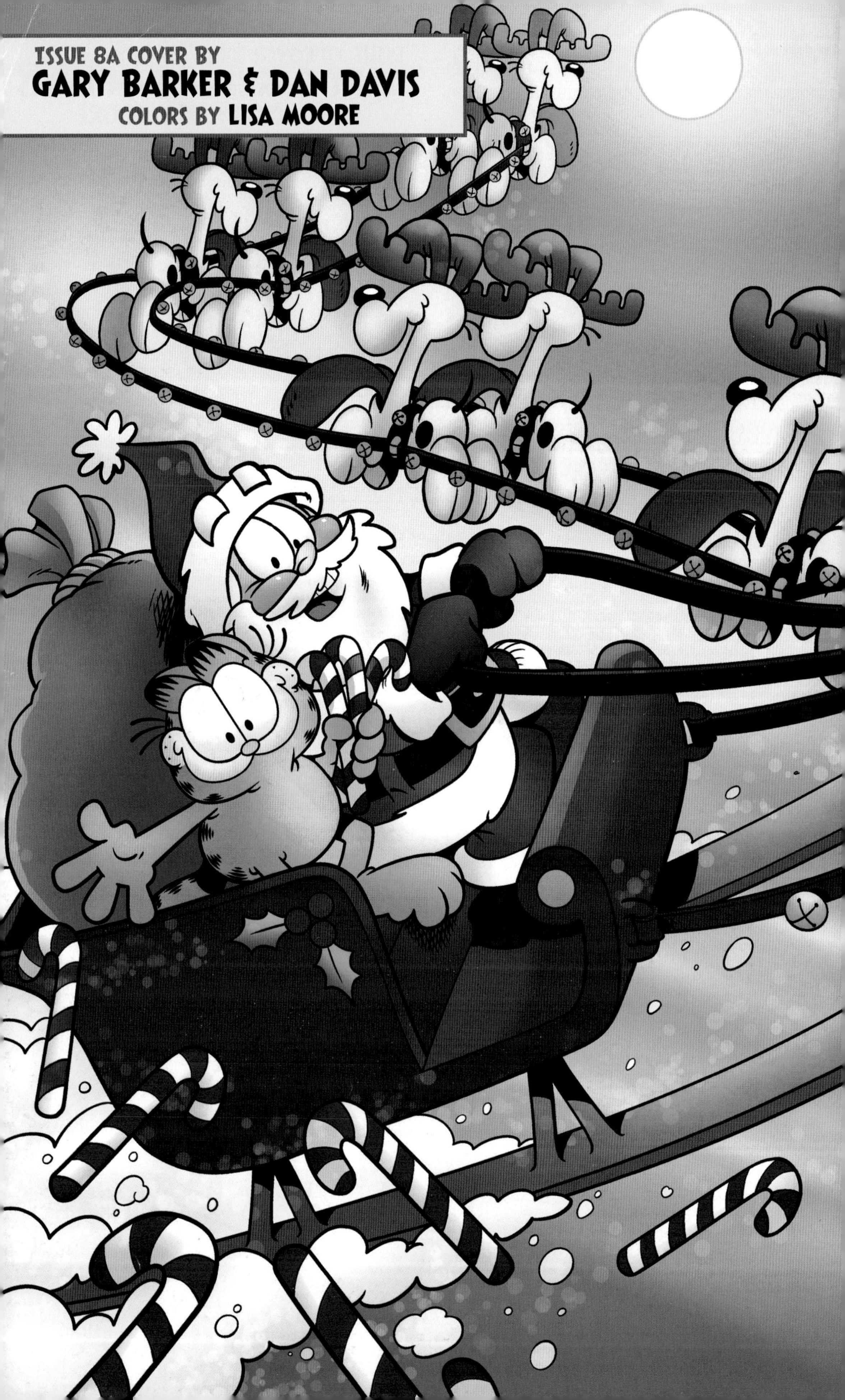

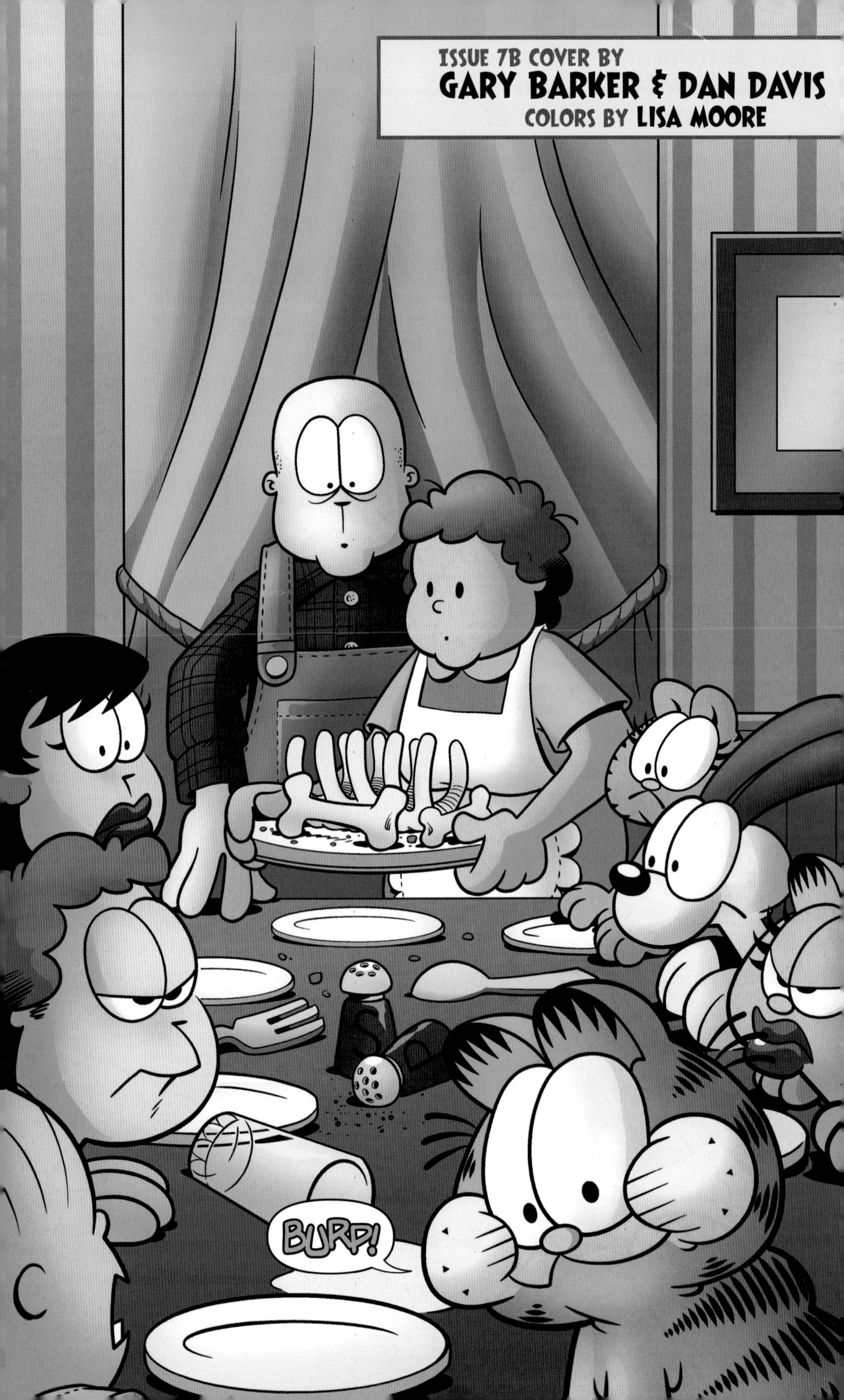
ISSUE 7B COVER BY
GARY BARKER & DAN DAVIS
COLORS BY LISA MOORE
BURP!

ISSUE 7A COVER BY
GARY BARKER & DAN DAVIS
COLORS BY LISA MOORE

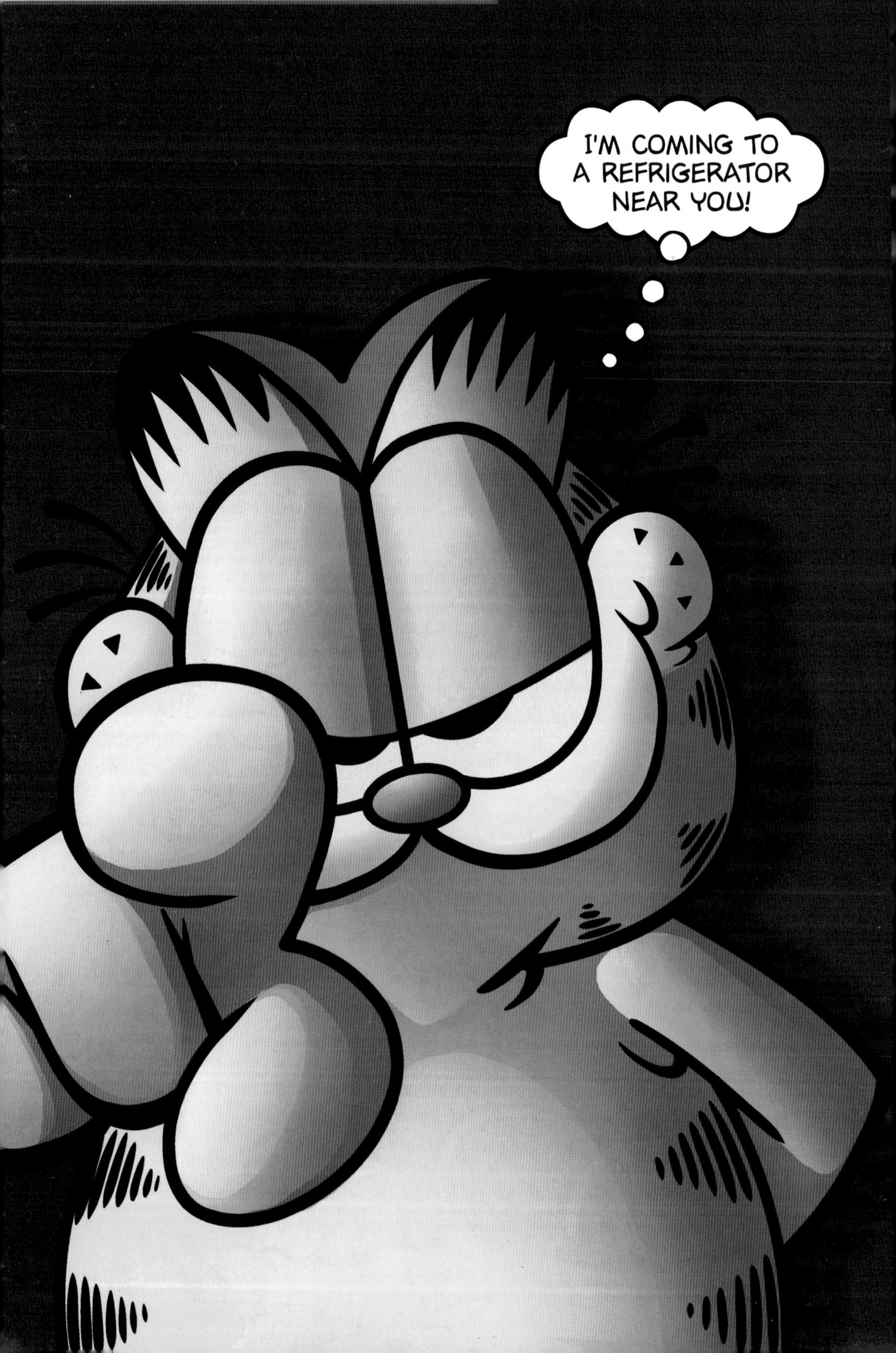
I'M COMING TO A REFRIGERATOR NEAR YOU!

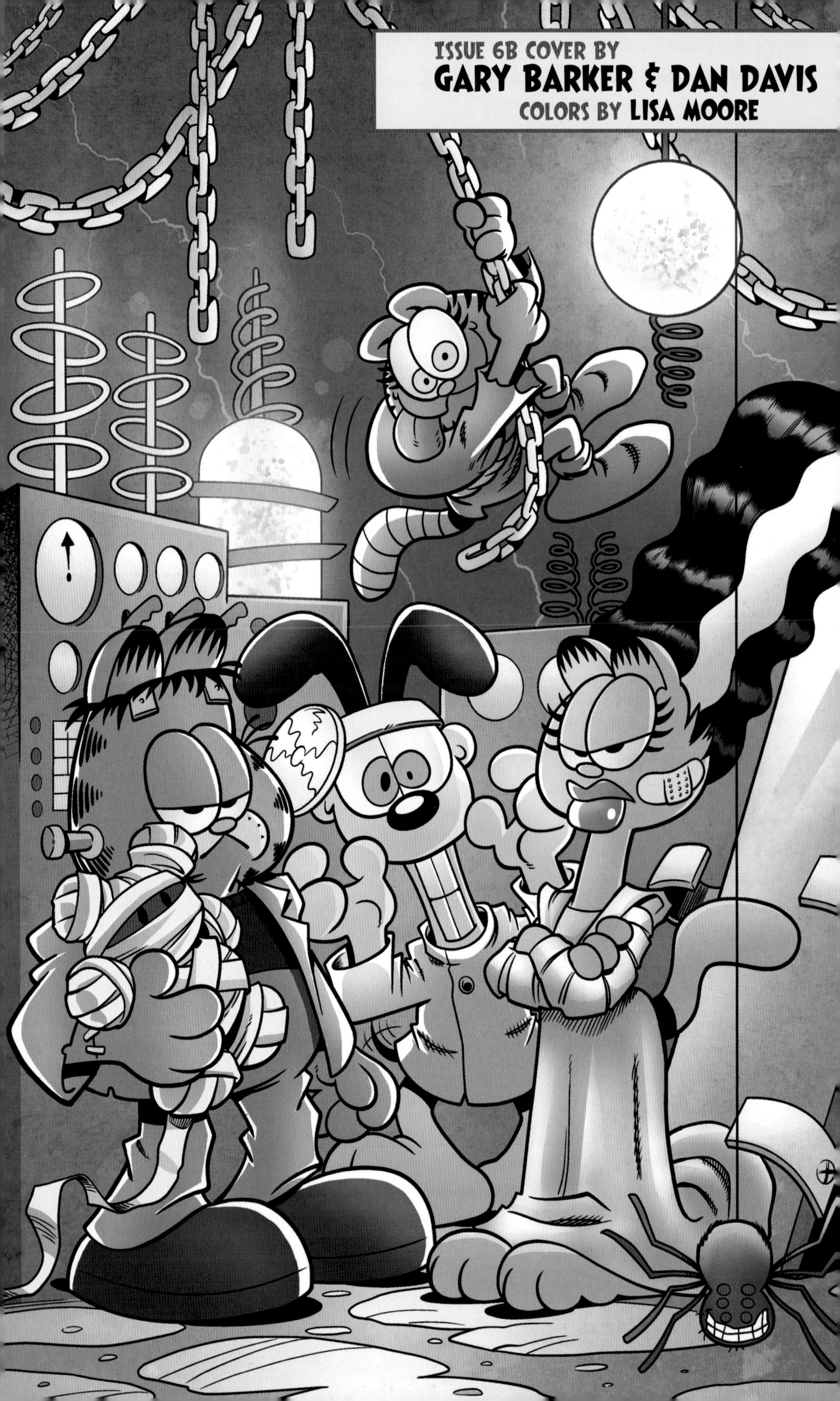
ISSUE 6B COVER BY
GARY BARKER & DAN DAVIS
COLORS BY LISA MOORE

ISSUE 6A COVER BY
GARY BARKER & DAN DAVIS
COLORS BY LISA MOORE

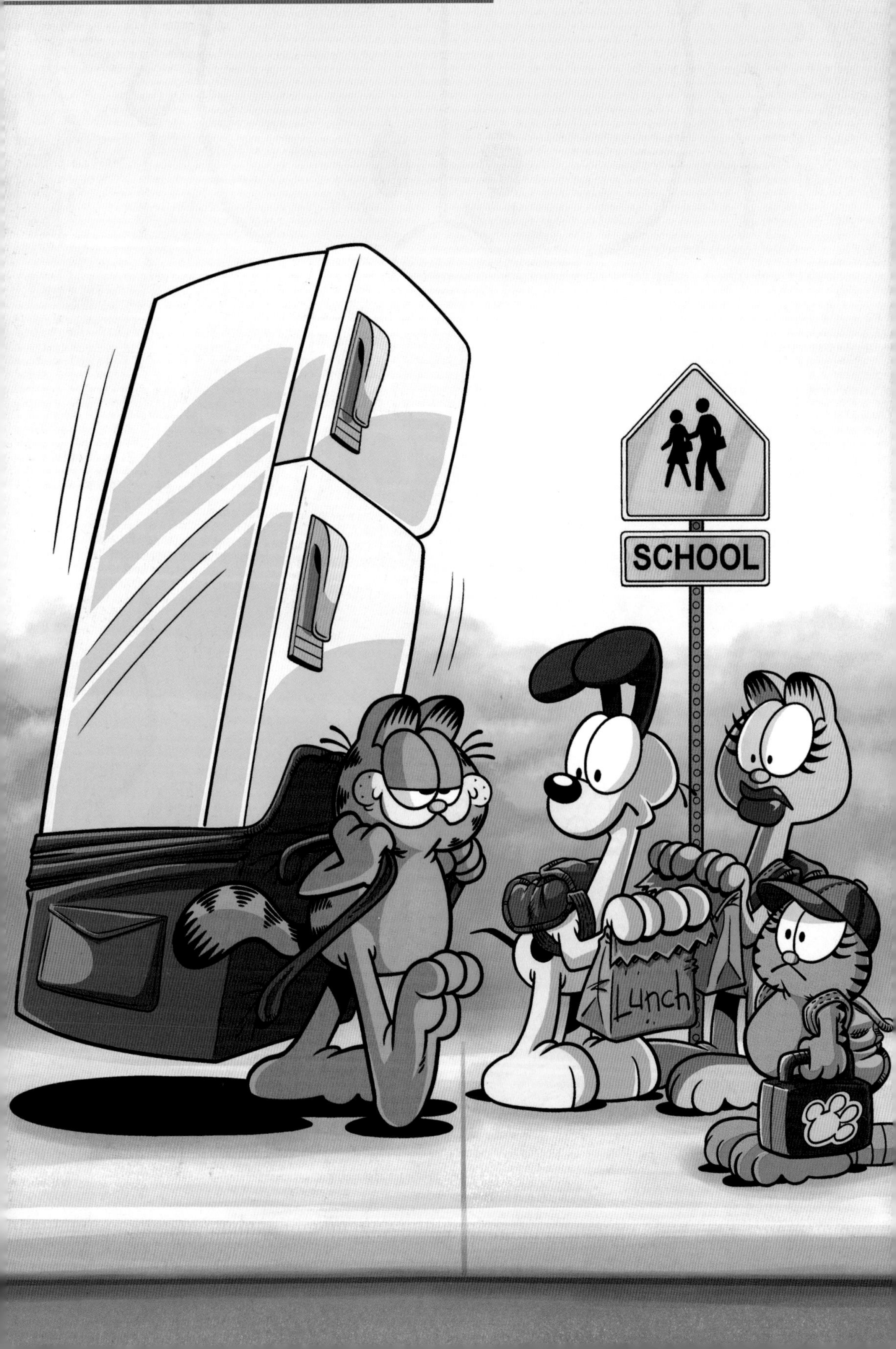
SCHOOL
Lunch

ISSUE 5B COVER BY
GARY BARKER & DAN DAVIS
COLORS BY **LISA MOORE**

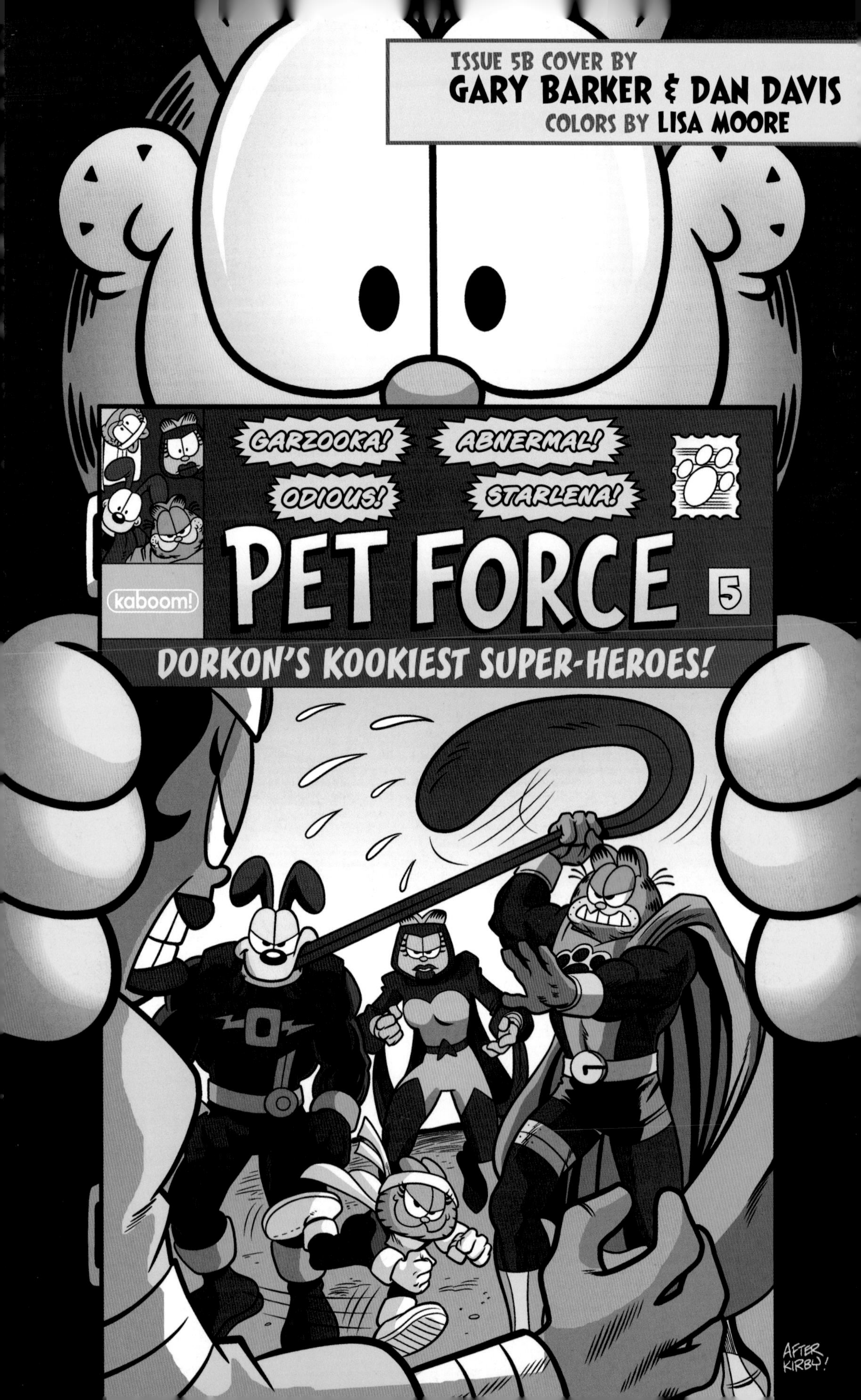
GARZOOKA!
ABNERMAL!
ODIOUS!
STARLENA!
PET FORCE
5
kaboom!
DORKON'S KOOKIEST SUPER-HEROES!
AFTER KIRBY!

ISSUE 5A COVER BY
GARY BARKER & DAN DAVIS
COLORS BY **LISA MOORE**

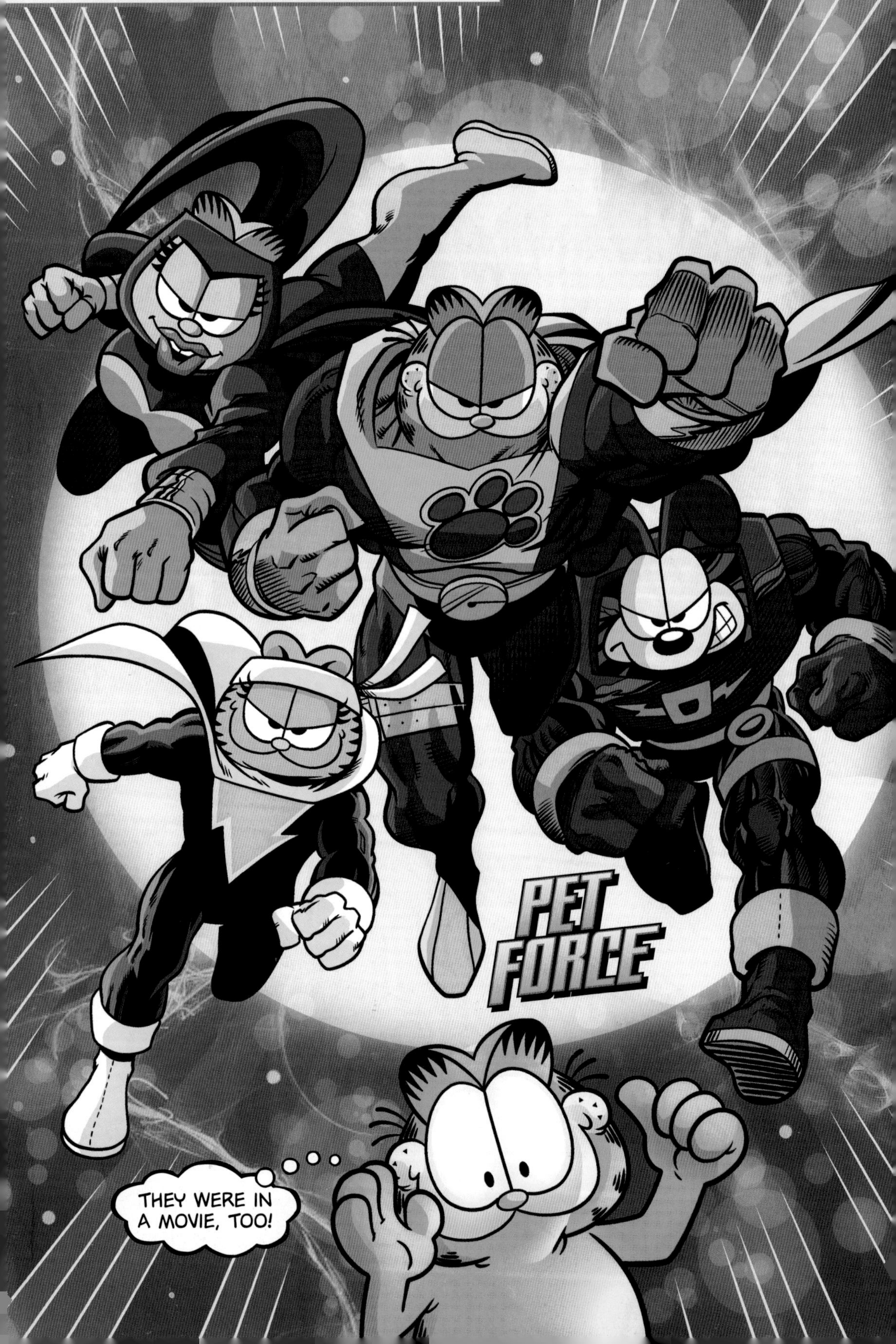
PET FORCE
THEY WERE IN A MOVIE, TOO!

COVER GALLERY

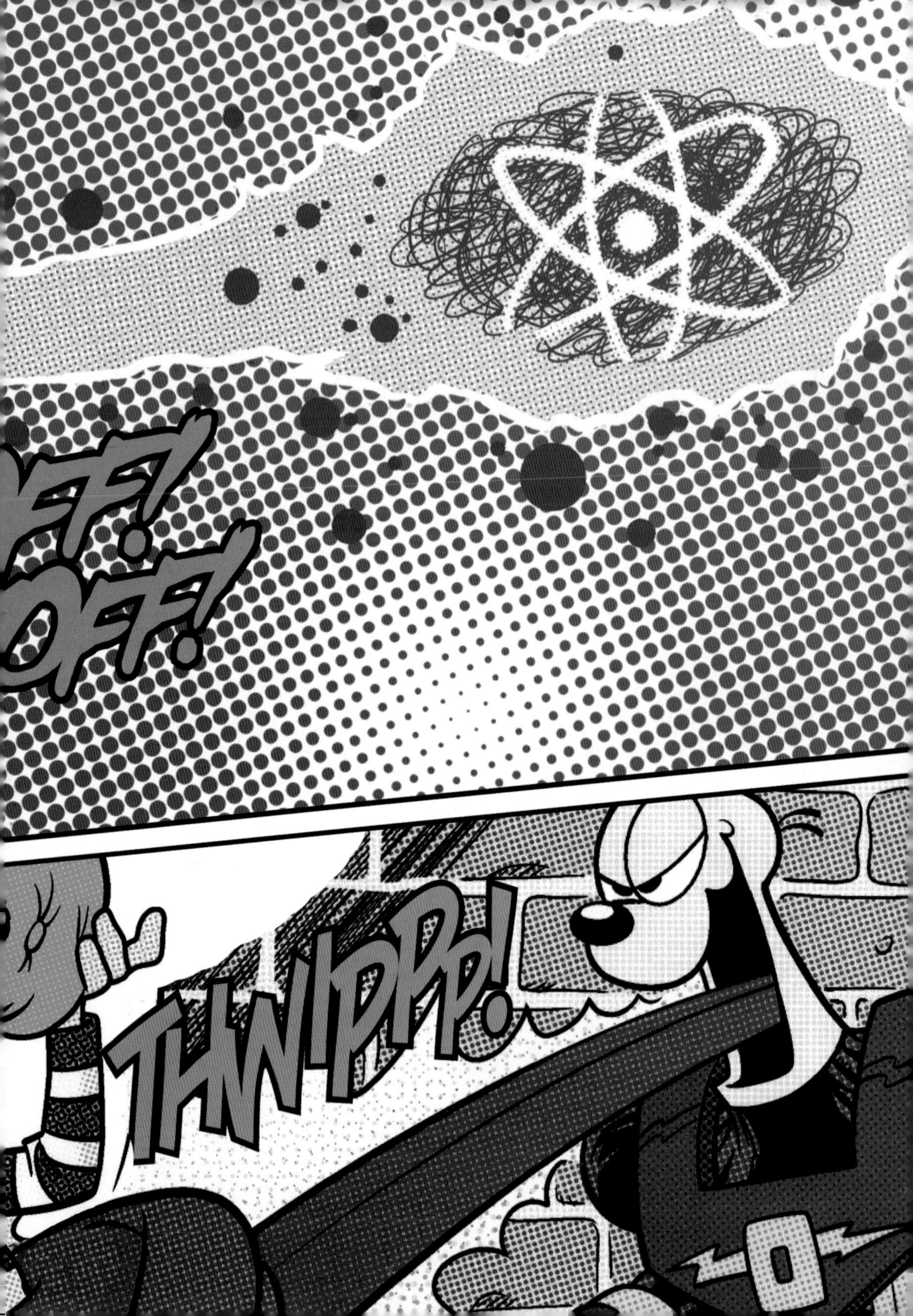
THWIPP!

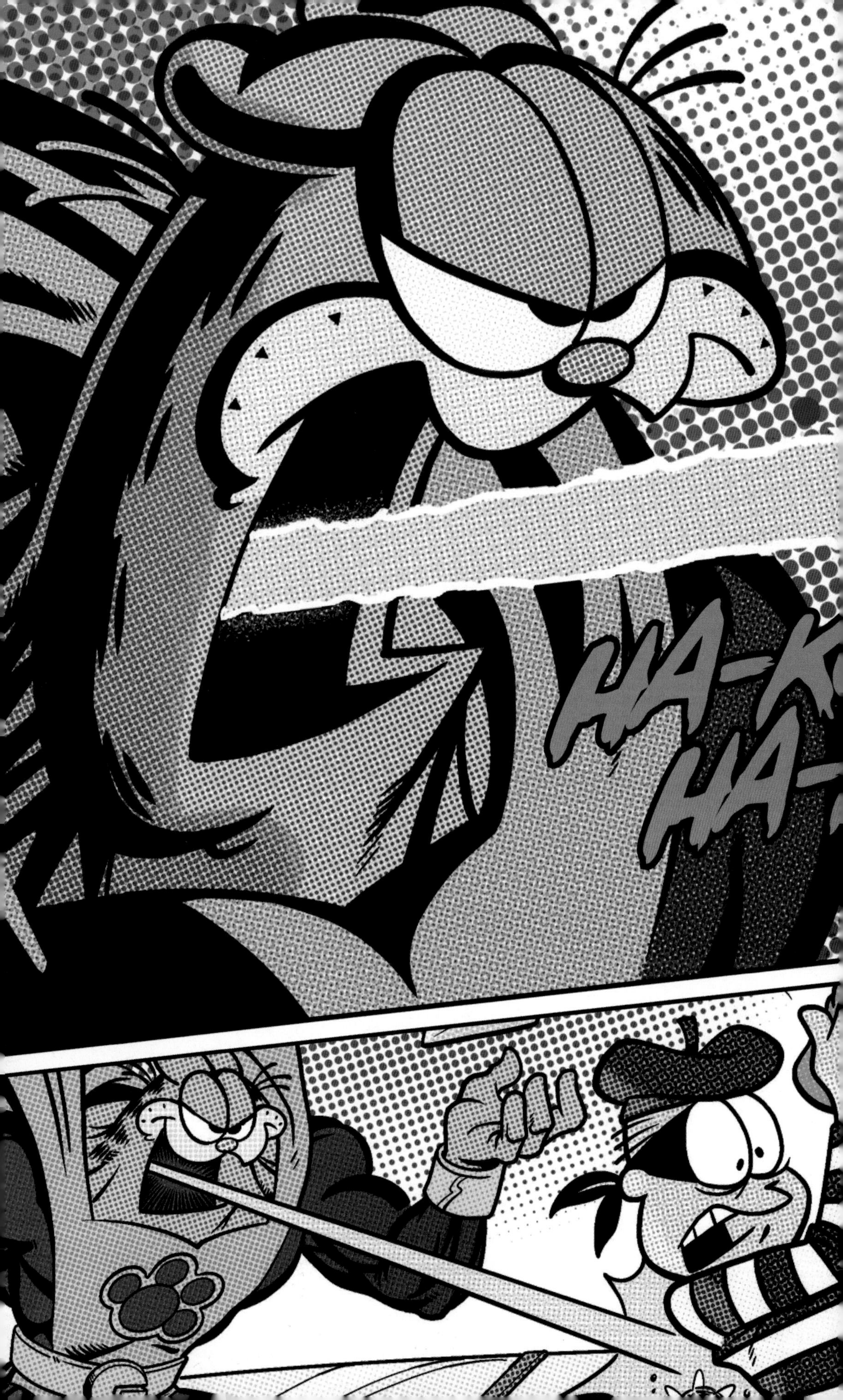
HA-K
HA-

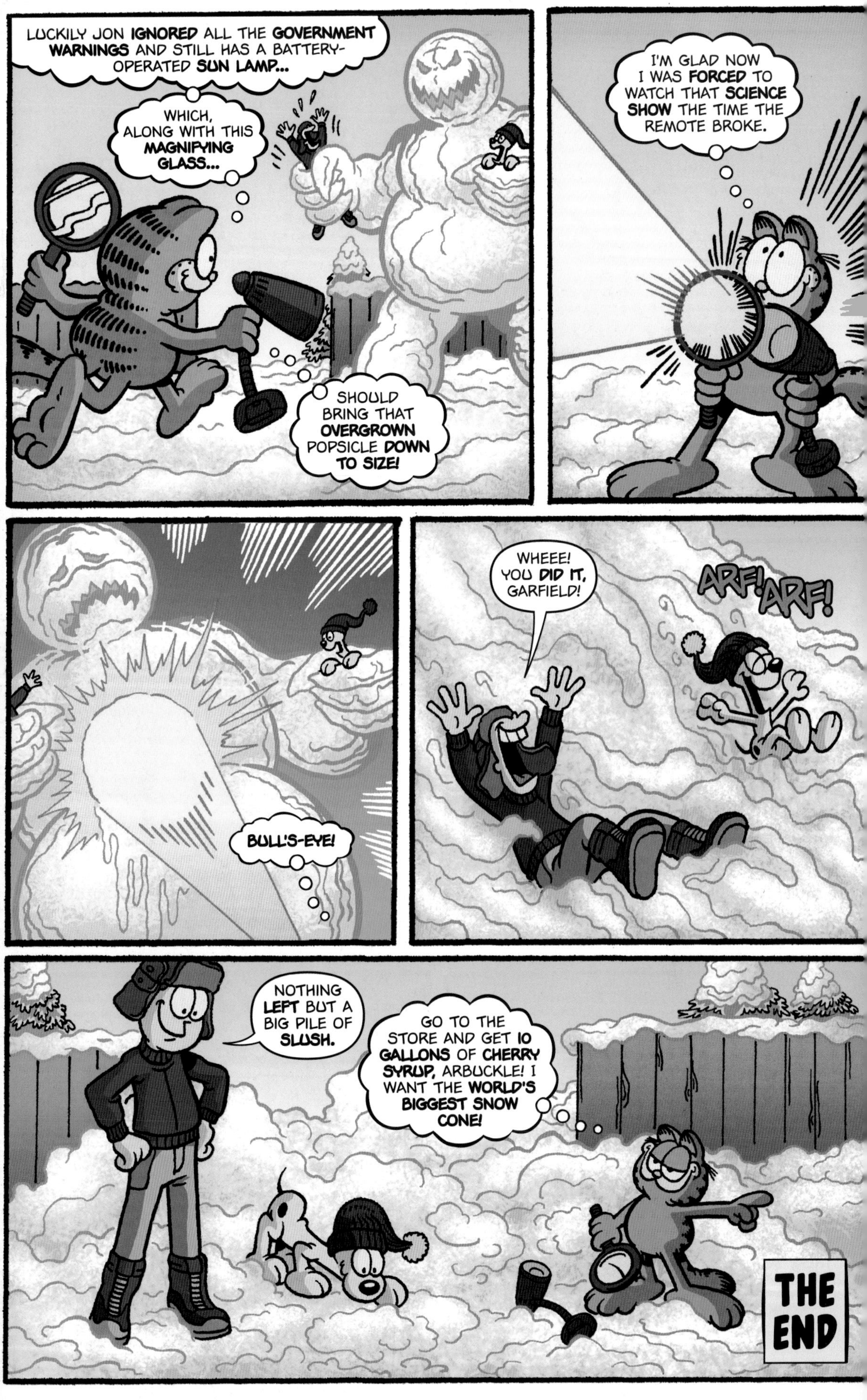
LUCKILY JON IGNORED ALL THE GOVERNMENT WARNINGS AND STILL HAS A BATTERY-OPERATED SUN LAMP...
WHICH, ALONG WITH THIS MAGNIFYING GLASS...
SHOULD BRING THAT OVERGROWN POPSICLE DOWN TO SIZE!
I'M GLAD NOW I WAS FORCED TO WATCH THAT SCIENCE SHOW THE TIME THE REMOTE BROKE.
BULL'S-EYE!
WHEEE! YOU DID IT, GARFIELD!
ARF! ARF!
NOTHING LEFT BUT A BIG PILE OF SLUSH.
GO TO THE STORE AND GET 10 GALLONS OF CHERRY SYRUP, ARBUCKLE! I WANT THE WORLD'S BIGGEST SNOW CONE!
THE END

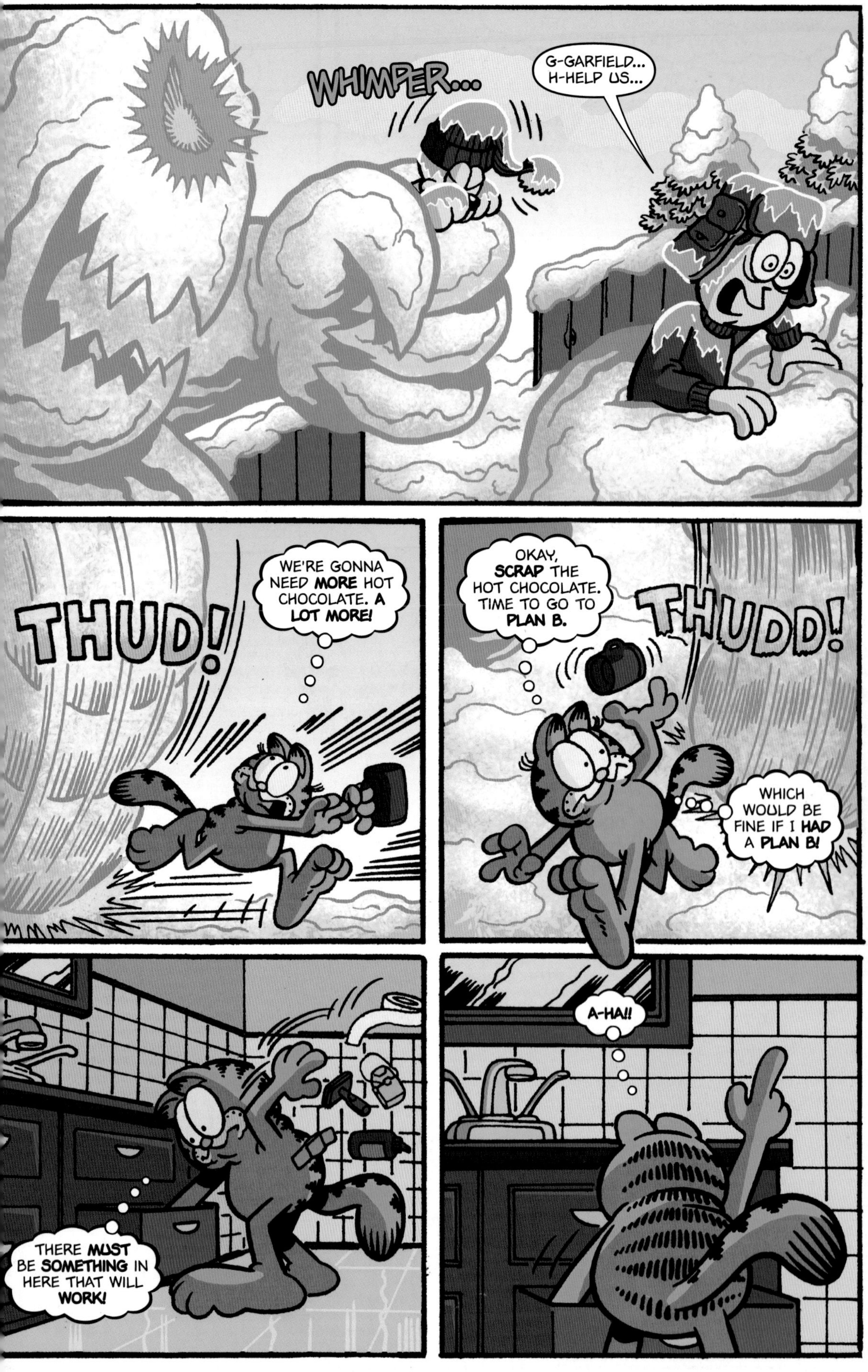
WHIMPER...
G-GARFIELD...
H-HELP US...
THUD!
WE'RE GONNA NEED MORE HOT CHOCOLATE. A LOT MORE!
OKAY, SCRAP THE HOT CHOCOLATE. TIME TO GO TO PLAN B.
THUDD!
WHICH WOULD BE FINE IF I HAD A PLAN B!
THERE MUST BE SOMETHING IN HERE THAT WILL WORK!
A-HA!!

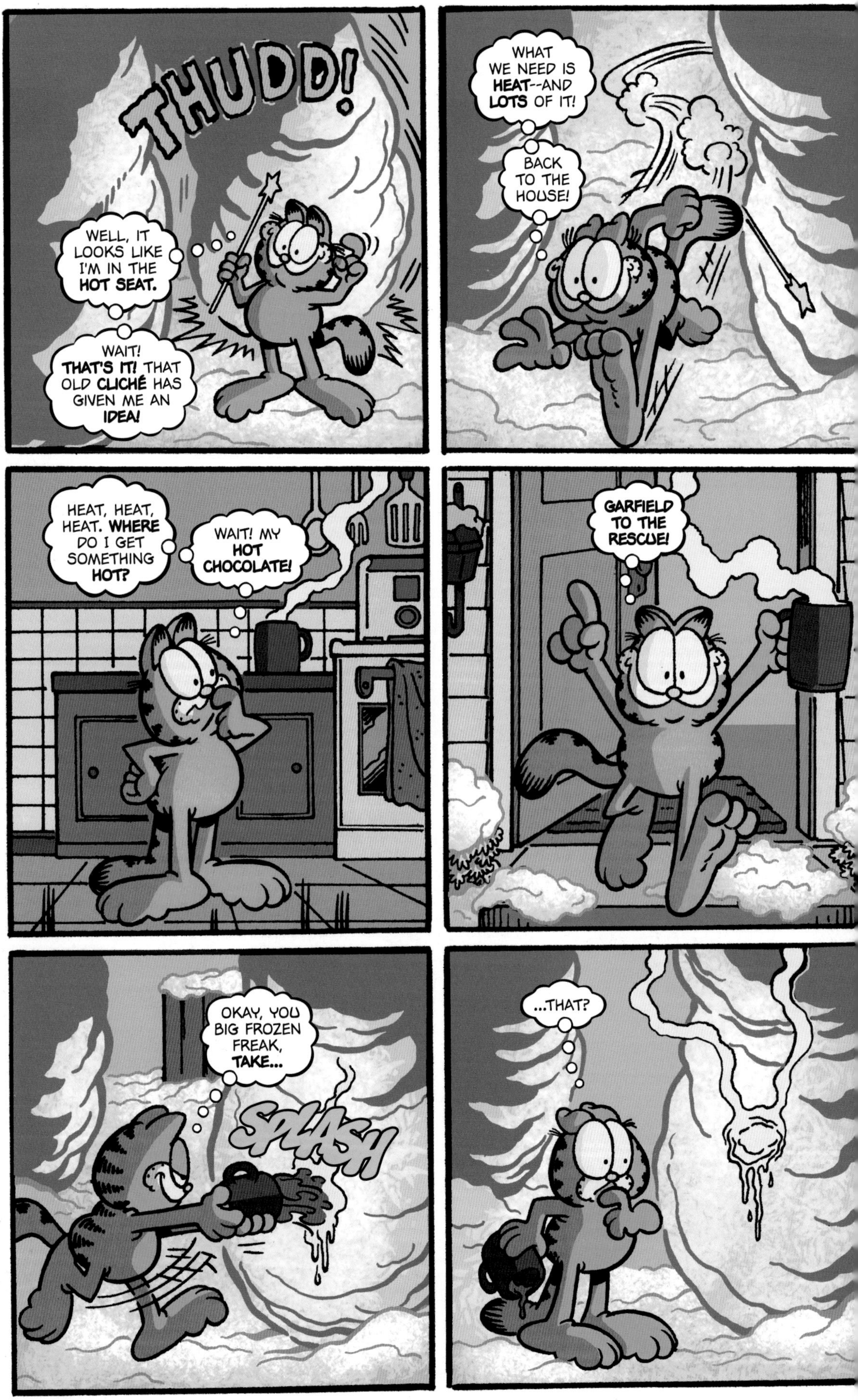
THUDD!
WELL, IT LOOKS LIKE I'M IN THE HOT SEAT.
WAIT! THAT'S IT! THAT OLD CLICHÉ HAS GIVEN ME AN IDEA!
WHAT WE NEED IS HEAT--AND LOTS OF IT!
BACK TO THE HOUSE!
HEAT, HEAT, HEAT. WHERE DO I GET SOMETHING HOT?
WAIT! MY HOT CHOCOLATE!
GARFIELD TO THE RESCUE!
OKAY, YOU BIG FROZEN FREAK, TAKE...
SPLASH
...THAT?

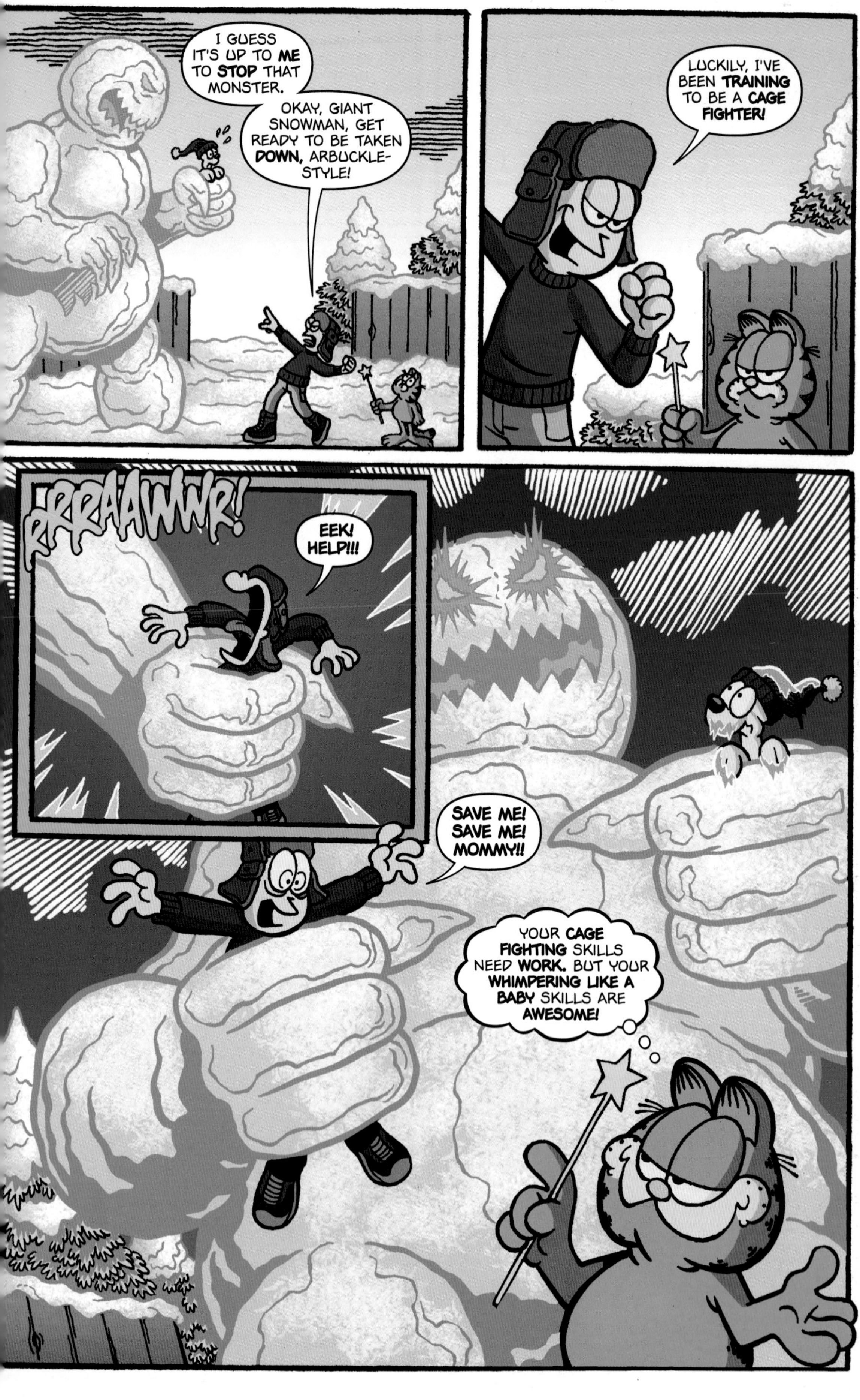

I GUESS IT'S UP TO **ME** TO **STOP** THAT MONSTER.
OKAY, GIANT SNOWMAN, GET READY TO BE TAKEN **DOWN,** ARBUCKLE-STYLE!
LUCKILY, I'VE BEEN **TRAINING** TO BE A **CAGE FIGHTER!**
RRRAAWWR!
EEK! HELP!!!
SAVE ME! SAVE ME! MOMMY!!
YOUR **CAGE FIGHTING** SKILLS NEED **WORK.** BUT YOUR **WHIMPERING LIKE A BABY** SKILLS ARE **AWESOME!**

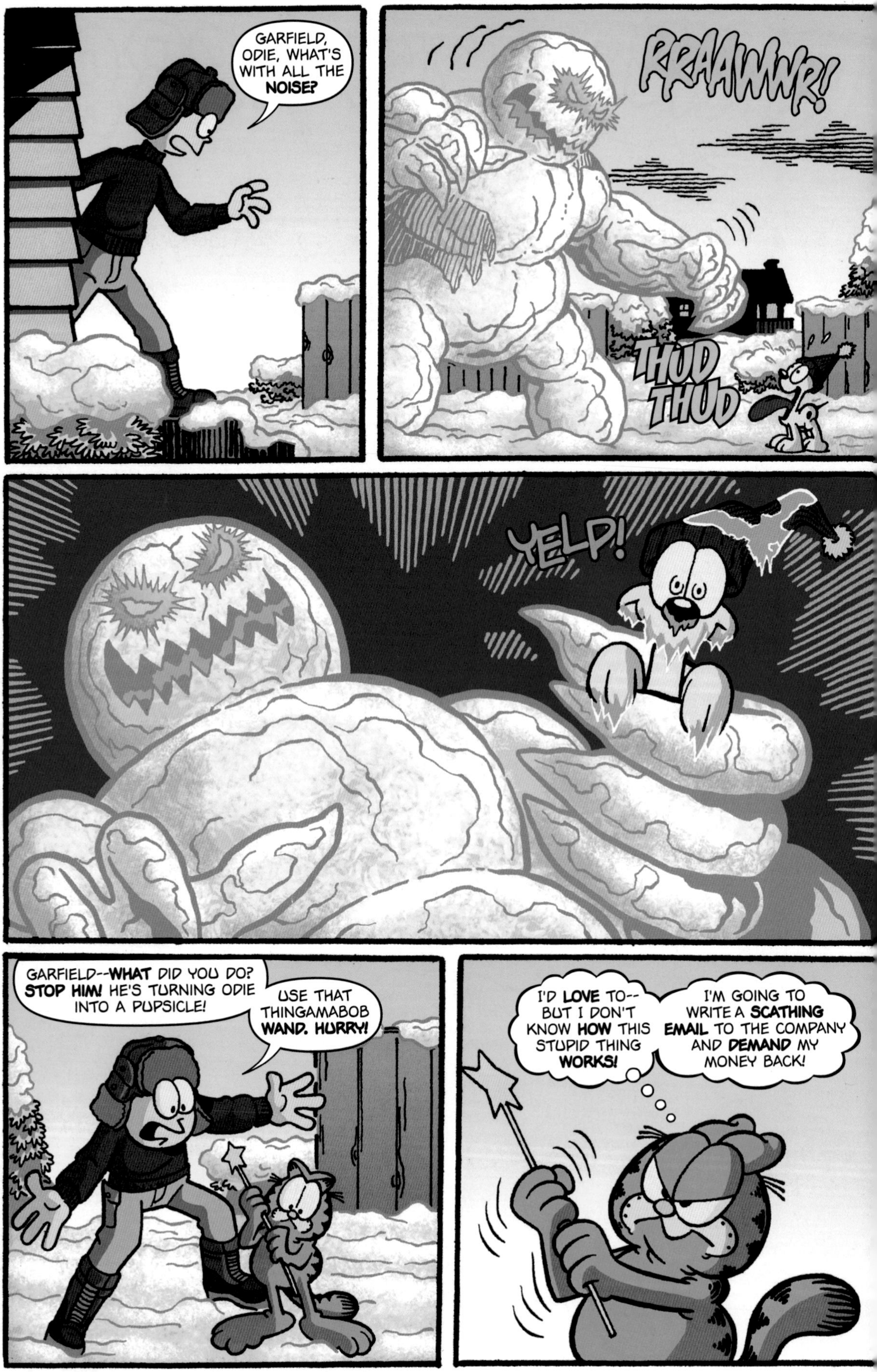
GARFIELD, ODIE, WHAT'S WITH ALL THE NOISE?
RRAAWWR!
THUD THUD
YELP!
GARFIELD--WHAT DID YOU DO? STOP HIM! HE'S TURNING ODIE INTO A PUPSICLE!
USE THAT THINGAMABOB WAND. HURRY!
I'D LOVE TO-- BUT I DON'T KNOW HOW THIS STUPID THING WORKS!
I'M GOING TO WRITE A SCATHING EMAIL TO THE COMPANY AND DEMAND MY MONEY BACK!

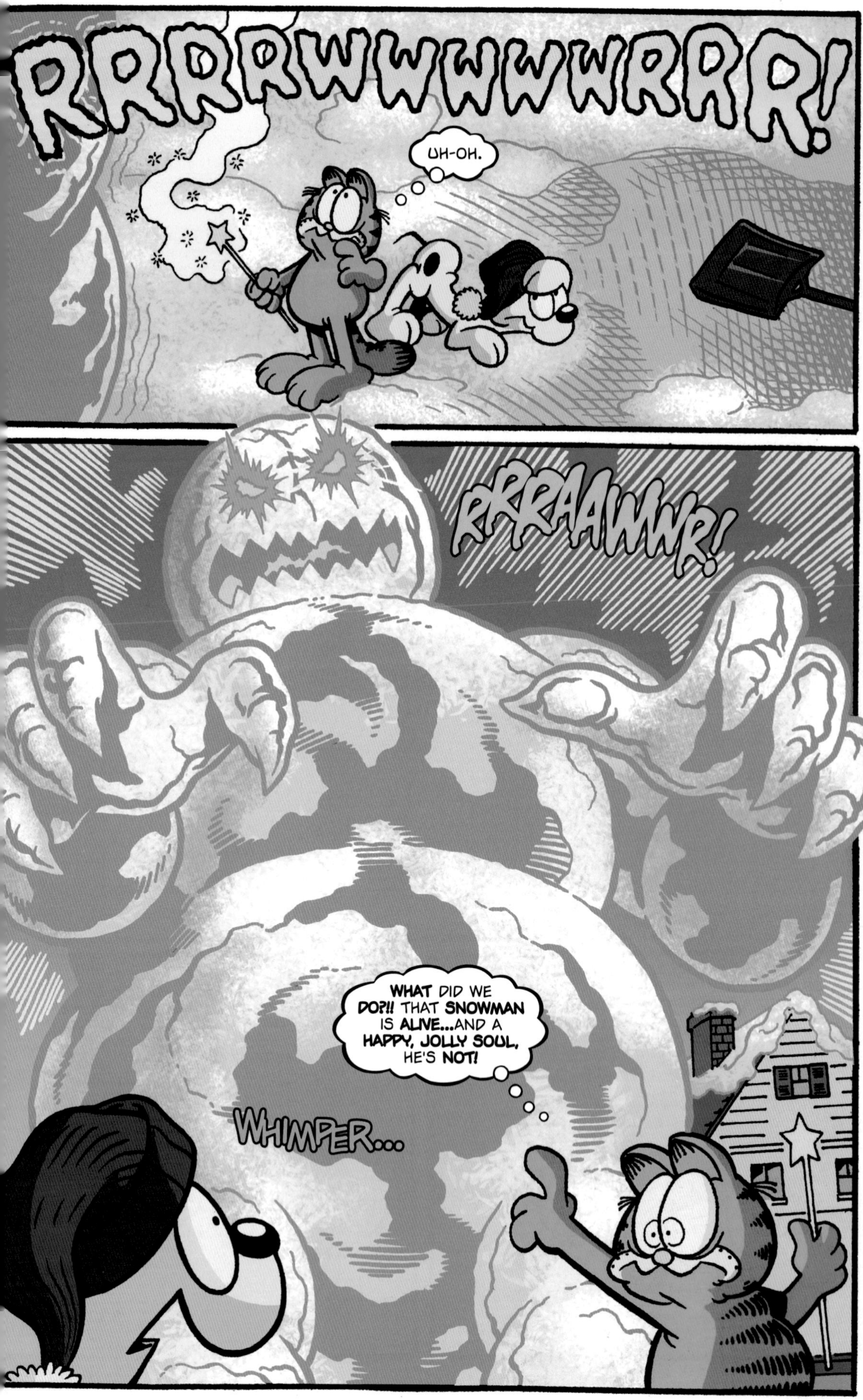
RRRRWWWWWRRRR!
UH-OH.
RRRAAWWR!
WHAT DID WE DO?!! THAT SNOWMAN IS ALIVE...AND A HAPPY, JOLLY SOUL, HE'S NOT!
WHIMPER...

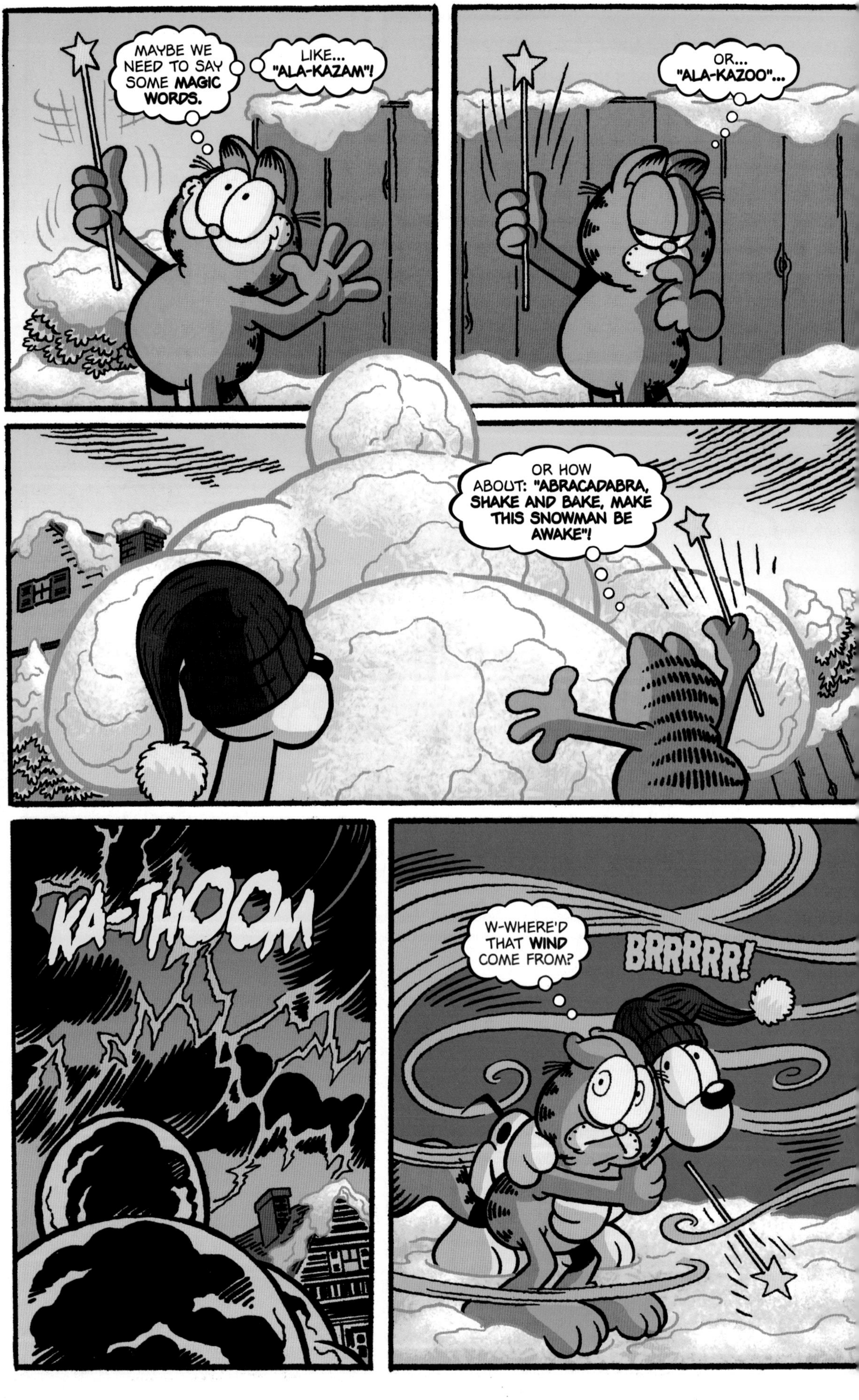

MAYBE WE NEED TO SAY SOME **MAGIC WORDS.**
LIKE... **"ALA-KAZAM"!**
OR... **"ALA-KAZOO"...**
OR HOW ABOUT: **"ABRACADABRA, SHAKE AND BAKE, MAKE THIS SNOWMAN BE AWAKE"!**
KA-THOOM
W-WHERE'D THAT **WIND** COME FROM?
BRRRRR!

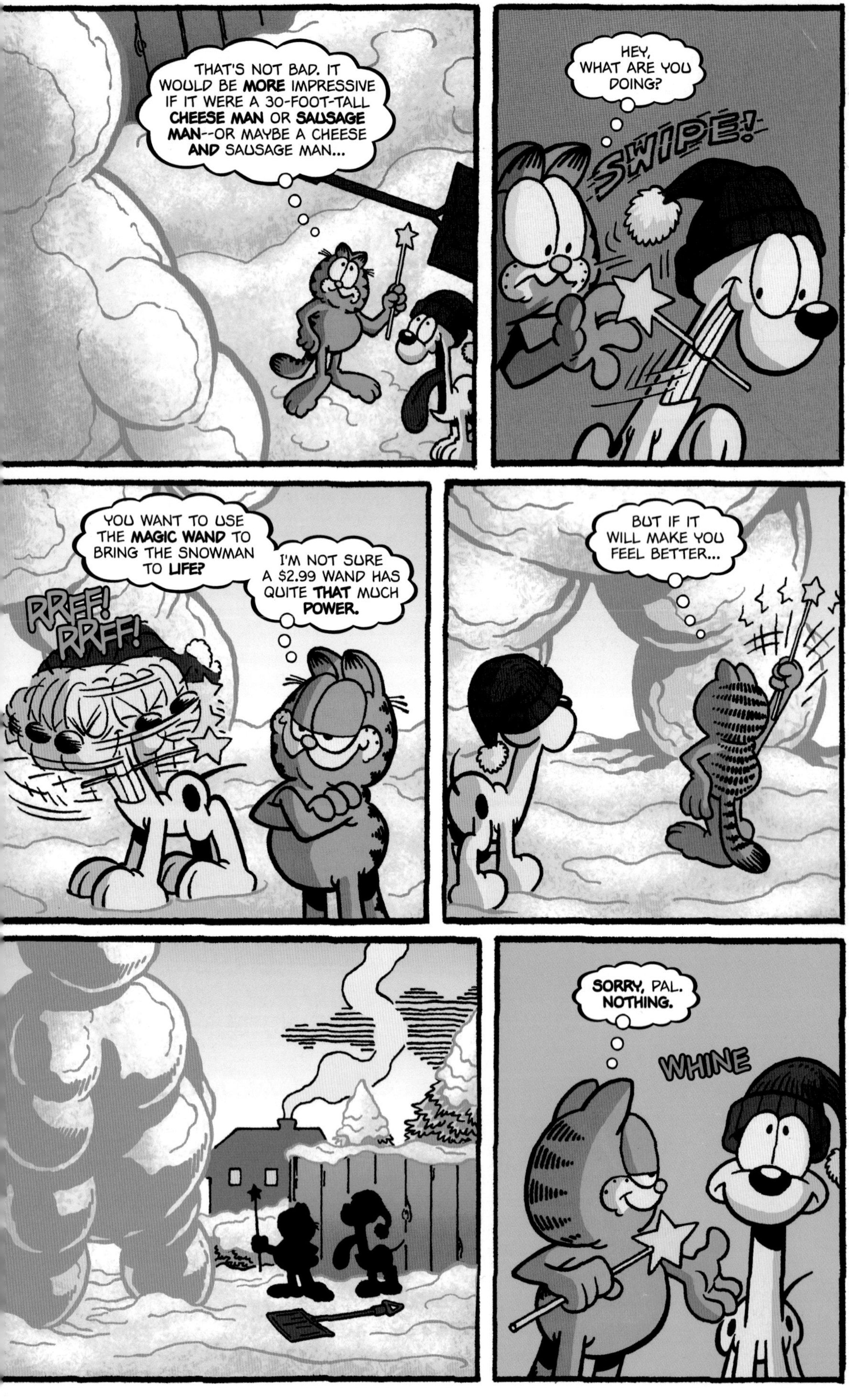

THAT'S NOT BAD. IT WOULD BE MORE IMPRESSIVE IF IT WERE A 30-FOOT-TALL CHEESE MAN OR SAUSAGE MAN--OR MAYBE A CHEESE AND SAUSAGE MAN...
HEY, WHAT ARE YOU DOING?
SWIPE!
YOU WANT TO USE THE MAGIC WAND TO BRING THE SNOWMAN TO LIFE?
RRFF! RRFF!
I'M NOT SURE A $2.99 WAND HAS QUITE THAT MUCH POWER.
BUT IF IT WILL MAKE YOU FEEL BETTER...
SORRY, PAL. NOTHING.
WHINE

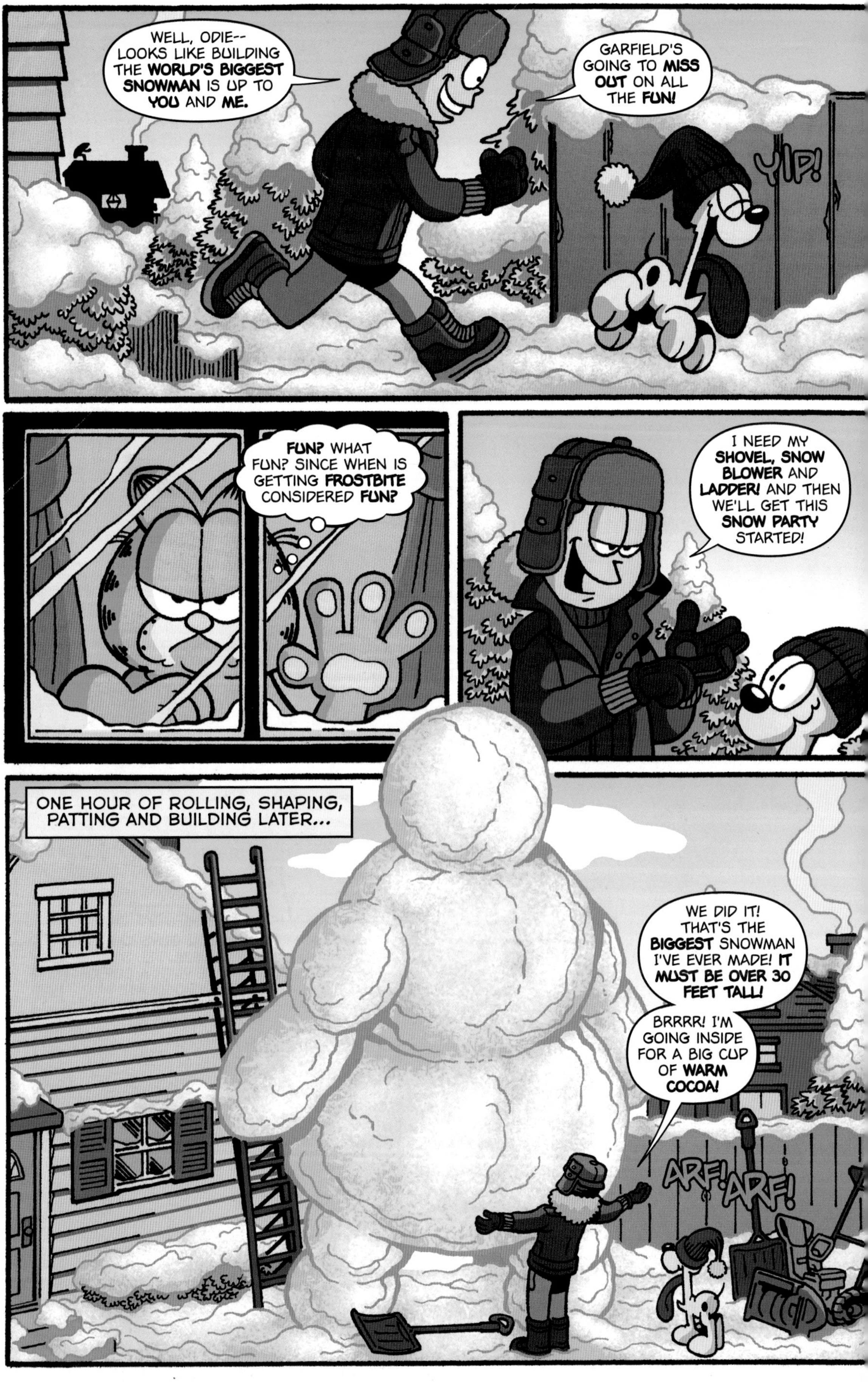
WELL, ODIE-- LOOKS LIKE BUILDING THE **WORLD'S BIGGEST SNOWMAN** IS UP TO **YOU** AND **ME.**
GARFIELD'S GOING TO **MISS OUT** ON ALL THE **FUN!**
YIP!
FUN? WHAT FUN? SINCE WHEN IS GETTING **FROSTBITE** CONSIDERED **FUN?**
I NEED MY **SHOVEL, SNOW BLOWER** AND **LADDER!** AND THEN WE'LL GET THIS **SNOW PARTY** STARTED!
ONE HOUR OF ROLLING, SHAPING, PATTING AND BUILDING LATER...
WE DID IT! THAT'S THE **BIGGEST** SNOWMAN I'VE EVER MADE! **IT MUST BE OVER 30 FEET TALL!**
BRRRR! I'M GOING INSIDE FOR A BIG CUP OF **WARM COCOA!**
ARF! ARF!

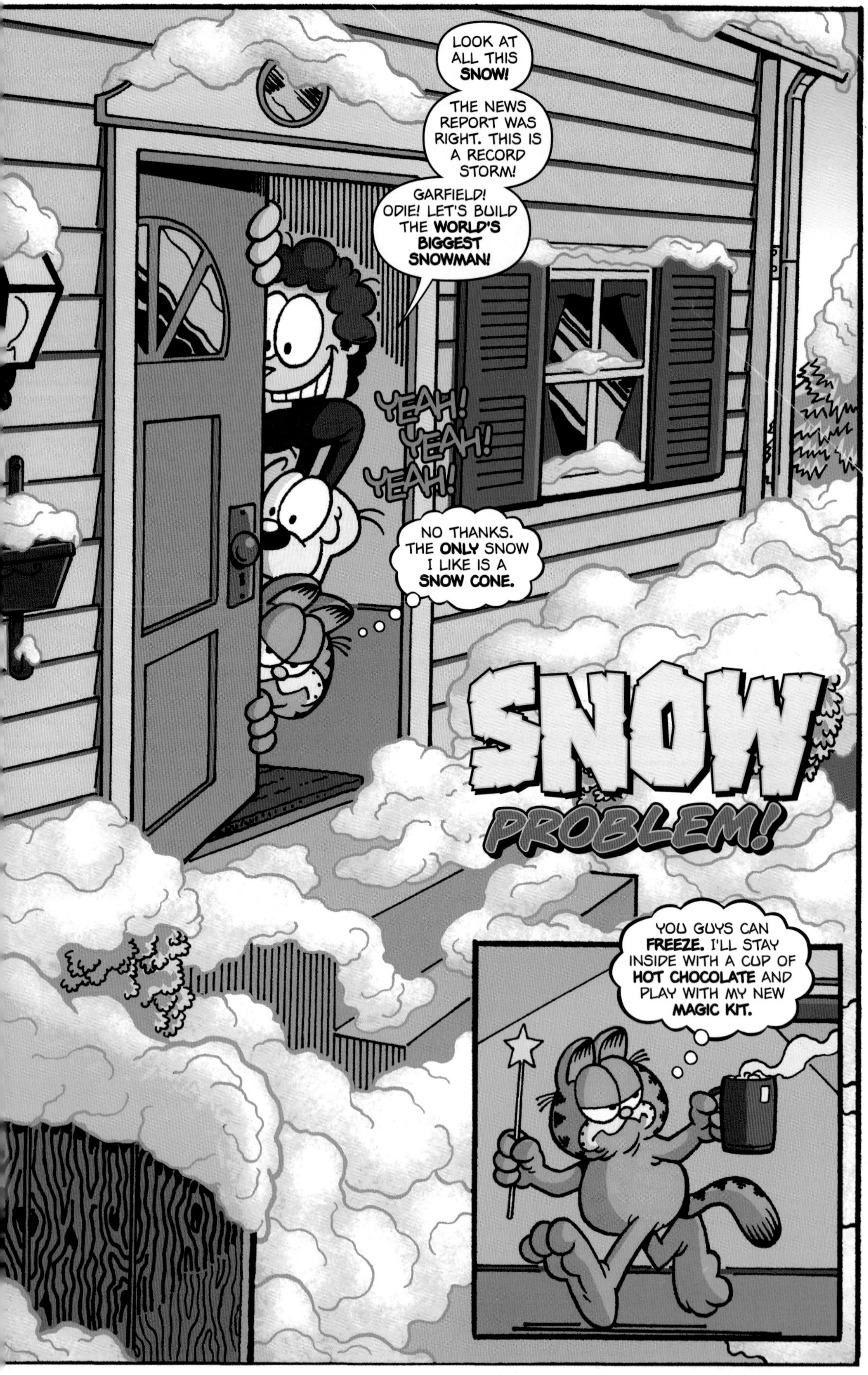

LOOK AT ALL THIS SNOW!
THE NEWS REPORT WAS RIGHT. THIS IS A RECORD STORM!
GARFIELD! ODIE! LET'S BUILD THE WORLD'S BIGGEST SNOWMAN!
YEAH! YEAH! YEAH!
NO THANKS. THE ONLY SNOW I LIKE IS A SNOW CONE.
SNOW PROBLEM!
YOU GUYS CAN FREEZE. I'LL STAY INSIDE WITH A CUP OF HOT CHOCOLATE AND PLAY WITH MY NEW MAGIC KIT.

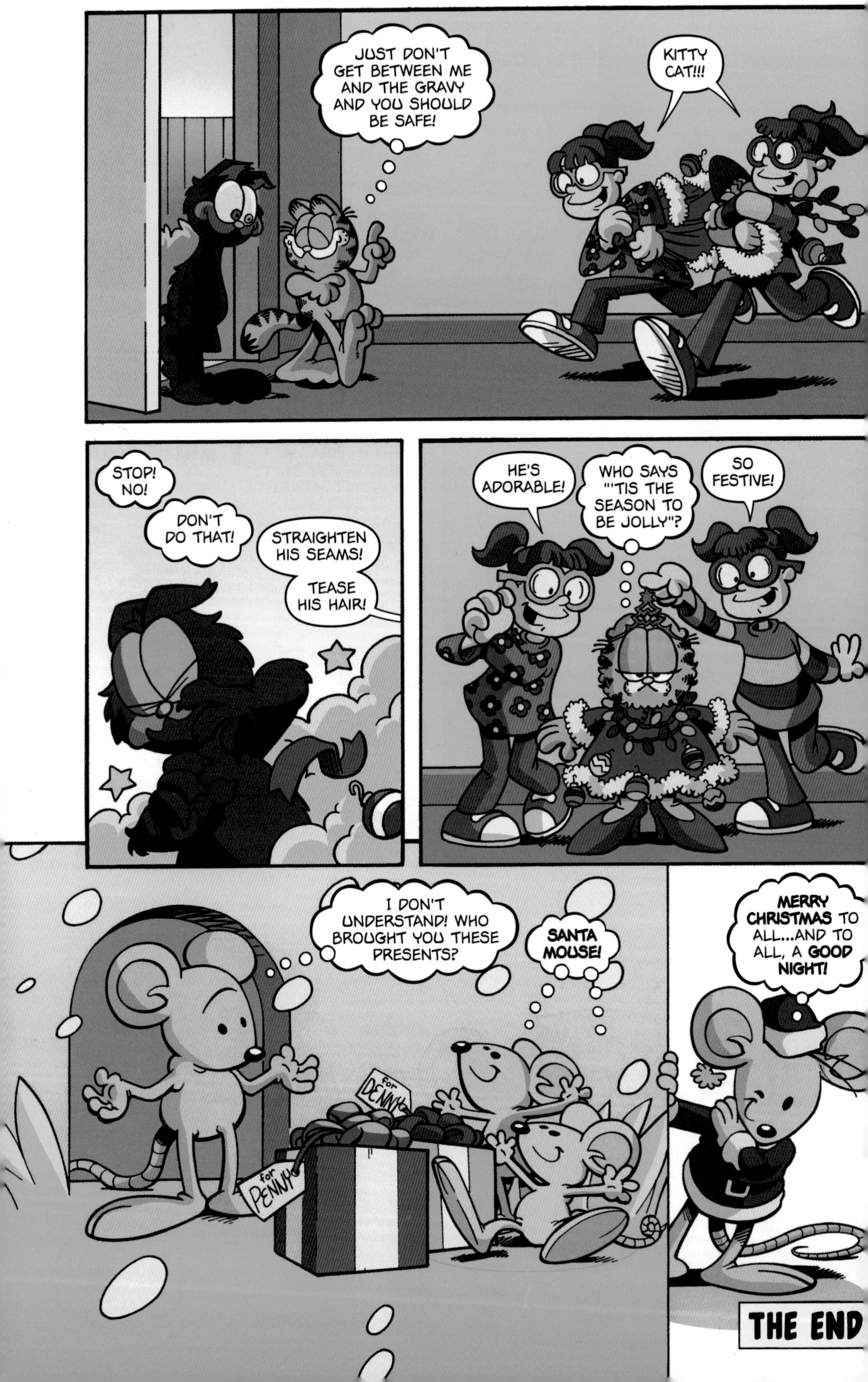
JUST DON'T GET BETWEEN ME AND THE GRAVY AND YOU SHOULD BE SAFE!
KITTY CAT!!!
STOP! NO!
DON'T DO THAT!
STRAIGHTEN HIS SEAMS!
TEASE HIS HAIR!
HE'S ADORABLE!
WHO SAYS "'TIS THE SEASON TO BE JOLLY"?
SO FESTIVE!
for DENNY
for PENNY
I DON'T UNDERSTAND! WHO BROUGHT YOU THESE PRESENTS?
SANTA MOUSE!
MERRY CHRISTMAS TO ALL...AND TO ALL, A GOOD NIGHT!
THE END

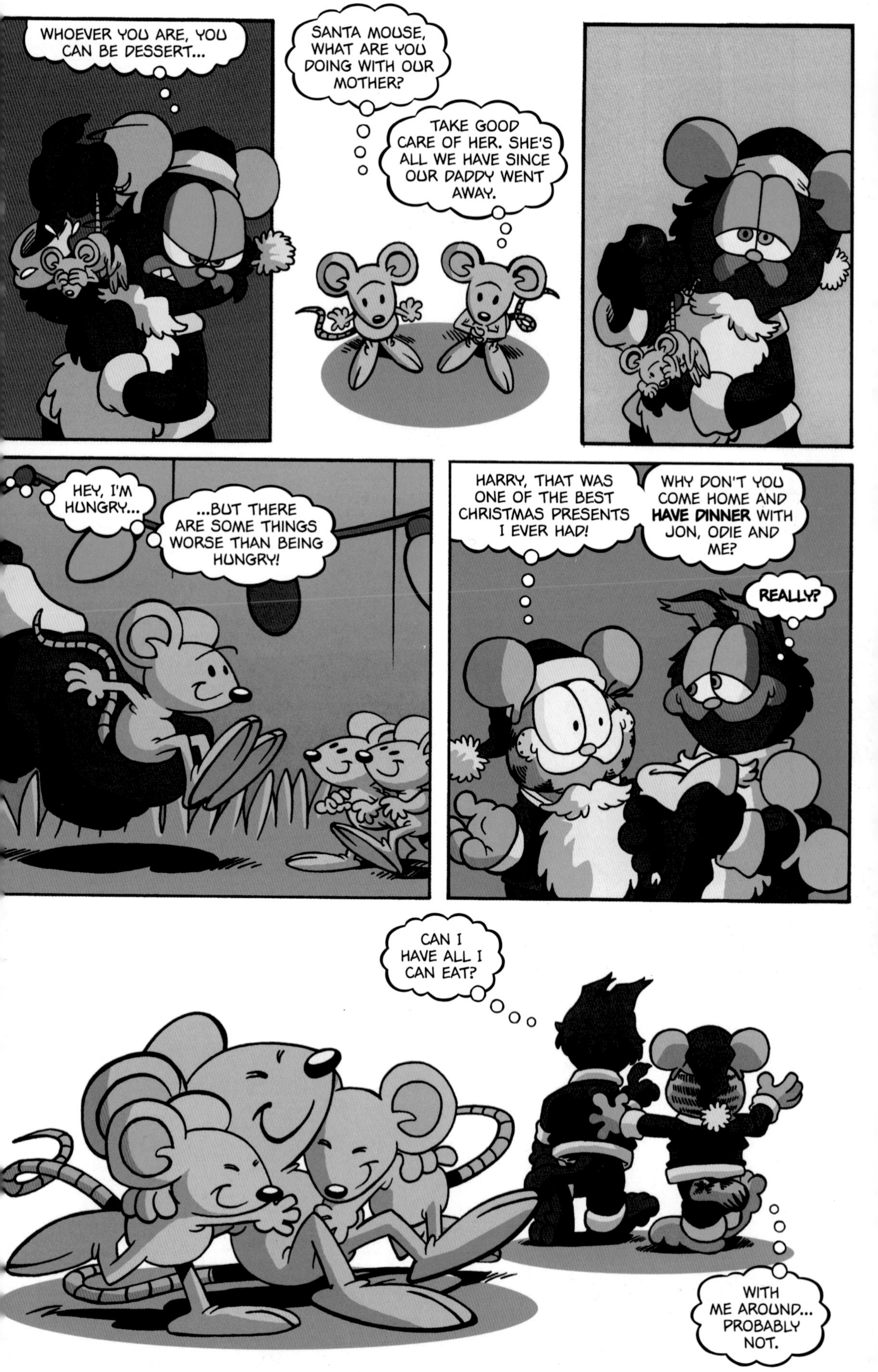

WHOEVER YOU ARE, YOU CAN BE DESSERT...
SANTA MOUSE, WHAT ARE YOU DOING WITH OUR MOTHER?
TAKE GOOD CARE OF HER. SHE'S ALL WE HAVE SINCE OUR DADDY WENT AWAY.
HEY, I'M HUNGRY...
...BUT THERE ARE SOME THINGS WORSE THAN BEING HUNGRY!
HARRY, THAT WAS ONE OF THE BEST CHRISTMAS PRESENTS I EVER HAD!
WHY DON'T YOU COME HOME AND HAVE DINNER WITH JON, ODIE AND ME?
REALLY?
CAN I HAVE ALL I CAN EAT?
WITH ME AROUND... PROBABLY NOT.

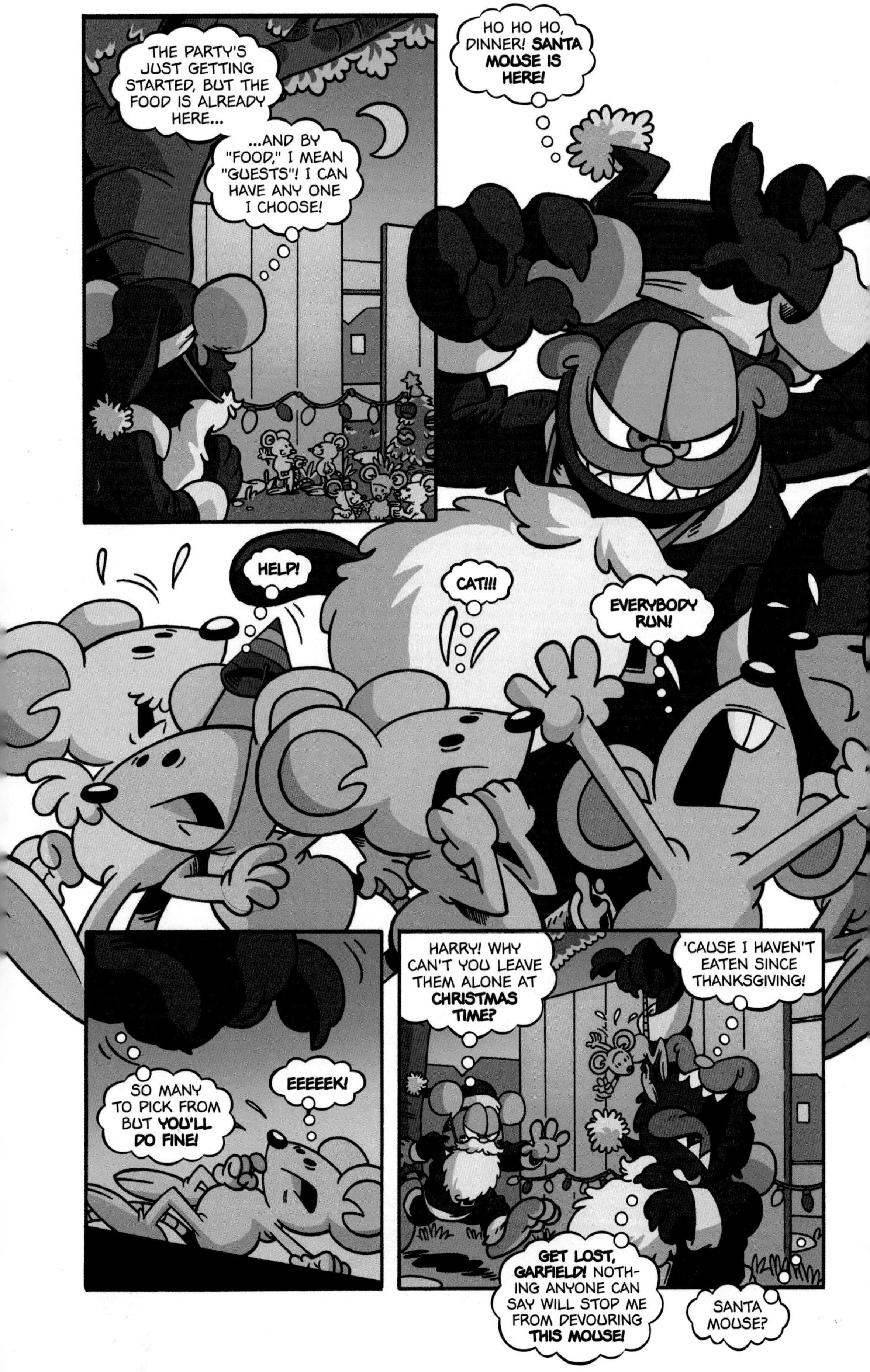
THE PARTY'S JUST GETTING STARTED, BUT THE FOOD IS ALREADY HERE...
...AND BY "FOOD," I MEAN "GUESTS"! I CAN HAVE ANY ONE I CHOOSE!
HO HO HO, DINNER! SANTA MOUSE IS HERE!
HELP!
CAT!!!
EVERYBODY RUN!
SO MANY TO PICK FROM BUT YOU'LL DO FINE!
EEEEEK!
HARRY! WHY CAN'T YOU LEAVE THEM ALONE AT CHRISTMAS TIME?
'CAUSE I HAVEN'T EATEN SINCE THANKSGIVING!
GET LOST, GARFIELD! NOTH-ING ANYONE CAN SAY WILL STOP ME FROM DEVOURING THIS MOUSE!
SANTA MOUSE?

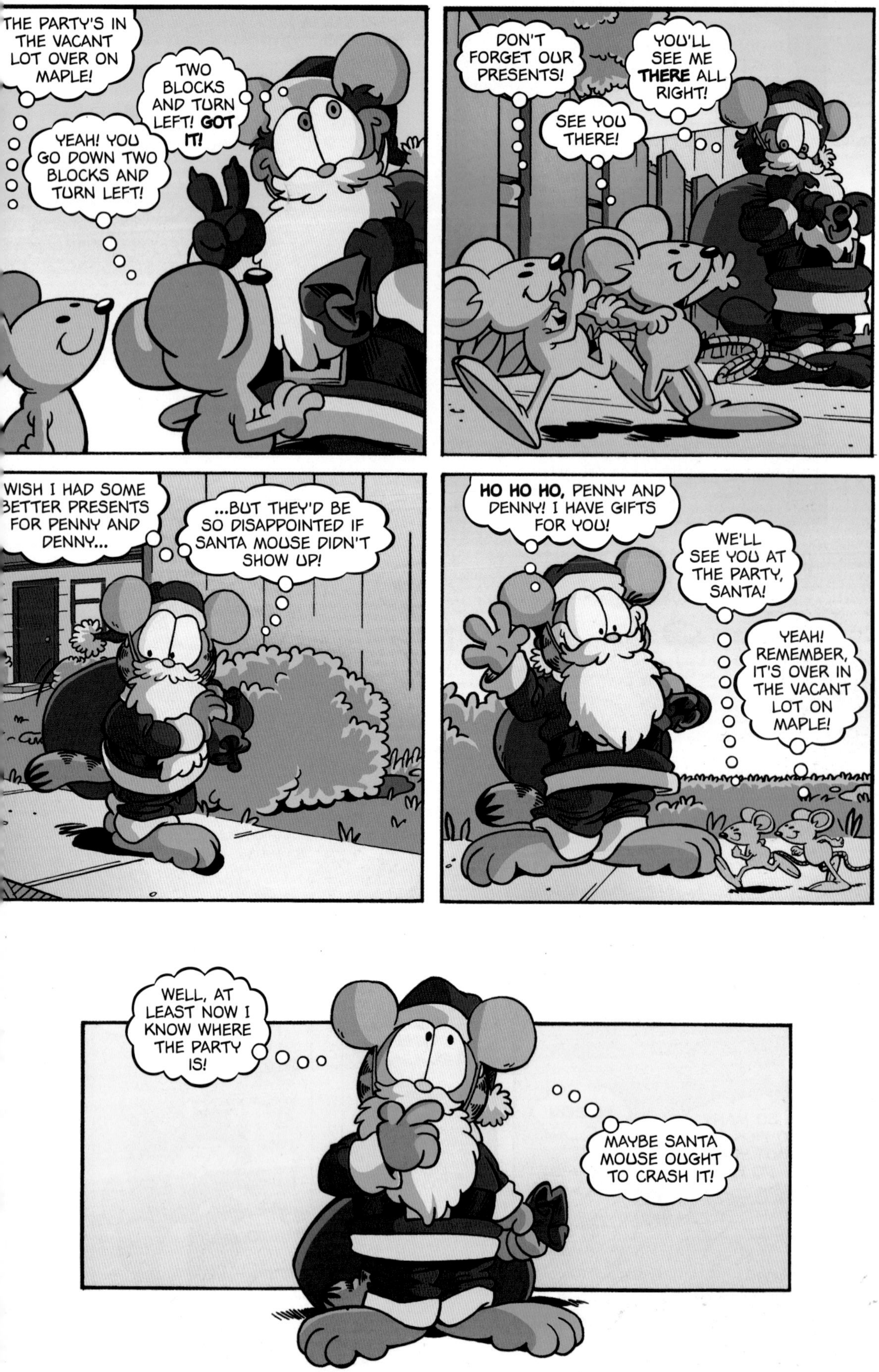

THE PARTY'S IN THE VACANT LOT OVER ON MAPLE!
TWO BLOCKS AND TURN LEFT! **GOT IT!**
YEAH! YOU GO DOWN TWO BLOCKS AND TURN LEFT!
DON'T FORGET OUR PRESENTS!
YOU'LL SEE ME **THERE** ALL RIGHT!
SEE YOU THERE!
WISH I HAD SOME BETTER PRESENTS FOR PENNY AND DENNY...
...BUT THEY'D BE SO DISAPPOINTED IF SANTA MOUSE DIDN'T SHOW UP!
HO HO HO, PENNY AND DENNY! I HAVE GIFTS FOR YOU!
WE'LL SEE YOU AT THE PARTY, SANTA!
YEAH! REMEMBER, IT'S OVER IN THE VACANT LOT ON MAPLE!
WELL, AT LEAST NOW I KNOW WHERE THE PARTY IS!
MAYBE SANTA MOUSE OUGHT TO CRASH IT!

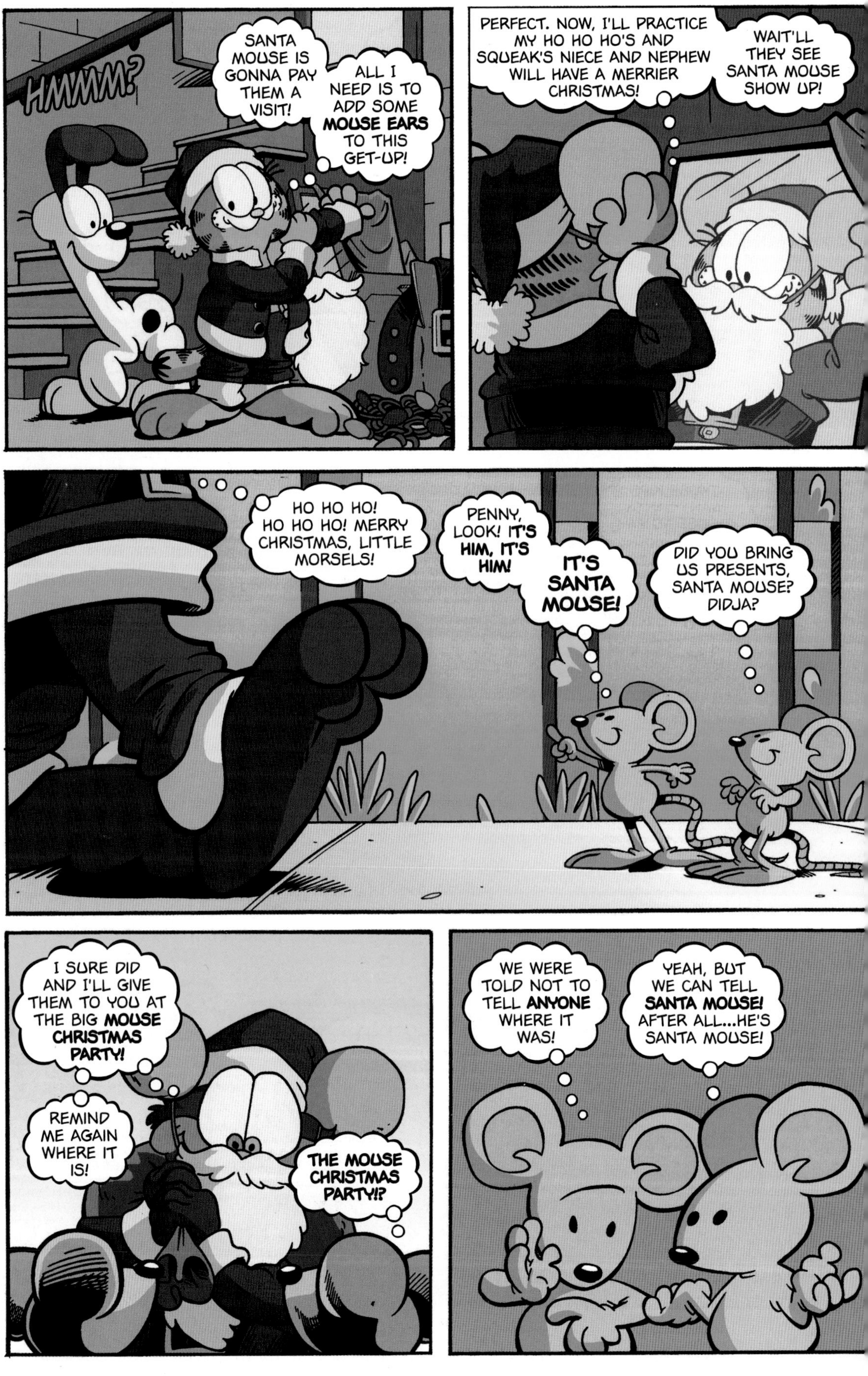
HMMM?
SANTA MOUSE IS GONNA PAY THEM A VISIT!
ALL I NEED IS TO ADD SOME MOUSE EARS TO THIS GET-UP!
PERFECT. NOW, I'LL PRACTICE MY HO HO HO'S AND SQUEAK'S NIECE AND NEPHEW WILL HAVE A MERRIER CHRISTMAS!
WAIT'LL THEY SEE SANTA MOUSE SHOW UP!
HO HO HO! HO HO HO! MERRY CHRISTMAS, LITTLE MORSELS!
PENNY, LOOK! IT'S HIM, IT'S HIM!
IT'S SANTA MOUSE!
DID YOU BRING US PRESENTS, SANTA MOUSE? DIDJA?
I SURE DID AND I'LL GIVE THEM TO YOU AT THE BIG MOUSE CHRISTMAS PARTY!
REMIND ME AGAIN WHERE IT IS!
THE MOUSE CHRISTMAS PARTY!?
WE WERE TOLD NOT TO TELL ANYONE WHERE IT WAS!
YEAH, BUT WE CAN TELL SANTA MOUSE! AFTER ALL...HE'S SANTA MOUSE!

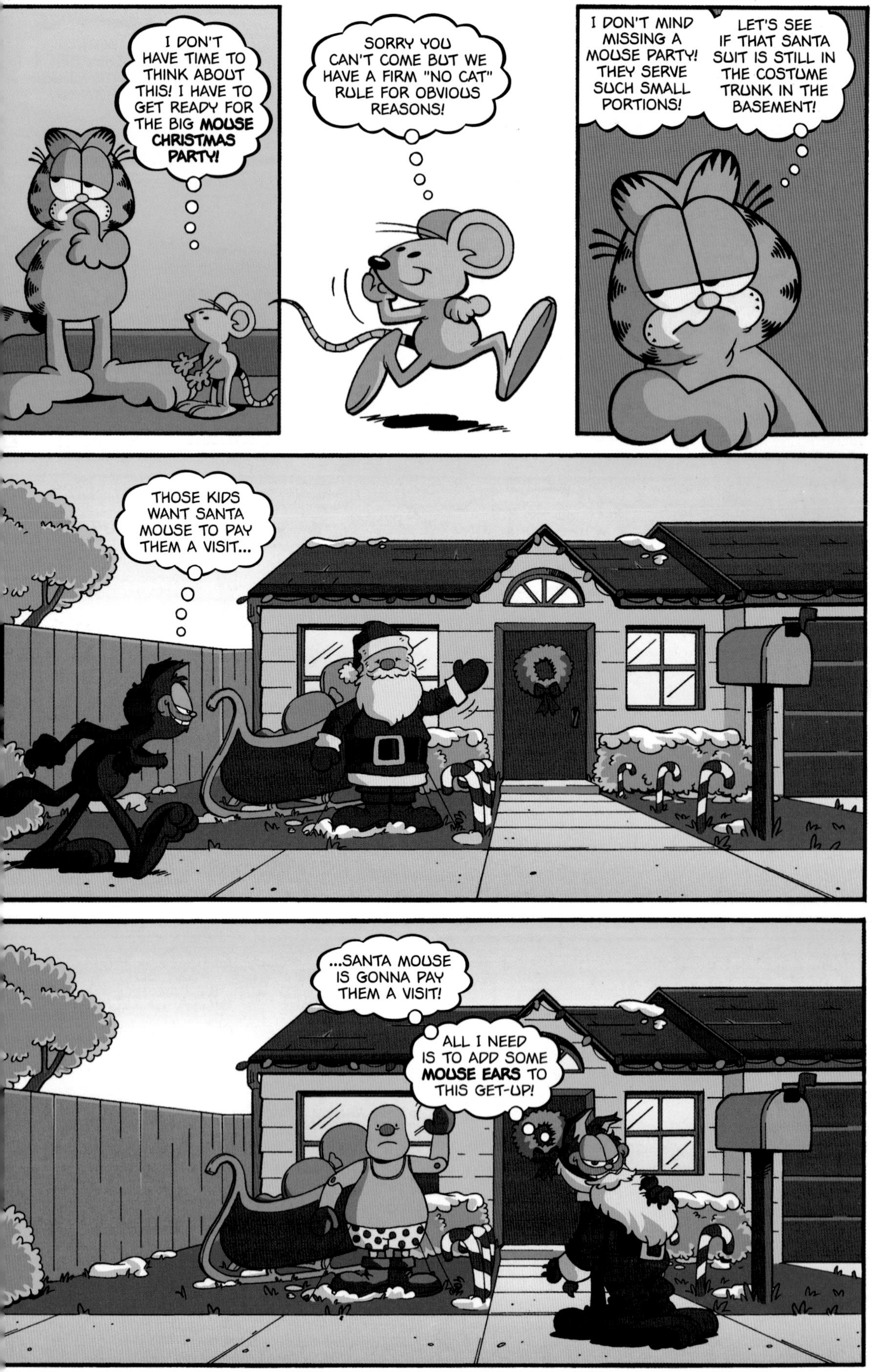
I DON'T HAVE TIME TO THINK ABOUT THIS! I HAVE TO GET READY FOR THE BIG MOUSE CHRISTMAS PARTY!
SORRY YOU CAN'T COME BUT WE HAVE A FIRM "NO CAT" RULE FOR OBVIOUS REASONS!
I DON'T MIND MISSING A MOUSE PARTY! THEY SERVE SUCH SMALL PORTIONS!
LET'S SEE IF THAT SANTA SUIT IS STILL IN THE COSTUME TRUNK IN THE BASEMENT!
THOSE KIDS WANT SANTA MOUSE TO PAY THEM A VISIT...
...SANTA MOUSE IS GONNA PAY THEM A VISIT!
ALL I NEED IS TO ADD SOME MOUSE EARS TO THIS GET-UP!

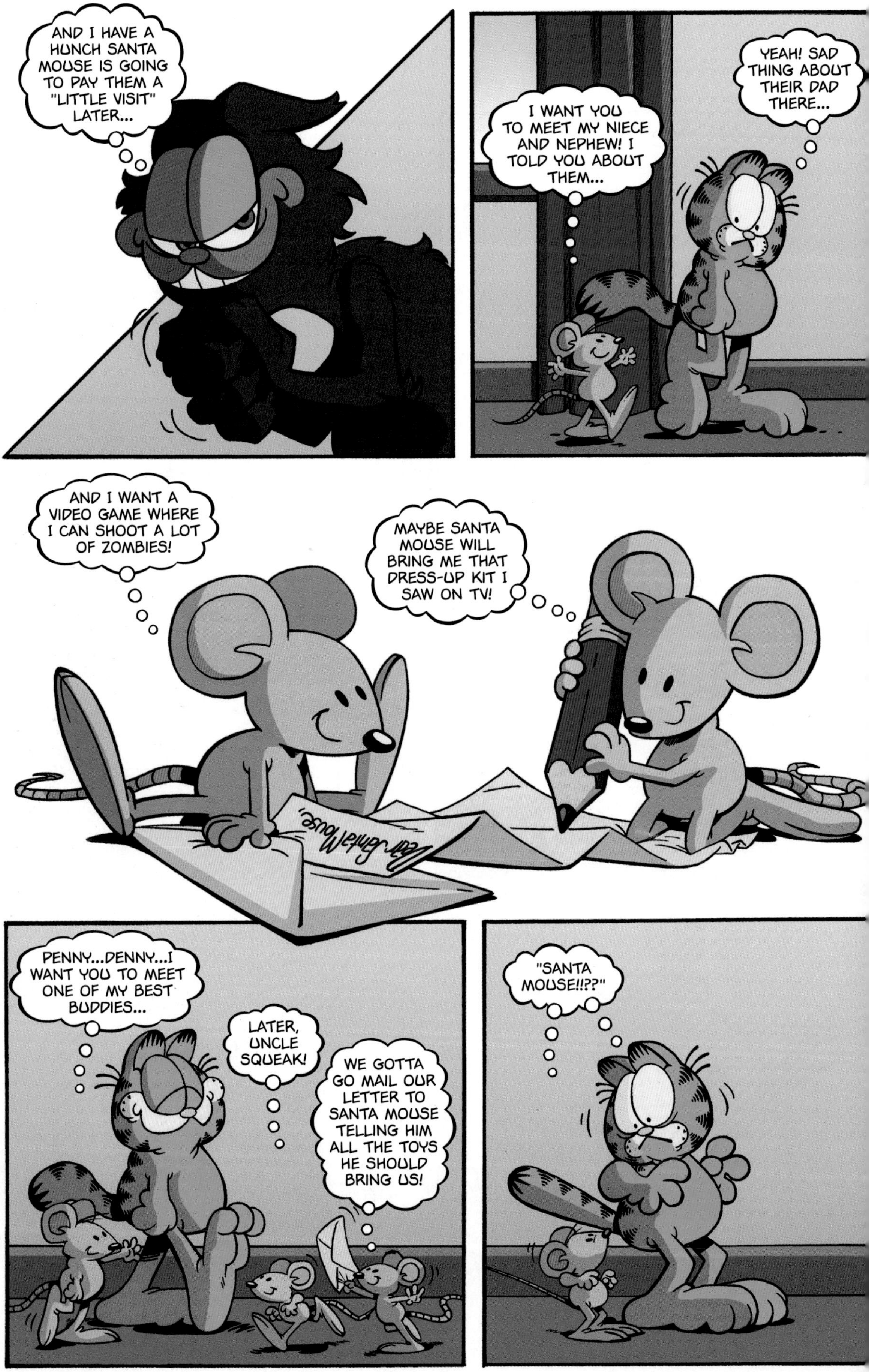
AND I HAVE A HUNCH SANTA MOUSE IS GOING TO PAY THEM A "LITTLE VISIT" LATER...
I WANT YOU TO MEET MY NIECE AND NEPHEW! I TOLD YOU ABOUT THEM...
YEAH! SAD THING ABOUT THEIR DAD THERE...
AND I WANT A VIDEO GAME WHERE I CAN SHOOT A LOT OF ZOMBIES!
MAYBE SANTA MOUSE WILL BRING ME THAT DRESS-UP KIT I SAW ON TV!
Dear Santa Mouse,
PENNY...DENNY...I WANT YOU TO MEET ONE OF MY BEST BUDDIES...
LATER, UNCLE SQUEAK!
WE GOTTA GO MAIL OUR LETTER TO SANTA MOUSE TELLING HIM ALL THE TOYS HE SHOULD BRING US!
"SANTA MOUSE!!??"

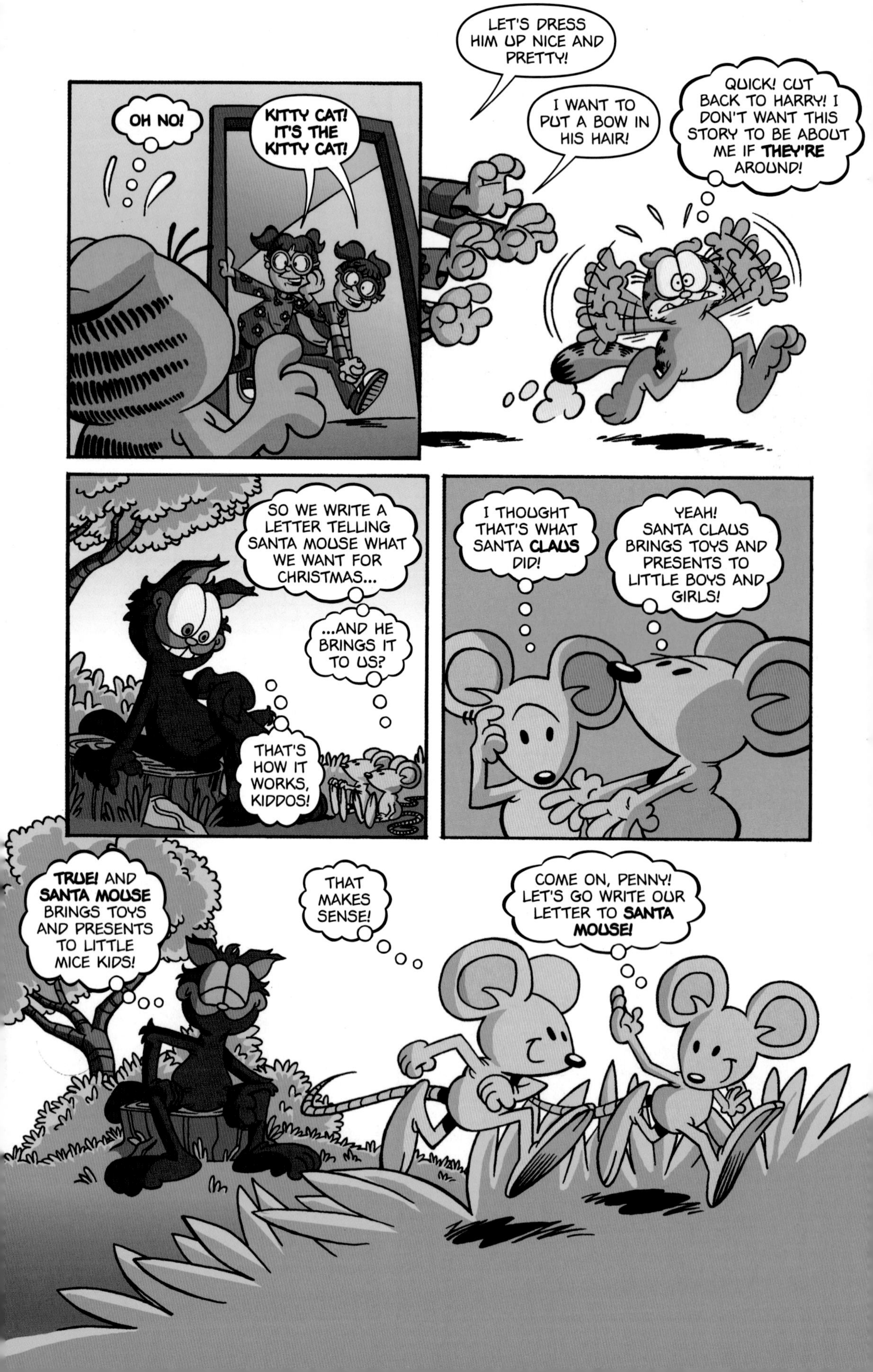
OH NO!
KITTY CAT! IT'S THE KITTY CAT!
LET'S DRESS HIM UP NICE AND PRETTY!
I WANT TO PUT A BOW IN HIS HAIR!
QUICK! CUT BACK TO HARRY! I DON'T WANT THIS STORY TO BE ABOUT ME IF THEY'RE AROUND!
SO WE WRITE A LETTER TELLING SANTA MOUSE WHAT WE WANT FOR CHRISTMAS...
...AND HE BRINGS IT TO US?
THAT'S HOW IT WORKS, KIDDOS!
I THOUGHT THAT'S WHAT SANTA CLAUS DID!
YEAH! SANTA CLAUS BRINGS TOYS AND PRESENTS TO LITTLE BOYS AND GIRLS!
TRUE! AND SANTA MOUSE BRINGS TOYS AND PRESENTS TO LITTLE MICE KIDS!
THAT MAKES SENSE!
COME ON, PENNY! LET'S GO WRITE OUR LETTER TO SANTA MOUSE!

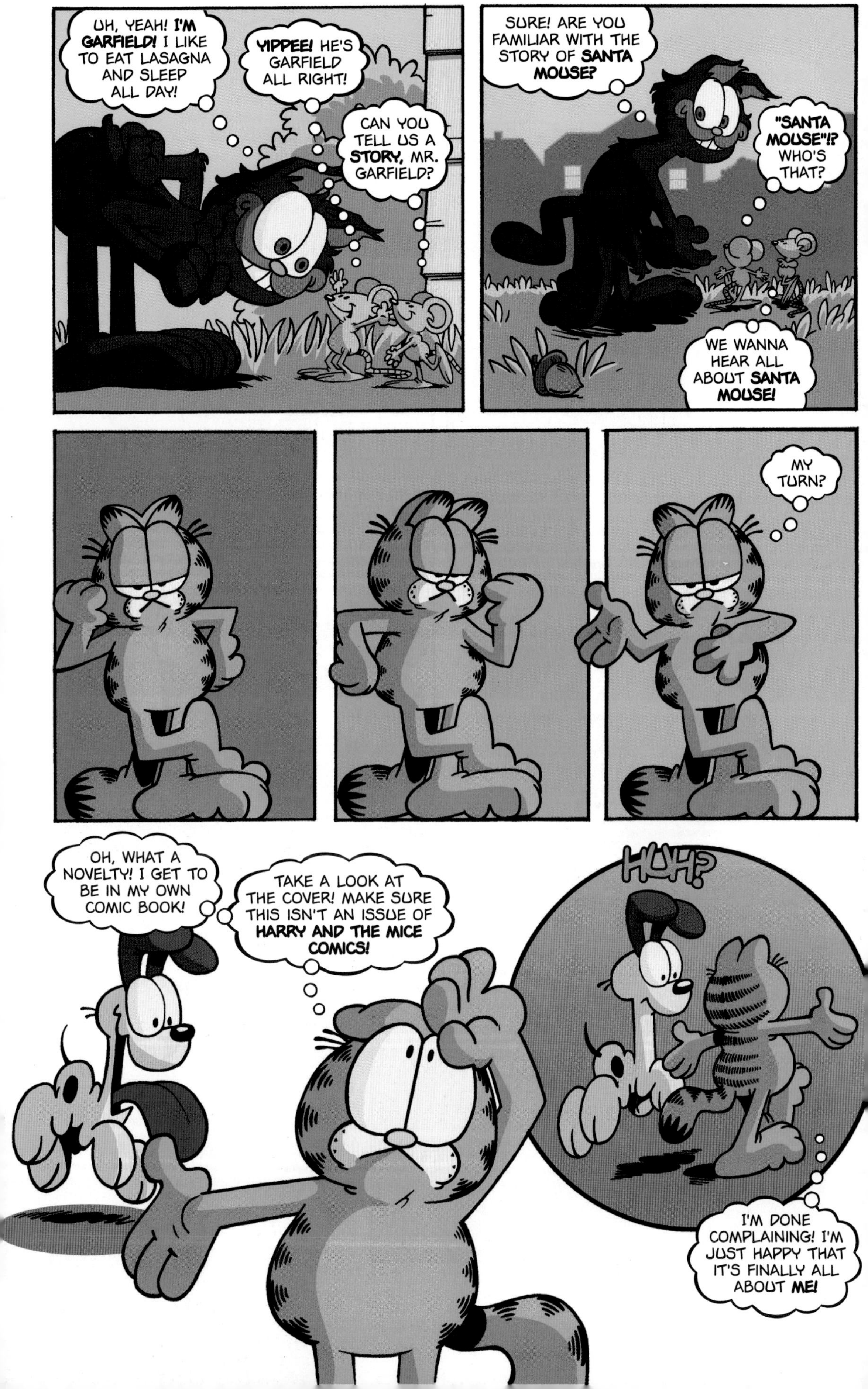

UH, YEAH! I'M GARFIELD! I LIKE TO EAT LASAGNA AND SLEEP ALL DAY!
YIPPEE! HE'S GARFIELD ALL RIGHT!
CAN YOU TELL US A STORY, MR. GARFIELD?
SURE! ARE YOU FAMILIAR WITH THE STORY OF SANTA MOUSE?
"SANTA MOUSE"!? WHO'S THAT?
WE WANNA HEAR ALL ABOUT SANTA MOUSE!
MY TURN?
OH, WHAT A NOVELTY! I GET TO BE IN MY OWN COMIC BOOK!
TAKE A LOOK AT THE COVER! MAKE SURE THIS ISN'T AN ISSUE OF HARRY AND THE MICE COMICS!
HUH?
I'M DONE COMPLAINING! I'M JUST HAPPY THAT IT'S FINALLY ALL ABOUT ME!

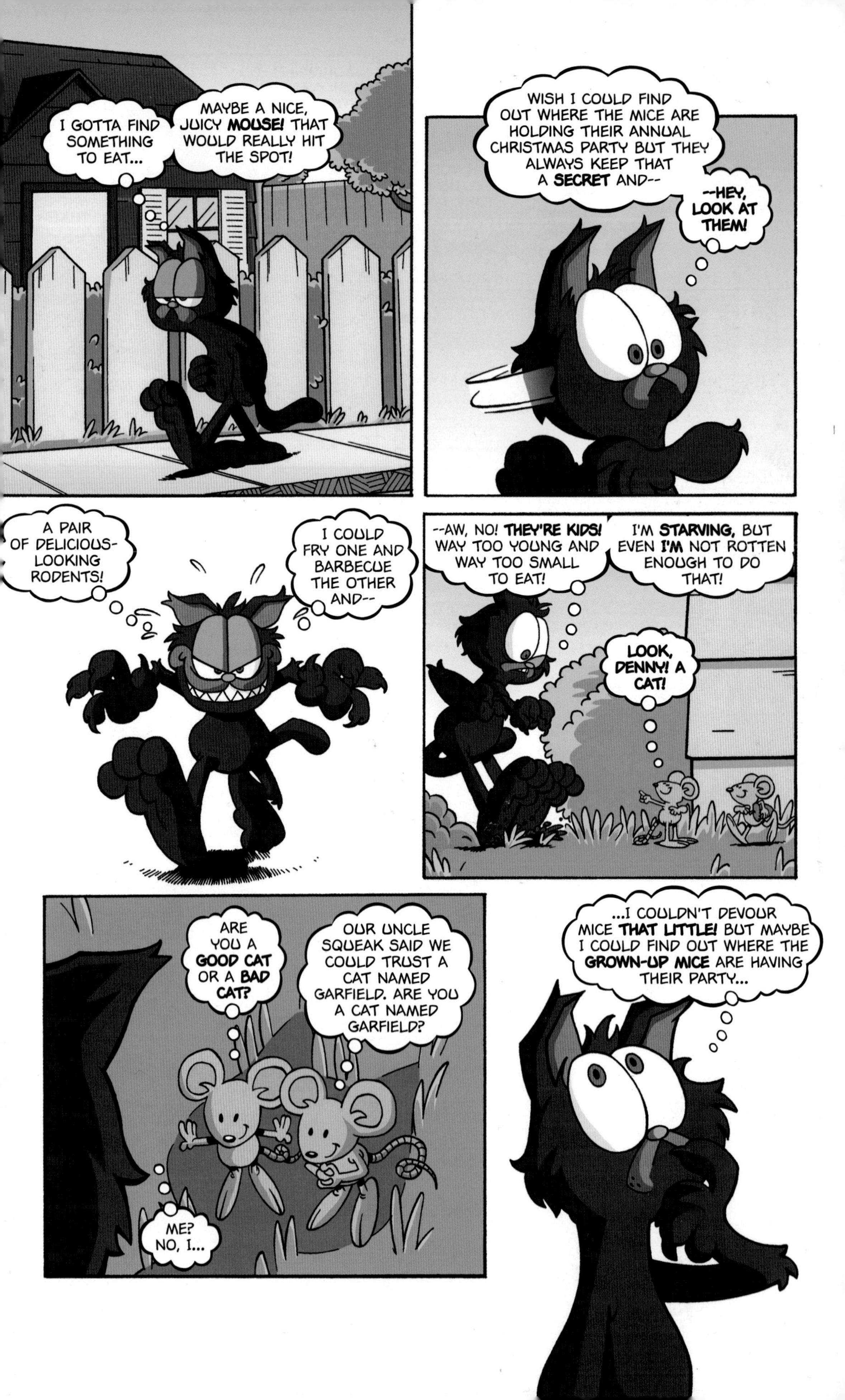
I GOTTA FIND SOMETHING TO EAT...
MAYBE A NICE, JUICY MOUSE! THAT WOULD REALLY HIT THE SPOT!
WISH I COULD FIND OUT WHERE THE MICE ARE HOLDING THEIR ANNUAL CHRISTMAS PARTY BUT THEY ALWAYS KEEP THAT A SECRET AND--
--HEY, LOOK AT THEM!
A PAIR OF DELICIOUS-LOOKING RODENTS!
I COULD FRY ONE AND BARBECUE THE OTHER AND--
--AW, NO! THEY'RE KIDS! WAY TOO YOUNG AND WAY TOO SMALL TO EAT!
I'M STARVING, BUT EVEN I'M NOT ROTTEN ENOUGH TO DO THAT!
LOOK, DENNY! A CAT!
ARE YOU A GOOD CAT OR A BAD CAT?
OUR UNCLE SQUEAK SAID WE COULD TRUST A CAT NAMED GARFIELD. ARE YOU A CAT NAMED GARFIELD?
ME? NO, I...
...I COULDN'T DEVOUR MICE THAT LITTLE! BUT MAYBE I COULD FIND OUT WHERE THE GROWN-UP MICE ARE HAVING THEIR PARTY...

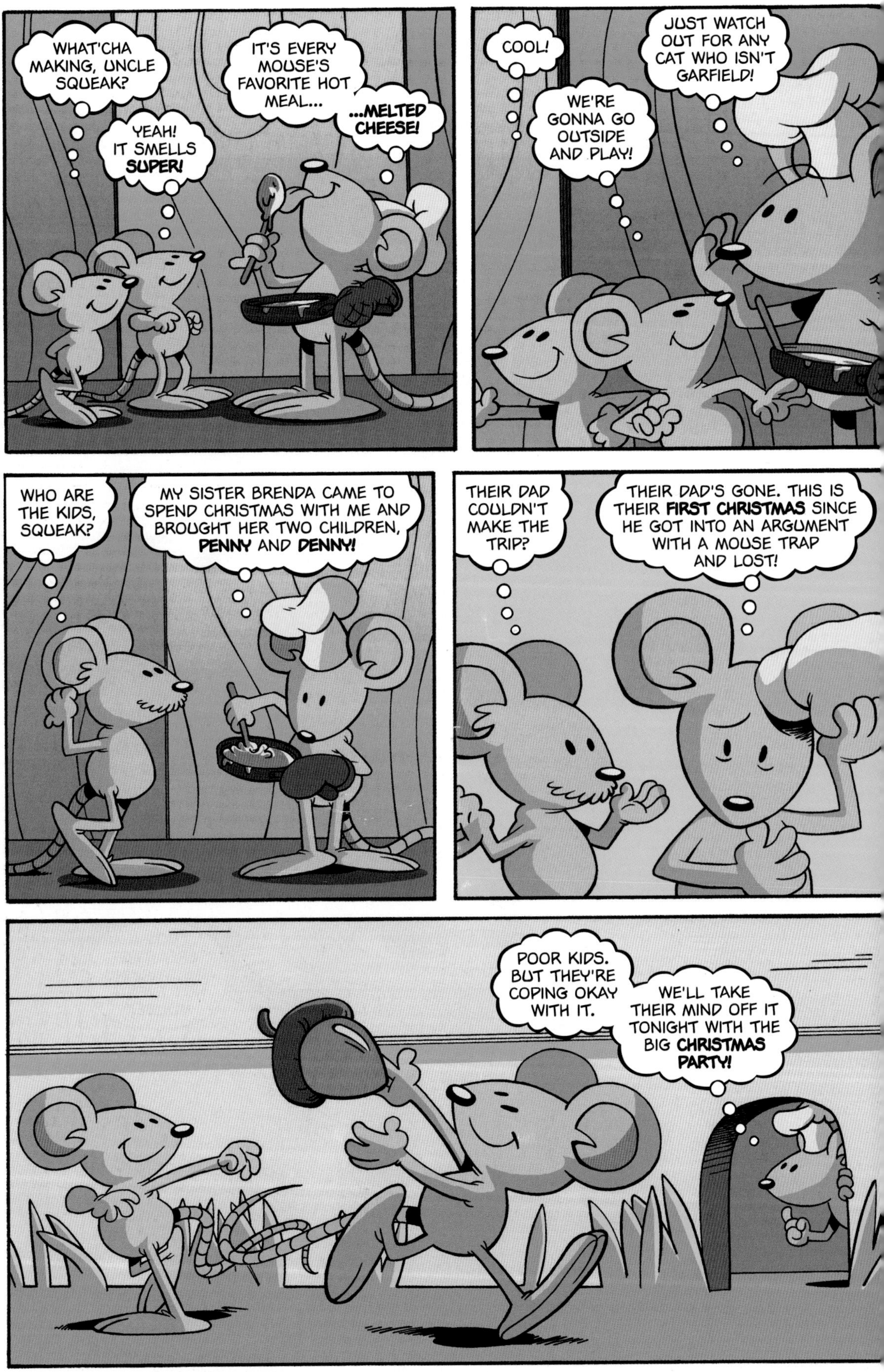
WHAT'CHA MAKING, UNCLE SQUEAK?
YEAH! IT SMELLS **SUPER!**
IT'S EVERY MOUSE'S FAVORITE HOT MEAL...
...MELTED CHEESE!
COOL!
WE'RE GONNA GO OUTSIDE AND PLAY!
JUST WATCH OUT FOR ANY CAT WHO ISN'T GARFIELD!
WHO ARE THE KIDS, SQUEAK?
MY SISTER BRENDA CAME TO SPEND CHRISTMAS WITH ME AND BROUGHT HER TWO CHILDREN, **PENNY** AND **DENNY!**
THEIR DAD COULDN'T MAKE THE TRIP?
THEIR DAD'S GONE. THIS IS THEIR **FIRST CHRISTMAS** SINCE HE GOT INTO AN ARGUMENT WITH A MOUSE TRAP AND LOST!
POOR KIDS. BUT THEY'RE COPING OKAY WITH IT.
WE'LL TAKE THEIR MIND OFF IT TONIGHT WITH THE BIG **CHRISTMAS PARTY!**

The Never-Ending Tale of Santa Mouse

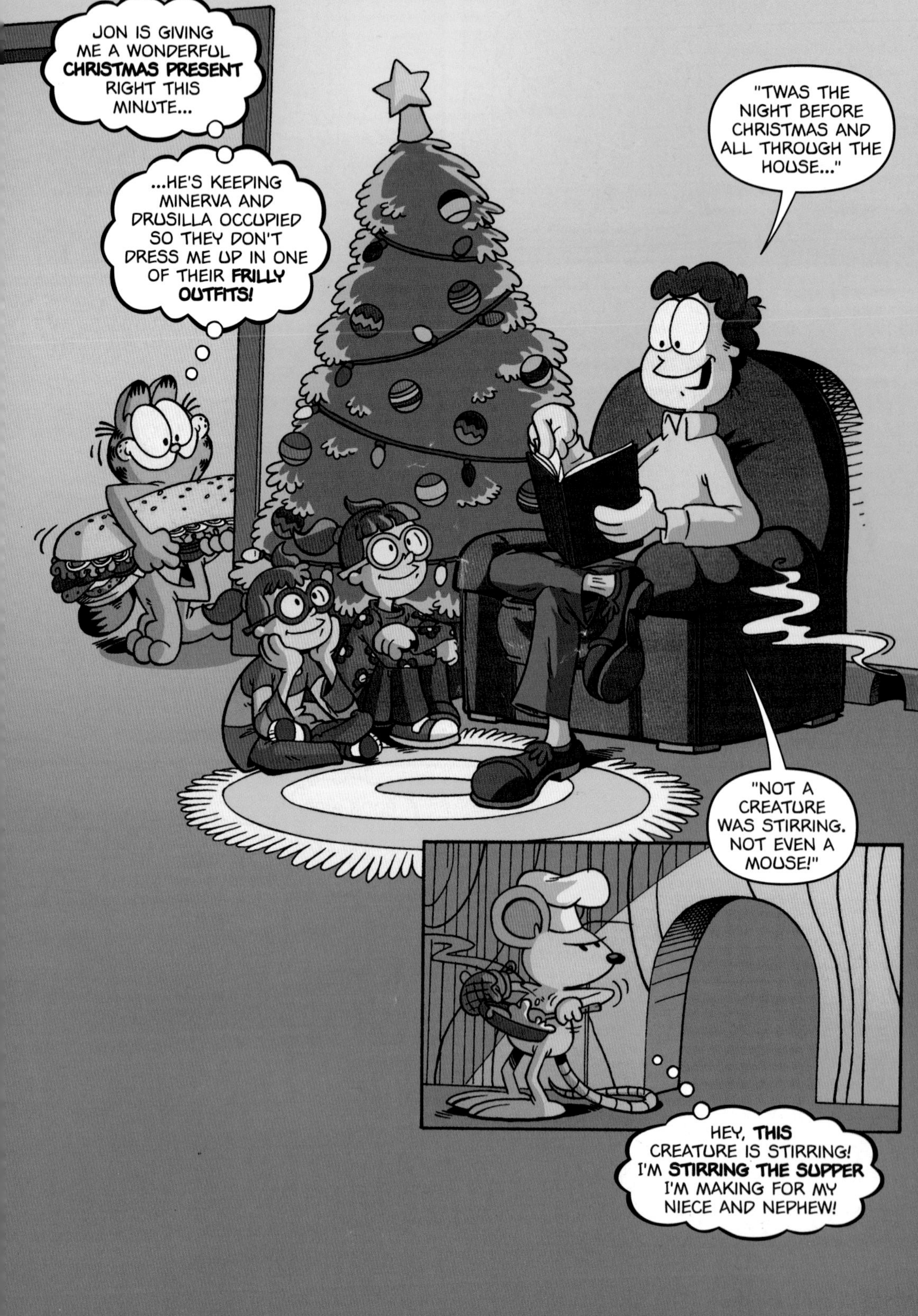
JON IS GIVING ME A WONDERFUL CHRISTMAS PRESENT RIGHT THIS MINUTE...
...HE'S KEEPING MINERVA AND DRUSILLA OCCUPIED SO THEY DON'T DRESS ME UP IN ONE OF THEIR FRILLY OUTFITS!
"TWAS THE NIGHT BEFORE CHRISTMAS AND ALL THROUGH THE HOUSE..."
"NOT A CREATURE WAS STIRRING. NOT EVEN A MOUSE!"
HEY, THIS CREATURE IS STIRRING! I'M STIRRING THE SUPPER I'M MAKING FOR MY NIECE AND NEPHEW!

CHAPTER 4

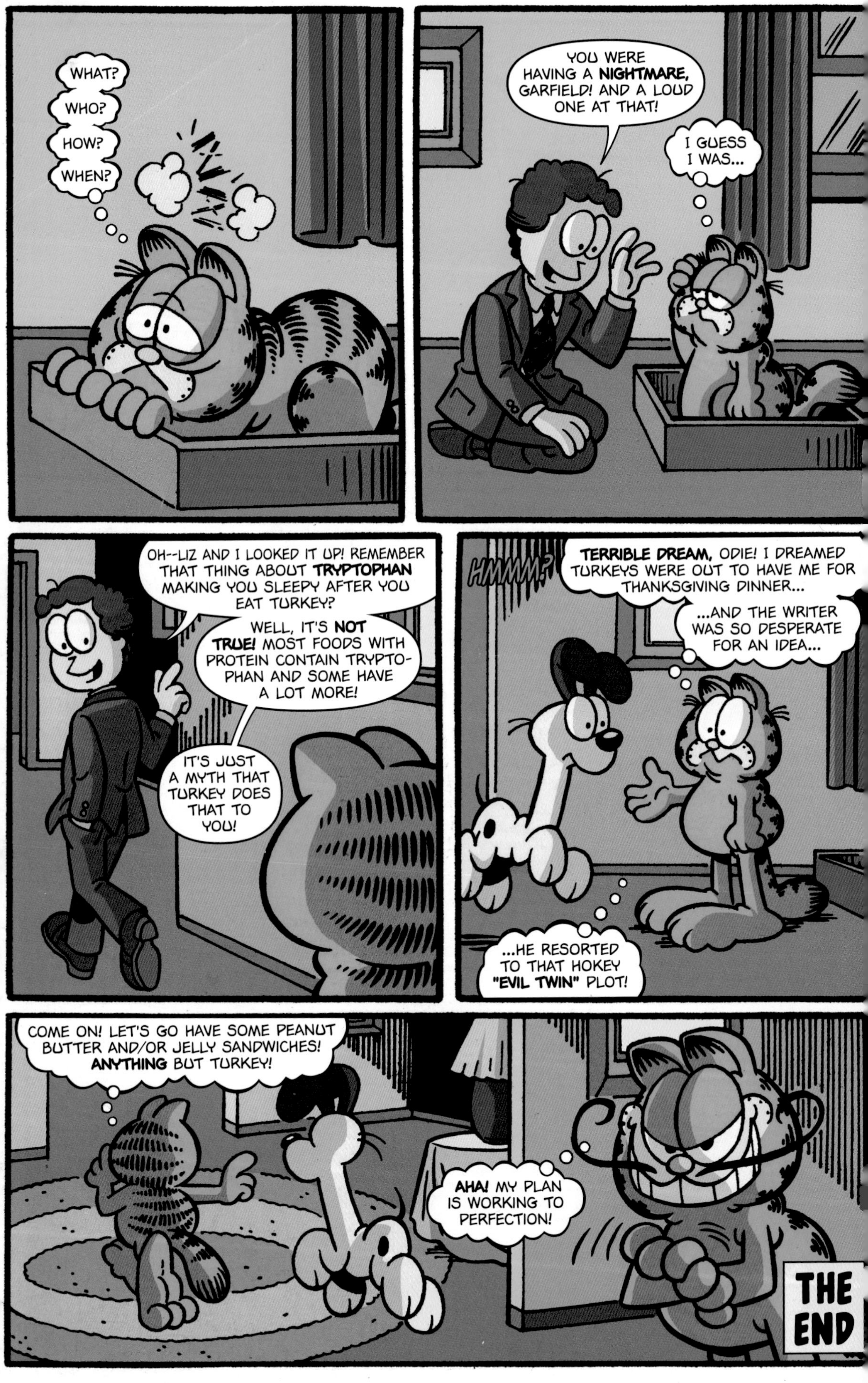
WHAT?
WHO?
HOW?
WHEN?
YOU WERE HAVING A **NIGHTMARE,** GARFIELD! AND A LOUD ONE AT THAT!
I GUESS I WAS...
OH--LIZ AND I LOOKED IT UP! REMEMBER THAT THING ABOUT **TRYPTOPHAN** MAKING YOU SLEEPY AFTER YOU EAT TURKEY?
WELL, IT'S **NOT TRUE!** MOST FOODS WITH PROTEIN CONTAIN TRYPTOPHAN AND SOME HAVE A LOT MORE!
IT'S JUST A MYTH THAT TURKEY DOES THAT TO YOU!
HMMM?
TERRIBLE DREAM, ODIE! I DREAMED TURKEYS WERE OUT TO HAVE ME FOR THANKSGIVING DINNER...
...AND THE WRITER WAS SO DESPERATE FOR AN IDEA...
...HE RESORTED TO THAT HOKEY **"EVIL TWIN"** PLOT!
COME ON! LET'S GO HAVE SOME PEANUT BUTTER AND/OR JELLY SANDWICHES! **ANYTHING** BUT TURKEY!
AHA! MY PLAN IS WORKING TO PERFECTION!
THE END

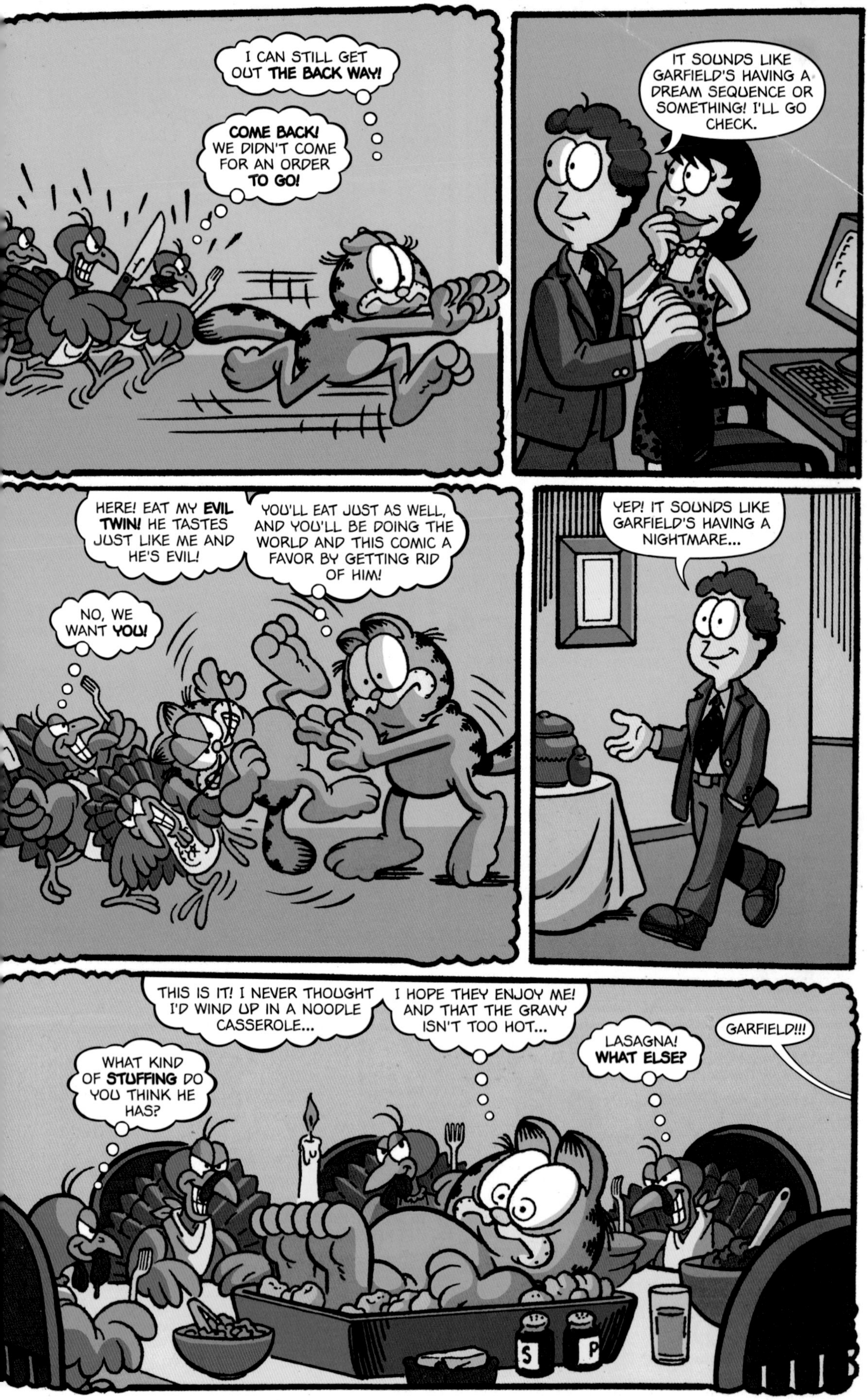
I CAN STILL GET OUT THE BACK WAY!
COME BACK! WE DIDN'T COME FOR AN ORDER TO GO!
IT SOUNDS LIKE GARFIELD'S HAVING A DREAM SEQUENCE OR SOMETHING! I'LL GO CHECK.
HERE! EAT MY EVIL TWIN! HE TASTES JUST LIKE ME AND HE'S EVIL!
YOU'LL EAT JUST AS WELL, AND YOU'LL BE DOING THE WORLD AND THIS COMIC A FAVOR BY GETTING RID OF HIM!
NO, WE WANT YOU!
YEP! IT SOUNDS LIKE GARFIELD'S HAVING A NIGHTMARE...
THIS IS IT! I NEVER THOUGHT I'D WIND UP IN A NOODLE CASSEROLE...
I HOPE THEY ENJOY ME! AND THAT THE GRAVY ISN'T TOO HOT...
WHAT KIND OF STUFFING DO YOU THINK HE HAS?
LASAGNA! WHAT ELSE?
GARFIELD!!!
S
P

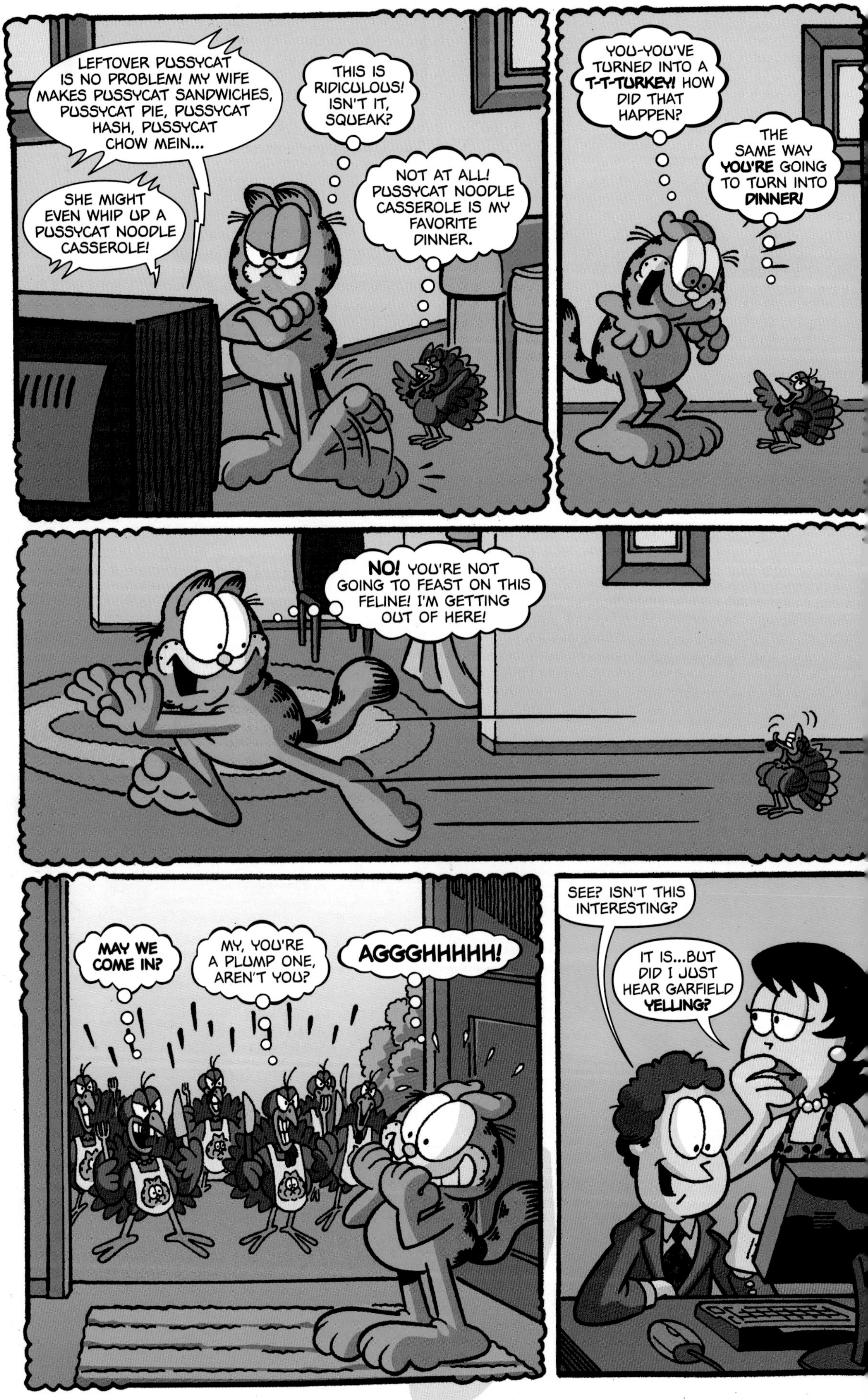
LEFTOVER PUSSYCAT IS NO PROBLEM! MY WIFE MAKES PUSSYCAT SANDWICHES, PUSSYCAT PIE, PUSSYCAT HASH, PUSSYCAT CHOW MEIN...
SHE MIGHT EVEN WHIP UP A PUSSYCAT NOODLE CASSEROLE!
THIS IS RIDICULOUS! ISN'T IT, SQUEAK?
NOT AT ALL! PUSSYCAT NOODLE CASSEROLE IS MY FAVORITE DINNER.
YOU-YOU'VE TURNED INTO A **T-T-TURKEY!** HOW DID THAT HAPPEN?
THE SAME WAY **YOU'RE** GOING TO TURN INTO **DINNER!**
NO! YOU'RE NOT GOING TO FEAST ON THIS FELINE! I'M GETTING OUT OF HERE!
MAY WE COME IN?
MY, YOU'RE A PLUMP ONE, AREN'T YOU?
AGGGHHHHH!
SEE? ISN'T THIS INTERESTING?
IT IS...BUT DID I JUST HEAR GARFIELD **YELLING?**

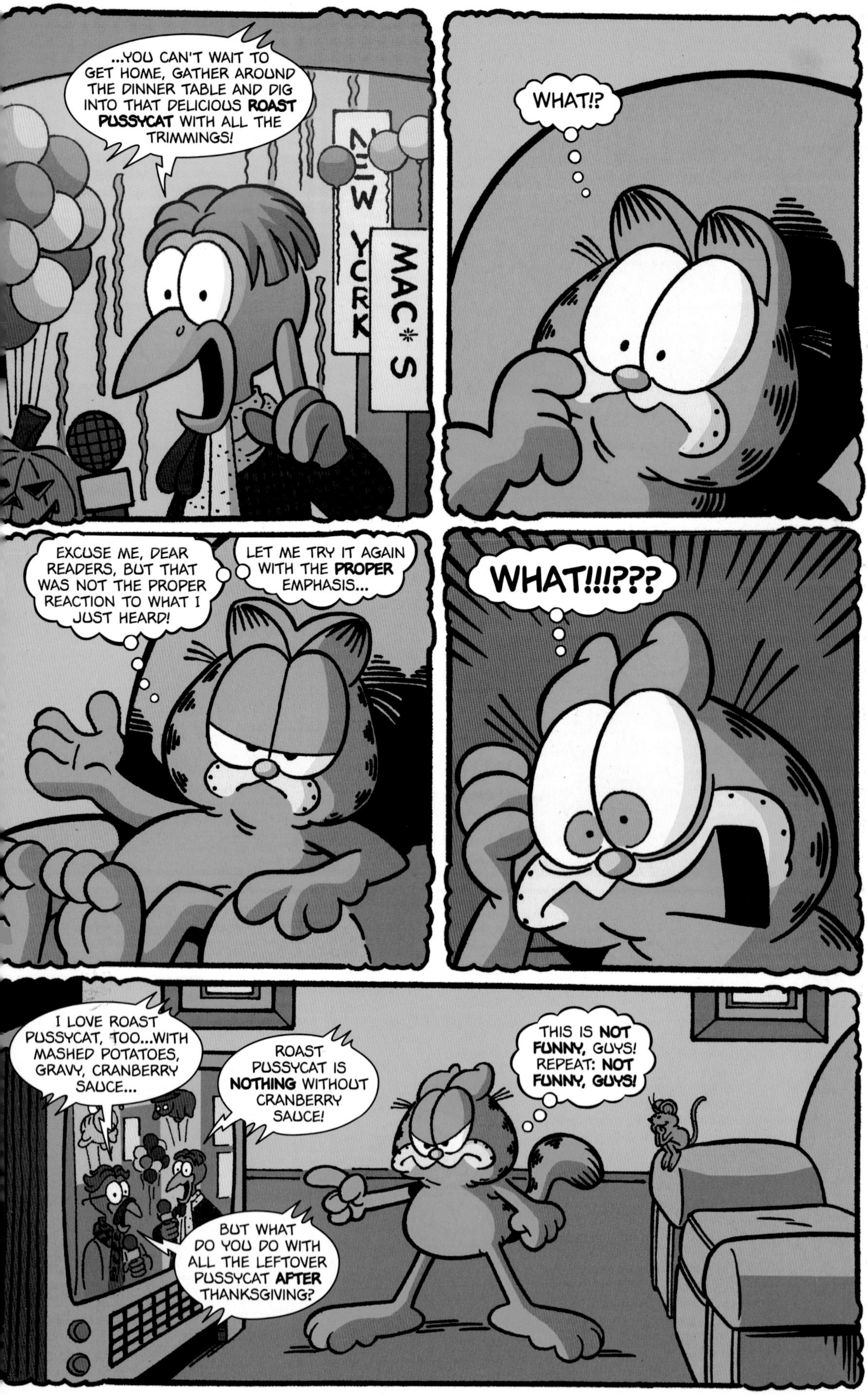
...YOU CAN'T WAIT TO GET HOME, GATHER AROUND THE DINNER TABLE AND DIG INTO THAT DELICIOUS **ROAST PUSSYCAT** WITH ALL THE TRIMMINGS!
NEW YORK
MAC*S
WHAT!?
EXCUSE ME, DEAR READERS, BUT THAT WAS NOT THE PROPER REACTION TO WHAT I JUST HEARD!
LET ME TRY IT AGAIN WITH THE **PROPER** EMPHASIS...
WHAT!!!???
I LOVE ROAST PUSSYCAT, TOO...WITH MASHED POTATOES, GRAVY, CRANBERRY SAUCE...
ROAST PUSSYCAT IS **NOTHING** WITHOUT CRANBERRY SAUCE!
BUT WHAT DO YOU DO WITH ALL THE LEFTOVER PUSSYCAT **AFTER** THANKSGIVING?
THIS IS **NOT FUNNY**, GUYS! REPEAT: **NOT FUNNY, GUYS!**

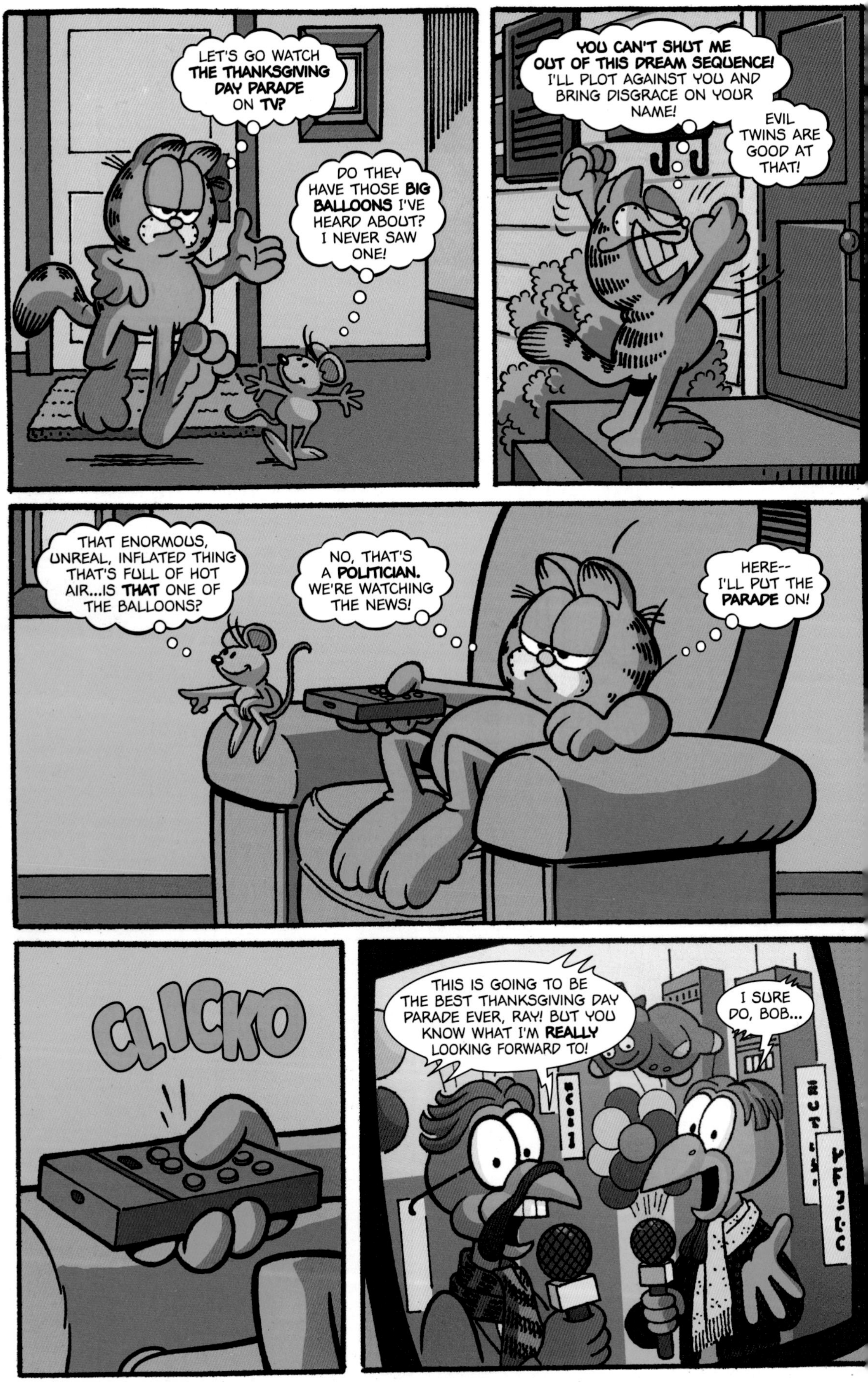
LET'S GO WATCH THE THANKSGIVING DAY PARADE ON TV?
DO THEY HAVE THOSE BIG BALLOONS I'VE HEARD ABOUT? I NEVER SAW ONE!
YOU CAN'T SHUT ME OUT OF THIS DREAM SEQUENCE! I'LL PLOT AGAINST YOU AND BRING DISGRACE ON YOUR NAME!
EVIL TWINS ARE GOOD AT THAT!
THAT ENORMOUS, UNREAL, INFLATED THING THAT'S FULL OF HOT AIR...IS THAT ONE OF THE BALLOONS?
NO, THAT'S A POLITICIAN. WE'RE WATCHING THE NEWS!
HERE-- I'LL PUT THE PARADE ON!
CLICKO
THIS IS GOING TO BE THE BEST THANKSGIVING DAY PARADE EVER, RAY! BUT YOU KNOW WHAT I'M REALLY LOOKING FORWARD TO!
I SURE DO, BOB...

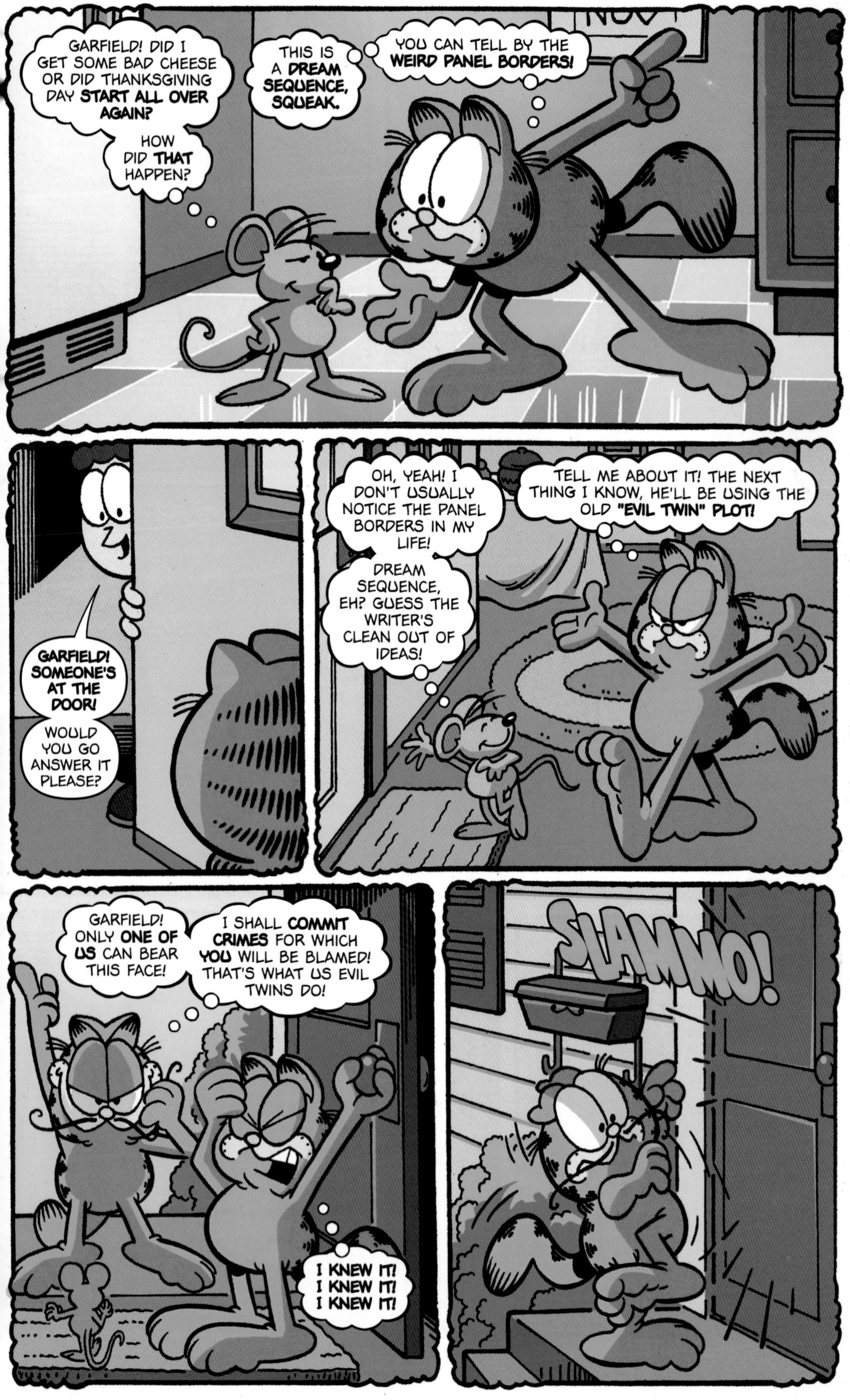
GARFIELD! DID I GET SOME BAD CHEESE OR DID THANKSGIVING DAY START ALL OVER AGAIN?
HOW DID THAT HAPPEN?
THIS IS A DREAM SEQUENCE, SQUEAK.
YOU CAN TELL BY THE WEIRD PANEL BORDERS!
GARFIELD! SOMEONE'S AT THE DOOR!
WOULD YOU GO ANSWER IT PLEASE?
OH, YEAH! I DON'T USUALLY NOTICE THE PANEL BORDERS IN MY LIFE!
DREAM SEQUENCE, EH? GUESS THE WRITER'S CLEAN OUT OF IDEAS!
TELL ME ABOUT IT! THE NEXT THING I KNOW, HE'LL BE USING THE OLD "EVIL TWIN" PLOT!
GARFIELD! ONLY ONE OF US CAN BEAR THIS FACE!
I SHALL COMMIT CRIMES FOR WHICH YOU WILL BE BLAMED! THAT'S WHAT US EVIL TWINS DO!
I KNEW IT! I KNEW IT! I KNEW IT!
SLAMMO!

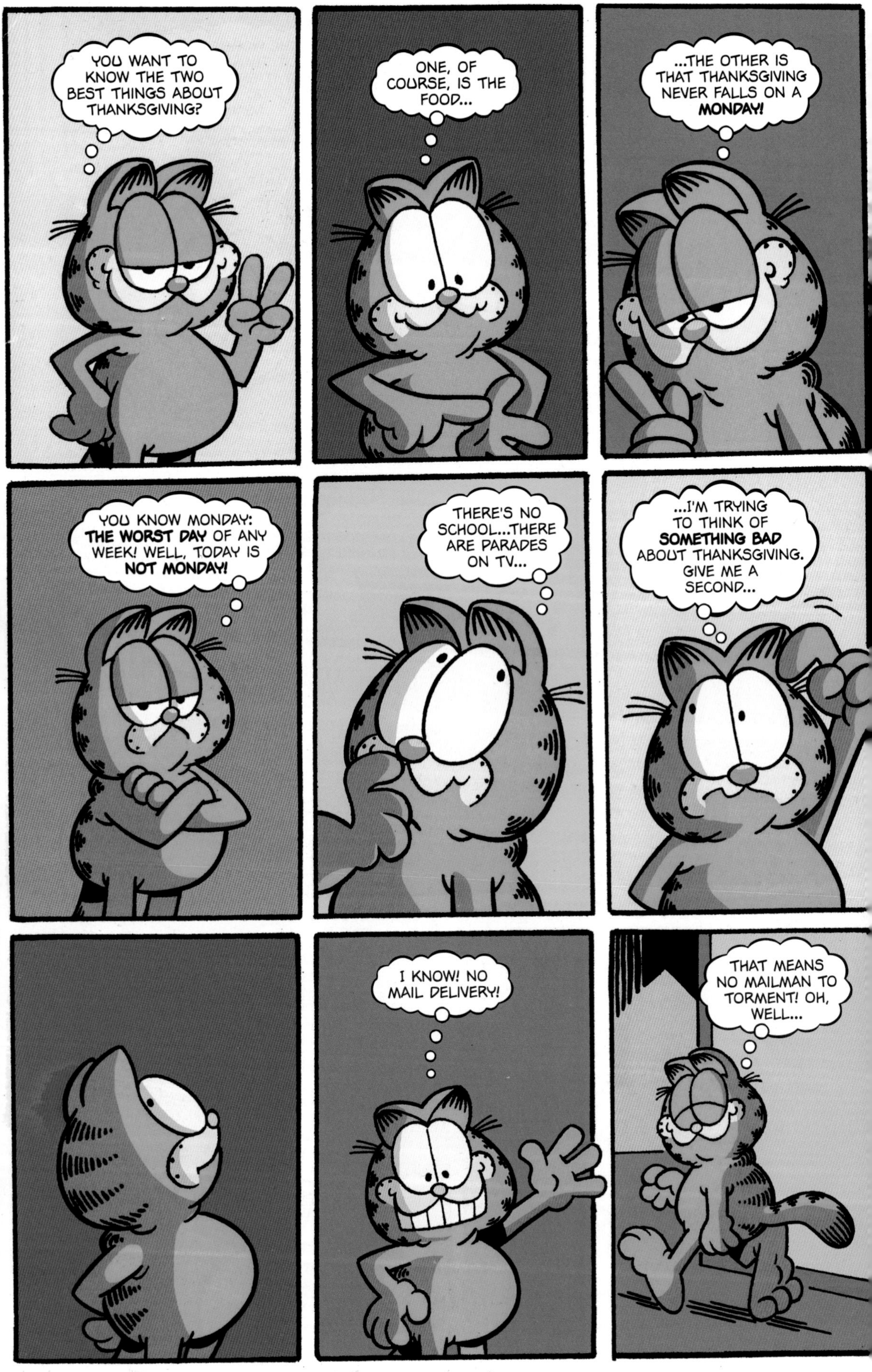
YOU WANT TO KNOW THE TWO BEST THINGS ABOUT THANKSGIVING?
ONE, OF COURSE, IS THE FOOD...
...THE OTHER IS THAT THANKSGIVING NEVER FALLS ON A **MONDAY!**
YOU KNOW MONDAY: **THE WORST DAY** OF ANY WEEK! WELL, TODAY IS **NOT MONDAY!**
THERE'S NO SCHOOL...THERE ARE PARADES ON TV...
...I'M TRYING TO THINK OF **SOMETHING BAD** ABOUT THANKSGIVING. GIVE ME A SECOND...
I KNOW! NO MAIL DELIVERY!
THAT MEANS NO MAILMAN TO TORMENT! OH, WELL...

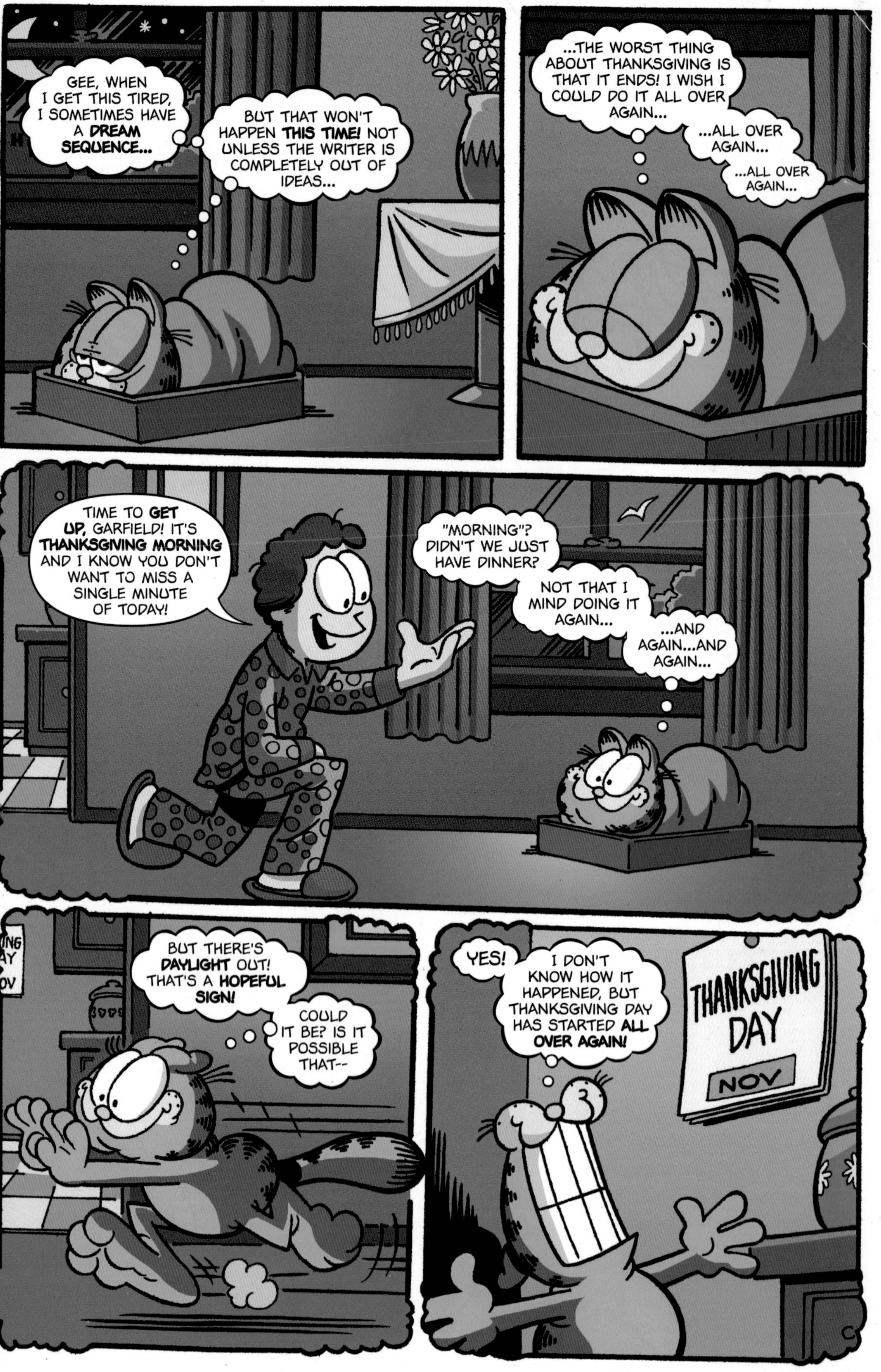
GEE, WHEN I GET THIS TIRED, I SOMETIMES HAVE A DREAM SEQUENCE...
BUT THAT WON'T HAPPEN THIS TIME! NOT UNLESS THE WRITER IS COMPLETELY OUT OF IDEAS...
...THE WORST THING ABOUT THANKSGIVING IS THAT IT ENDS! I WISH I COULD DO IT ALL OVER AGAIN...
...ALL OVER AGAIN...
...ALL OVER AGAIN...
TIME TO GET UP, GARFIELD! IT'S THANKSGIVING MORNING AND I KNOW YOU DON'T WANT TO MISS A SINGLE MINUTE OF TODAY!
"MORNING"? DIDN'T WE JUST HAVE DINNER?
NOT THAT I MIND DOING IT AGAIN...
...AND AGAIN...AND AGAIN...
BUT THERE'S DAYLIGHT OUT! THAT'S A HOPEFUL SIGN!
COULD IT BE? IS IT POSSIBLE THAT--
YES!
I DON'T KNOW HOW IT HAPPENED, BUT THANKSGIVING DAY HAS STARTED ALL OVER AGAIN!
THANKSGIVING DAY
NOV

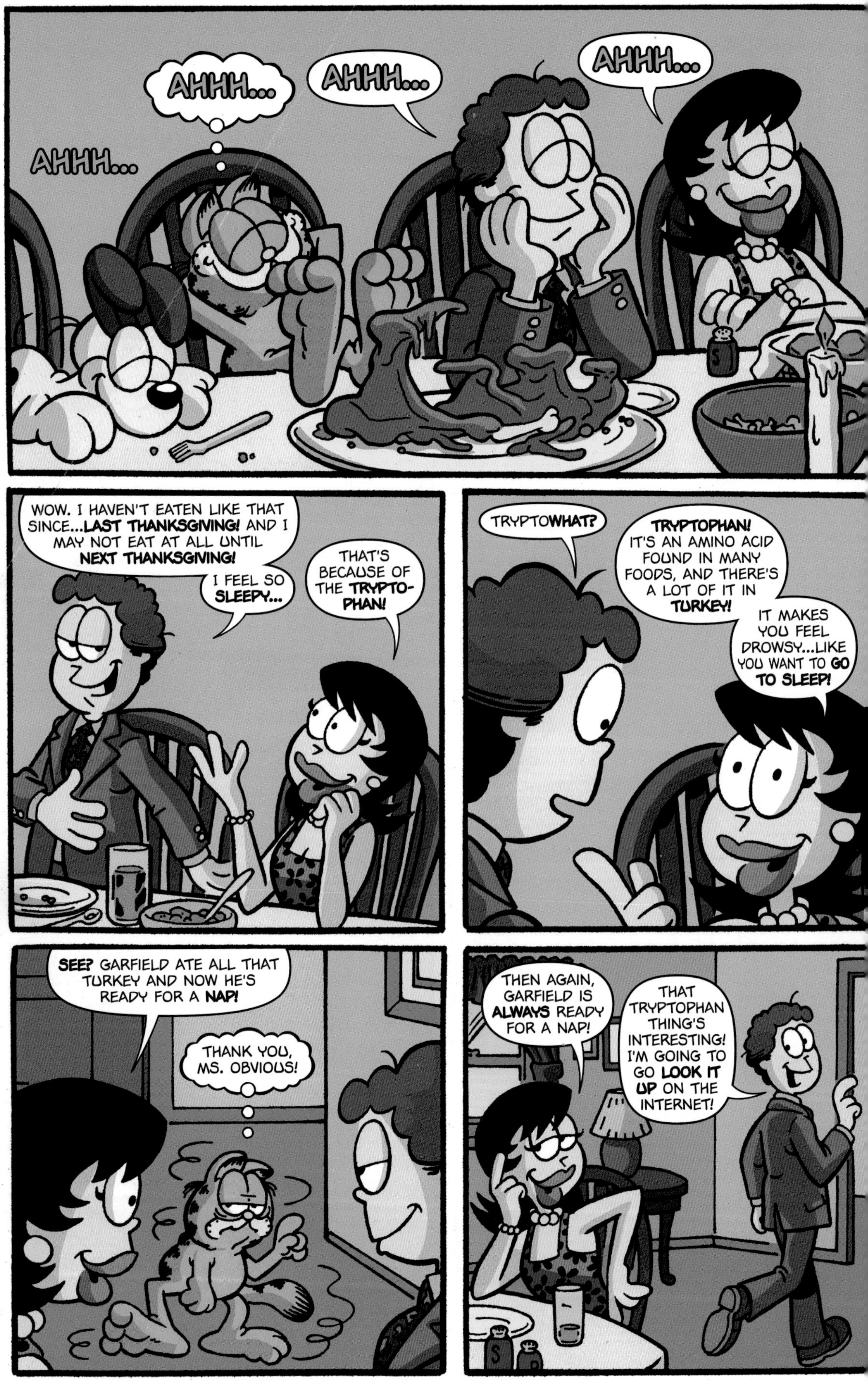
AHHH...
AHHH...
AHHH...
AHHH...
WOW. I HAVEN'T EATEN LIKE THAT SINCE...LAST THANKSGIVING! AND I MAY NOT EAT AT ALL UNTIL NEXT THANKSGIVING!
I FEEL SO SLEEPY...
THAT'S BECAUSE OF THE TRYPTO-PHAN!
TRYPTOWHAT?
TRYPTOPHAN! IT'S AN AMINO ACID FOUND IN MANY FOODS, AND THERE'S A LOT OF IT IN TURKEY!
IT MAKES YOU FEEL DROWSY...LIKE YOU WANT TO GO TO SLEEP!
SEE? GARFIELD ATE ALL THAT TURKEY AND NOW HE'S READY FOR A NAP!
THANK YOU, MS. OBVIOUS!
THEN AGAIN, GARFIELD IS ALWAYS READY FOR A NAP!
THAT TRYPTOPHAN THING'S INTERESTING! I'M GOING TO GO LOOK IT UP ON THE INTERNET!

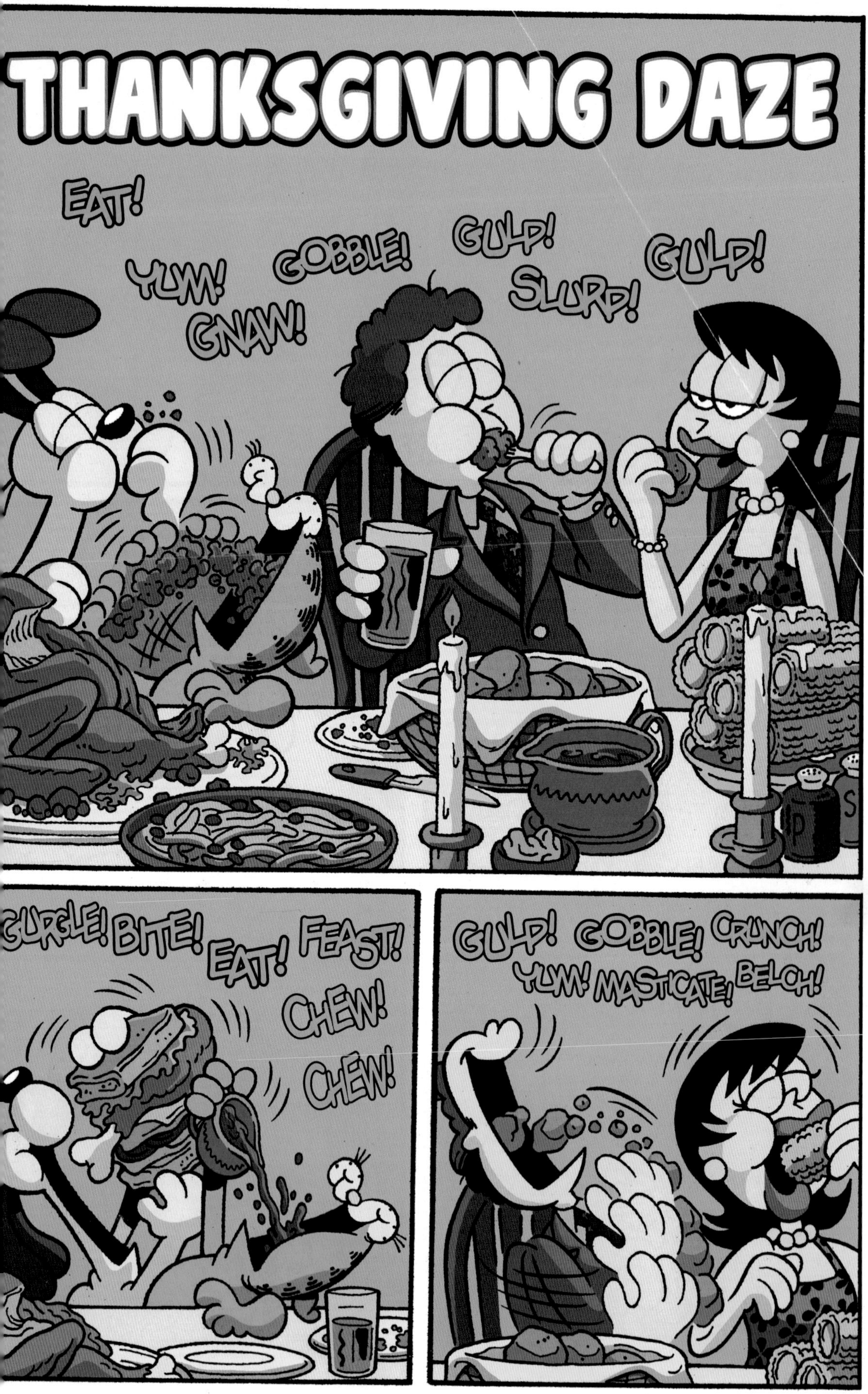
THANKSGIVING DAZE
EAT!
YUM!
GNAW!
GOBBLE!
GULP!
SLURP!
GULP!
GURGLE!
BITE!
EAT!
FEAST!
CHEW!
CHEW!
GULP!
GOBBLE!
CRUNCH!
YUM!
MASTICATE!
BELCH!

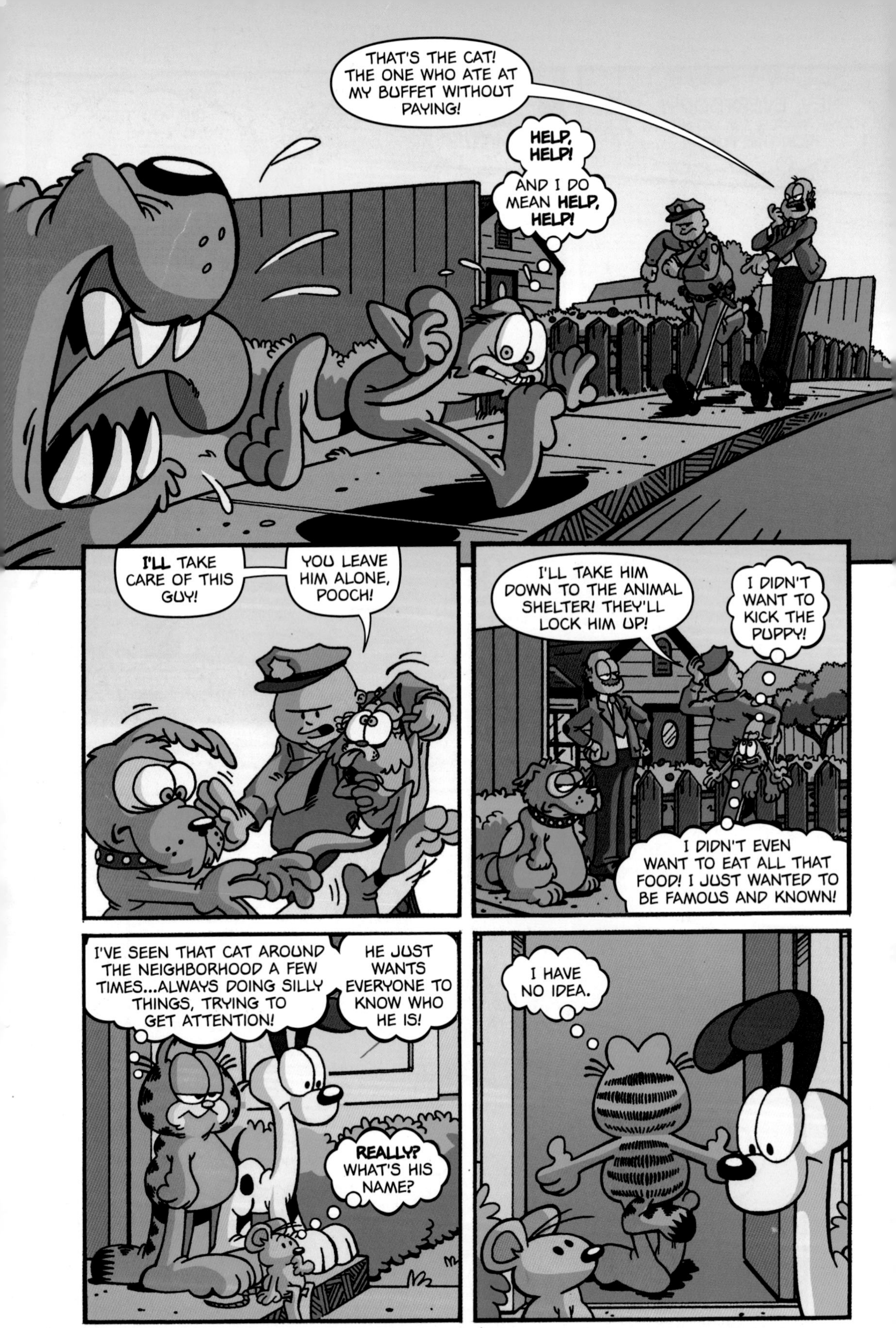
THAT'S THE CAT! THE ONE WHO ATE AT MY BUFFET WITHOUT PAYING!
HELP, HELP!
AND I DO MEAN HELP, HELP!
I'LL TAKE CARE OF THIS GUY!
YOU LEAVE HIM ALONE, POOCH!
I'LL TAKE HIM DOWN TO THE ANIMAL SHELTER! THEY'LL LOCK HIM UP!
I DIDN'T WANT TO KICK THE PUPPY!
I DIDN'T EVEN WANT TO EAT ALL THAT FOOD! I JUST WANTED TO BE FAMOUS AND KNOWN!
I'VE SEEN THAT CAT AROUND THE NEIGHBORHOOD A FEW TIMES...ALWAYS DOING SILLY THINGS, TRYING TO GET ATTENTION!
HE JUST WANTS EVERYONE TO KNOW WHO HE IS!
REALLY? WHAT'S HIS NAME?
I HAVE NO IDEA.

THE END

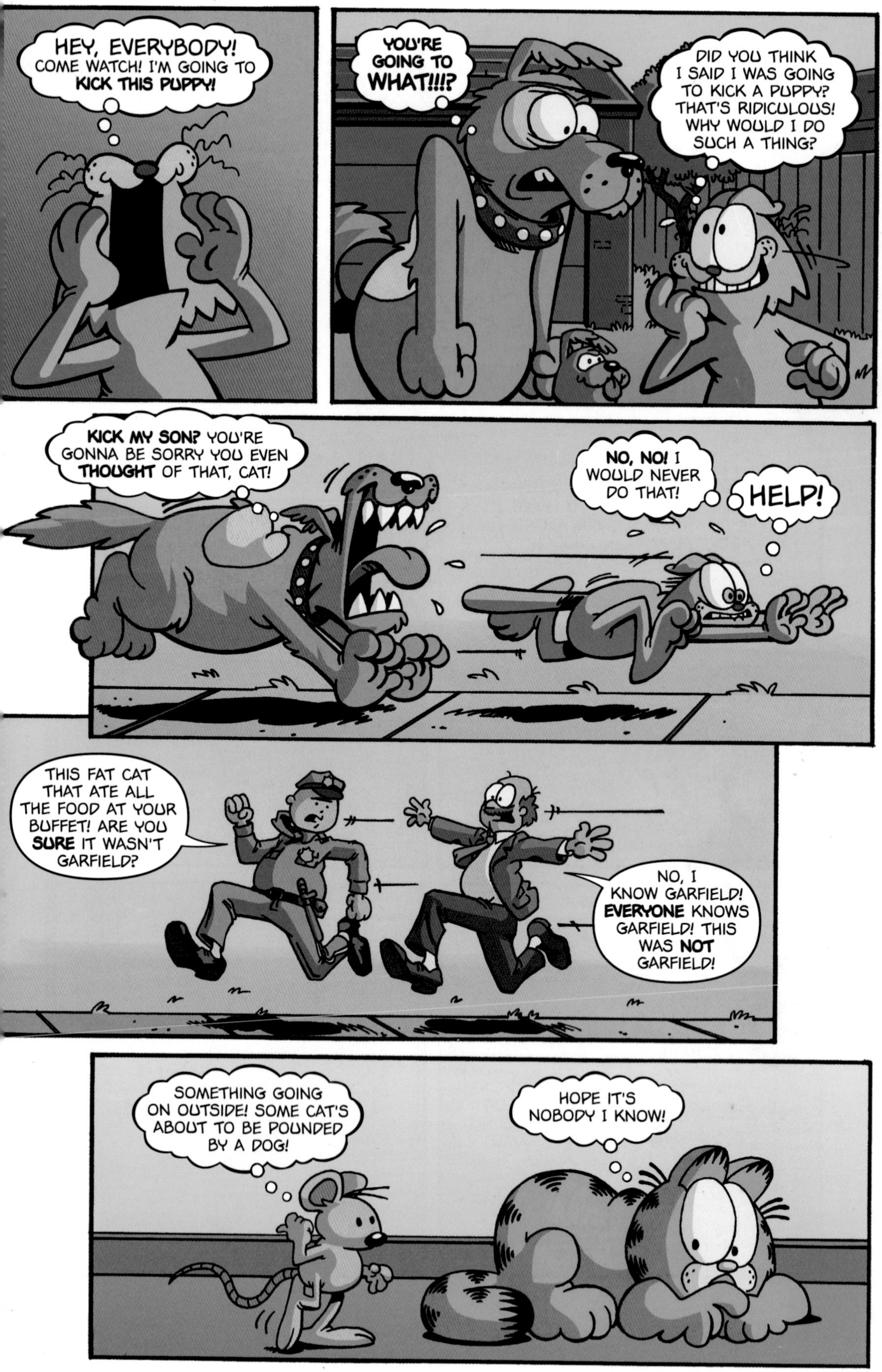
HEY, EVERYBODY! COME WATCH! I'M GOING TO KICK THIS PUPPY!
YOU'RE GOING TO WHAT!!!?
DID YOU THINK I SAID I WAS GOING TO KICK A PUPPY? THAT'S RIDICULOUS! WHY WOULD I DO SUCH A THING?
KICK MY SON? YOU'RE GONNA BE SORRY YOU EVEN THOUGHT OF THAT, CAT!
NO, NO! I WOULD NEVER DO THAT!
HELP!
THIS FAT CAT THAT ATE ALL THE FOOD AT YOUR BUFFET! ARE YOU SURE IT WASN'T GARFIELD?
NO, I KNOW GARFIELD! EVERYONE KNOWS GARFIELD! THIS WAS NOT GARFIELD!
SOMETHING GOING ON OUTSIDE! SOME CAT'S ABOUT TO BE POUNDED BY A DOG!
HOPE IT'S NOBODY I KNOW!

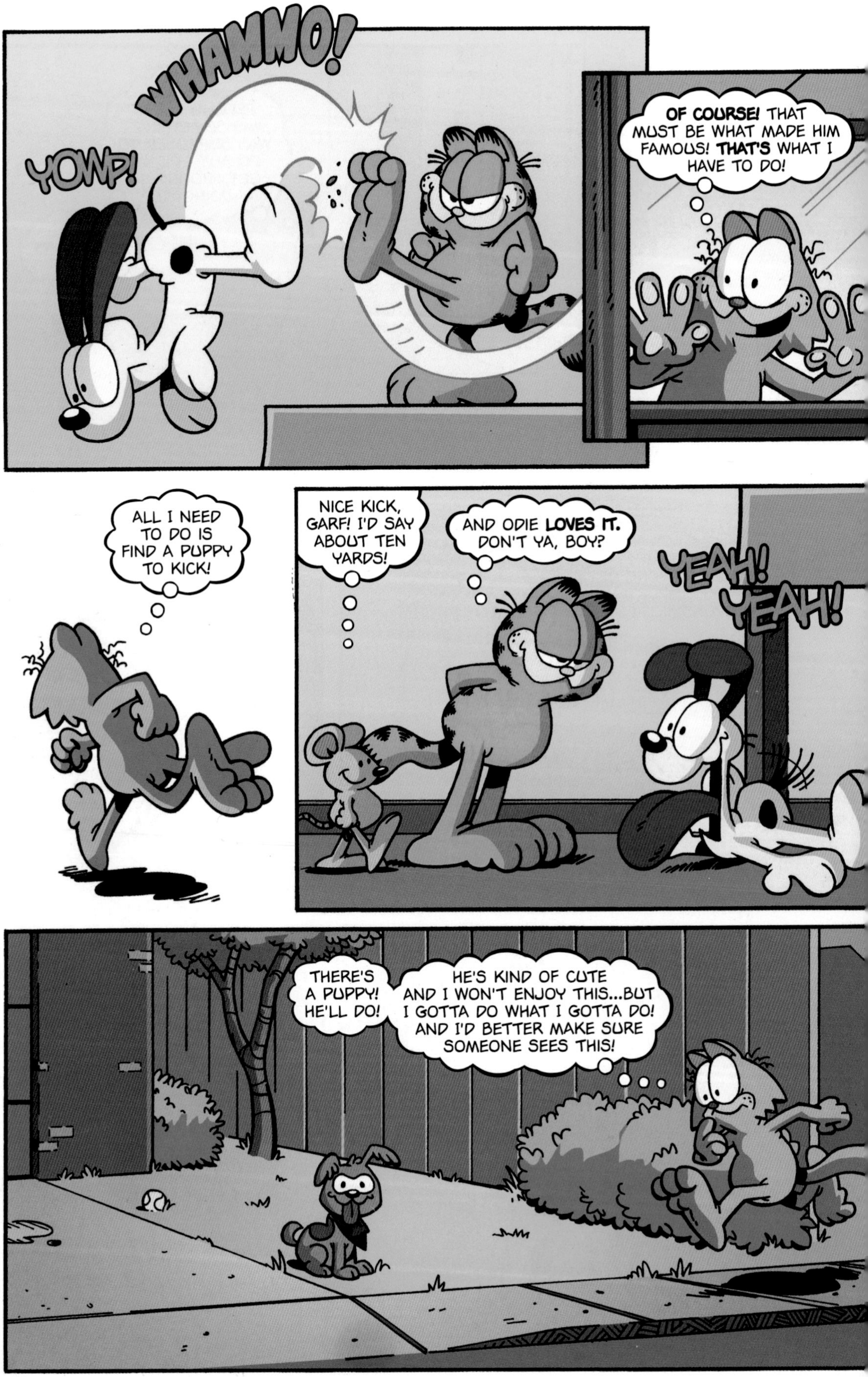
WHAMMO!
YOWP!
OF COURSE! THAT MUST BE WHAT MADE HIM FAMOUS! THAT'S WHAT I HAVE TO DO!
ALL I NEED TO DO IS FIND A PUPPY TO KICK!
NICE KICK, GARF! I'D SAY ABOUT TEN YARDS!
AND ODIE LOVES IT. DON'T YA, BOY?
YEAH! YEAH!
THERE'S A PUPPY! HE'LL DO!
HE'S KIND OF CUTE AND I WON'T ENJOY THIS...BUT I GOTTA DO WHAT I GOTTA DO! AND I'D BETTER MAKE SURE SOMEONE SEES THIS!

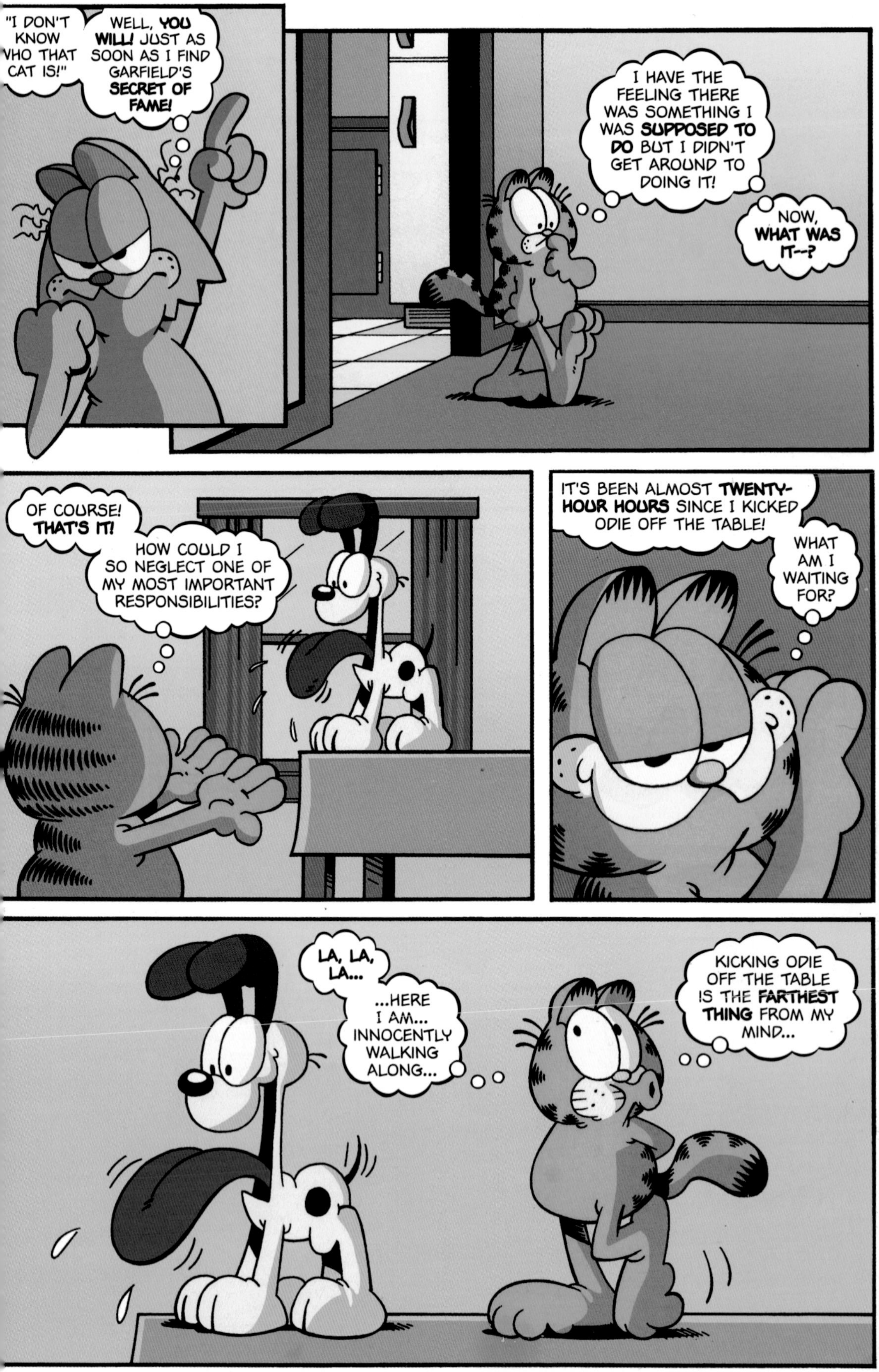
"I DON'T KNOW WHO THAT CAT IS!"
WELL, YOU WILL! JUST AS SOON AS I FIND GARFIELD'S SECRET OF FAME!
I HAVE THE FEELING THERE WAS SOMETHING I WAS SUPPOSED TO DO BUT I DIDN'T GET AROUND TO DOING IT!
NOW, WHAT WAS IT--?
OF COURSE! THAT'S IT!
HOW COULD I SO NEGLECT ONE OF MY MOST IMPORTANT RESPONSIBILITIES?
IT'S BEEN ALMOST TWENTY-HOUR HOURS SINCE I KICKED ODIE OFF THE TABLE!
WHAT AM I WAITING FOR?
LA, LA, LA...
...HERE I AM... INNOCENTLY WALKING ALONG...
KICKING ODIE OFF THE TABLE IS THE FARTHEST THING FROM MY MIND...

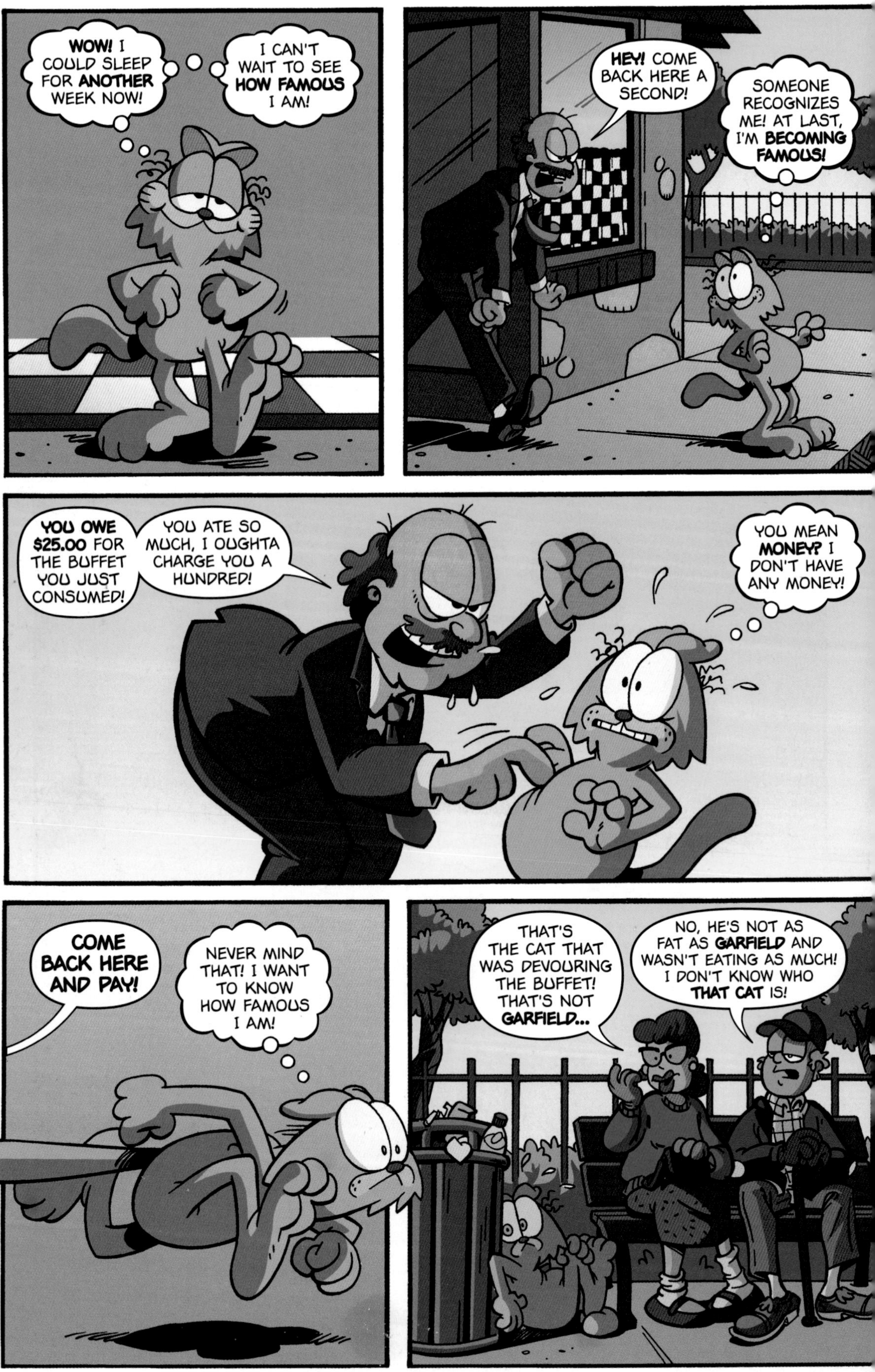
WOW! I COULD SLEEP FOR ANOTHER WEEK NOW!
I CAN'T WAIT TO SEE HOW FAMOUS I AM!
HEY! COME BACK HERE A SECOND!
SOMEONE RECOGNIZES ME! AT LAST, I'M BECOMING FAMOUS!
YOU OWE $25.00 FOR THE BUFFET YOU JUST CONSUMED!
YOU ATE SO MUCH, I OUGHTA CHARGE YOU A HUNDRED!
YOU MEAN MONEY? I DON'T HAVE ANY MONEY!
COME BACK HERE AND PAY!
NEVER MIND THAT! I WANT TO KNOW HOW FAMOUS I AM!
THAT'S THE CAT THAT WAS DEVOURING THE BUFFET! THAT'S NOT GARFIELD...
NO, HE'S NOT AS FAT AS GARFIELD AND WASN'T EATING AS MUCH! I DON'T KNOW WHO THAT CAT IS!

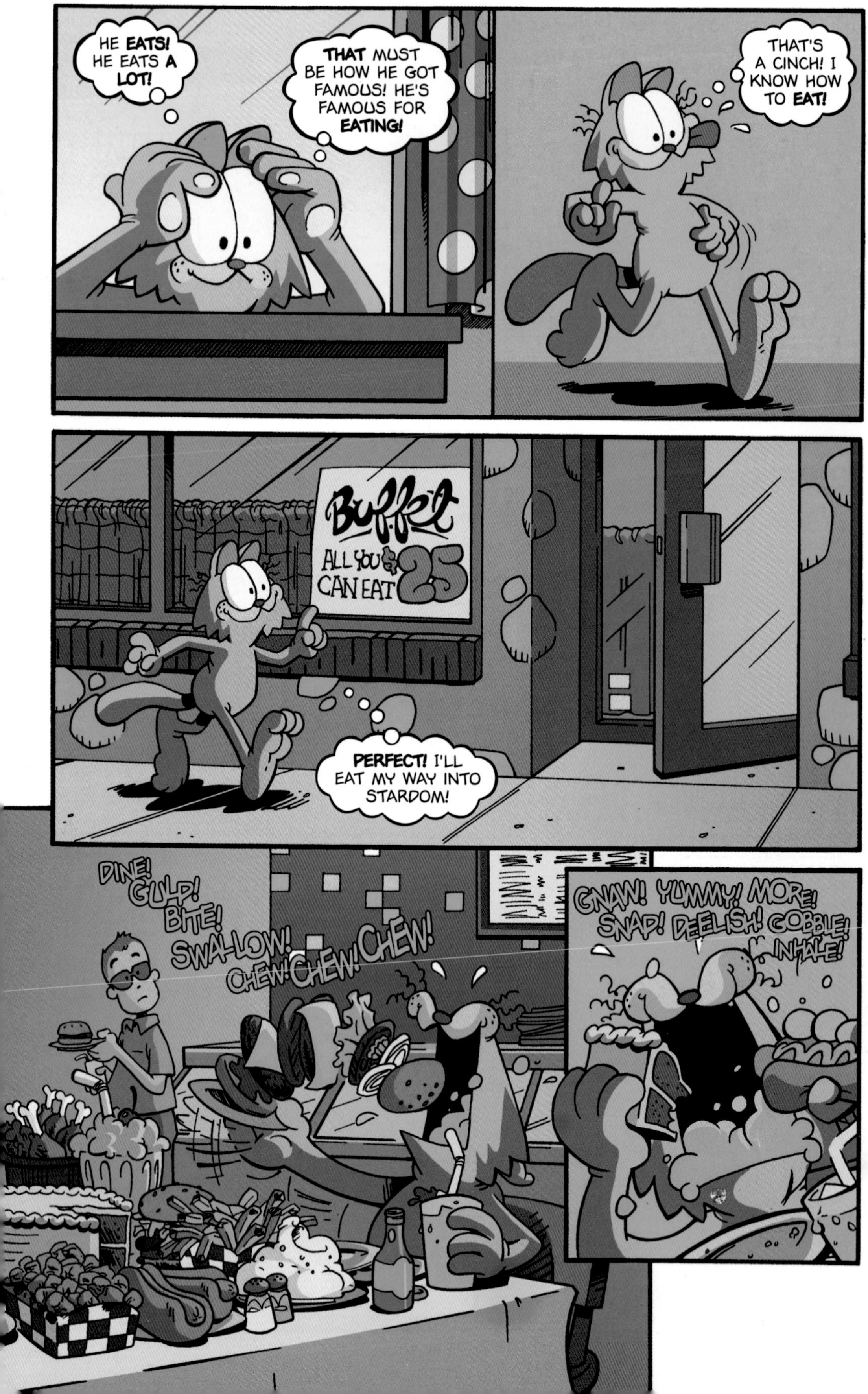
HE EATS! HE EATS A LOT!
THAT MUST BE HOW HE GOT FAMOUS! HE'S FAMOUS FOR EATING!
THAT'S A CINCH! I KNOW HOW TO EAT!
Buffet
ALL YOU CAN EAT $25
PERFECT! I'LL EAT MY WAY INTO STARDOM!
DINE! GULP! BITE! SWALLOW! CHEW! CHEW! CHEW!
GNAW! YUMMY! MORE! SNAP! DEELISH! GOBBLE! INHALE!

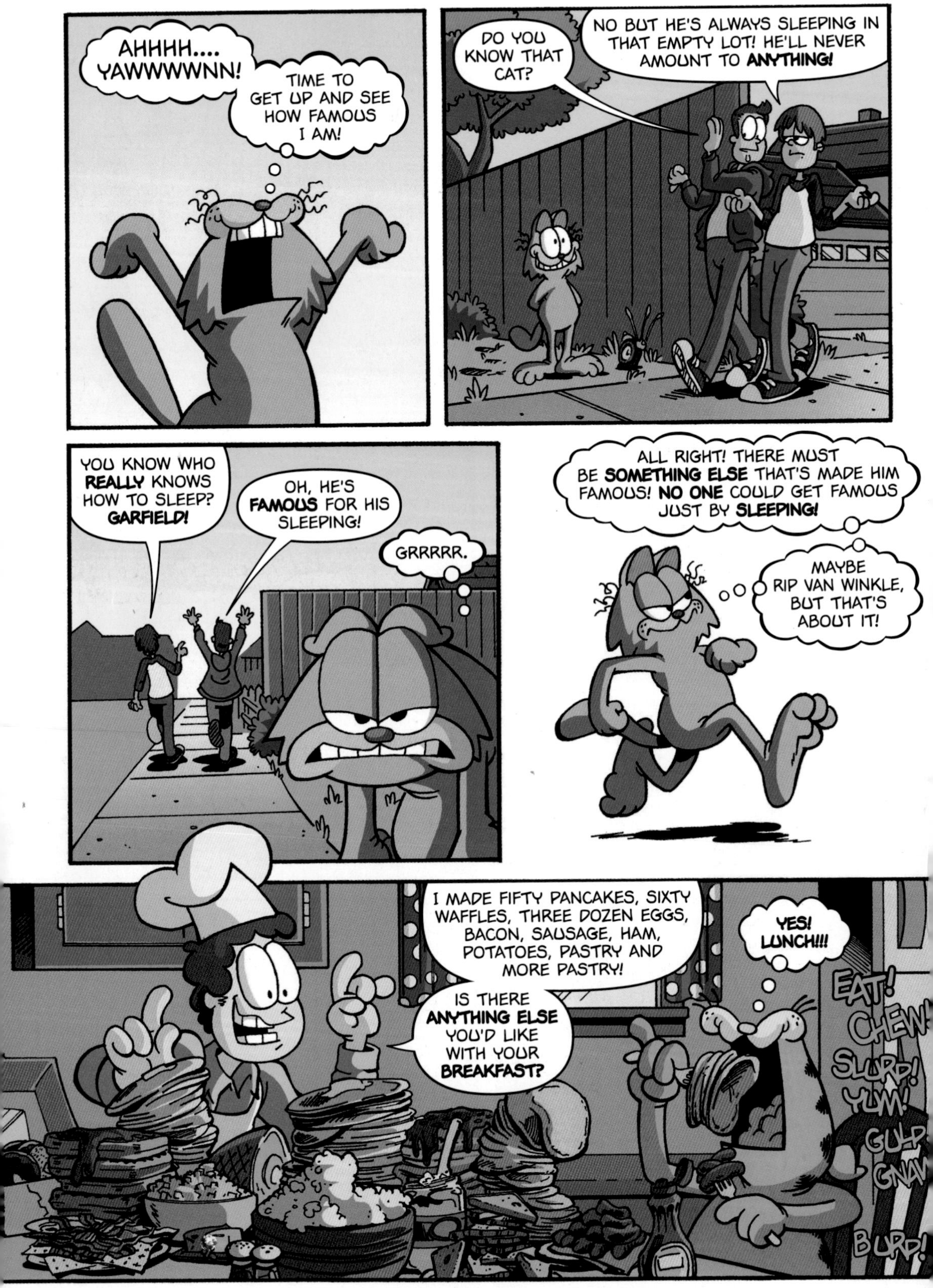
AHHHH.... YAWWWWNN!
TIME TO GET UP AND SEE HOW FAMOUS I AM!
DO YOU KNOW THAT CAT?
NO BUT HE'S ALWAYS SLEEPING IN THAT EMPTY LOT! HE'LL NEVER AMOUNT TO **ANYTHING!**
YOU KNOW WHO **REALLY** KNOWS HOW TO SLEEP? **GARFIELD!**
OH, HE'S **FAMOUS** FOR HIS SLEEPING!
GRRRRR.
ALL RIGHT! THERE MUST BE **SOMETHING ELSE** THAT'S MADE HIM FAMOUS! **NO ONE** COULD GET FAMOUS JUST BY **SLEEPING!**
MAYBE RIP VAN WINKLE, BUT THAT'S ABOUT IT!
I MADE FIFTY PANCAKES, SIXTY WAFFLES, THREE DOZEN EGGS, BACON, SAUSAGE, HAM, POTATOES, PASTRY AND MORE PASTRY!
IS THERE **ANYTHING ELSE** YOU'D LIKE WITH YOUR **BREAKFAST?**
YES! LUNCH!!!
EAT!
CHEW
SLURP!
YUM!
GULP
GNAW
BURP!

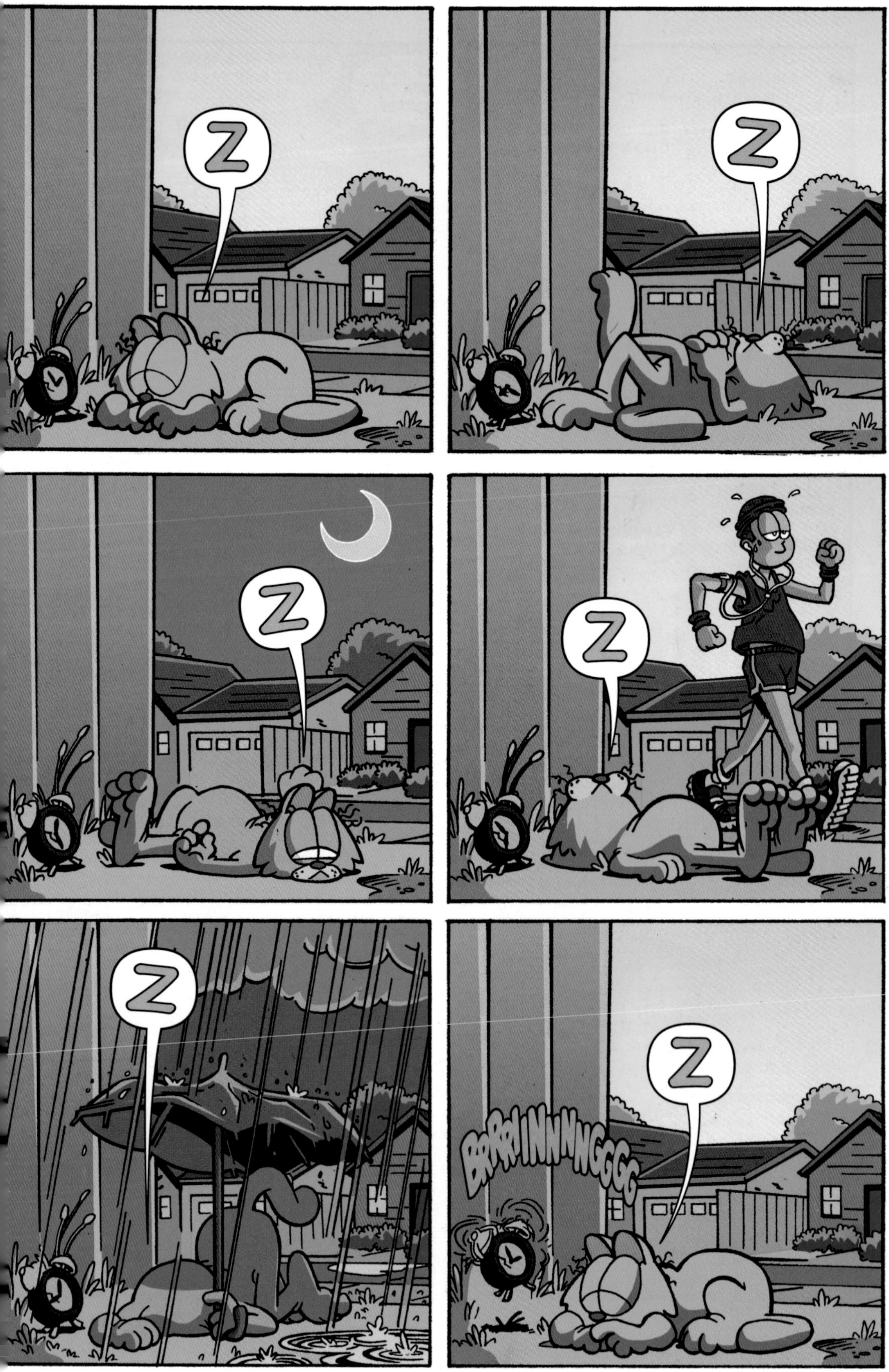
Z
Z
Z
Z
Z
BRRRIINNNNGGGG
Z

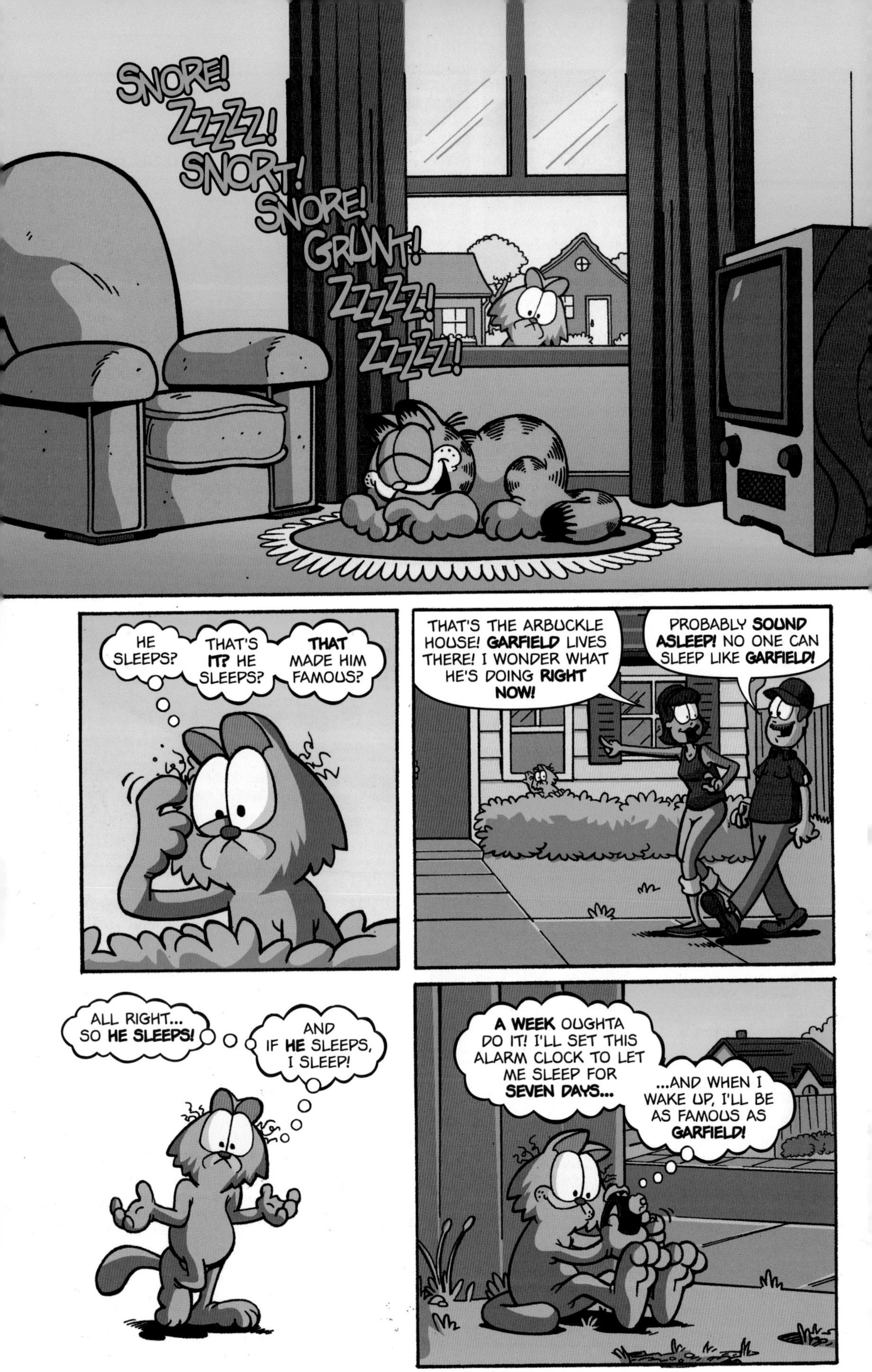
SNORE! ZZZZZ! SNORT! SNORE! GRUNT! ZZZZZ! ZZZZZ!
HE SLEEPS?
THAT'S IT? HE SLEEPS?
THAT MADE HIM FAMOUS?
THAT'S THE ARBUCKLE HOUSE! GARFIELD LIVES THERE! I WONDER WHAT HE'S DOING RIGHT NOW!
PROBABLY SOUND ASLEEP! NO ONE CAN SLEEP LIKE GARFIELD!
ALL RIGHT... SO HE SLEEPS!
AND IF HE SLEEPS, I SLEEP!
A WEEK OUGHTA DO IT! I'LL SET THIS ALARM CLOCK TO LET ME SLEEP FOR SEVEN DAYS...
...AND WHEN I WAKE UP, I'LL BE AS FAMOUS AS GARFIELD!

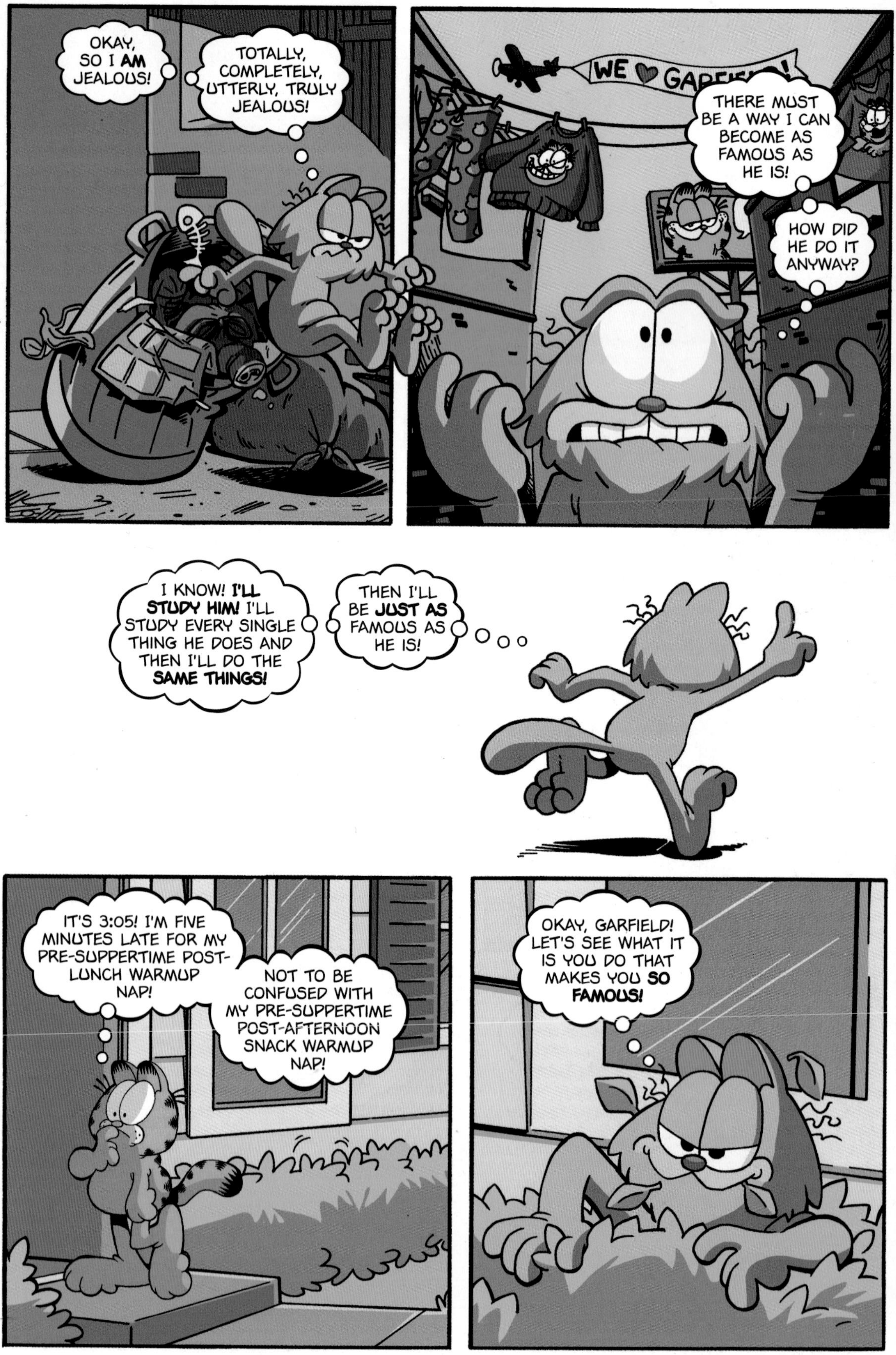
OKAY, SO I AM JEALOUS!
TOTALLY, COMPLETELY, UTTERLY, TRULY JEALOUS!
WE ♥ GAR
THERE MUST BE A WAY I CAN BECOME AS FAMOUS AS HE IS!
HOW DID HE DO IT ANYWAY?
I KNOW! I'LL STUDY HIM! I'LL STUDY EVERY SINGLE THING HE DOES AND THEN I'LL DO THE SAME THINGS!
THEN I'LL BE JUST AS FAMOUS AS HE IS!
IT'S 3:05! I'M FIVE MINUTES LATE FOR MY PRE-SUPPERTIME POST-LUNCH WARMUP NAP!
NOT TO BE CONFUSED WITH MY PRE-SUPPERTIME POST-AFTERNOON SNACK WARMUP NAP!
OKAY, GARFIELD! LET'S SEE WHAT IT IS YOU DO THAT MAKES YOU SO FAMOUS!

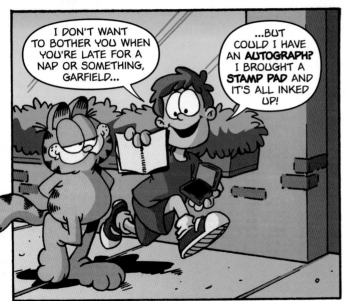

I DON'T WANT TO BOTHER YOU WHEN YOU'RE LATE FOR A NAP OR SOMETHING, GARFIELD...

...BUT COULD I HAVE AN **AUTOGRAPH?** I BROUGHT A **STAMP PAD** AND IT'S ALL INKED UP!

ANYTHING FOR MY PUBLIC!

NEATO! THANKS!

SUCH A LITTLE GESTURE! BUT IT MAKES SOME PEOPLE SO HAPPY!

IT'S NOT LIKE I'M **JEALOUS** OR ANYTHING...

SEE? **LOOK WHAT I GOT!** I'M GOING TO LOVE IT AND TREASURE IT AND ADMIRE IT...

...I MAY EVEN WAIT A **WHOLE MONTH** BEFORE I AUCTION IT OFF ON THE INTERNET!

THAT'S GREAT! I LOVE GARFIELD SO MUCH!

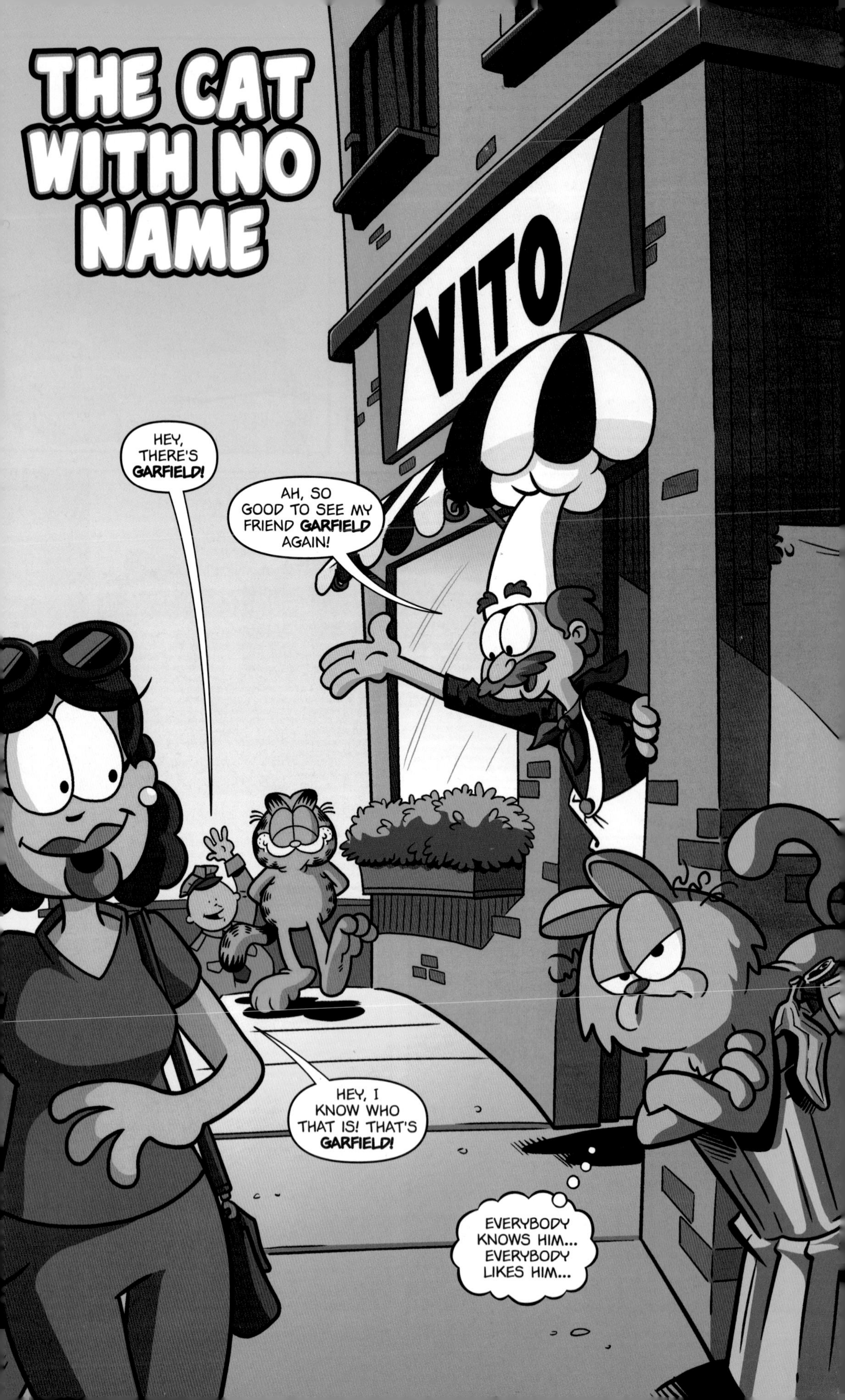
THE CAT WITH NO NAME
VITO
HEY, THERE'S GARFIELD!
AH, SO GOOD TO SEE MY FRIEND GARFIELD AGAIN!
HEY, I KNOW WHO THAT IS! THAT'S GARFIELD!
EVERYBODY KNOWS HIM... EVERYBODY LIKES HIM...

CHAPTER 3

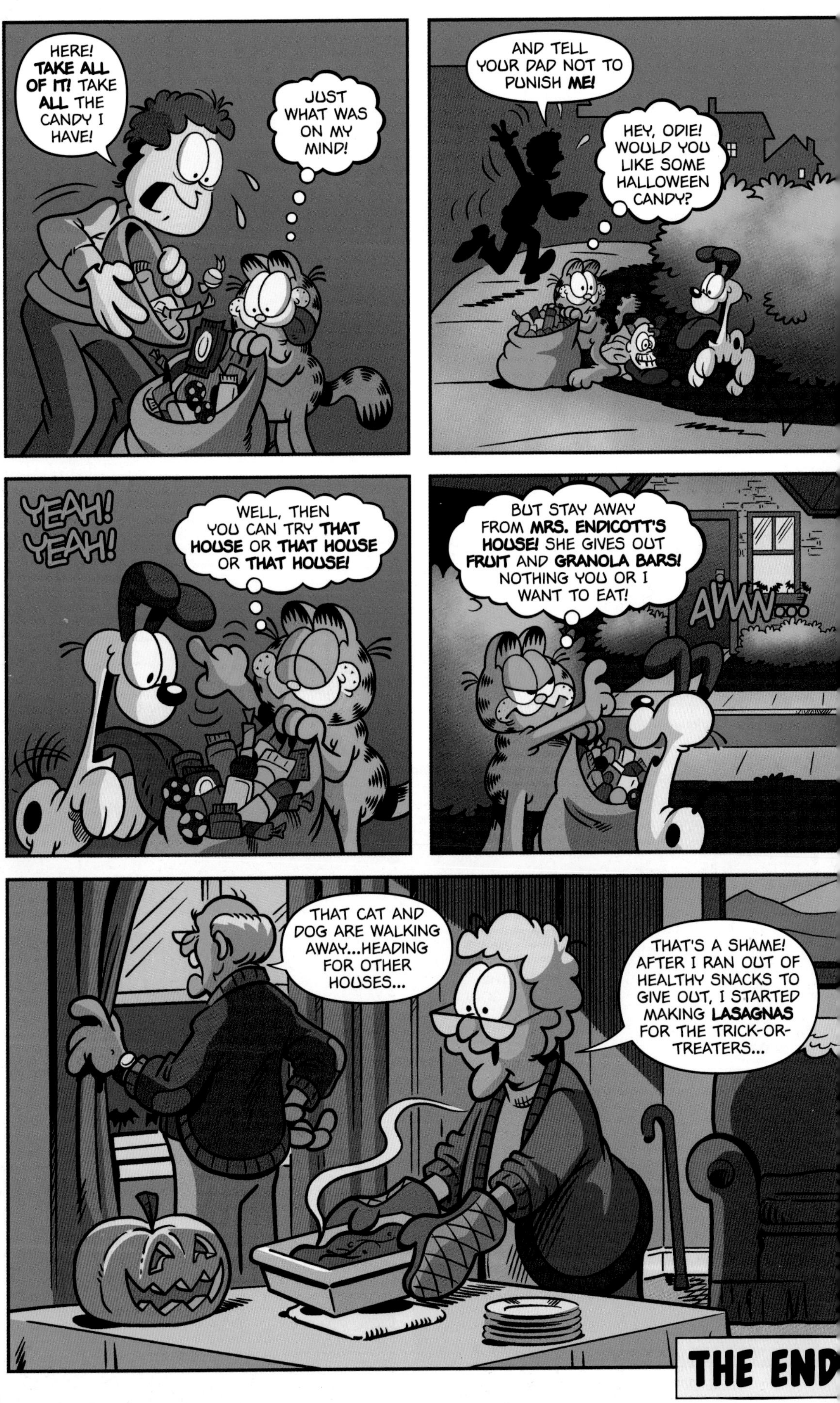
HERE! TAKE ALL OF IT! TAKE ALL THE CANDY I HAVE!
JUST WHAT WAS ON MY MIND!
AND TELL YOUR DAD NOT TO PUNISH ME!
HEY, ODIE! WOULD YOU LIKE SOME HALLOWEEN CANDY?
YEAH! YEAH!
WELL, THEN YOU CAN TRY THAT HOUSE OR THAT HOUSE OR THAT HOUSE!
BUT STAY AWAY FROM MRS. ENDICOTT'S HOUSE! SHE GIVES OUT FRUIT AND GRANOLA BARS! NOTHING YOU OR I WANT TO EAT!
AWW...
THAT CAT AND DOG ARE WALKING AWAY...HEADING FOR OTHER HOUSES...
THAT'S A SHAME! AFTER I RAN OUT OF HEALTHY SNACKS TO GIVE OUT, I STARTED MAKING LASAGNAS FOR THE TRICK-OR-TREATERS...
THE END

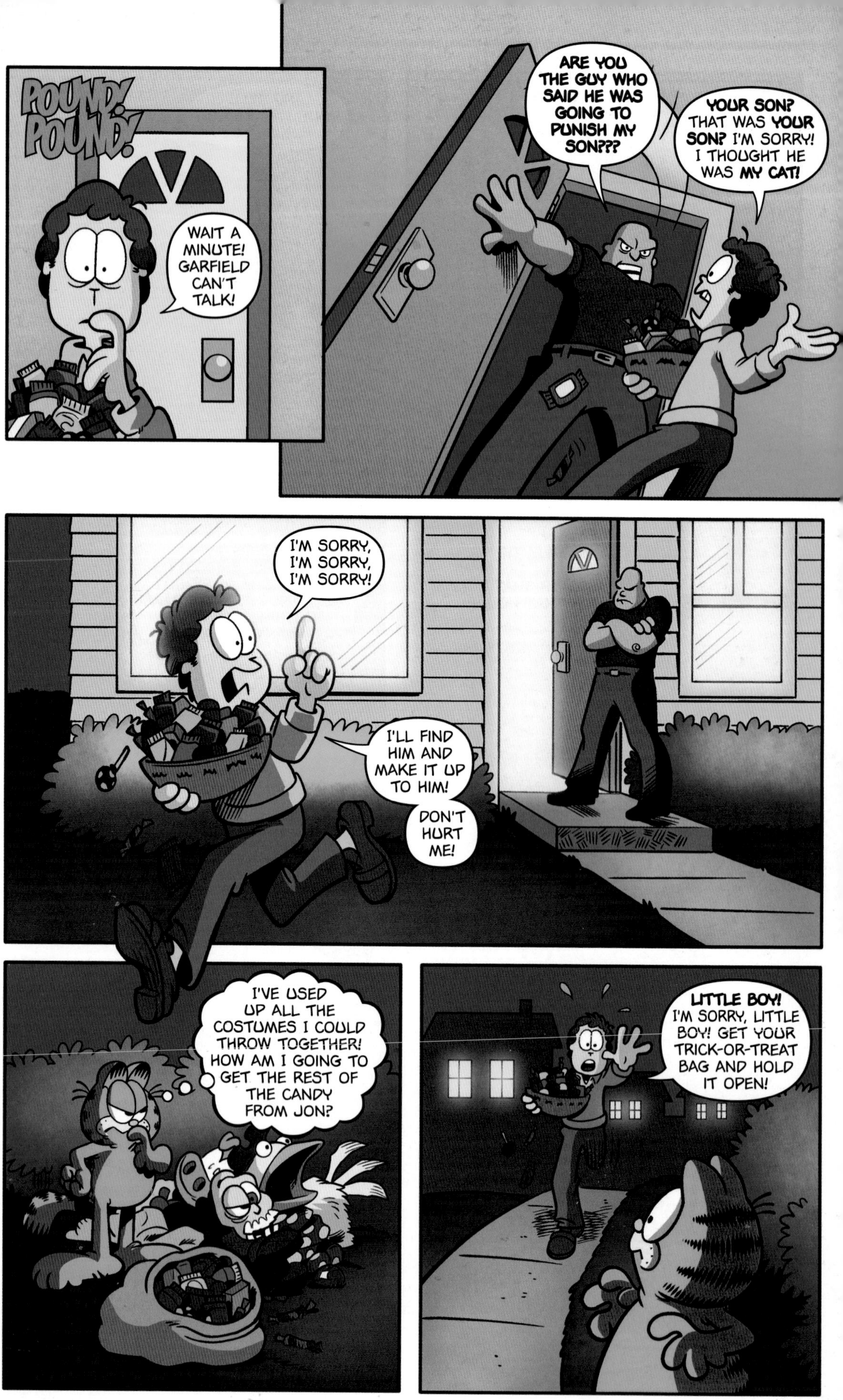
POUND! POUND!
WAIT A MINUTE! GARFIELD CAN'T TALK!
ARE YOU THE GUY WHO SAID HE WAS GOING TO PUNISH MY SON???
YOUR SON? THAT WAS YOUR SON? I'M SORRY! I THOUGHT HE WAS MY CAT!
I'M SORRY, I'M SORRY, I'M SORRY!
I'LL FIND HIM AND MAKE IT UP TO HIM!
DON'T HURT ME!
I'VE USED UP ALL THE COSTUMES I COULD THROW TOGETHER! HOW AM I GOING TO GET THE REST OF THE CANDY FROM JON?
LITTLE BOY! I'M SORRY, LITTLE BOY! GET YOUR TRICK-OR-TREAT BAG AND HOLD IT OPEN!

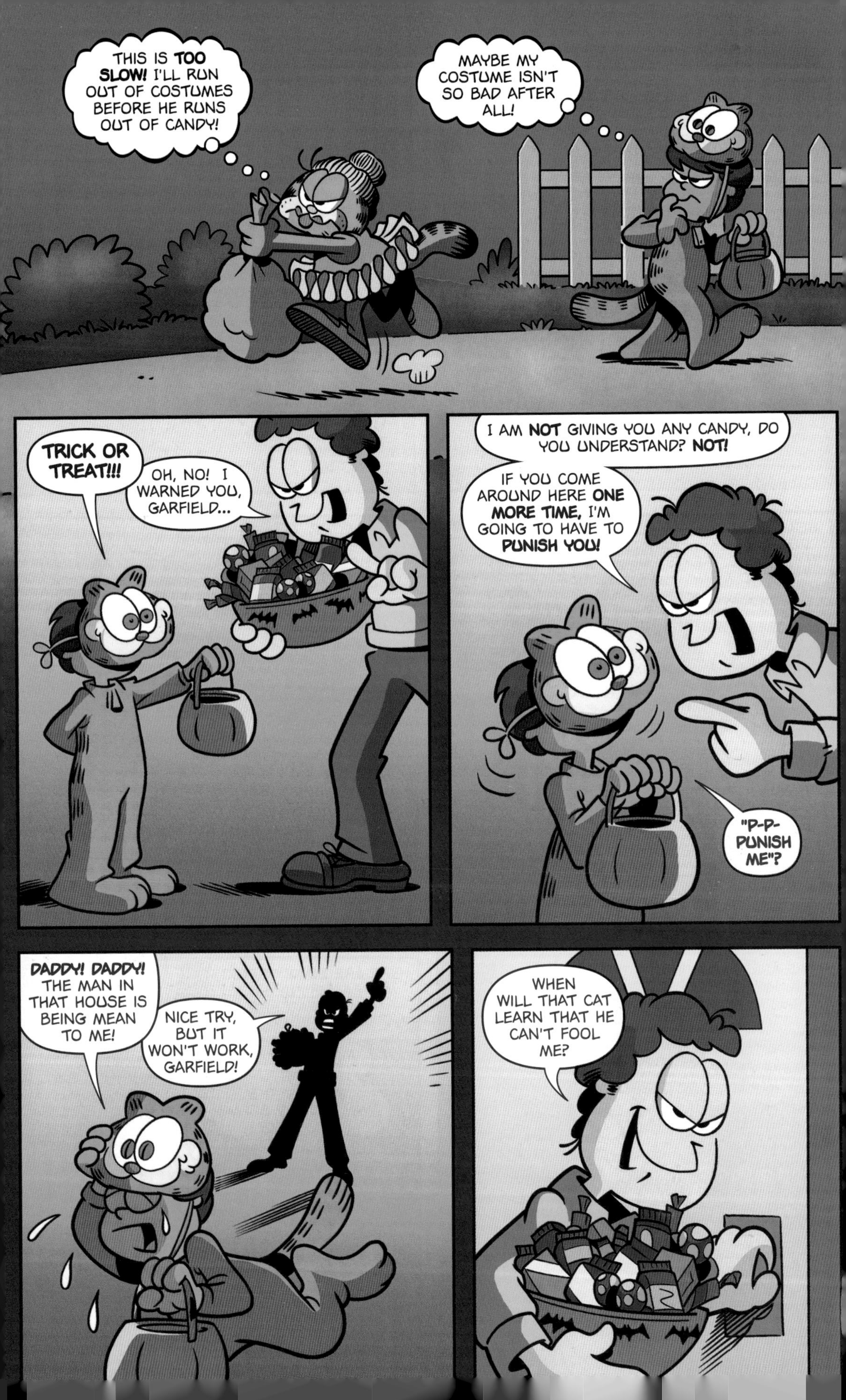
THIS IS **TOO SLOW!** I'LL RUN OUT OF COSTUMES BEFORE HE RUNS OUT OF CANDY!
MAYBE MY COSTUME ISN'T SO BAD AFTER ALL!
TRICK OR TREAT!!!
OH, NO! I WARNED YOU, GARFIELD...
I AM **NOT** GIVING YOU ANY CANDY, DO YOU UNDERSTAND? **NOT!**
IF YOU COME AROUND HERE **ONE MORE TIME,** I'M GOING TO HAVE TO **PUNISH YOU!**
"P-P-PUNISH ME"?
DADDY! DADDY! THE MAN IN THAT HOUSE IS BEING MEAN TO ME!
NICE TRY, BUT IT WON'T WORK, GARFIELD!
WHEN WILL THAT CAT LEARN THAT HE CAN'T FOOL ME?

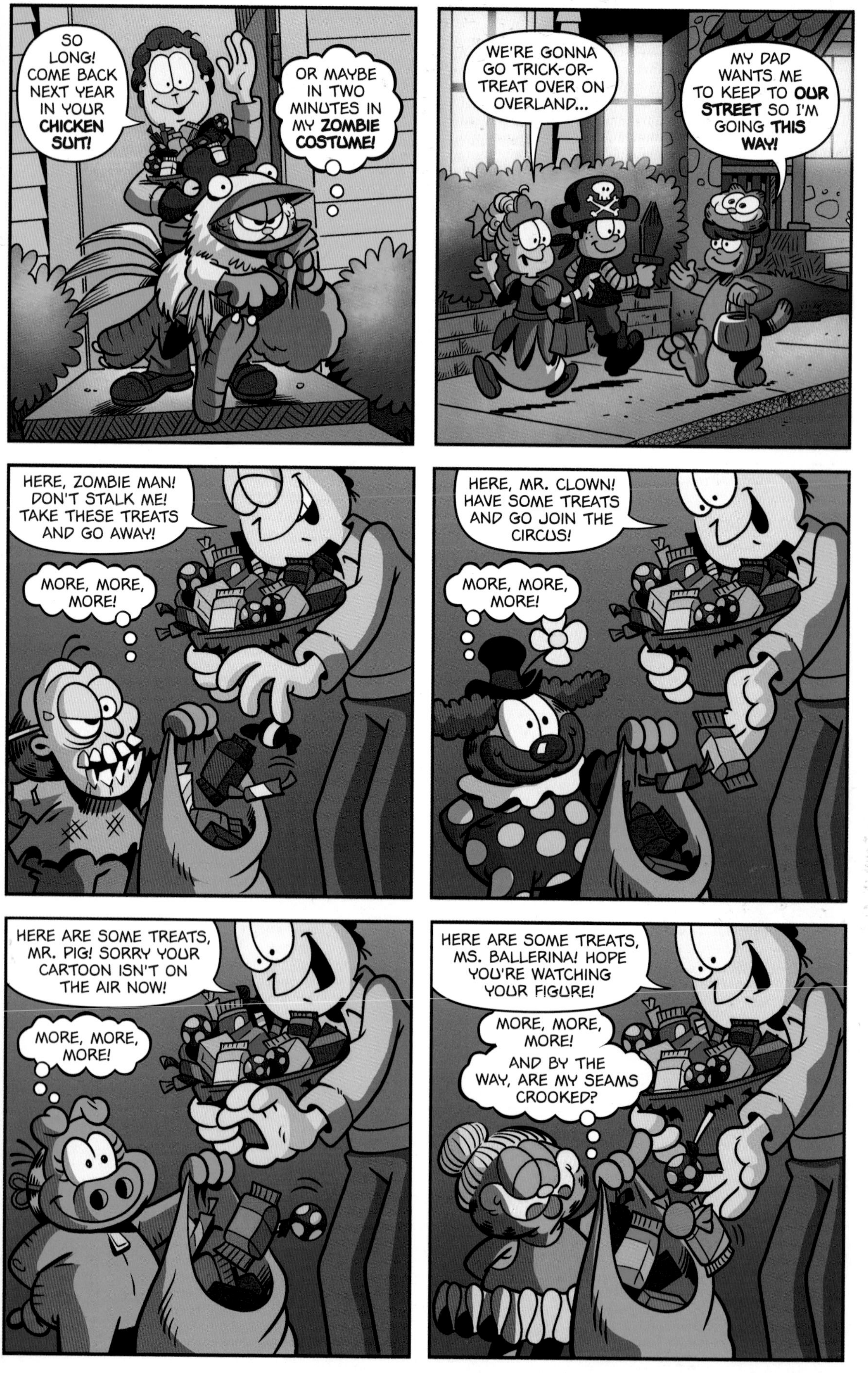
SO LONG! COME BACK NEXT YEAR IN YOUR **CHICKEN SUIT!**
OR MAYBE IN TWO MINUTES IN MY **ZOMBIE COSTUME!**
WE'RE GONNA GO TRICK-OR-TREAT OVER ON OVERLAND...
MY DAD WANTS ME TO KEEP TO **OUR STREET** SO I'M GOING **THIS WAY!**
HERE, ZOMBIE MAN! DON'T STALK ME! TAKE THESE TREATS AND GO AWAY!
MORE, MORE, MORE!
HERE, MR. CLOWN! HAVE SOME TREATS AND GO JOIN THE CIRCUS!
MORE, MORE, MORE!
HERE ARE SOME TREATS, MR. PIG! SORRY YOUR CARTOON ISN'T ON THE AIR NOW!
MORE, MORE, MORE!
HERE ARE SOME TREATS, MS. BALLERINA! HOPE YOU'RE WATCHING YOUR FIGURE!
MORE, MORE, MORE!
AND BY THE WAY, ARE MY SEAMS CROOKED?

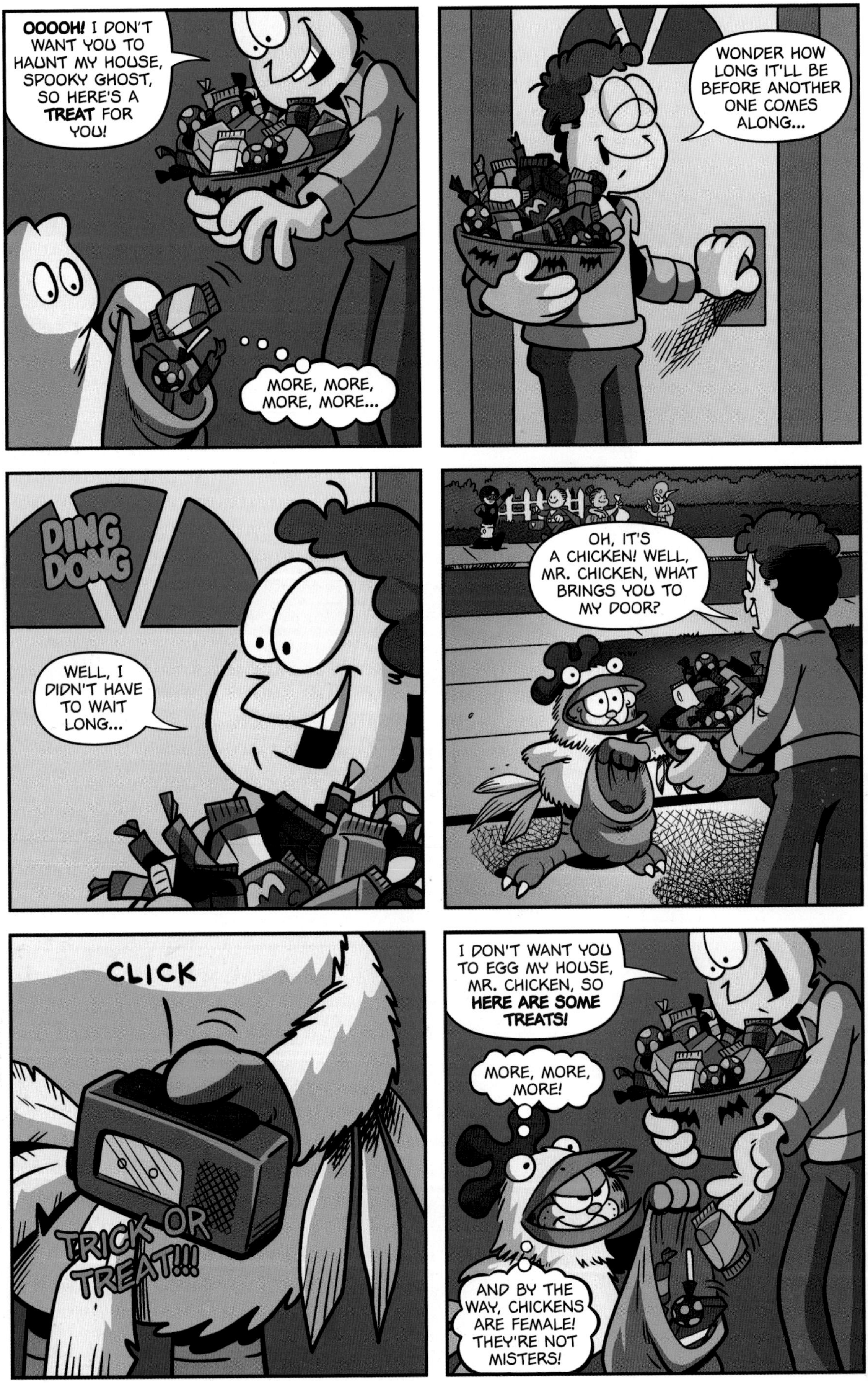
OOOOH! I DON'T WANT YOU TO HAUNT MY HOUSE, SPOOKY GHOST, SO HERE'S A TREAT FOR YOU!
MORE, MORE, MORE, MORE...
WONDER HOW LONG IT'LL BE BEFORE ANOTHER ONE COMES ALONG...
DING DONG
WELL, I DIDN'T HAVE TO WAIT LONG...
OH, IT'S A CHICKEN! WELL, MR. CHICKEN, WHAT BRINGS YOU TO MY DOOR?
CLICK
TRICK OR TREAT!!!
I DON'T WANT YOU TO EGG MY HOUSE, MR. CHICKEN, SO HERE ARE SOME TREATS!
MORE, MORE, MORE!
AND BY THE WAY, CHICKENS ARE FEMALE! THEY'RE NOT MISTERS!

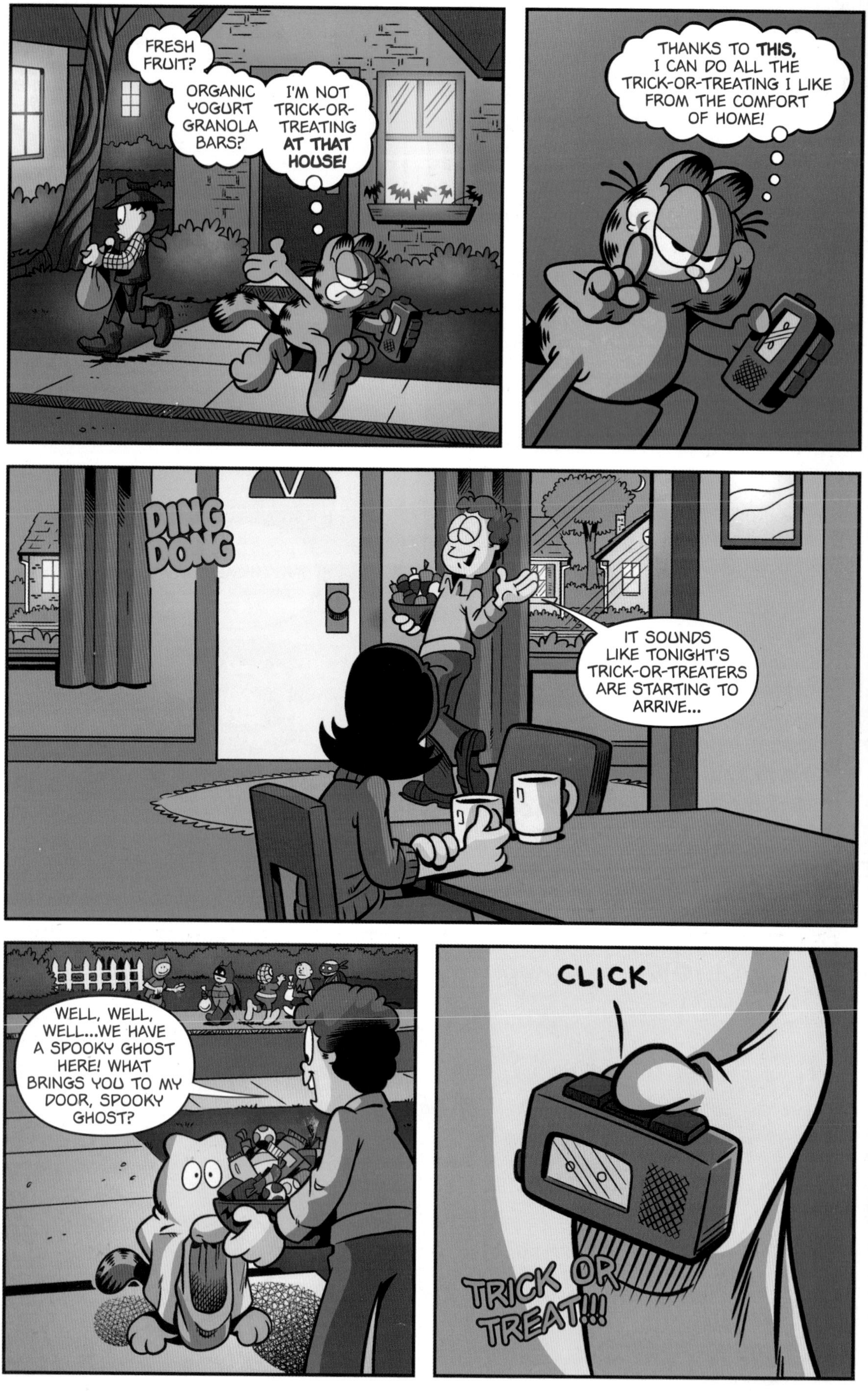
FRESH FRUIT?
ORGANIC YOGURT GRANOLA BARS?
I'M NOT TRICK-OR-TREATING **AT THAT HOUSE!**
THANKS TO **THIS,** I CAN DO ALL THE TRICK-OR-TREATING I LIKE FROM THE COMFORT OF HOME!
DING DONG
IT SOUNDS LIKE TONIGHT'S TRICK-OR-TREATERS ARE STARTING TO ARRIVE...
WELL, WELL, WELL...WE HAVE A SPOOKY GHOST HERE! WHAT BRINGS YOU TO MY DOOR, SPOOKY GHOST?
CLICK
TRICK OR TREAT!!!

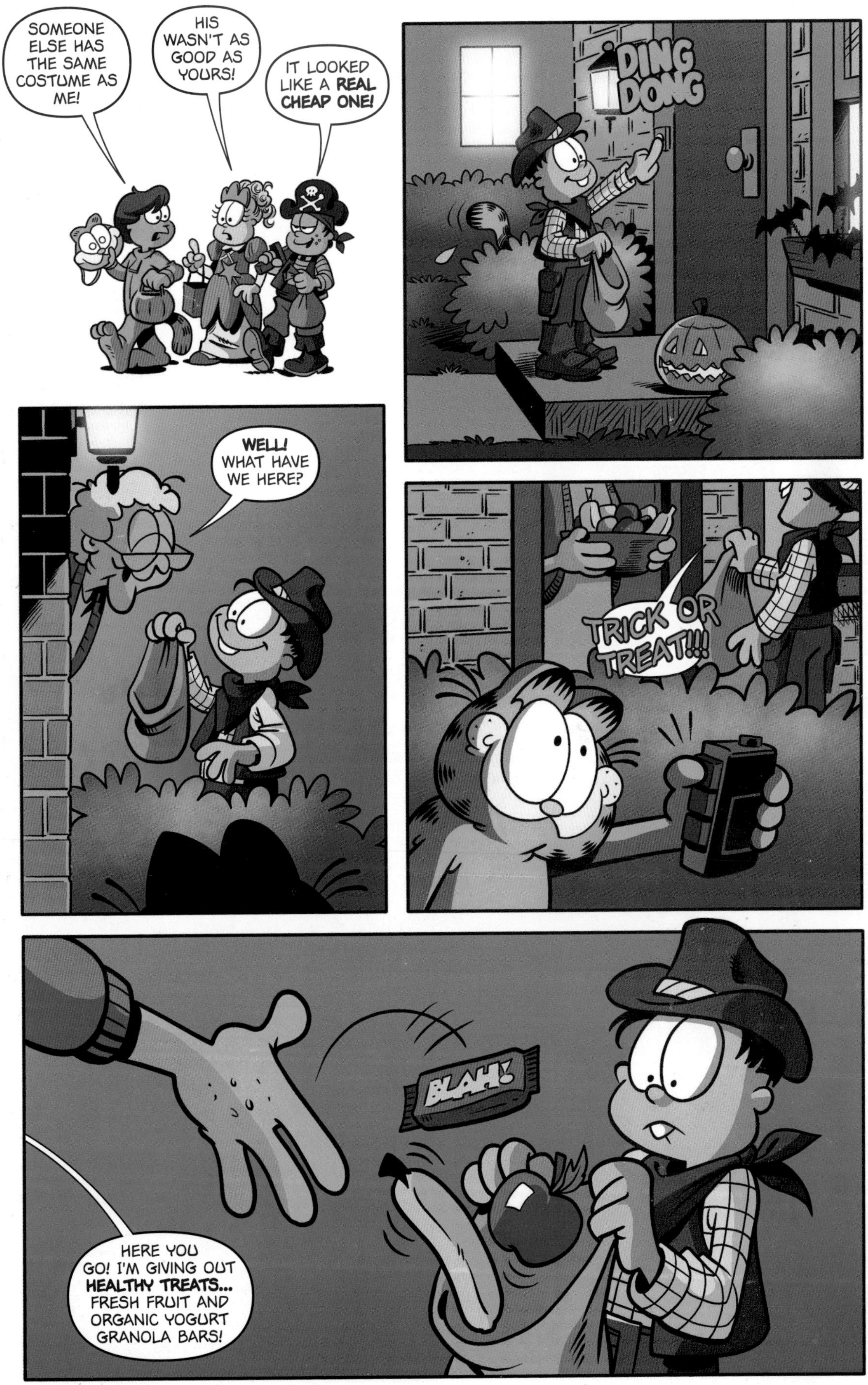

SOMEONE ELSE HAS THE SAME COSTUME AS ME!
HIS WASN'T AS GOOD AS YOURS!
IT LOOKED LIKE A **REAL CHEAP ONE!**
DING DONG
WELL! WHAT HAVE WE HERE?
TRICK OR TREAT!!!
BLAH!
HERE YOU GO! I'M GIVING OUT **HEALTHY TREATS...** FRESH FRUIT AND ORGANIC YOGURT GRANOLA BARS!

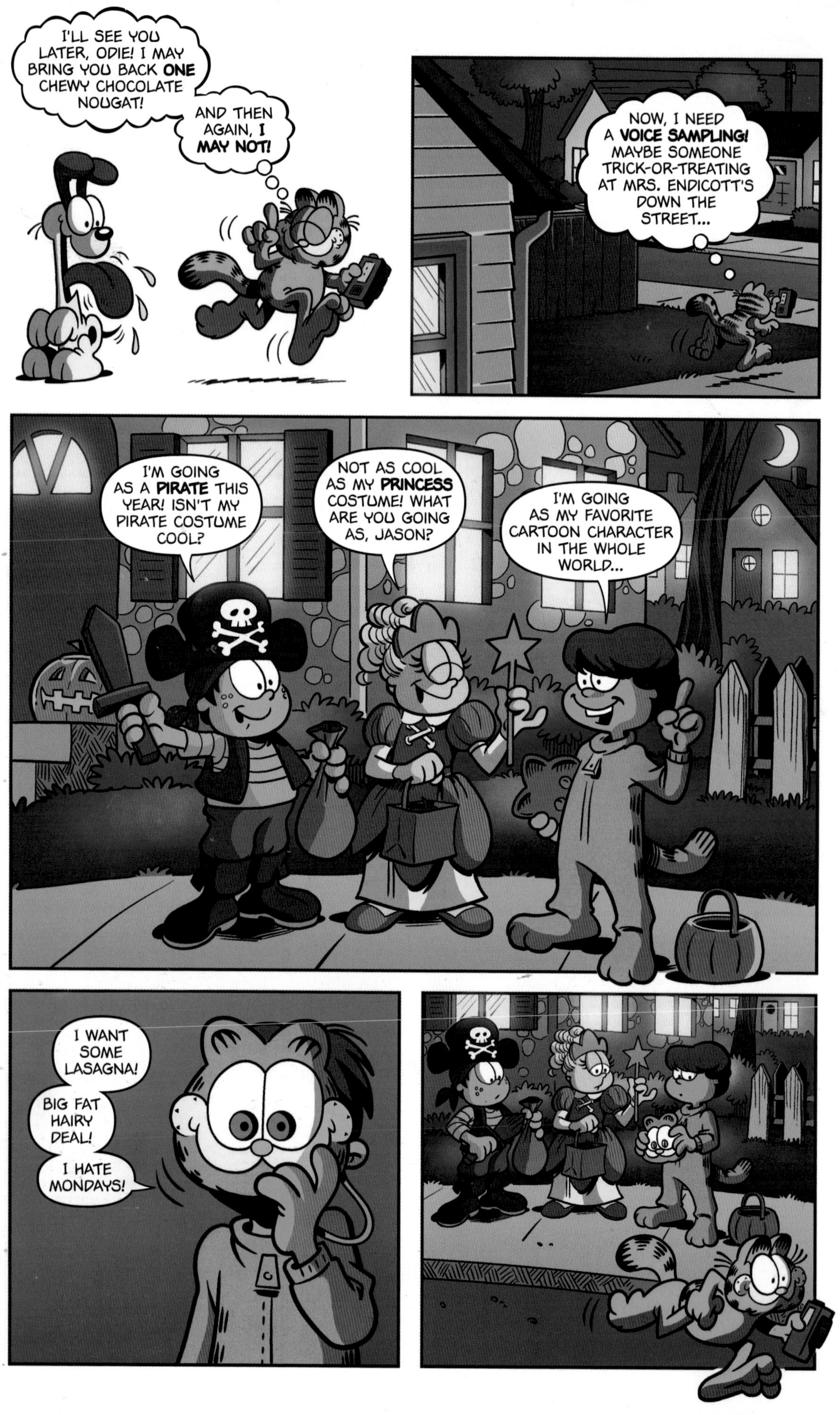

I'LL SEE YOU LATER, ODIE! I MAY BRING YOU BACK **ONE** CHEWY CHOCOLATE NOUGAT!
AND THEN AGAIN, **I MAY NOT!**
NOW, I NEED A **VOICE SAMPLING!** MAYBE SOMEONE TRICK-OR-TREATING AT MRS. ENDICOTT'S DOWN THE STREET...
I'M GOING AS A **PIRATE** THIS YEAR! ISN'T MY PIRATE COSTUME COOL?
NOT AS COOL AS MY **PRINCESS** COSTUME! WHAT ARE YOU GOING AS, JASON?
I'M GOING AS MY FAVORITE CARTOON CHARACTER IN THE WHOLE WORLD...
I WANT SOME LASAGNA!
BIG FAT HAIRY DEAL!
I HATE MONDAYS!

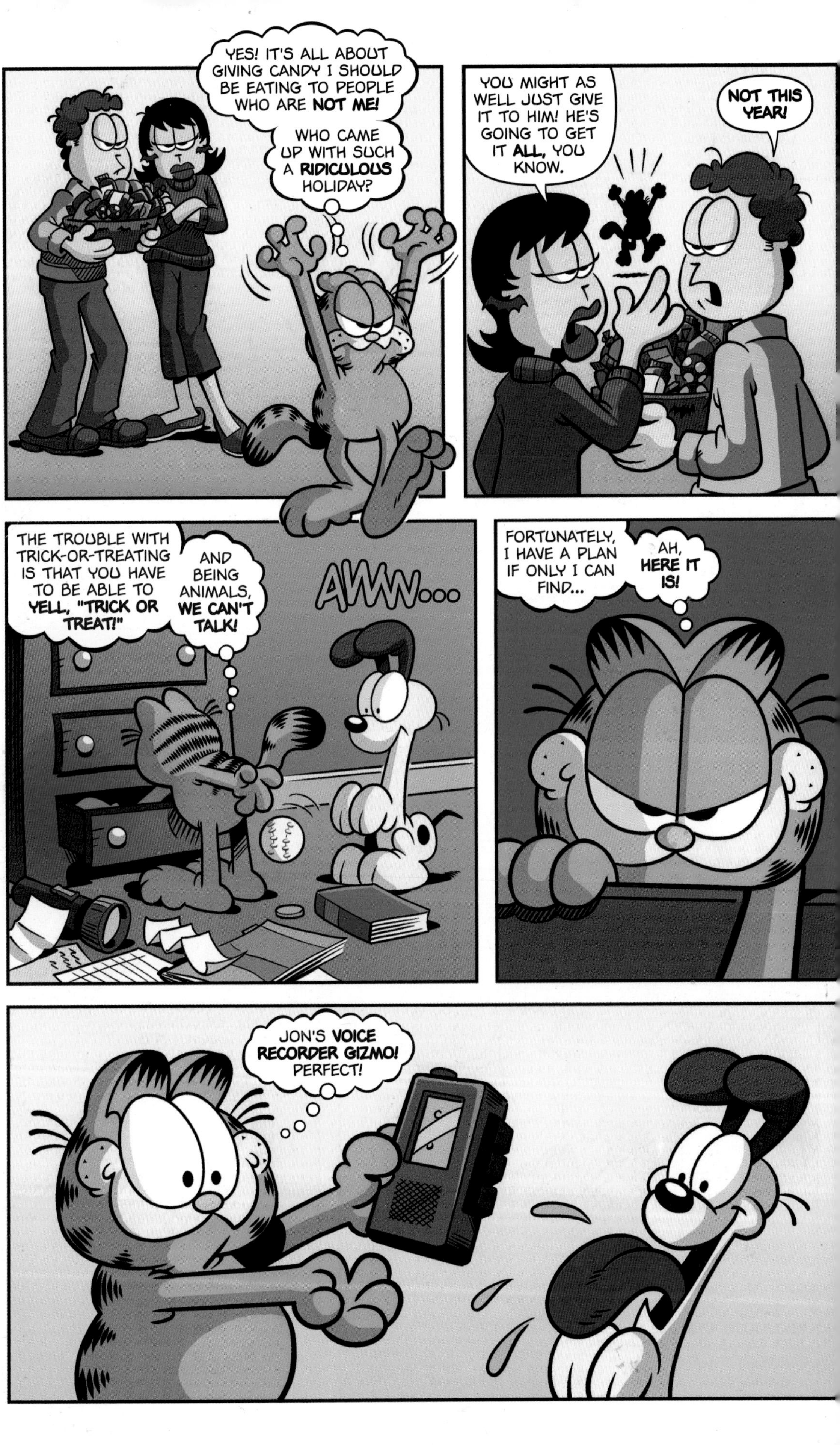
YES! IT'S ALL ABOUT GIVING CANDY I SHOULD BE EATING TO PEOPLE WHO ARE NOT ME!
WHO CAME UP WITH SUCH A RIDICULOUS HOLIDAY?
YOU MIGHT AS WELL JUST GIVE IT TO HIM! HE'S GOING TO GET IT ALL, YOU KNOW.
NOT THIS YEAR!
THE TROUBLE WITH TRICK-OR-TREATING IS THAT YOU HAVE TO BE ABLE TO YELL, "TRICK OR TREAT!"
AND BEING ANIMALS, WE CAN'T TALK!
AWW...
FORTUNATELY, I HAVE A PLAN IF ONLY I CAN FIND...
AH, HERE IT IS!
JON'S VOICE RECORDER GIZMO! PERFECT!

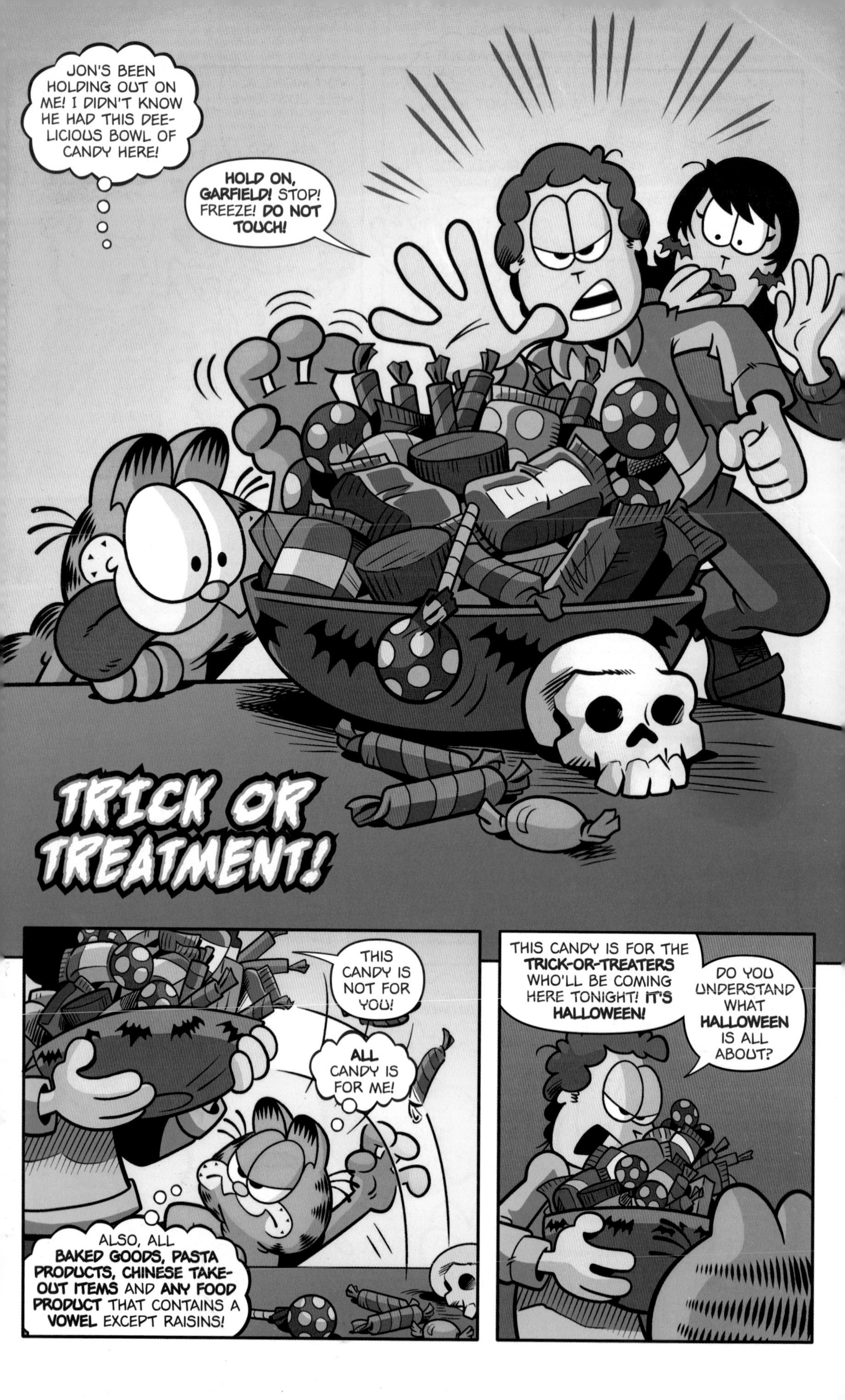
JON'S BEEN HOLDING OUT ON ME! I DIDN'T KNOW HE HAD THIS DEE-LICIOUS BOWL OF CANDY HERE!
HOLD ON, GARFIELD! STOP! FREEZE! DO NOT TOUCH!
TRICK OR TREATMENT!
THIS CANDY IS NOT FOR YOU!
ALL CANDY IS FOR ME!
ALSO, ALL BAKED GOODS, PASTA PRODUCTS, CHINESE TAKE-OUT ITEMS AND ANY FOOD PRODUCT THAT CONTAINS A VOWEL EXCEPT RAISINS!
THIS CANDY IS FOR THE TRICK-OR-TREATERS WHO'LL BE COMING HERE TONIGHT! IT'S HALLOWEEN!
DO YOU UNDERSTAND WHAT HALLOWEEN IS ALL ABOUT?

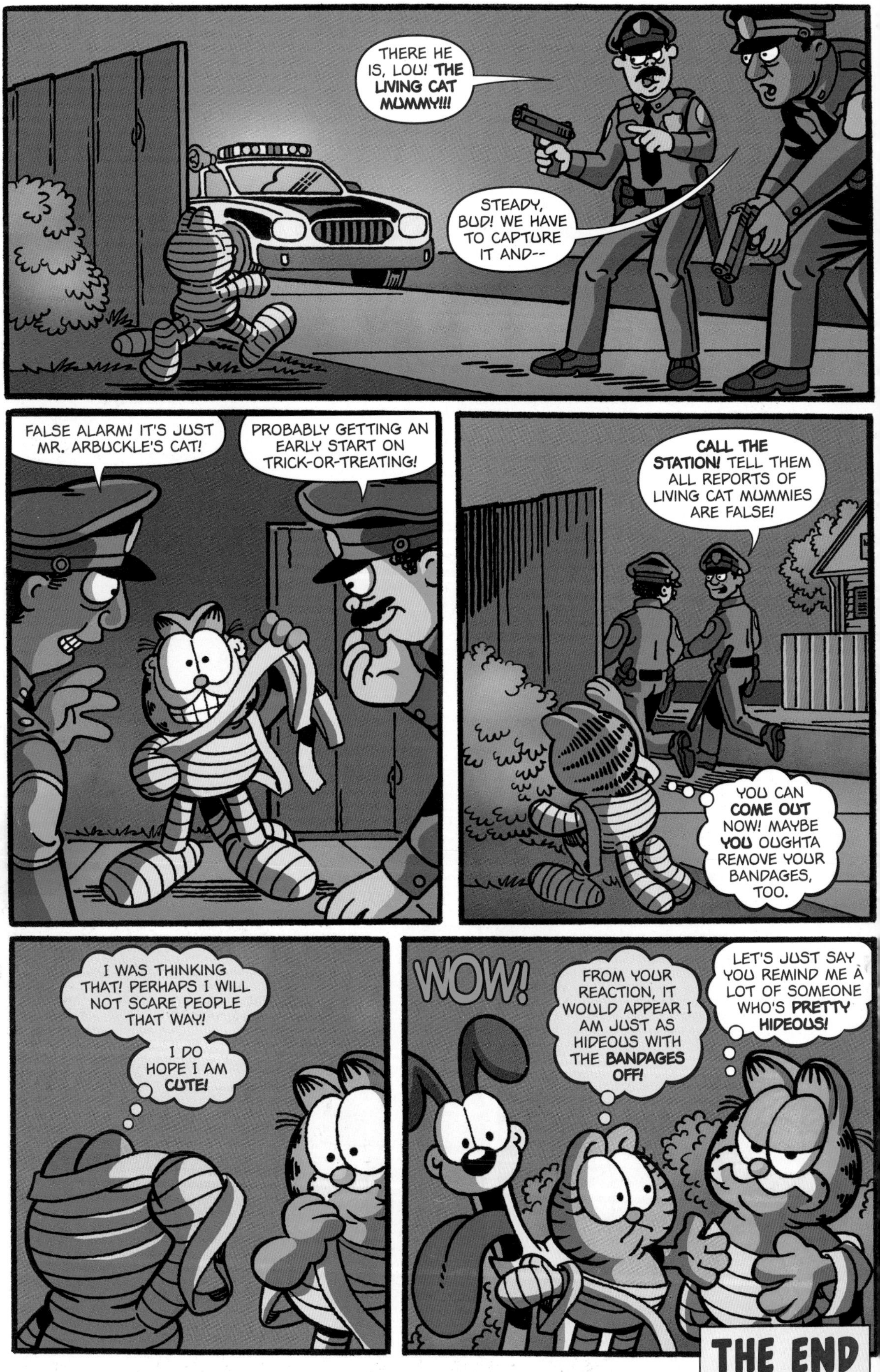

THERE HE IS, LOU! **THE LIVING CAT MUMMY!!!**
STEADY, BUD! WE HAVE TO CAPTURE IT AND--
FALSE ALARM! IT'S JUST MR. ARBUCKLE'S CAT!
PROBABLY GETTING AN EARLY START ON TRICK-OR-TREATING!
CALL THE STATION! TELL THEM ALL REPORTS OF LIVING CAT MUMMIES ARE FALSE!
YOU CAN **COME OUT** NOW! MAYBE **YOU** OUGHTA REMOVE YOUR BANDAGES, TOO.
I WAS THINKING THAT! PERHAPS I WILL NOT SCARE PEOPLE THAT WAY!
I DO HOPE I AM **CUTE!**
WOW!
FROM YOUR REACTION, IT WOULD APPEAR I AM JUST AS HIDEOUS WITH THE **BANDAGES OFF!**
LET'S JUST SAY YOU REMIND ME A LOT OF SOMEONE WHO'S **PRETTY HIDEOUS!**
THE END

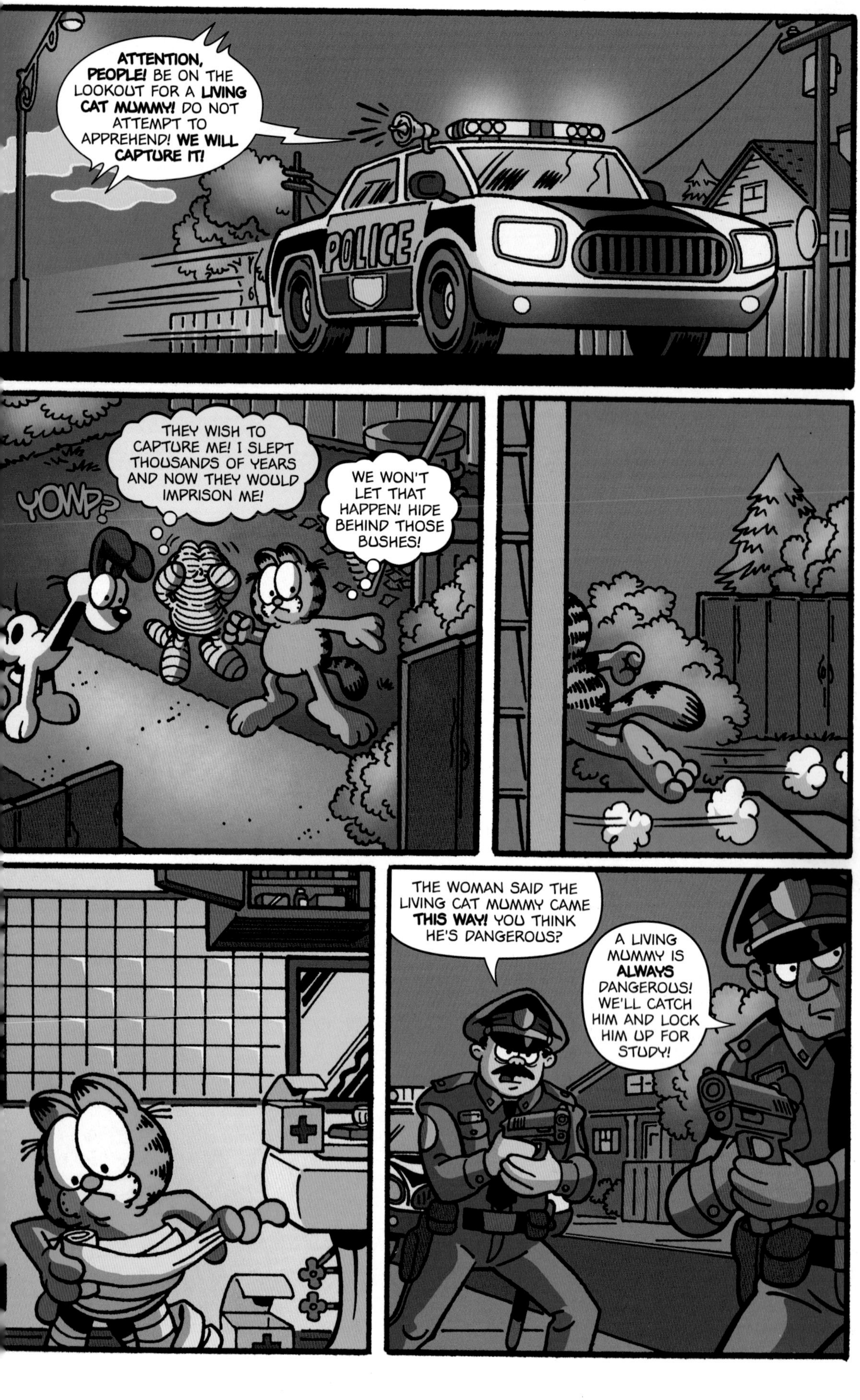

ATTENTION, PEOPLE! BE ON THE LOOKOUT FOR A LIVING CAT MUMMY! DO NOT ATTEMPT TO APPREHEND! WE WILL CAPTURE IT!
POLICE
THEY WISH TO CAPTURE ME! I SLEPT THOUSANDS OF YEARS AND NOW THEY WOULD IMPRISON ME!
YOWP?
WE WON'T LET THAT HAPPEN! HIDE BEHIND THOSE BUSHES!
THE WOMAN SAID THE LIVING CAT MUMMY CAME THIS WAY! YOU THINK HE'S DANGEROUS?
A LIVING MUMMY IS ALWAYS DANGEROUS! WE'LL CATCH HIM AND LOCK HIM UP FOR STUDY!

AGGGHH!
GOTCHA!
THAT WAS CLOSE! NOW, AS FOR SAMSON...
IF YOU MEAN THE TALLER CAT, HE IS FAR IN THE DISTANCE!
HE RUNS FROM ME AS DO SO MANY!
YOU...YOU'RE THAT MUMMY WE SAW AT THE MUSEUM! HOW DID YOU...?
THE TONGUE MOISTURE OF THE CANINE HERE SEEMS TO HAVE RE-ANIMATED ME!
I MEAN NO HARM, BUT PEOPLE FLEE FROM ME, SO...
...I ONLY WISH TO LEARN OF THIS TIME AND PLACE...
HIDE! QUICK! I SEE POLICE CARS COMING!

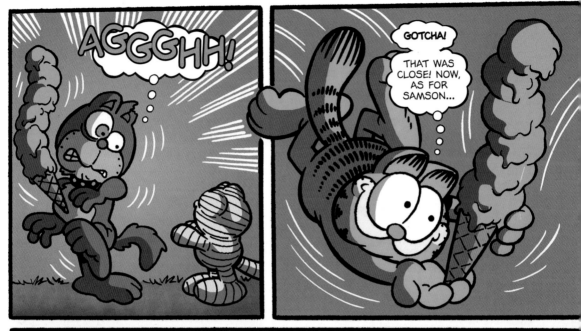

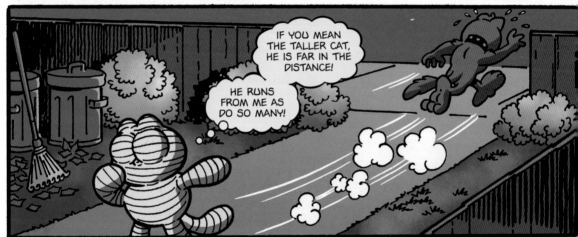

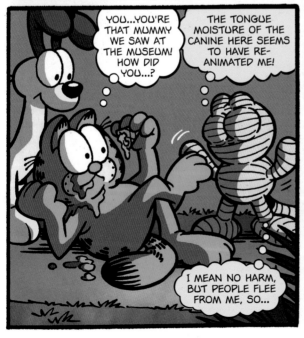

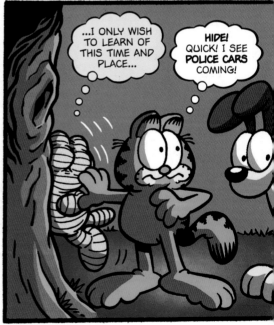

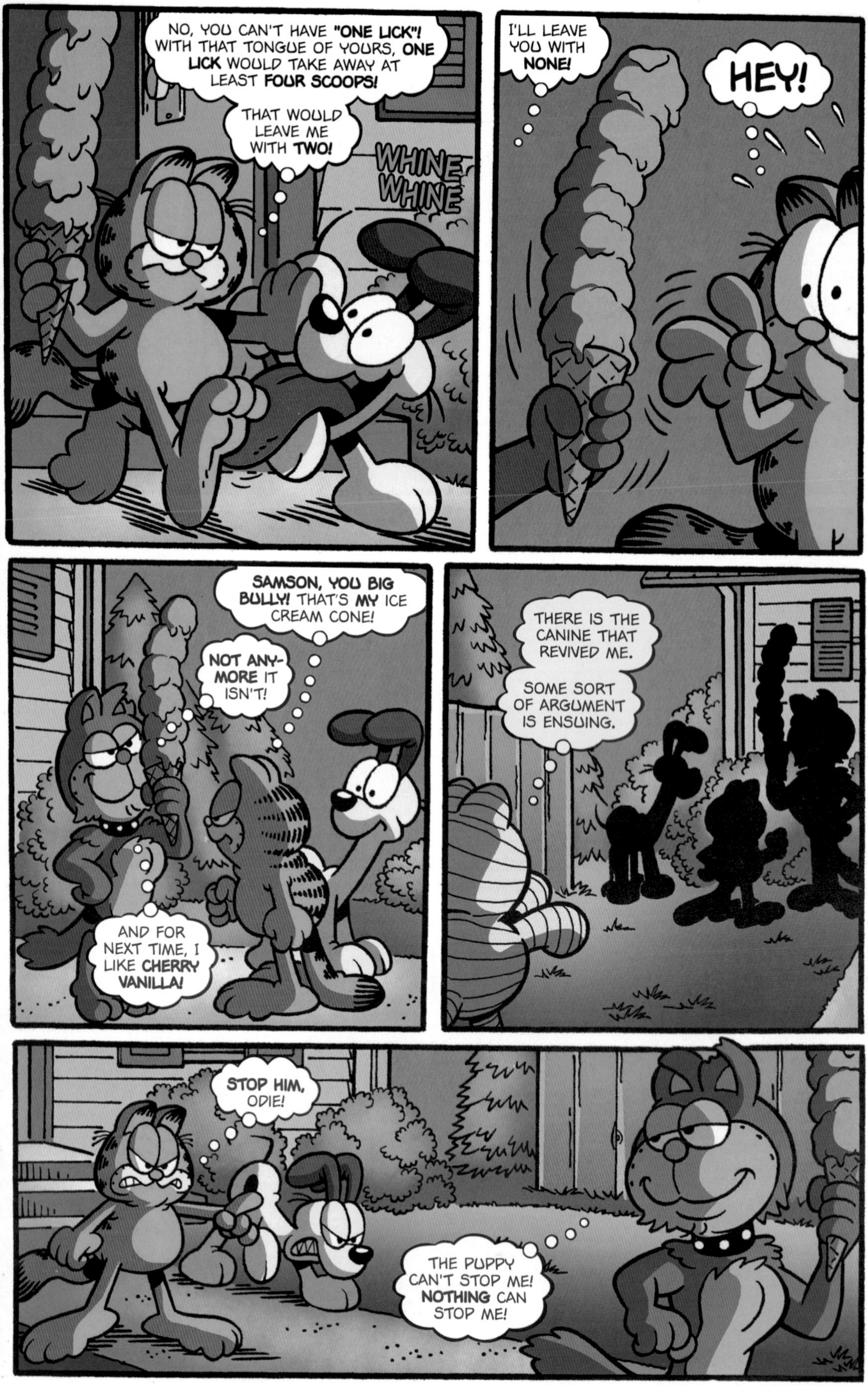

NO, YOU CAN'T HAVE "ONE LICK"! WITH THAT TONGUE OF YOURS, ONE LICK WOULD TAKE AWAY AT LEAST FOUR SCOOPS!
THAT WOULD LEAVE ME WITH TWO!
WHINE WHINE
I'LL LEAVE YOU WITH NONE!
HEY!
SAMSON, YOU BIG BULLY! THAT'S MY ICE CREAM CONE!
NOT ANY-MORE IT ISN'T!
AND FOR NEXT TIME, I LIKE CHERRY VANILLA!
THERE IS THE CANINE THAT REVIVED ME.
SOME SORT OF ARGUMENT IS ENSUING.
STOP HIM, ODIE!
THE PUPPY CAN'T STOP ME! NOTHING CAN STOP ME!

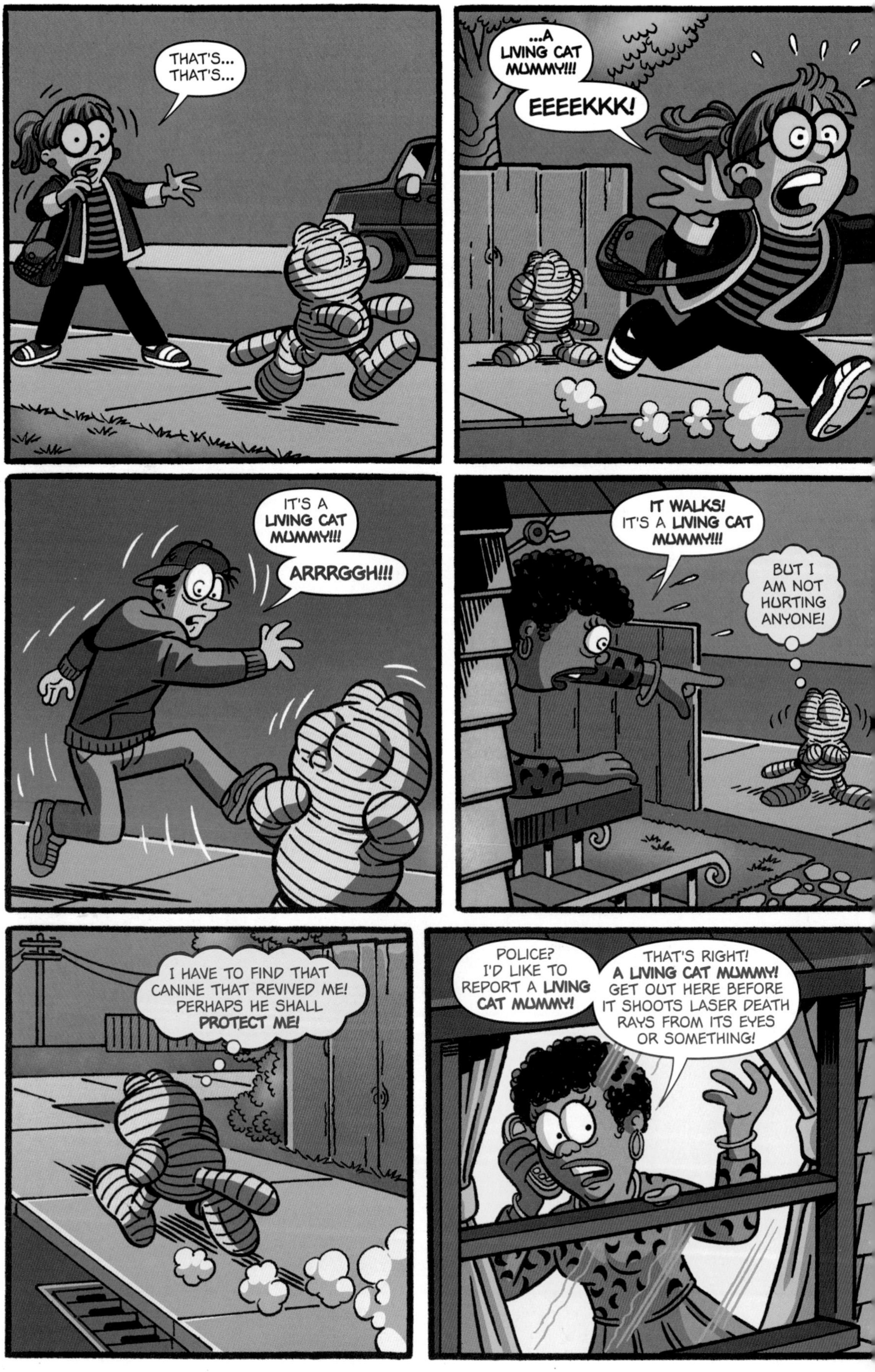
THAT'S... THAT'S...
...A LIVING CAT MUMMY!!!
EEEEKKK!
IT'S A LIVING CAT MUMMY!!!
ARRRGGH!!!
IT WALKS! IT'S A LIVING CAT MUMMY!!!
BUT I AM NOT HURTING ANYONE!
I HAVE TO FIND THAT CANINE THAT REVIVED ME! PERHAPS HE SHALL PROTECT ME!
POLICE? I'D LIKE TO REPORT A LIVING CAT MUMMY!
THAT'S RIGHT! A LIVING CAT MUMMY! GET OUT HERE BEFORE IT SHOOTS LASER DEATH RAYS FROM ITS EYES OR SOMETHING!

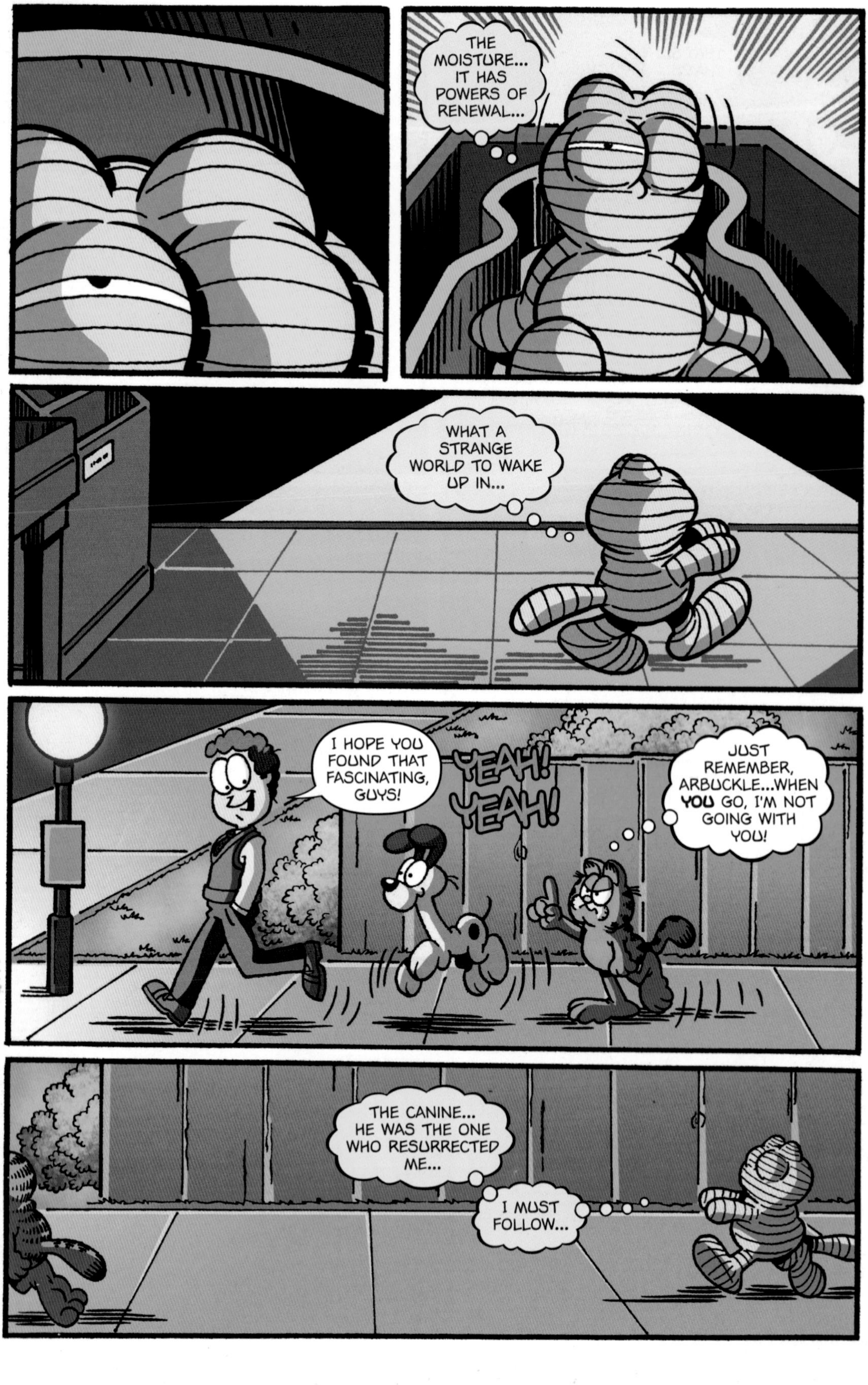
THE MOISTURE... IT HAS POWERS OF RENEWAL...
WHAT A STRANGE WORLD TO WAKE UP IN...
I HOPE YOU FOUND THAT FASCINATING, GUYS!
YEAH! YEAH!
JUST REMEMBER, ARBUCKLE...WHEN YOU GO, I'M NOT GOING WITH YOU!
THE CANINE... HE WAS THE ONE WHO RESURRECTED ME...
I MUST FOLLOW...

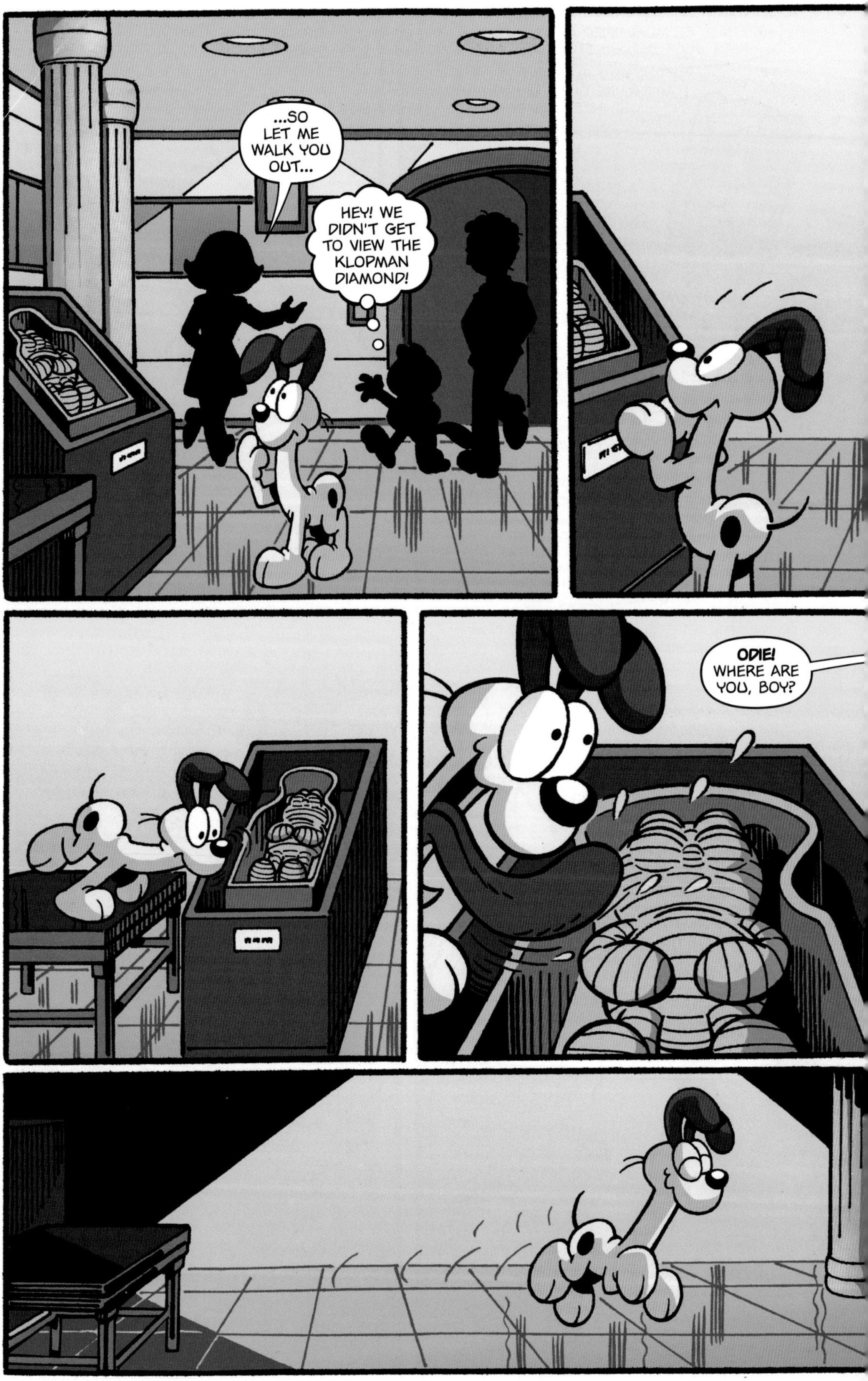
...SO LET ME WALK YOU OUT...
HEY! WE DIDN'T GET TO VIEW THE KLOPMAN DIAMOND!
ODIE! WHERE ARE YOU, BOY?

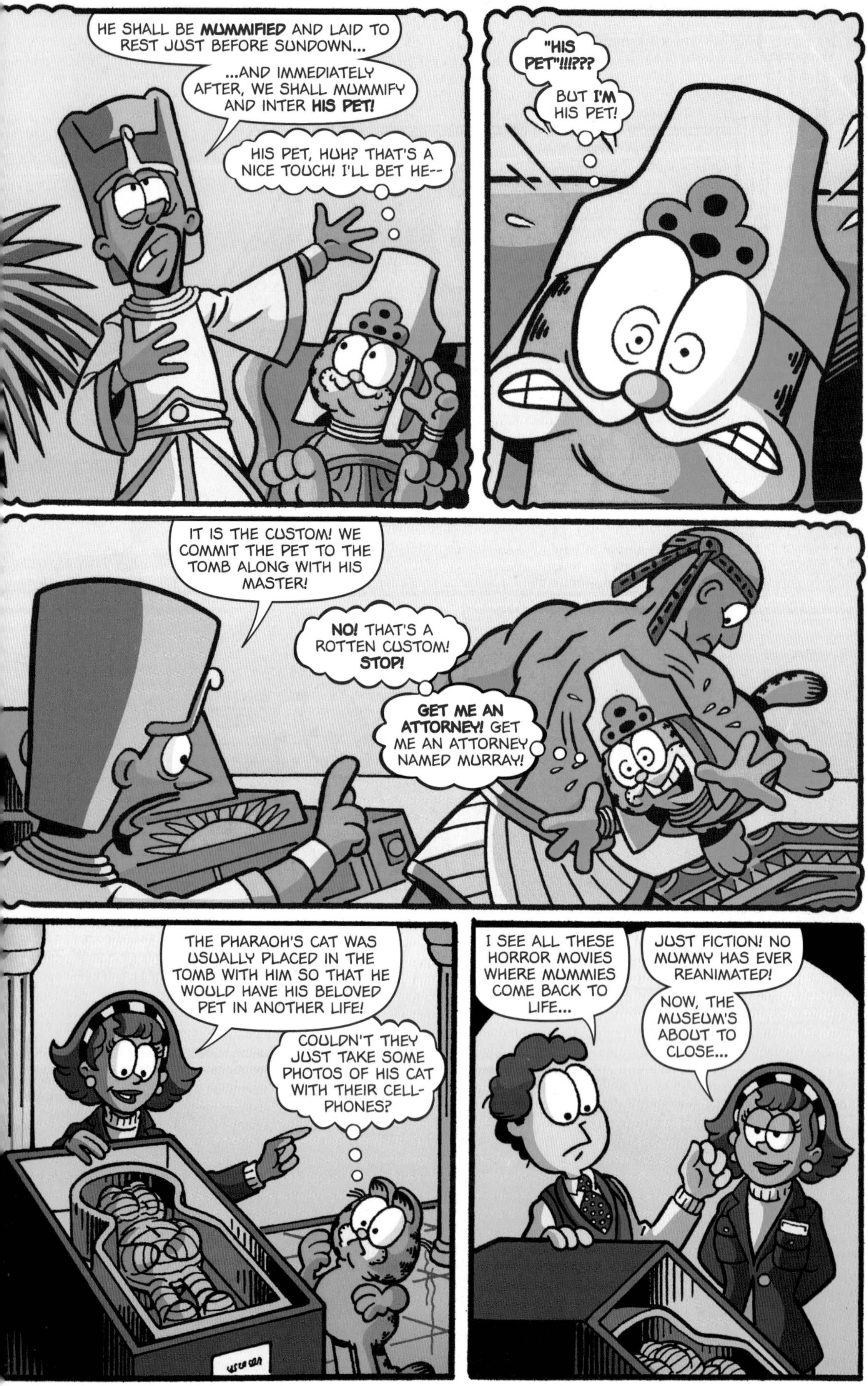
HE SHALL BE **MUMMIFIED** AND LAID TO REST JUST BEFORE SUNDOWN...
...AND IMMEDIATELY AFTER, WE SHALL MUMMIFY AND INTER **HIS PET!**
HIS PET, HUH? THAT'S A NICE TOUCH! I'LL BET HE--
"HIS PET"!!!???
BUT **I'M** HIS PET!
IT IS THE CUSTOM! WE COMMIT THE PET TO THE TOMB ALONG WITH HIS MASTER!
NO! THAT'S A ROTTEN CUSTOM! **STOP!**
GET ME AN ATTORNEY! GET ME AN ATTORNEY NAMED MURRAY!
THE PHARAOH'S CAT WAS USUALLY PLACED IN THE TOMB WITH HIM SO THAT HE WOULD HAVE HIS BELOVED PET IN ANOTHER LIFE!
COULDN'T THEY JUST TAKE SOME PHOTOS OF HIS CAT WITH THEIR CELL-PHONES?
I SEE ALL THESE HORROR MOVIES WHERE MUMMIES COME BACK TO LIFE...
JUST FICTION! NO MUMMY HAS EVER REANIMATED!
NOW, THE MUSEUM'S ABOUT TO CLOSE...

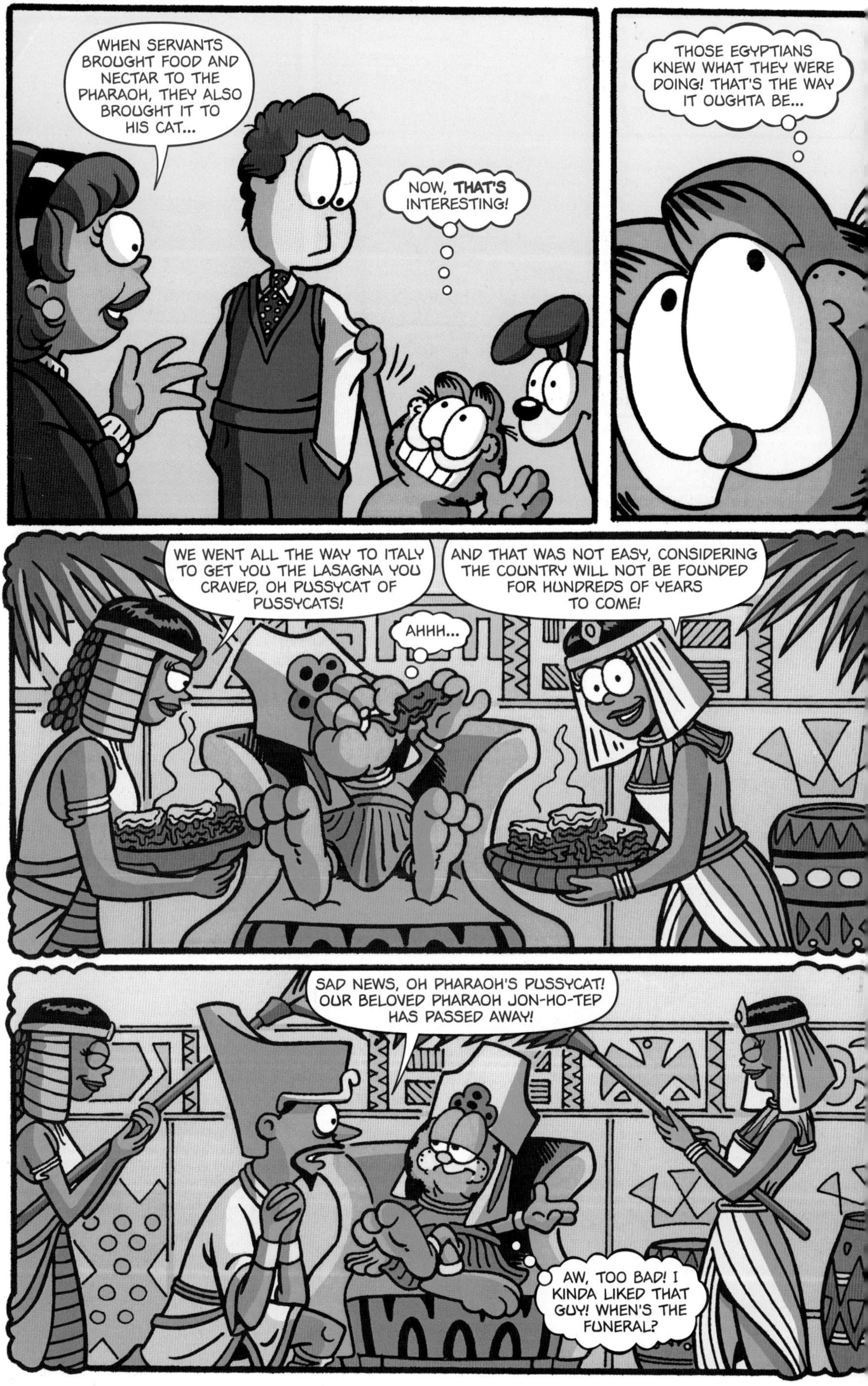
WHEN SERVANTS BROUGHT FOOD AND NECTAR TO THE PHARAOH, THEY ALSO BROUGHT IT TO HIS CAT...
NOW, **THAT'S** INTERESTING!
THOSE EGYPTIANS KNEW WHAT THEY WERE DOING! THAT'S THE WAY IT OUGHTA BE...
WE WENT ALL THE WAY TO ITALY TO GET YOU THE LASAGNA YOU CRAVED, OH PUSSYCAT OF PUSSYCATS!
AND THAT WAS NOT EASY, CONSIDERING THE COUNTRY WILL NOT BE FOUNDED FOR HUNDREDS OF YEARS TO COME!
AHHH...
SAD NEWS, OH PHARAOH'S PUSSYCAT! OUR BELOVED PHARAOH JON-HO-TEP HAS PASSED AWAY!
AW, TOO BAD! I KINDA LIKED THAT GUY! WHEN'S THE FUNERAL?

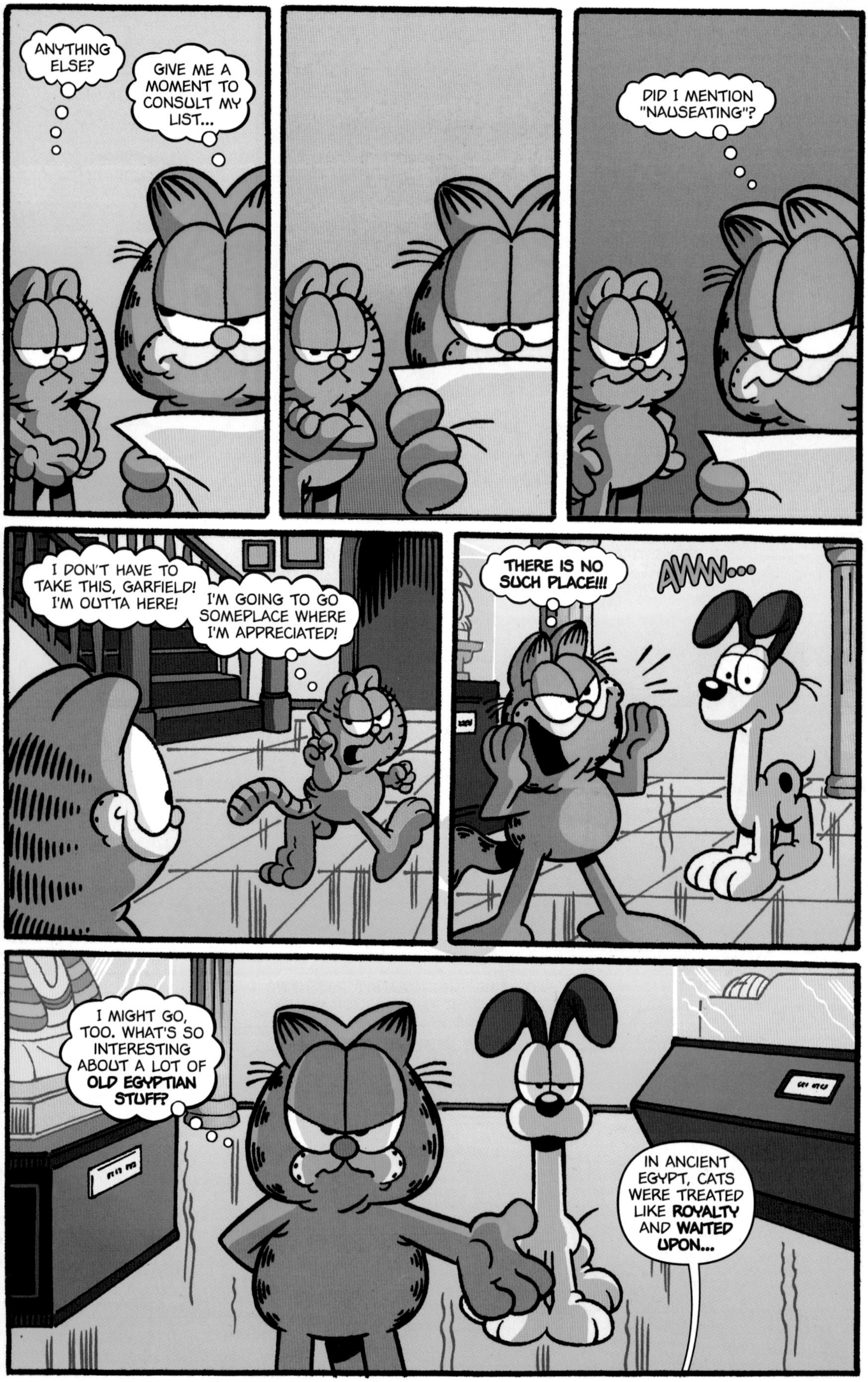
ANYTHING ELSE?
GIVE ME A MOMENT TO CONSULT MY LIST...
DID I MENTION "NAUSEATING"?
I DON'T HAVE TO TAKE THIS, GARFIELD! I'M OUTTA HERE!
I'M GOING TO GO SOMEPLACE WHERE I'M APPRECIATED!
THERE IS NO SUCH PLACE!!!
AWWW...
I MIGHT GO, TOO. WHAT'S SO INTERESTING ABOUT A LOT OF OLD EGYPTIAN STUFF?
IN ANCIENT EGYPT, CATS WERE TREATED LIKE ROYALTY AND WAITED UPON...

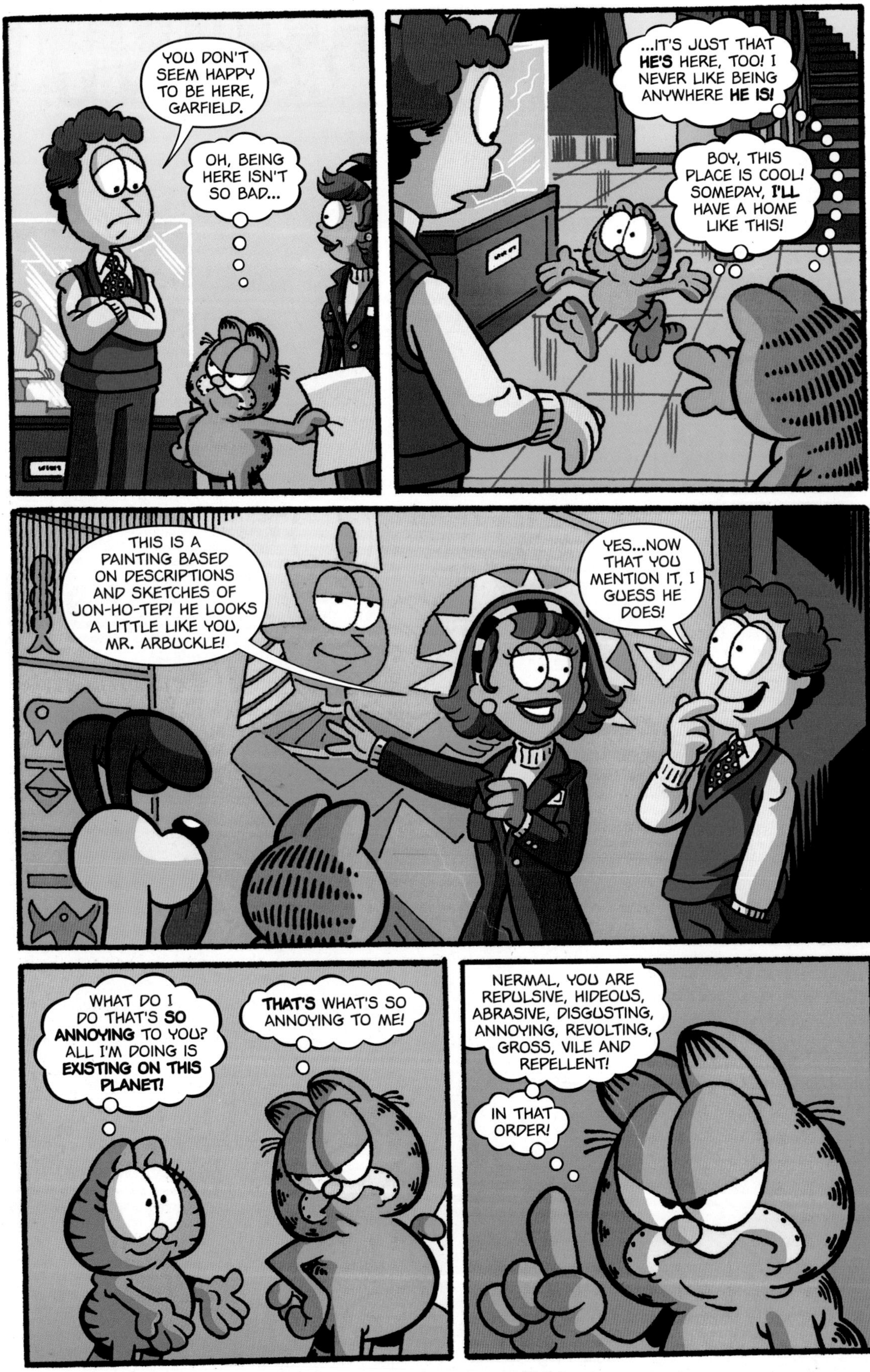

YOU DON'T SEEM HAPPY TO BE HERE, GARFIELD.
OH, BEING HERE ISN'T SO BAD...
...IT'S JUST THAT HE'S HERE, TOO! I NEVER LIKE BEING ANYWHERE HE IS!
BOY, THIS PLACE IS COOL! SOMEDAY, I'LL HAVE A HOME LIKE THIS!
THIS IS A PAINTING BASED ON DESCRIPTIONS AND SKETCHES OF JON-HO-TEP! HE LOOKS A LITTLE LIKE YOU, MR. ARBUCKLE!
YES...NOW THAT YOU MENTION IT, I GUESS HE DOES!
WHAT DO I DO THAT'S SO ANNOYING TO YOU? ALL I'M DOING IS EXISTING ON THIS PLANET!
THAT'S WHAT'S SO ANNOYING TO ME!
NERMAL, YOU ARE REPULSIVE, HIDEOUS, ABRASIVE, DISGUSTING, ANNOYING, REVOLTING, GROSS, VILE AND REPELLENT!
IN THAT ORDER!

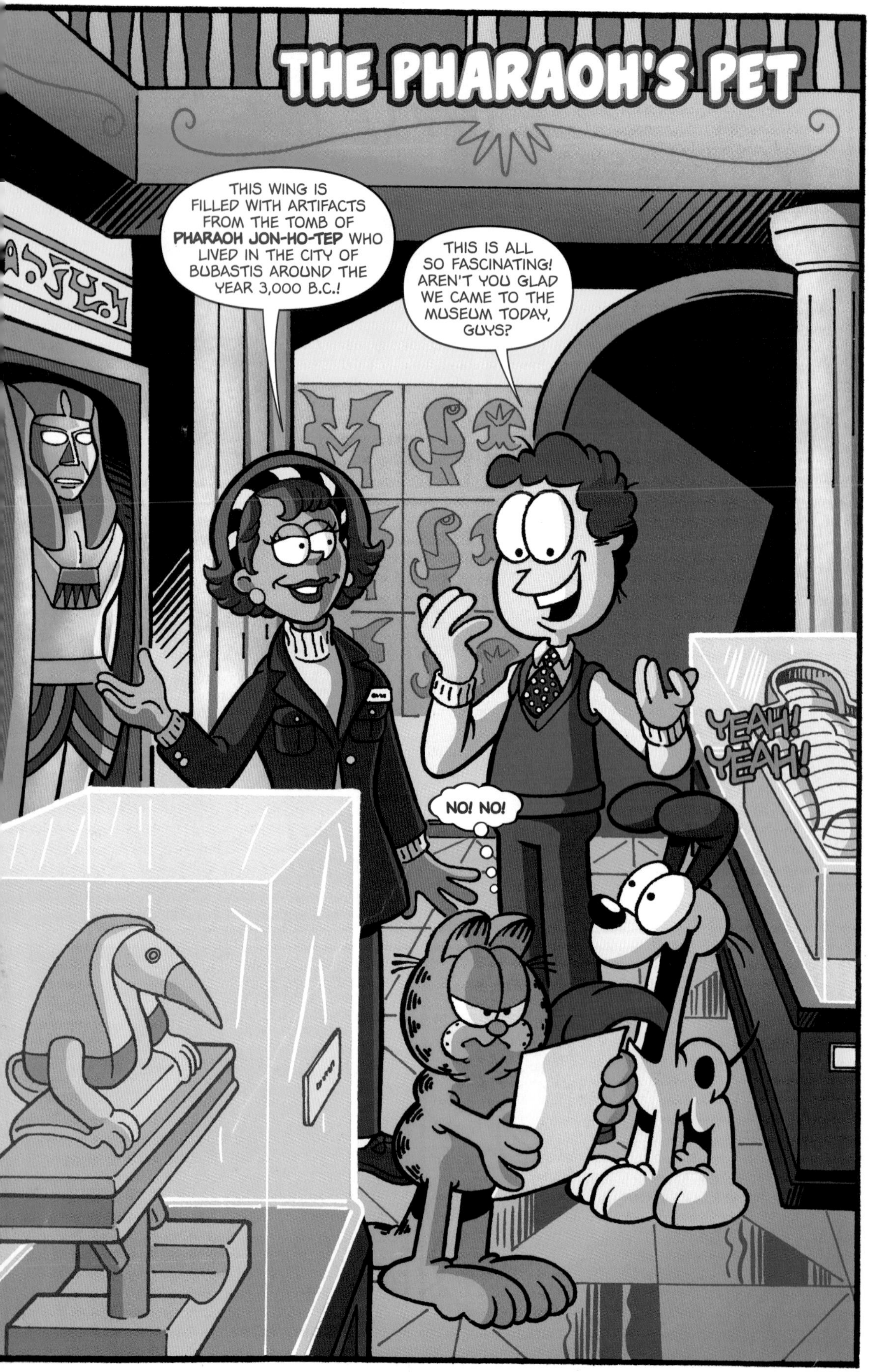
THE PHARAOH'S PET
THIS WING IS FILLED WITH ARTIFACTS FROM THE TOMB OF PHARAOH JON-HO-TEP WHO LIVED IN THE CITY OF BUBASTIS AROUND THE YEAR 3,000 B.C.!
THIS IS ALL SO FASCINATING! AREN'T YOU GLAD WE CAME TO THE MUSEUM TODAY, GUYS?
NO! NO!
YEAH! YEAH!

CHAPTER 2

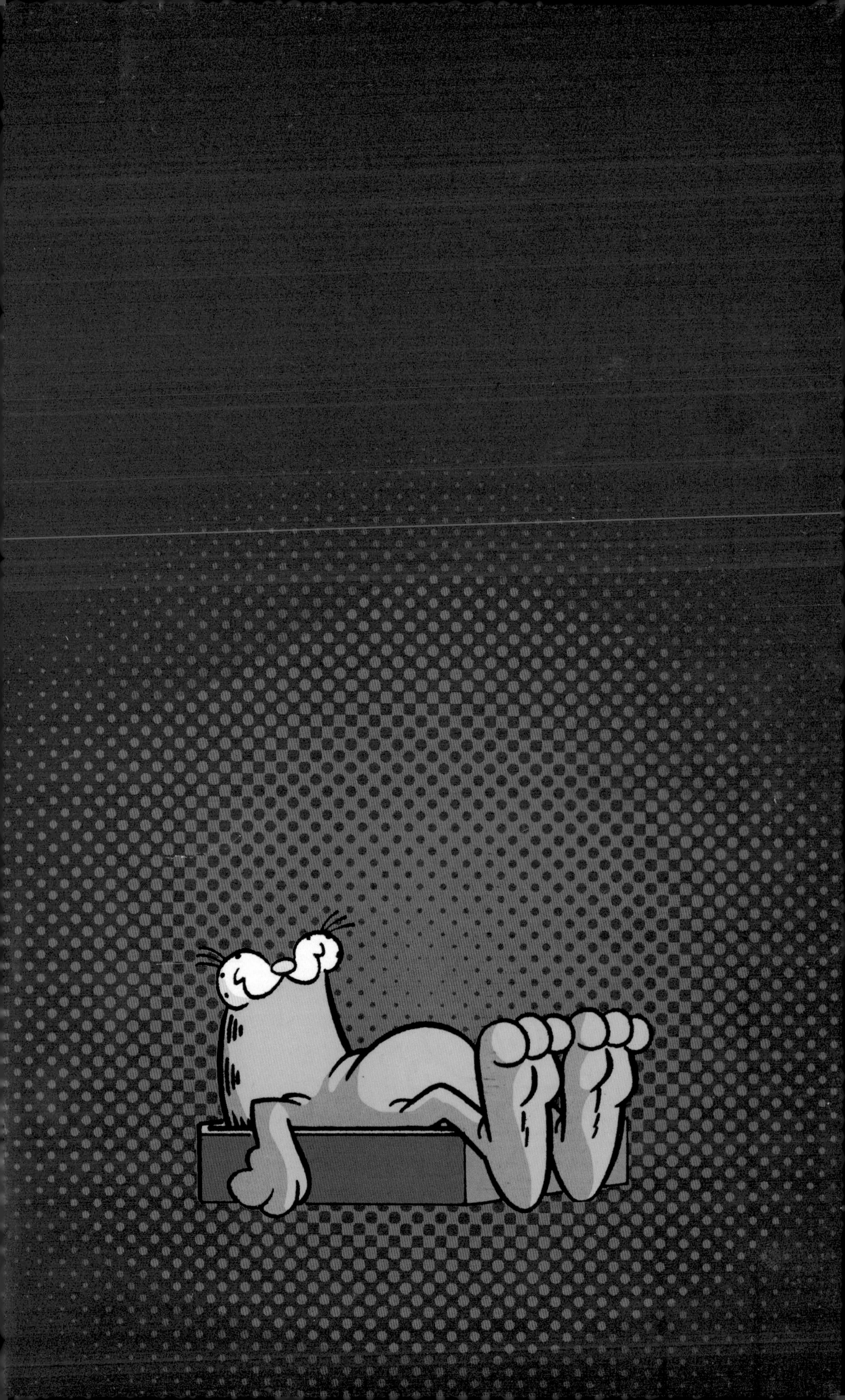

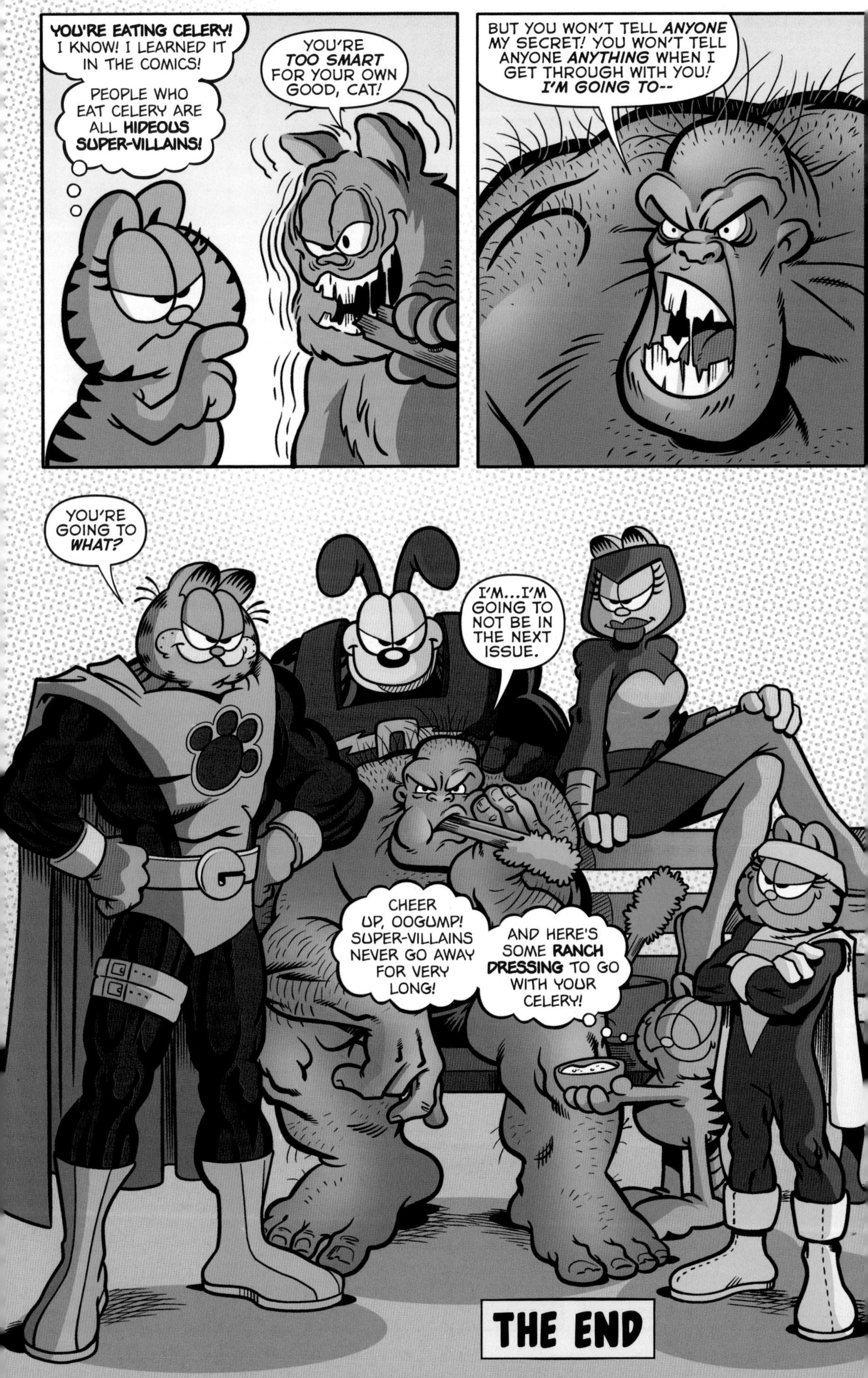
YOU'RE EATING CELERY! I KNOW! I LEARNED IT IN THE COMICS!
PEOPLE WHO EAT CELERY ARE ALL HIDEOUS SUPER-VILLAINS!
YOU'RE TOO SMART FOR YOUR OWN GOOD, CAT!
BUT YOU WON'T TELL ANYONE MY SECRET! YOU WON'T TELL ANYONE ANYTHING WHEN I GET THROUGH WITH YOU! I'M GOING TO--
YOU'RE GOING TO WHAT?
I'M...I'M GOING TO NOT BE IN THE NEXT ISSUE.
CHEER UP, OOGUMP! SUPER-VILLAINS NEVER GO AWAY FOR VERY LONG!
AND HERE'S SOME RANCH DRESSING TO GO WITH YOUR CELERY!
THE END

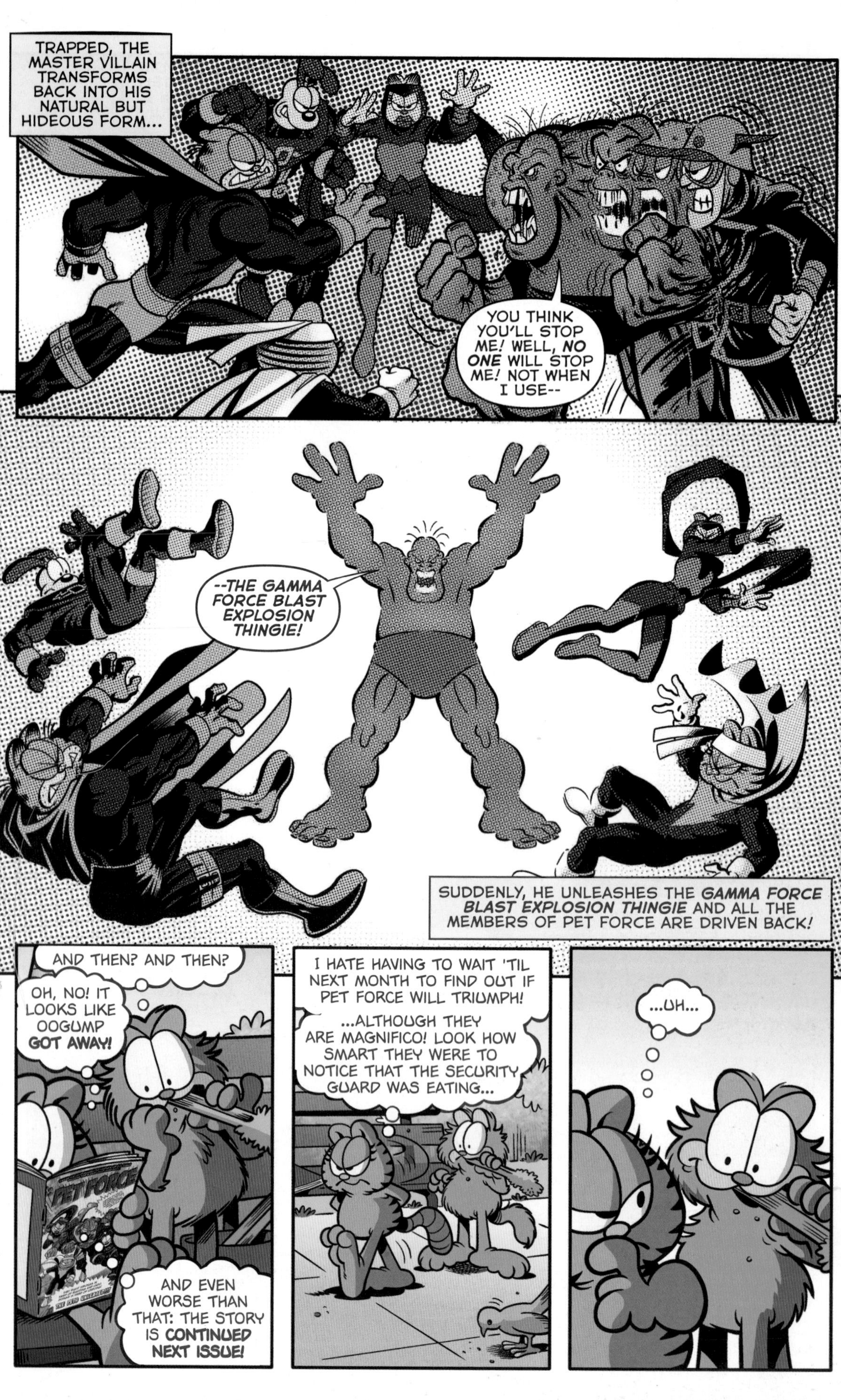
TRAPPED, THE MASTER VILLAIN TRANSFORMS BACK INTO HIS NATURAL BUT HIDEOUS FORM...
YOU THINK YOU'LL STOP ME! WELL, NO ONE WILL STOP ME! NOT WHEN I USE--
--THE GAMMA FORCE BLAST EXPLOSION THINGIE!
SUDDENLY, HE UNLEASHES THE GAMMA FORCE BLAST EXPLOSION THINGIE AND ALL THE MEMBERS OF PET FORCE ARE DRIVEN BACK!
AND THEN? AND THEN?
OH, NO! IT LOOKS LIKE OOGUMP GOT AWAY!
AND EVEN WORSE THAN THAT: THE STORY IS CONTINUED NEXT ISSUE!
I HATE HAVING TO WAIT 'TIL NEXT MONTH TO FIND OUT IF PET FORCE WILL TRIUMPH!
...ALTHOUGH THEY ARE MAGNIFICO! LOOK HOW SMART THEY WERE TO NOTICE THAT THE SECURITY GUARD WAS EATING...
...UH...

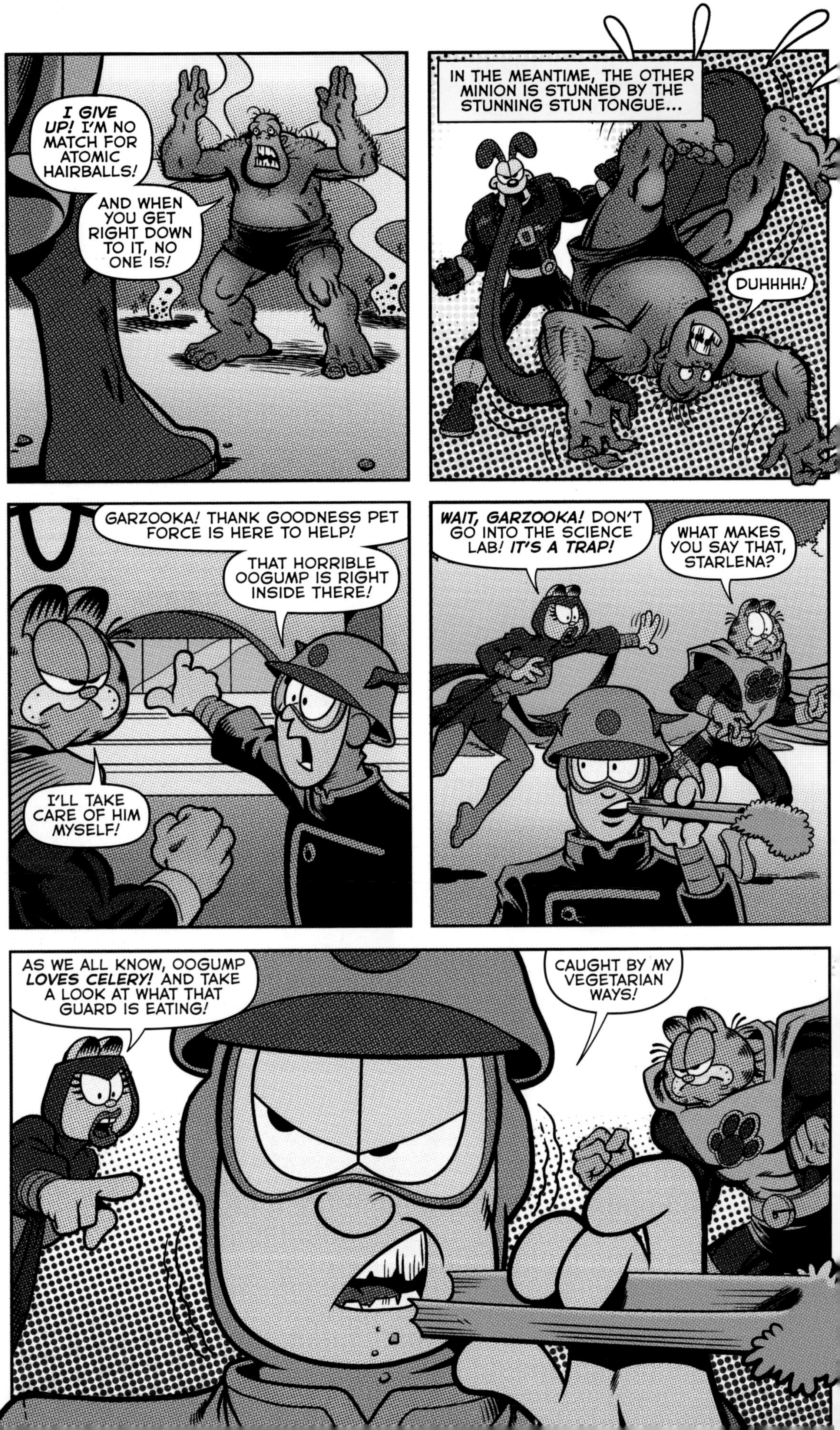

I GIVE UP! I'M NO MATCH FOR ATOMIC HAIRBALLS!
AND WHEN YOU GET RIGHT DOWN TO IT, NO ONE IS!
IN THE MEANTIME, THE OTHER MINION IS STUNNED BY THE STUNNING STUN TONGUE...
DUHHHH!
GARZOOKA! THANK GOODNESS PET FORCE IS HERE TO HELP!
THAT HORRIBLE OOGUMP IS RIGHT INSIDE THERE!
I'LL TAKE CARE OF HIM MYSELF!
WAIT, GARZOOKA! DON'T GO INTO THE SCIENCE LAB! IT'S A TRAP!
WHAT MAKES YOU SAY THAT, STARLENA?
AS WE ALL KNOW, OOGUMP LOVES CELERY! AND TAKE A LOOK AT WHAT THAT GUARD IS EATING!
CAUGHT BY MY VEGETARIAN WAYS!

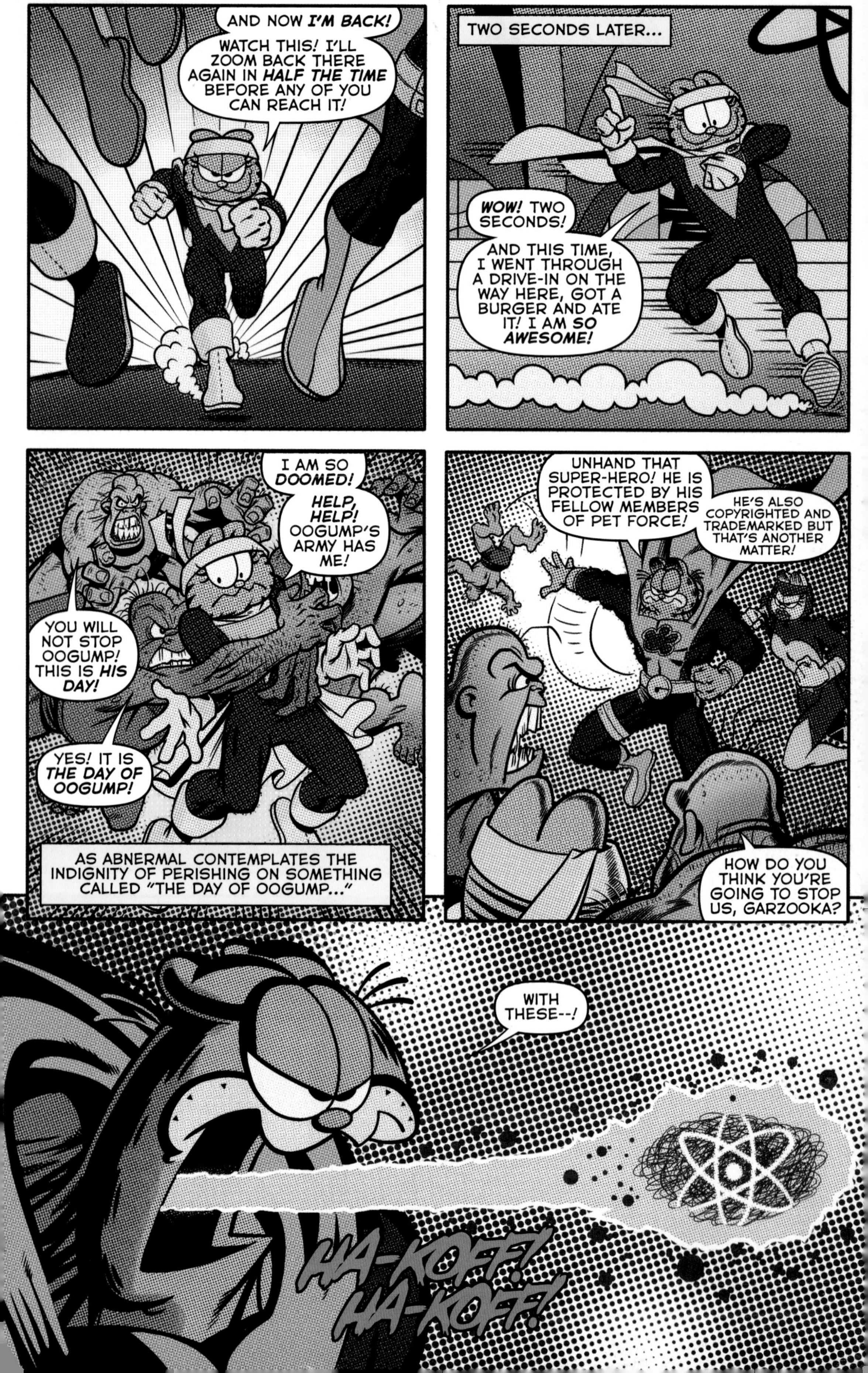
AND NOW I'M BACK!
WATCH THIS! I'LL ZOOM BACK THERE AGAIN IN HALF THE TIME BEFORE ANY OF YOU CAN REACH IT!
TWO SECONDS LATER...
WOW! TWO SECONDS!
AND THIS TIME, I WENT THROUGH A DRIVE-IN ON THE WAY HERE, GOT A BURGER AND ATE IT! I AM SO AWESOME!
I AM SO DOOMED!
HELP, HELP! OOGUMP'S ARMY HAS ME!
YOU WILL NOT STOP OOGUMP! THIS IS HIS DAY!
YES! IT IS THE DAY OF OOGUMP!
AS ABNERMAL CONTEMPLATES THE INDIGNITY OF PERISHING ON SOMETHING CALLED "THE DAY OF OOGUMP..."
UNHAND THAT SUPER-HERO! HE IS PROTECTED BY HIS FELLOW MEMBERS OF PET FORCE!
HE'S ALSO COPYRIGHTED AND TRADEMARKED BUT THAT'S ANOTHER MATTER!
HOW DO YOU THINK YOU'RE GOING TO STOP US, GARZOOKA?
WITH THESE--!
HA-KOFF! HA-KOFF!

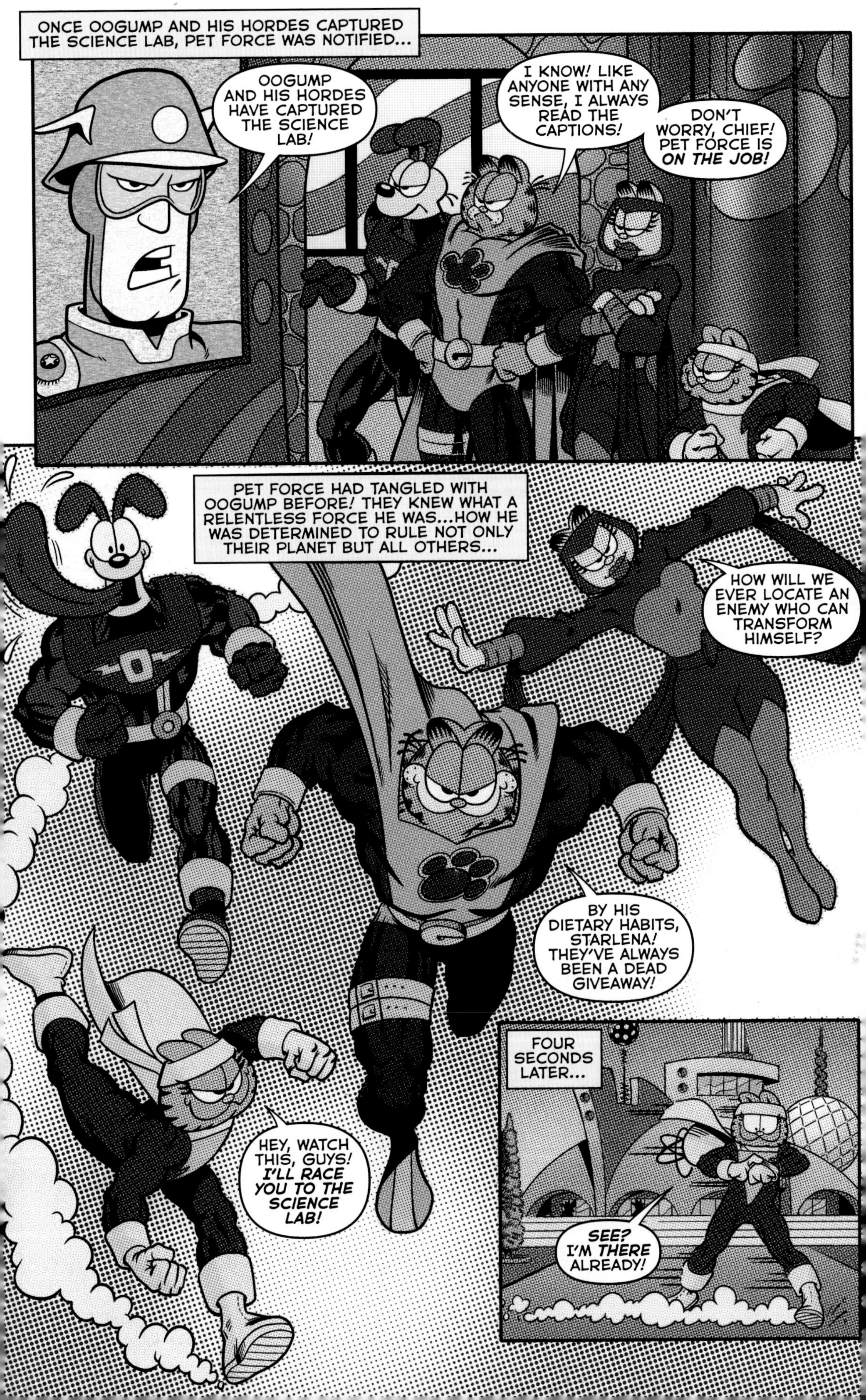
ONCE OOGUMP AND HIS HORDES CAPTURED THE SCIENCE LAB, PET FORCE WAS NOTIFIED...
OOGUMP AND HIS HORDES HAVE CAPTURED THE SCIENCE LAB!
I KNOW! LIKE ANYONE WITH ANY SENSE, I ALWAYS READ THE CAPTIONS!
DON'T WORRY, CHIEF! PET FORCE IS ON THE JOB!
PET FORCE HAD TANGLED WITH OOGUMP BEFORE! THEY KNEW WHAT A RELENTLESS FORCE HE WAS...HOW HE WAS DETERMINED TO RULE NOT ONLY THEIR PLANET BUT ALL OTHERS...
HOW WILL WE EVER LOCATE AN ENEMY WHO CAN TRANSFORM HIMSELF?
BY HIS DIETARY HABITS, STARLENA! THEY'VE ALWAYS BEEN A DEAD GIVEAWAY!
HEY, WATCH THIS, GUYS! I'LL RACE YOU TO THE SCIENCE LAB!
FOUR SECONDS LATER...
SEE? I'M THERE ALREADY!

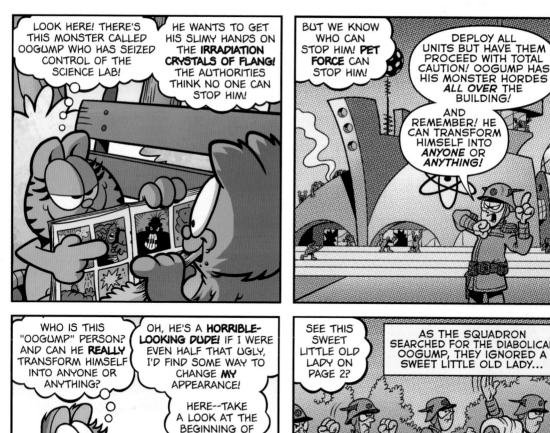

LOOK HERE! THERE'S THIS MONSTER CALLED OOGUMP WHO HAS SEIZED CONTROL OF THE SCIENCE LAB!

HE WANTS TO GET HIS SLIMY HANDS ON THE **IRRADIATION CRYSTALS OF FLANG!** THE AUTHORITIES THINK NO ONE CAN STOP HIM!

BUT WE KNOW WHO CAN STOP HIM! **PET FORCE** CAN STOP HIM!

DEPLOY ALL UNITS BUT HAVE THEM PROCEED WITH TOTAL CAUTION! OOGUMP HAS HIS MONSTER HORDES *ALL OVER* THE BUILDING!

AND REMEMBER! HE CAN TRANSFORM HIMSELF INTO *ANYONE OR ANYTHING!*

WHO IS THIS "OOGUMP" PERSON? AND CAN HE **REALLY** TRANSFORM HIMSELF INTO ANYONE OR ANYTHING?

OH, HE'S A **HORRIBLE-LOOKING DUDE!** IF I WERE EVEN HALF THAT UGLY, I'D FIND SOME WAY TO CHANGE **MY** APPEARANCE!

HERE--TAKE A LOOK AT THE BEGINNING OF THIS ISSUE...

SEE THIS SWEET LITTLE OLD LADY ON PAGE 2?

AS THE SQUADRON SEARCHED FOR THE DIABOLICAL OOGUMP, THEY IGNORED A SWEET LITTLE OLD LADY...

MY STARS! WHAT IS ALL THIS FUSS ABOUT?

WELL, LOOK WHAT "SHE" TURNS INTO ON **PAGE 4!**

...FOR WHEN NO ONE WAS LOOKING, THE SWEET LITTLE OLD LADY TRANSFORMED BACK INTO...

ONCE AGAIN, I AM *OOGUMP*-- SOON TO BE THE *RULER OF THIS PLANET!*

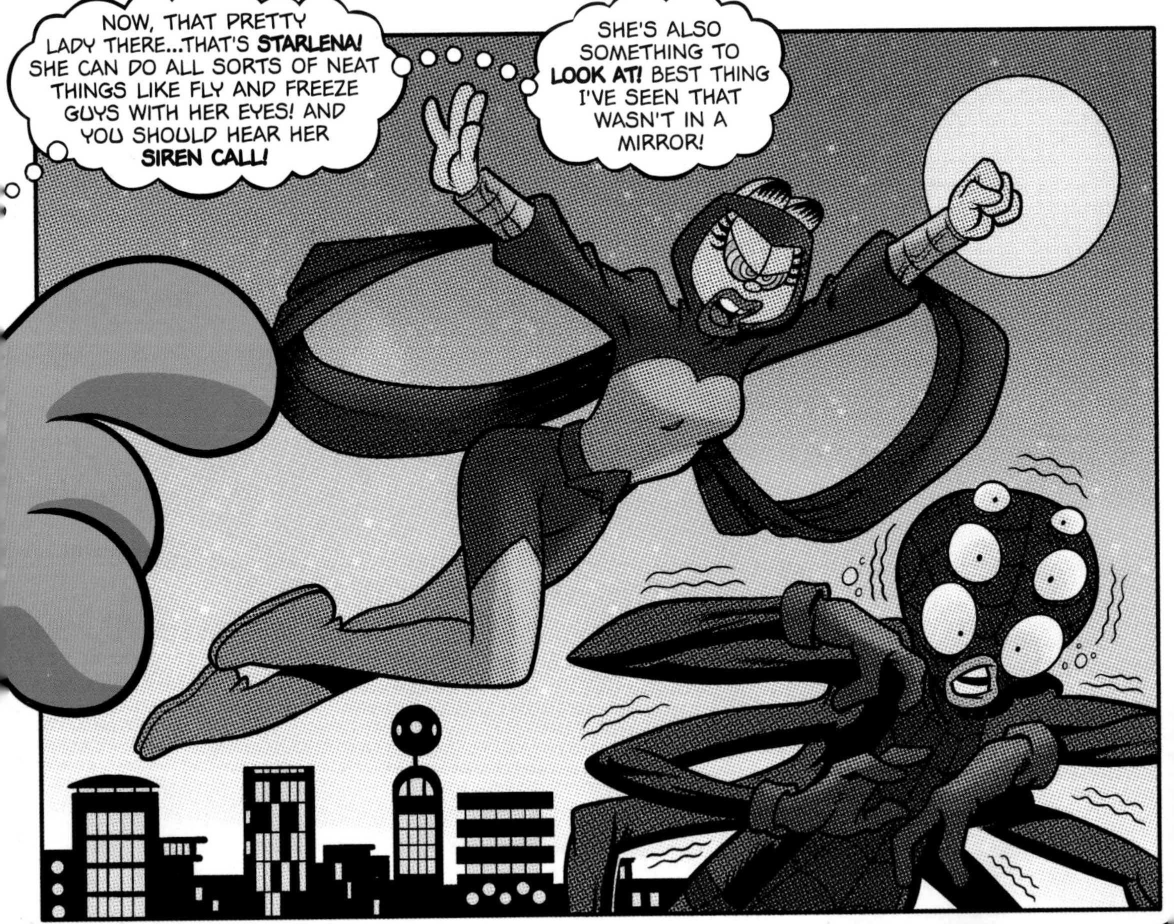
NOW, THAT PRETTY LADY THERE...THAT'S STARLENA! SHE CAN DO ALL SORTS OF NEAT THINGS LIKE FLY AND FREEZE GUYS WITH HER EYES! AND YOU SHOULD HEAR HER SIREN CALL!
SHE'S ALSO SOMETHING TO LOOK AT! BEST THING I'VE SEEN THAT WASN'T IN A MIRROR!

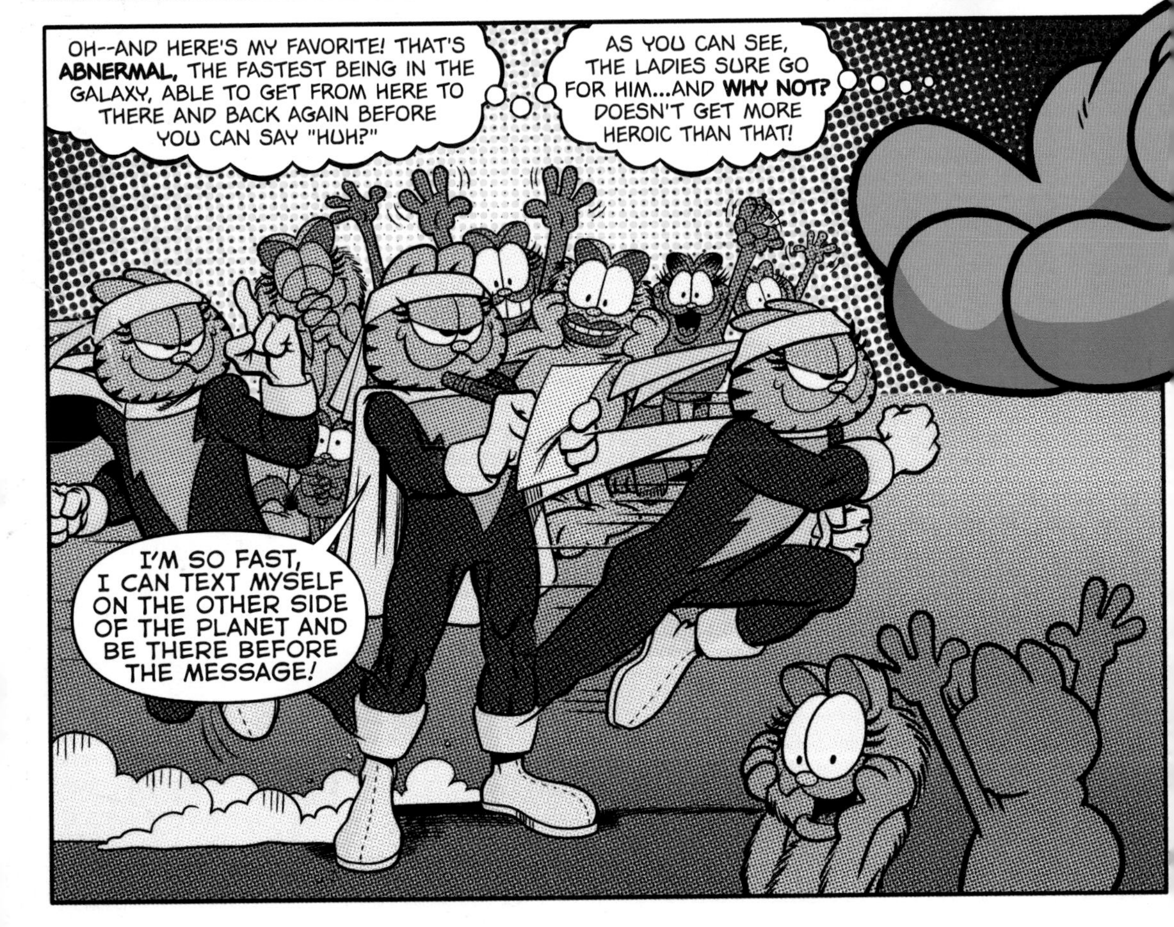
OH--AND HERE'S MY FAVORITE! THAT'S ABNERMAL, THE FASTEST BEING IN THE GALAXY, ABLE TO GET FROM HERE TO THERE AND BACK AGAIN BEFORE YOU CAN SAY "HUH?"
AS YOU CAN SEE, THE LADIES SURE GO FOR HIM...AND WHY NOT? DOESN'T GET MORE HEROIC THAN THAT!
I'M SO FAST, I CAN TEXT MYSELF ON THE OTHER SIDE OF THE PLANET AND BE THERE BEFORE THE MESSAGE!

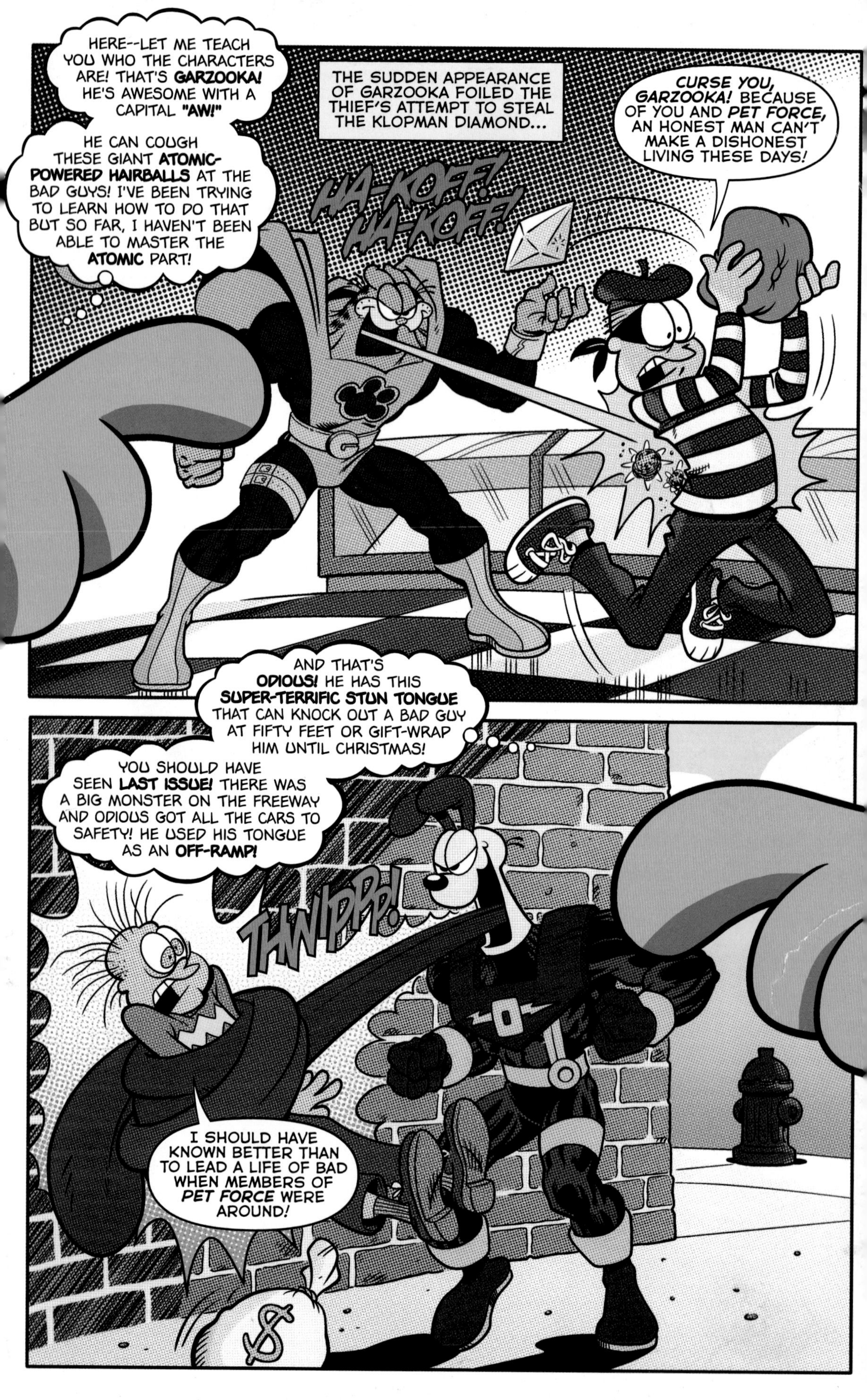
HERE--LET ME TEACH YOU WHO THE CHARACTERS ARE! THAT'S **GARZOOKA!** HE'S AWESOME WITH A CAPITAL **"AW!"**
HE CAN COUGH THESE GIANT **ATOMIC-POWERED HAIRBALLS** AT THE BAD GUYS! I'VE BEEN TRYING TO LEARN HOW TO DO THAT BUT SO FAR, I HAVEN'T BEEN ABLE TO MASTER THE **ATOMIC** PART!
THE SUDDEN APPEARANCE OF GARZOOKA FOILED THE THIEF'S ATTEMPT TO STEAL THE KLOPMAN DIAMOND...
HA-KOFF! HA-KOFF!
CURSE YOU, GARZOOKA! BECAUSE OF YOU AND *PET FORCE*, AN HONEST MAN CAN'T MAKE A DISHONEST LIVING THESE DAYS!
AND THAT'S **ODIOUS!** HE HAS THIS **SUPER-TERRIFIC STUN TONGUE** THAT CAN KNOCK OUT A BAD GUY AT FIFTY FEET OR GIFT-WRAP HIM UNTIL CHRISTMAS!
YOU SHOULD HAVE SEEN **LAST ISSUE!** THERE WAS A BIG MONSTER ON THE FREEWAY AND ODIOUS GOT ALL THE CARS TO SAFETY! HE USED HIS TONGUE AS AN **OFF-RAMP!**
THWIPPP!
I SHOULD HAVE KNOWN BETTER THAN TO LEAD A LIFE OF BAD WHEN MEMBERS OF *PET FORCE* WERE AROUND!

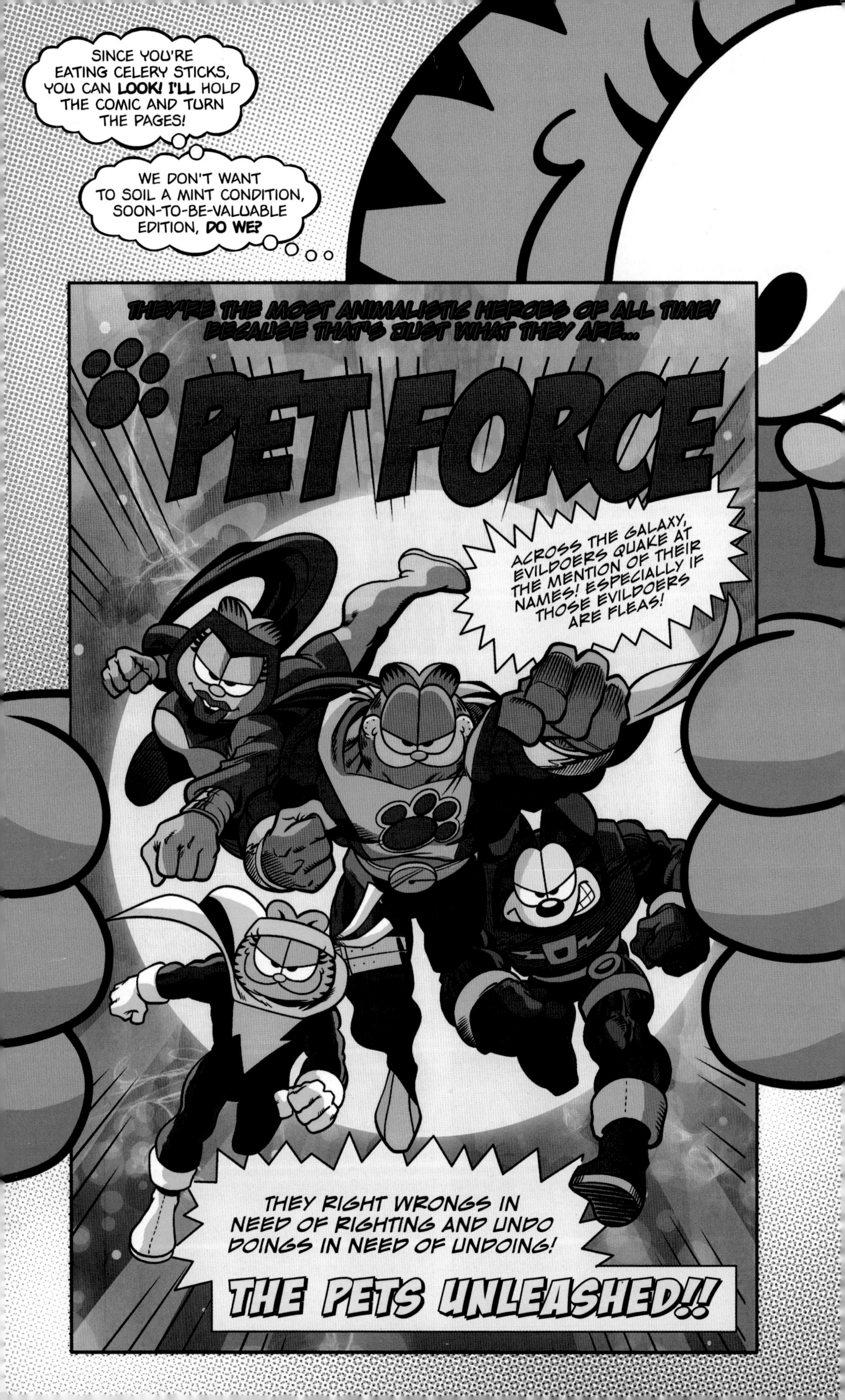
SINCE YOU'RE EATING CELERY STICKS, YOU CAN LOOK! I'LL HOLD THE COMIC AND TURN THE PAGES!
WE DON'T WANT TO SOIL A MINT CONDITION, SOON-TO-BE-VALUABLE EDITION, DO WE?
THEY'RE THE MOST ANIMALISTIC HEROES OF ALL TIME! BECAUSE THAT'S JUST WHAT THEY ARE...
PET FORCE
ACROSS THE GALAXY, EVILDOERS QUAKE AT THE MENTION OF THEIR NAMES! ESPECIALLY IF THOSE EVILDOERS ARE FLEAS!
THEY RIGHT WRONGS IN NEED OF RIGHTING AND UNDO DOINGS IN NEED OF UNDOING!
THE PETS UNLEASHED!!

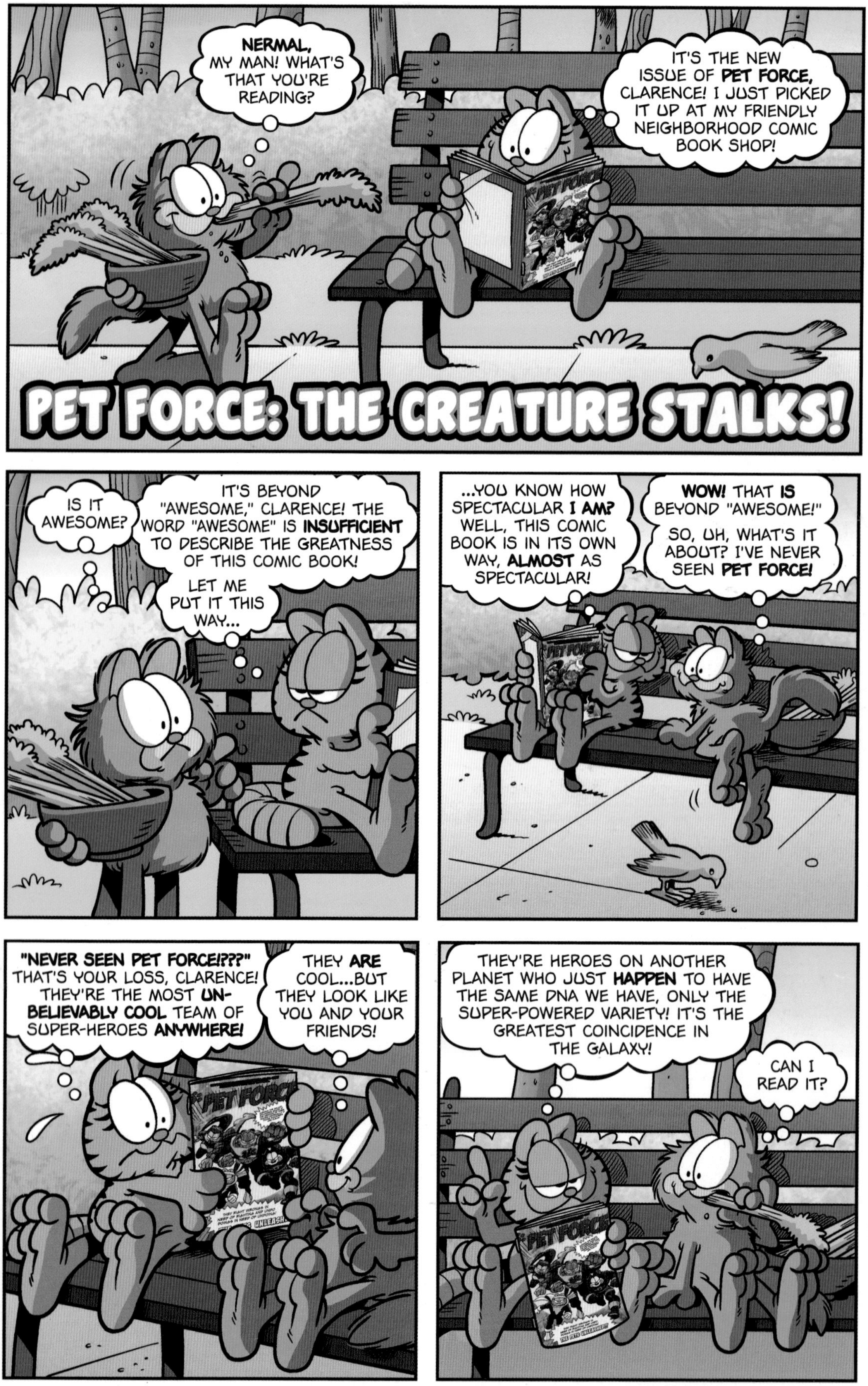
NERMAL, MY MAN! WHAT'S THAT YOU'RE READING?
IT'S THE NEW ISSUE OF PET FORCE, CLARENCE! I JUST PICKED IT UP AT MY FRIENDLY NEIGHBORHOOD COMIC BOOK SHOP!
PET FORCE: THE CREATURE STALKS!
IS IT AWESOME?
IT'S BEYOND "AWESOME," CLARENCE! THE WORD "AWESOME" IS INSUFFICIENT TO DESCRIBE THE GREATNESS OF THIS COMIC BOOK!
LET ME PUT IT THIS WAY...
...YOU KNOW HOW SPECTACULAR I AM? WELL, THIS COMIC BOOK IS IN ITS OWN WAY, ALMOST AS SPECTACULAR!
WOW! THAT IS BEYOND "AWESOME!"
SO, UH, WHAT'S IT ABOUT? I'VE NEVER SEEN PET FORCE!
"NEVER SEEN PET FORCE!???" THAT'S YOUR LOSS, CLARENCE! THEY'RE THE MOST UN-BELIEVABLY COOL TEAM OF SUPER-HEROES ANYWHERE!
THEY ARE COOL...BUT THEY LOOK LIKE YOU AND YOUR FRIENDS!
THEY'RE HEROES ON ANOTHER PLANET WHO JUST HAPPEN TO HAVE THE SAME DNA WE HAVE, ONLY THE SUPER-POWERED VARIETY! IT'S THE GREATEST COINCIDENCE IN THE GALAXY!
CAN I READ IT?

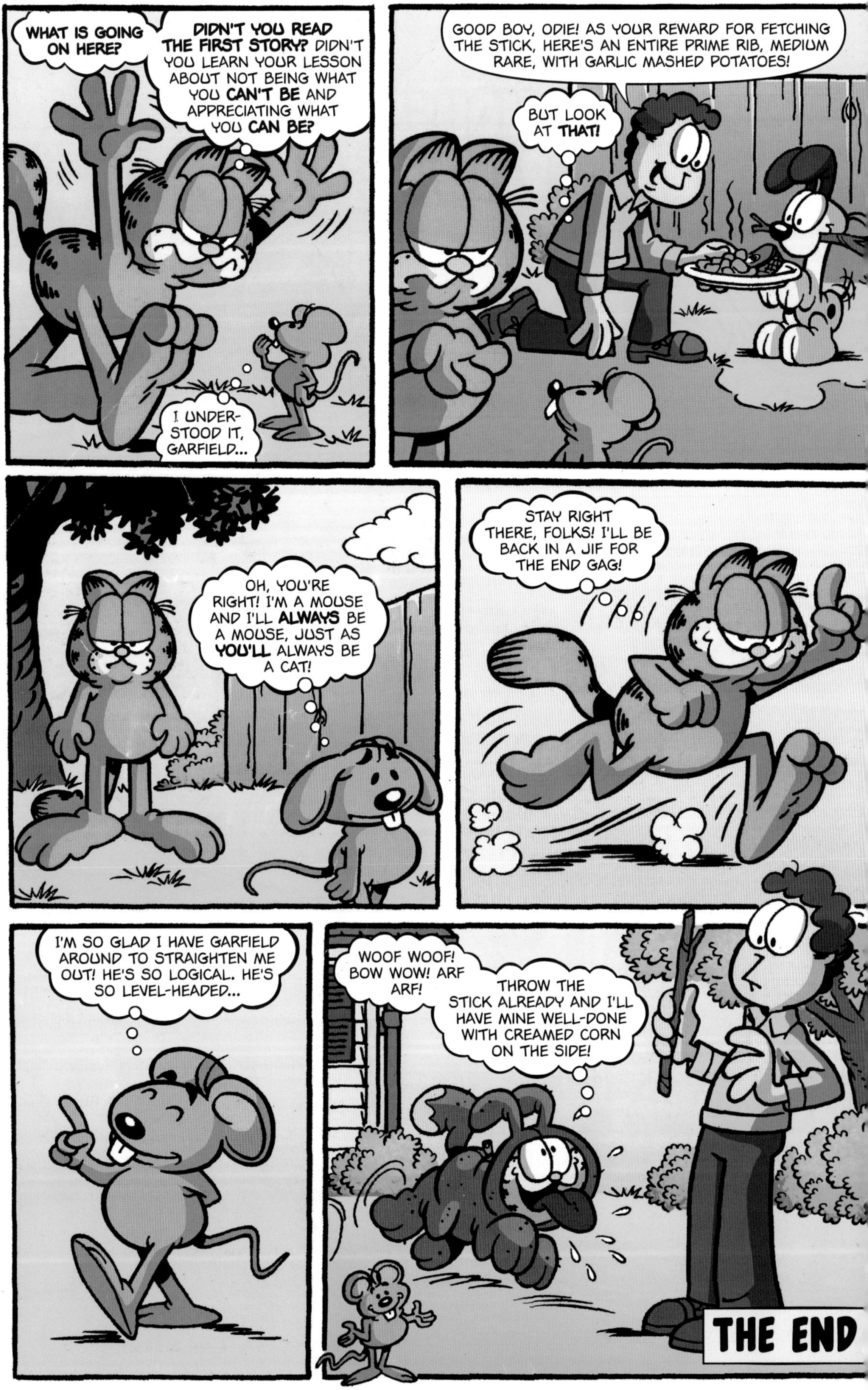
WHAT IS GOING ON HERE?
DIDN'T YOU READ THE FIRST STORY? DIDN'T YOU LEARN YOUR LESSON ABOUT NOT BEING WHAT YOU CAN'T BE AND APPRECIATING WHAT YOU CAN BE?
I UNDERSTOOD IT, GARFIELD...
GOOD BOY, ODIE! AS YOUR REWARD FOR FETCHING THE STICK, HERE'S AN ENTIRE PRIME RIB, MEDIUM RARE, WITH GARLIC MASHED POTATOES!
BUT LOOK AT THAT!
OH, YOU'RE RIGHT! I'M A MOUSE AND I'LL ALWAYS BE A MOUSE, JUST AS YOU'LL ALWAYS BE A CAT!
STAY RIGHT THERE, FOLKS! I'LL BE BACK IN A JIF FOR THE END GAG!
I'M SO GLAD I HAVE GARFIELD AROUND TO STRAIGHTEN ME OUT! HE'S SO LOGICAL. HE'S SO LEVEL-HEADED...
WOOF WOOF! BOW WOW! ARF ARF!
THROW THE STICK ALREADY AND I'LL HAVE MINE WELL-DONE WITH CREAMED CORN ON THE SIDE!
THE END

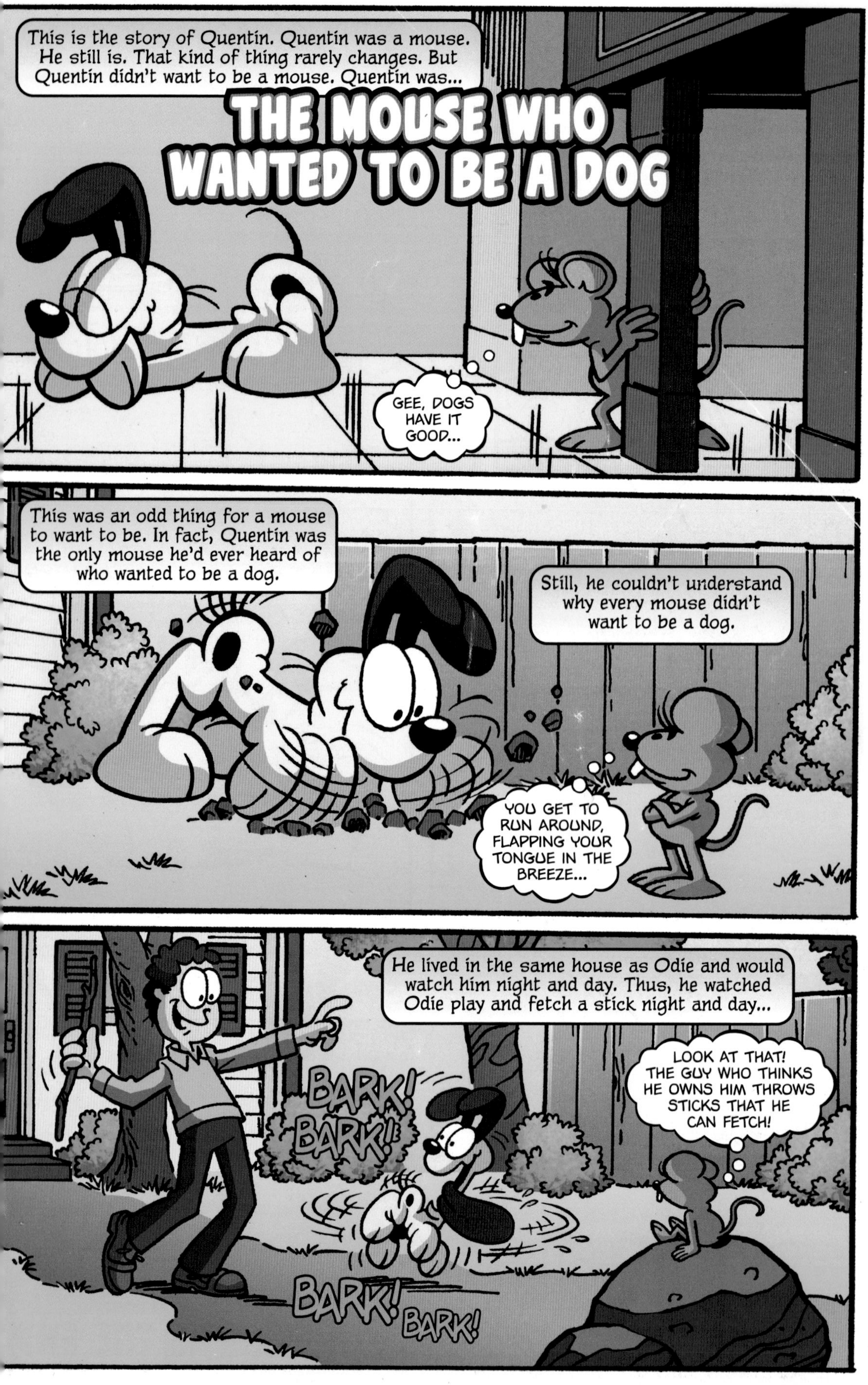
This is the story of Quentin. Quentin was a mouse. He still is. That kind of thing rarely changes. But Quentin didn't want to be a mouse. Quentin was...
THE MOUSE WHO WANTED TO BE A DOG
GEE, DOGS HAVE IT GOOD...
This was an odd thing for a mouse to want to be. In fact, Quentin was the only mouse he'd ever heard of who wanted to be a dog.
Still, he couldn't understand why every mouse didn't want to be a dog.
YOU GET TO RUN AROUND, FLAPPING YOUR TONGUE IN THE BREEZE...
He lived in the same house as Odie and would watch him night and day. Thus, he watched Odie play and fetch a stick night and day...
BARK! BARK!
LOOK AT THAT! THE GUY WHO THINKS HE OWNS HIM THROWS STICKS THAT HE CAN FETCH!
BARK! BARK!

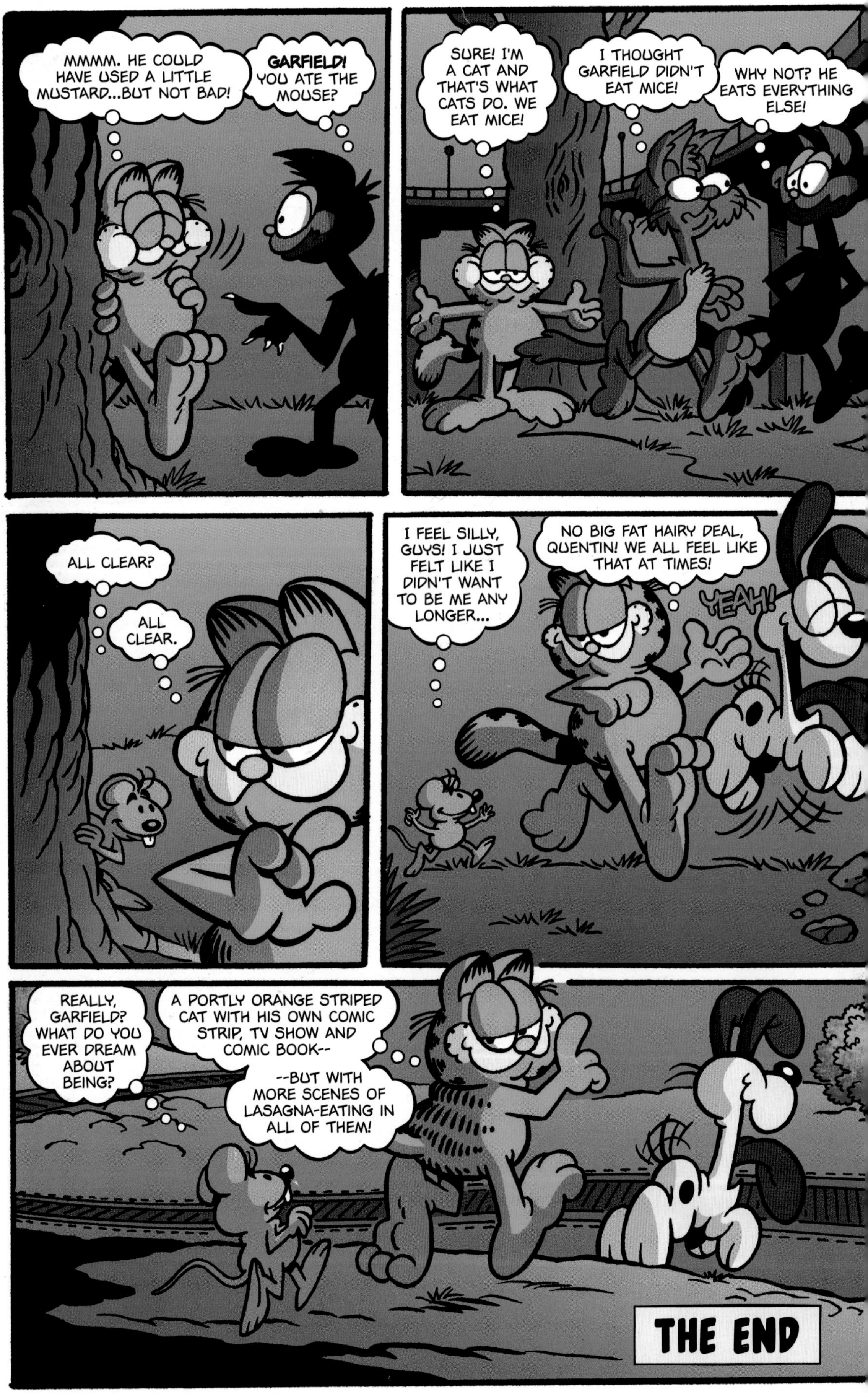
MMMM. HE COULD HAVE USED A LITTLE MUSTARD...BUT NOT BAD!
GARFIELD! YOU ATE THE MOUSE?
SURE! I'M A CAT AND THAT'S WHAT CATS DO. WE EAT MICE!
I THOUGHT GARFIELD DIDN'T EAT MICE!
WHY NOT? HE EATS EVERYTHING ELSE!
ALL CLEAR?
ALL CLEAR.
I FEEL SILLY, GUYS! I JUST FELT LIKE I DIDN'T WANT TO BE ME ANY LONGER...
NO BIG FAT HAIRY DEAL, QUENTIN! WE ALL FEEL LIKE THAT AT TIMES!
YEAH!
REALLY, GARFIELD? WHAT DO YOU EVER DREAM ABOUT BEING?
A PORTLY ORANGE STRIPED CAT WITH HIS OWN COMIC STRIP, TV SHOW AND COMIC BOOK--
--BUT WITH MORE SCENES OF LASAGNA-EATING IN ALL OF THEM!
THE END

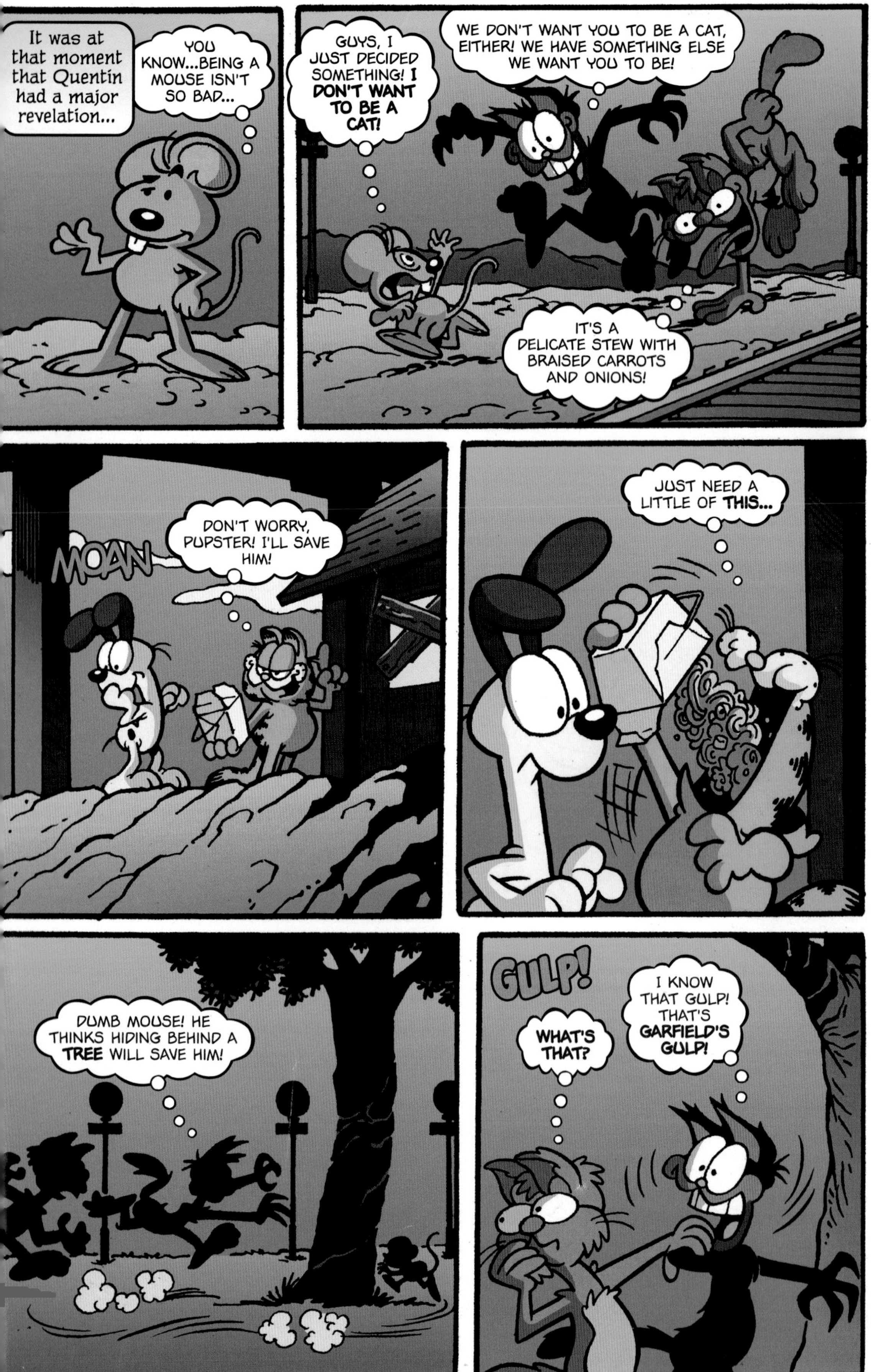
It was at that moment that Quentin had a major revelation...
YOU KNOW...BEING A MOUSE ISN'T SO BAD...
GUYS, I JUST DECIDED SOMETHING! I DON'T WANT TO BE A CAT!
WE DON'T WANT YOU TO BE A CAT, EITHER! WE HAVE SOMETHING ELSE WE WANT YOU TO BE!
IT'S A DELICATE STEW WITH BRAISED CARROTS AND ONIONS!
MOAN
DON'T WORRY, PUPSTER! I'LL SAVE HIM!
JUST NEED A LITTLE OF THIS...
DUMB MOUSE! HE THINKS HIDING BEHIND A TREE WILL SAVE HIM!
GULP!
WHAT'S THAT?
I KNOW THAT GULP! THAT'S GARFIELD'S GULP!

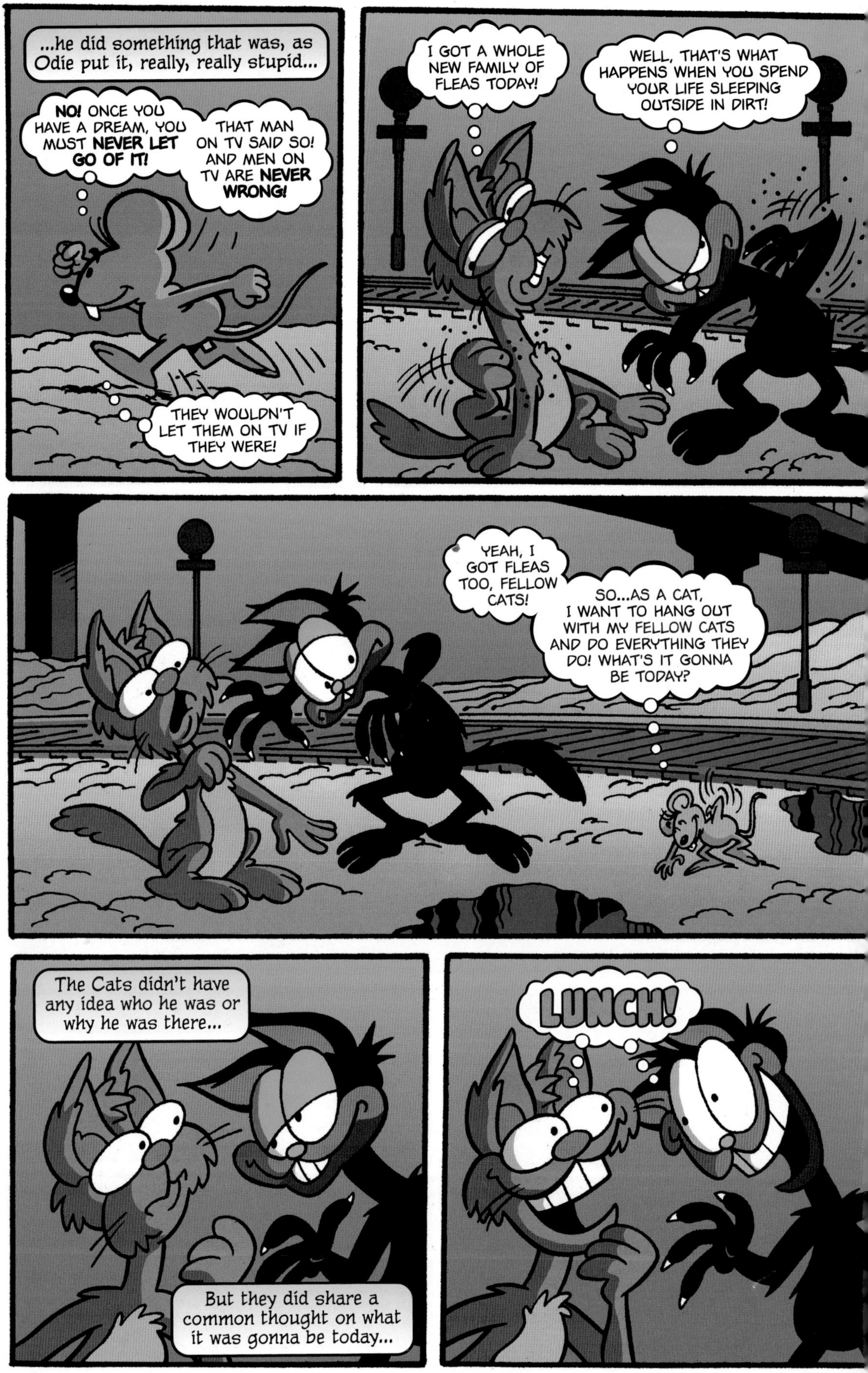

...he did something that was, as Odie put it, really, really stupid...
NO! ONCE YOU HAVE A DREAM, YOU MUST NEVER LET GO OF IT!
THAT MAN ON TV SAID SO! AND MEN ON TV ARE NEVER WRONG!
THEY WOULDN'T LET THEM ON TV IF THEY WERE!
I GOT A WHOLE NEW FAMILY OF FLEAS TODAY!
WELL, THAT'S WHAT HAPPENS WHEN YOU SPEND YOUR LIFE SLEEPING OUTSIDE IN DIRT!
YEAH, I GOT FLEAS TOO, FELLOW CATS!
SO...AS A CAT, I WANT TO HANG OUT WITH MY FELLOW CATS AND DO EVERYTHING THEY DO! WHAT'S IT GONNA BE TODAY?
The Cats didn't have any idea who he was or why he was there...
But they did share a common thought on what it was gonna be today...
LUNCH!

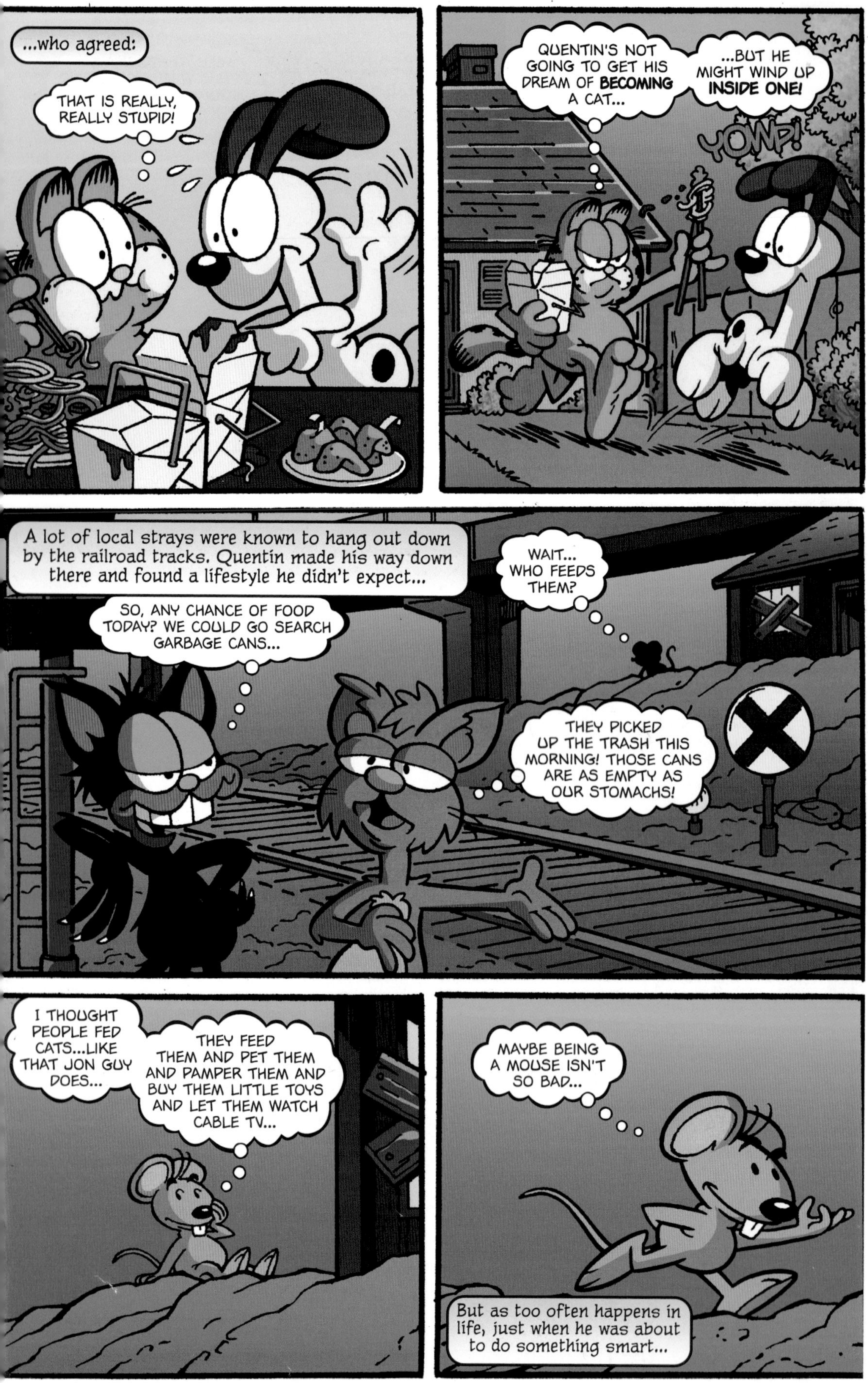
...who agreed:
THAT IS REALLY, REALLY STUPID!
QUENTIN'S NOT GOING TO GET HIS DREAM OF BECOMING A CAT...
...BUT HE MIGHT WIND UP INSIDE ONE!
YOMP!
A lot of local strays were known to hang out down by the railroad tracks. Quentin made his way down there and found a lifestyle he didn't expect...
SO, ANY CHANCE OF FOOD TODAY? WE COULD GO SEARCH GARBAGE CANS...
WAIT... WHO FEEDS THEM?
THEY PICKED UP THE TRASH THIS MORNING! THOSE CANS ARE AS EMPTY AS OUR STOMACHS!
I THOUGHT PEOPLE FED CATS...LIKE THAT JON GUY DOES...
THEY FEED THEM AND PET THEM AND PAMPER THEM AND BUY THEM LITTLE TOYS AND LET THEM WATCH CABLE TV...
MAYBE BEING A MOUSE ISN'T SO BAD...
But as too often happens in life, just when he was about to do something smart...

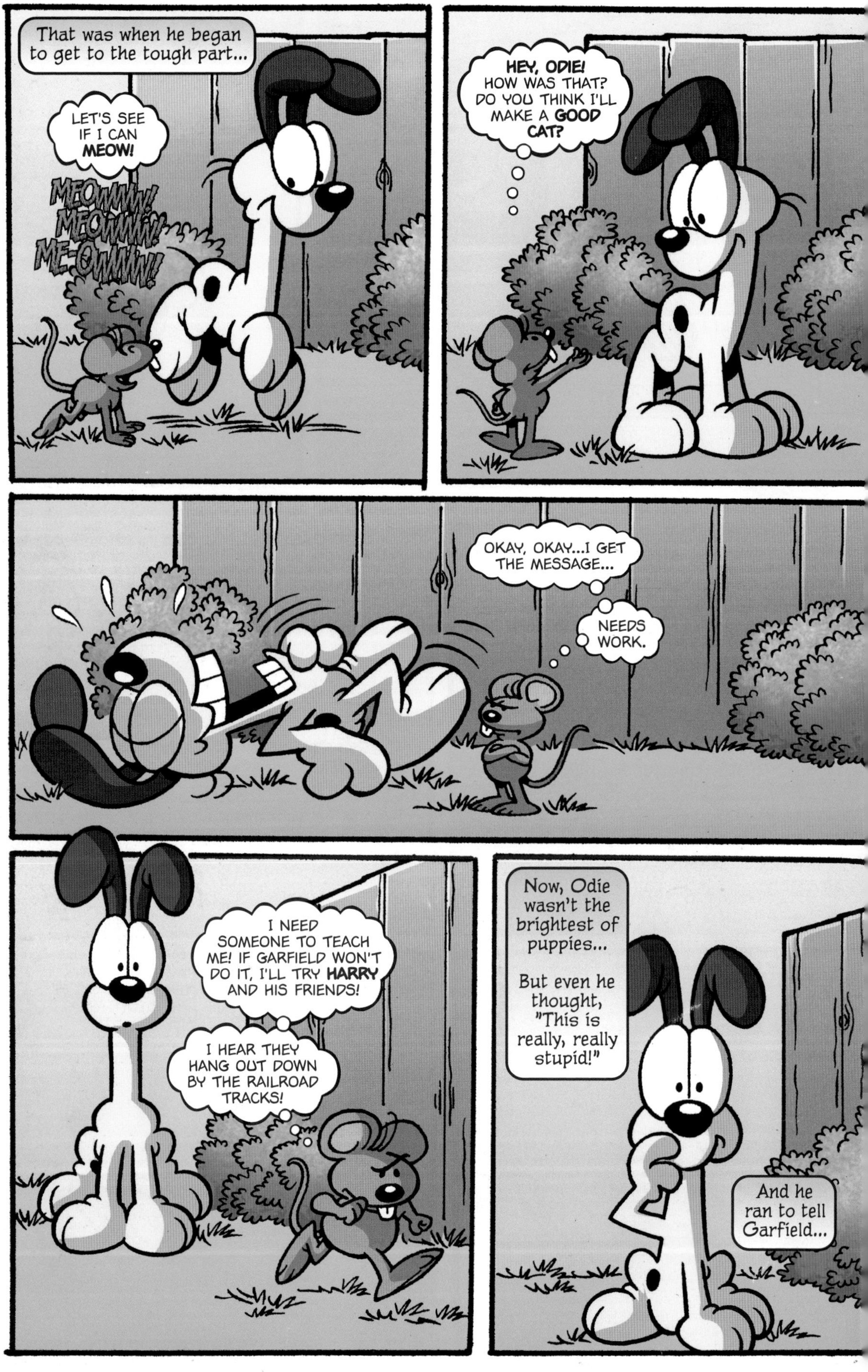
That was when he began to get to the tough part...
LET'S SEE IF I CAN MEOW!
MEOWWW! MEOWWW! ME-OWWW!
HEY, ODIE! HOW WAS THAT? DO YOU THINK I'LL MAKE A GOOD CAT?
OKAY, OKAY...I GET THE MESSAGE...
NEEDS WORK.
I NEED SOMEONE TO TEACH ME! IF GARFIELD WON'T DO IT, I'LL TRY HARRY AND HIS FRIENDS!
I HEAR THEY HANG OUT DOWN BY THE RAILROAD TRACKS!
Now, Odie wasn't the brightest of puppies...
But even he thought, "This is really, really stupid!"
And he ran to tell Garfield...

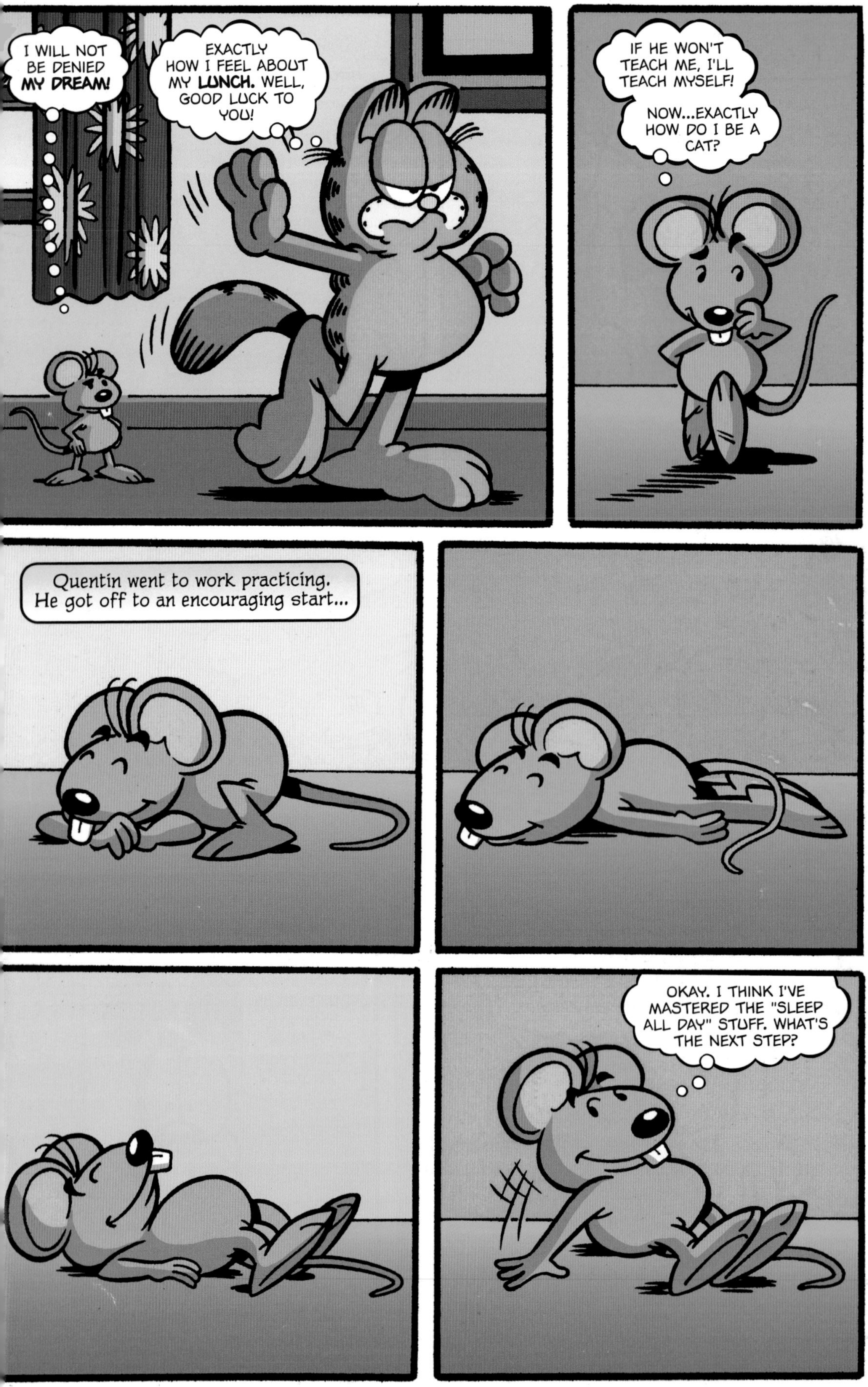
I WILL NOT BE DENIED **MY DREAM!**
EXACTLY HOW I FEEL ABOUT MY **LUNCH.** WELL, GOOD LUCK TO YOU!
IF HE WON'T TEACH ME, I'LL TEACH MYSELF!
NOW...EXACTLY HOW DO I BE A CAT?
Quentin went to work practicing. He got off to an encouraging start...
OKAY. I THINK I'VE MASTERED THE "SLEEP ALL DAY" STUFF. WHAT'S THE NEXT STEP?

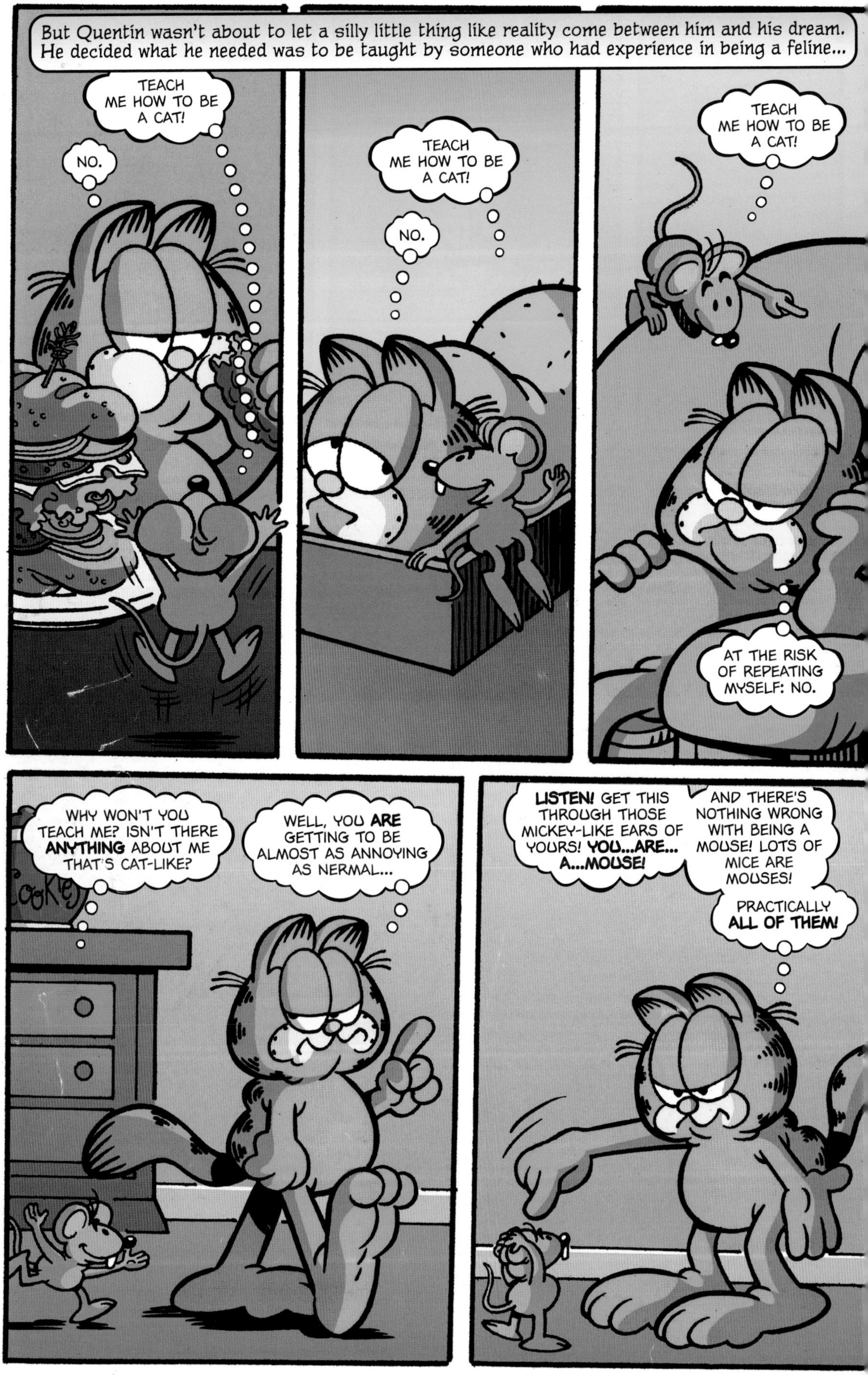
But Quentin wasn't about to let a silly little thing like reality come between him and his dream. He decided what he needed was to be taught by someone who had experience in being a feline...
TEACH ME HOW TO BE A CAT!
NO.
TEACH ME HOW TO BE A CAT!
NO.
TEACH ME HOW TO BE A CAT!
AT THE RISK OF REPEATING MYSELF: NO.
WHY WON'T YOU TEACH ME? ISN'T THERE ANYTHING ABOUT ME THAT'S CAT-LIKE?
WELL, YOU ARE GETTING TO BE ALMOST AS ANNOYING AS NERMAL...
COOKIES
LISTEN! GET THIS THROUGH THOSE MICKEY-LIKE EARS OF YOURS! YOU...ARE... A...MOUSE!
AND THERE'S NOTHING WRONG WITH BEING A MOUSE! LOTS OF MICE ARE MOUSES!
PRACTICALLY ALL OF THEM!

I WANT TO BE A COWBOY!

I WANT TO BE A FAMOUS BALLERINA!

I WANT TO BE A SENATOR!

REMEMBER! ONCE YOU HAVE A DREAM, YOU MUST **NEVER LET GO** OF IT!

SAD TO SEE THAT LAST KID ALREADY EMBARKING ON A LIFE OF CRIME!

HEY, GARFIELD! YOU KNOW WHAT **I'M** GOING TO BE?

I'LL GO WAY OUT ON A LIMB AND GUESS "A MOUSE"!

NO, **A CAT!** I HEARD THE MAN ON TV! HE SAID IF I WANT IT BADLY ENOUGH AND I WORK HARD, IT **WILL HAPPEN!**

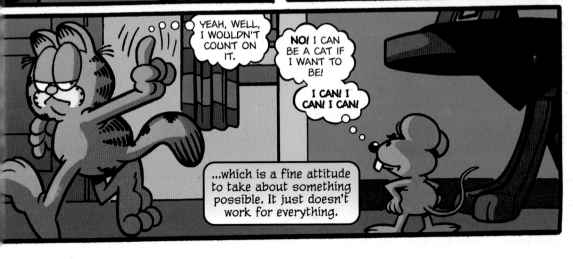

YEAH, WELL, I WOULDN'T COUNT ON IT.

NO! I CAN BE A CAT IF I WANT TO BE!

I CAN! I CAN! I CAN!

...which is a fine attitude to take about something possible. It just doesn't work for everything.

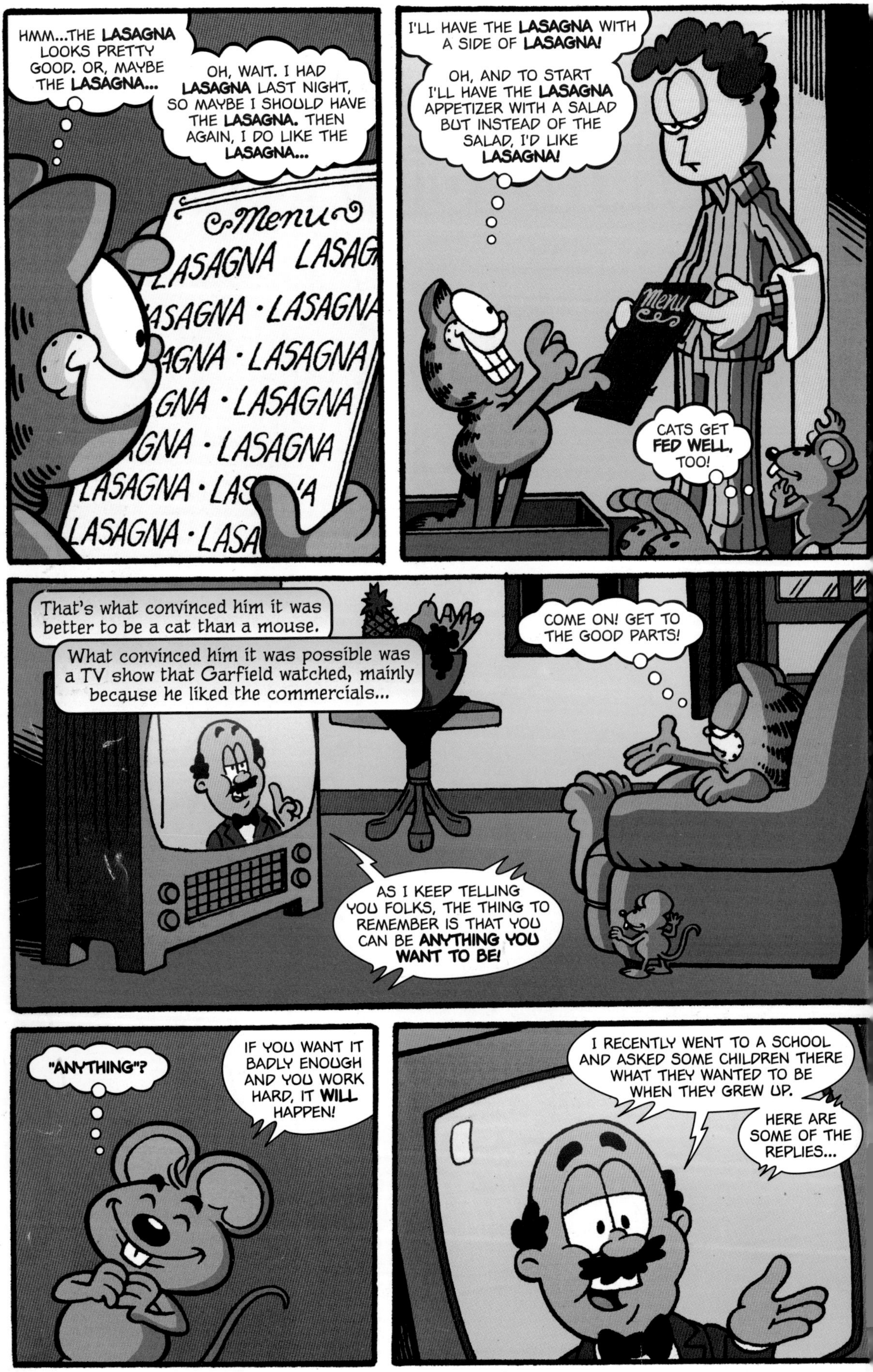
HMM...THE **LASAGNA** LOOKS PRETTY GOOD. OR, MAYBE THE **LASAGNA...**
OH, WAIT. I HAD **LASAGNA** LAST NIGHT, SO MAYBE I SHOULD HAVE THE **LASAGNA.** THEN AGAIN, I DO LIKE THE **LASAGNA...**
Menu
LASAGNA LASAG
ASAGNA · LASAGNA
AGNA · LASAGNA
GNA · LASAGNA
GNA · LASAGNA
LASAGNA · LA A
LASAGNA · LASA
I'LL HAVE THE **LASAGNA** WITH A SIDE OF **LASAGNA!**
OH, AND TO START I'LL HAVE THE **LASAGNA** APPETIZER WITH A SALAD BUT INSTEAD OF THE SALAD, I'D LIKE **LASAGNA!**
Menu
CATS GET **FED WELL,** TOO!
That's what convinced him it was better to be a cat than a mouse.
What convinced him it was possible was a TV show that Garfield watched, mainly because he liked the commercials...
COME ON! GET TO THE GOOD PARTS!
AS I KEEP TELLING YOU FOLKS, THE THING TO REMEMBER IS THAT YOU CAN BE **ANYTHING YOU WANT TO BE!**
"ANYTHING"?
IF YOU WANT IT BADLY ENOUGH AND YOU WORK HARD, IT **WILL** HAPPEN!
I RECENTLY WENT TO A SCHOOL AND ASKED SOME CHILDREN THERE WHAT THEY WANTED TO BE WHEN THEY GREW UP.
HERE ARE SOME OF THE REPLIES...

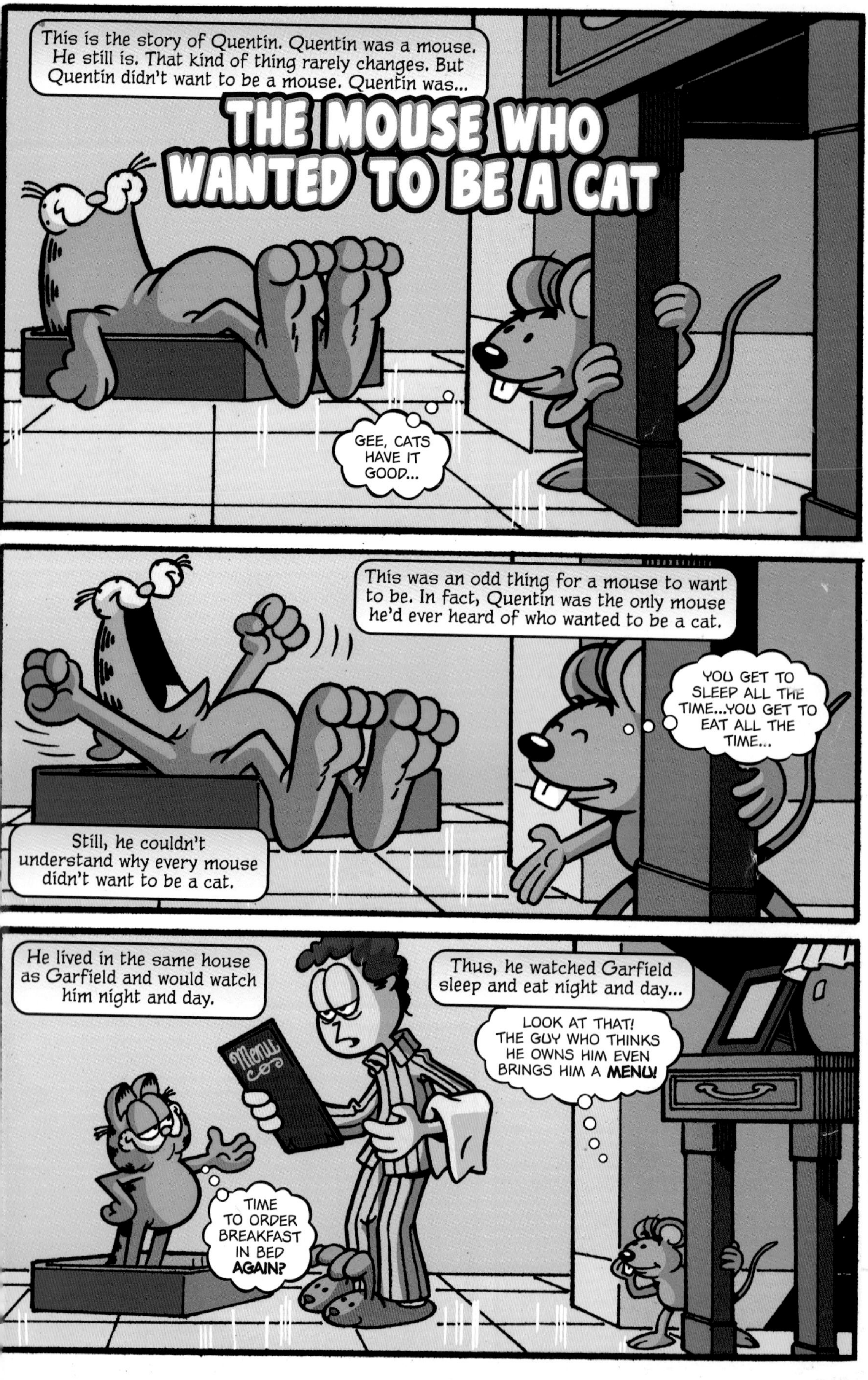
This is the story of Quentin. Quentin was a mouse. He still is. That kind of thing rarely changes. But Quentin didn't want to be a mouse. Quentin was...
THE MOUSE WHO WANTED TO BE A CAT
GEE, CATS HAVE IT GOOD...
This was an odd thing for a mouse to want to be. In fact, Quentin was the only mouse he'd ever heard of who wanted to be a cat.
YOU GET TO SLEEP ALL THE TIME...YOU GET TO EAT ALL THE TIME...
Still, he couldn't understand why every mouse didn't want to be a cat.
He lived in the same house as Garfield and would watch him night and day.
Thus, he watched Garfield sleep and eat night and day...
LOOK AT THAT! THE GUY WHO THINKS HE OWNS HIM EVEN BRINGS HIM A MENU!
Menu
TIME TO ORDER BREAKFAST IN BED AGAIN?

CHAPTER 1

WRITTEN BY
MARK EVANIER

"SNOW PROBLEM" WRITTEN BY SCOTT NICKEL

ART BY
GARY BARKER (CHAPTERS 5,6)
DAN DAVIS (CHAPTERS 5,6,7)
ANDY HIRSCH (CHAPTERS 7,8)
MARK & STEPHANIE HEIKE (CHAPTERS 7,8)
AND MIKE DECARLO (CHAPTERS 5-8)

COLORS BY
LISA MOORE

LETTERS BY
STEVE WANDS

COVER BY
GARY BARKER
AND DAN DAVIS
COLORS BY BRADEN LAMB

EDITOR: MATT GAGNON
ASSISTANT EDITOR: CHRIS ROSA
TRADE DESIGNER: KASSANDRA HELLER

GARFIELD CREATED BY
JIM DAVIS

SPECIAL THANKS TO SCOTT NICKEL, DAVID REDDICK, AND THE ENTIRE PAWS, INC. TE